THE BRINK

A novel

BY MARK FADDEN

iUniverse, Inc.
New York   Bloomington

iUniverse books may be ordered through booksellers or by contacting:

iUniverse
1663 Liberty Drive
Bloomington, IN 47403
www.iuniverse.com
1-800-Authors (1-800-288-4677)

ISBN: 978-1-4502-1048-5 (sc)
ISBN: 978-1-4502-1049-2 (ebook)
ISBN: 978-1-4502-1047-8 (dj)

Library of Congress Controll Number: 2010902205

Printed in the United States of America

iUniverse rev. date: 03/18/2010

For my family

"Never doubt that a small group of
thoughtful citizens can change the world.
Indeed, it is the only thing that ever has."—Margaret Mead

Chapter 1

Joel Basher crashed through the front doors of the Library of Congress. The gnawing chill in the night air hit him like a raw slap. As he hit the stairs running, he tightened his grip on the stolen parcel inside his coat.

The door burst open behind him. Joel heard the cop shouting, but the voice in his head was louder: *You're supposed to get caught.*

He tore through the first landing, exploded down the next section of stairs, but then halted on the next landing. The cop did the same on the landing above him. Joel clenched the icy granite railing in front of him. He hurled himself over it. His shoes cracked the water's surface in the fountain below. He turned, saw the policeman with his gun raised, and knew it was time to dump the package.

"Freeze!" the cop barked as he raced down to the landing above the tank.

That's exactly what Joel was doing, standing here in the shin-deep water next to Neptune and his two fishy henchmen.

"Hands up!" the cop shouted as he braced himself against the railing, his outstretched pistol pointed at Joel's chest.

Joel nodded. He spread his jacket wide to show he had no weapon. As he did, the book inside tumbled down his body into the water.

The cop's eyes exploded. Joel knew what he was thinking. *Water. Paper. A deadly combination.*

The cop made the mistake of trying to keep his gun on Joel as he stiff-armed the railing. His hand slipped on the ice, and gravity took care of the rest. By the time the cop's flailing body crashed into the water, Joel was gone.

He sprinted across First Street into the awaiting darkness behind a cluster of spruce trees. As soon as he nestled in their shadows, he turned to watch the show. The shivering policeman sat down on the edge of the fountain and opened the book. He plucked out the leather pouch and studied it a moment before an older man dressed in an elegant suit, who showed incredible agility for his age, flew down the stairs. He ripped the pouch from the cop's hands. Even from his distance, Joel saw the concern consume the old man's face.

Chapter 2

Simon Shilling, the obsessive, overly protective chief of staff, shook President Jack Butcher awake.

"What the hell is it? The goddamn place on fire?" Butcher was disgusted, but he was also fully awake. "Simon? Christ, man, don't you ever sleep?"

"I'll sleep when I'm—"

"Don't," Jack interrupted. "You'll be working even harder without a body slowing you down."

"There's been an incident, Mr. President," Simon said.

Jack instinctively glanced at the other side of the bed, where the First Lady's spot was empty.

"It's not the First Lady," Simon said, reading the president's concern about his wife. She was in the middle of a goodwill trip to the Middle East. "She's fine."

Jack felt the presence of others in the room. The hallway light dug into his eyes as he peered into the open doorway. Peter Devon, his spit-shined Secret Service chief, eclipsed much of the glow. He dwarfed the man standing next to him.

"What is it?" Jack uttered.

"There was an attempted robbery at the Library of Congress," Simon replied.

Jack blinked to clear his vision. "Attempted robbery? What's so important about—" He stopped as he finally recognized Julius Brennan. Brennan was the Library of Congress's head librarian. Jack rose, strapped on his bathrobe, and stepped into his slippers. He motioned for Pete to hit the lights. Jack waited for his eyes to adjust and then approached Brennan.

"Mr. President," the librarian said, outstretching his hand.

"Julius, what happened?" Jack asked, shaking hands.

"There was an attempt to steal documents from the Rare Book Reading Room, sir."

"You all keep saying it was an attempt. So was the thief caught?"

"One of our library police officers was able to retrieve the documents," Julius replied. "But the thief got away."

Jack turned to Simon. The two had long ago mastered the ability to read each other's faces.

"Let's not beat around the bush, Julius. Please show the president what's so important about these documents to wake him in the middle of the night."

Jack hadn't noticed the briefcase hanging at Julius's side until now. Julius crossed to Thomas Jefferson's coffee table. It usually provided visitors with a place to set their drinks inside the mayor's office at Philadelphia's city hall, but it was being loaned to the city's favorite son while he was a tenant here.

Julius placed the briefcase on the table as if there was a crystal bomb inside it. He clicked open the left latch. His nervous fingers barely touched the right one before Peter Devon's words made him stop.

"Mr. President."

Jack could tell he was simultaneously listening to a voice in his earpiece. "Yeah, Pete?"

"Sir, I'm being told that Howard Fielding is here to see you."

Chapter 3

The door that led into the Oval Office opened, and Director of National Intelligence Howard Fielding launched off the couch that flanked JFK's rattan rocker into a fully upright and locked stance. The two men sitting on the other couch across the coffee table followed Fielding's lead. Although it was the original coffee table from George Washington's sitting room at Mount Vernon, it was somewhat less impressive than the one upstairs in the president's bedroom.

Jack recognized Hunter Atkinson from his picture on the back of his book jackets. He had no clue as to the other man's identity. Even at nearly four in the morning, they were both dressed in what looked like their best suits and ties. Simon was also dressed in a suit. Jack felt a little underdressed, having thrown on a pair of dark slacks and a long sleeve polo shirt embroidered with the presidential seal in record time.

Jack addressed them as he crossed the room. "Gentlemen." No one shook hands. The shared concern in the room trumped any ritual of good manners for the moment.

"Mr. President," Fielding started, "approximately three hours ago, two armed suspects broke into Monticello. They shot and killed the two security guards on duty. They proceeded to the South Square Room, where they smashed a drawing table to pieces. This table had a secret compartment in it. We believe they took whatever was inside it."

Jack asked the most important question first. "Are the guards' families being attended to?"

"We have agents outside their homes as we speak, sir," Fielding replied. "I wanted to inform you first."

"Let's make the families as comfortable as possible, Howard."

"Of course, sir." Fielding whipped out his BlackBerry from his jacket pocket and began pecking away.

Jack looked at Simon. Simon nodded but not because he approved this show of sympathy from the White House. He knew why Jack's instinct was to put families first.

"So, what are we thinking was stolen?"

Fielding had already made the BlackBerry disappear. "Mr. President, this is Bubba Durant and Hunter Atkinson." Jack nodded at them as Fielding continued. "Bubba is the head of the American History department at GWU and Hunter is an author that—"

"Specializes in the history of the American presidency," Jack finished. "I'm a big fan."

Hunter beamed. "It's an honor to meet you, sir."

"Although I'm not yet certain why you're here, thank you both for coming in the middle of the night."

"They're here to help us figure out what exactly was stolen from Monticello, sir," Fielding replied.

Jack edged around to the rocker and motioned for all of them to sit. Simon took up his normal post at the far end of the couch from the president.

"Forgive me," Jack started, "I know this sounds heartless, but how does the murder of two Monticello guards involve the White House?"

Simon cleared his throat. "Mr. President, it looks as if this event is tied to the robbery attempt at the LOC."

"There was a robbery at the Library of Congress?" Bubba blurted out. Silence crashed into the room as Bubba realized his faux pas. He sunk back into the couch cushions. His reaction only intensified Jack's glares at Simon and Fielding.

Reading Jack's reaction to his spilling the news, Simon said, "These men are here to help us figure out the connection between these two events, Mr. President." The president nodded and Simon continued. "I called Admiral Fielding shortly after I received news of the robbery attempt at the LOC. I told him if anything else should surface that could be tied to the robbery to please notify us immediately."

"And that's what he's doing here now?" Jack asked.

"Yes, sir," Simon replied. "He called me approximately ninety minutes ago with the report of the Monticello break-in. I wanted to verify everything before getting you involved."

"And Mr. Atkinson and Mr. Durant just happened to be here taking the tour in the middle of the night?"

"They're on a short list of consultants we use, Mr. President," Fielding replied.

"Wonderful. The United States government pays for on-call history detectives. Imagine if the press got a hold of that one." As they tended to do wherever Jack went, all eyes were glued on the president. It allowed Simon to begin a silent conversation with him. He only needed to arch one of his thin, silver eyebrows.

Jack sighed. "Mr. Atkinson, Mr. Durant ... may we have the room for a few minutes please?"

Chapter 4

So as not to arouse the suspicions of a college professor and a writer, Simon Shilling had Julius Brennan enter the Oval from the side door that led directly to his office. They met for fifty-five minutes before the decision was made to let Bubba and Hunter back in.

Jack allowed them to get comfortable on the couch before he issued his warning. "Gentlemen, what we are about to discuss has been verified by Director of National Intelligence Howard Fielding as pertinent to our national security and is therefore classified information. You are forbidden by law to disclose any part of this conversation to any persons." Jack paused to let the words soak in. Then he stared at Hunter Atkinson. "Or include it in the pages of your next best seller."

"Yes, sir," both men said simultaneously. Jack nodded at Julius. He retrieved the briefcase from his feet and set it on the coffee table. His hands trembled again as he fumbled with both locks. He opened the briefcase and scooped out the plastic bag containing the brown, legal size file folder. Jack noticed the words "ACID-FREE" and "BUFFERED" that ran along the bottom of the folder's spine.

Julius extracted the folder from the bag. He set it down on the table and then dove back into his briefcase again. He retrieved three pairs of white cotton gloves and slipped one pair on his hands. Hunter and Bubba looked at the gloves and then at the president.

"Be my guest," Jack said. He motioned toward Simon. "We've already seen it."

Julius waited until the two wriggled on their gloves before continuing. He moved to open the folder when Howard Fielding leaned forward.

"Gentlemen." With that one word, Fielding stole the attention away from the documents waiting for them inside the folder. "May

I remind you that breaking laws pertaining to national security can, and in this case will, be punishable by life sentences in prison. Not even the highest-paid attorney or the loudest protests from the ACLU will change that fact."

Hunter nodded first. Then Bubba. Again, all eyes focused on Jack, and he nodded at Julius to open the folder. As he did, the faint letters at the top blazed with impossibility.

Article VIII.

After both men read through both documents, Julius closed the folder. He eased it back into the plastic bag and then shucked his gloves. As his actions punctured the crescendo of silence, all eyes were not on the president. Instead, they were firmly focused on the two pieces of parchment that were now safe from the dangers of both theft and exposure.

"A lost article of the Constitution." The words fell out of Atkinson's mouth. "I can't believe it." He gazed at the president. "Mr. President, you will have it tested to ensure its authenticity?"

"We have a Constitution expert from the National Archives on standby," Simon Shilling answered.

"This is," Atkinson muttered, his eyes back on the folder. "It's unthinkable."

"But here it is all the same," Bubba said. Over the next few minutes, Bubba regaled his audience with exactly why there would be an Eighth Article in existence and, more important, why it had been separated from the rest of the Constitution. He concluded by stating that there had to be copies. Copies no doubt hidden by Thomas Jefferson in his hallowed Virginia residence. Other pieces of parchment. Words for which people had just killed.

The room once again fell silent for well over a minute, an eternity in the Oval Office. Simon gazed at the president and pierced the hush. "You look like you're considering a new theory, Mr. President."

"Not a new theory but a new question," Jack replied.

"Which is?" Simon asked.

"What in God's name were the Founding Fathers thinking?"

Chapter 5

Lake Guerrero, Mexico
165 miles south of the Texas border
Three weeks later

The private resort nestled atop the tallest of the rolling hills in this quiet section of northern Mexico seemed an ironic place to Stefan Taber. It had been a monastery before an American corporation, Phoenix Oil, bought it from the struggling *Iglesia Católica Mejicana*, the Catholic Church of Mexico. What was once a humble dwelling to a handful of pious men who had devoted their lives and their passion to Jesus Christ had been transformed into a plush bird-hunting outpost for American executives.

Hunting season was still months away. Nathan Broederlam, head of the finance chamber for the International Court of Justice, had promised the other two chamber members who accompanied him to this place that they could meet in complete privacy.

But Taber was fully aware that privacy was Broederlam's secondary concern. His first concern was to gauge the other judges' reactions to the lawsuit he had presented this morning. It was all part of the plan set in motion by Broederlam's and Taber's *other* employer, a faction only referred to as The Group.

The meeting was not even an hour old before Sydney Dumas, the only female judge on the ICJ, urged them to table their discussions and consider the case independently before reconvening that afternoon. Joseph Ambrose, the third judge who made up the chamber, had agreed.

Now, as Taber stared at the elaborate stained-glass window depicting Christ's crucifixion that accented the end of the hallway near Joseph Ambrose's quarters, he couldn't help thinking about trust. Like Jesus Christ, both Joseph Ambrose and Sydney Dumas had trusted their fellow man. They trusted Nathan Broederlam had picked this desolate location because of the unnerving sensitivity this lawsuit demanded. Instead, Broederlam wanted an isolated place where the deaths of his colleagues could be explained. Death here in a monastery, a place originally built to celebrate the Giver of Life. Ironic indeed.

Trust was also the reason why Taber was waiting out here in the hallway. He glanced at his watch. The stopwatch function was engaged. It had now passed the one-minute mark. *He's taking too much time*, Taber thought. Too much time meant problems, the least of which was the fact that Declan Drake, Taber's new protégé, might be having second thoughts.

Taber reminded himself about the target. Joseph Ambrose was a German civil rights lawyer before serving on the ICJ. He had made a name for himself in his home country, winning several landmark civil rights cases, including one that made international headlines. He had led a group of German lawyers that sued the U.S. government to turn over a half dozen CIA agents sought in the alleged kidnapping of a German citizen with suspected ties to a terrorist cell. The case strained relations between the two countries for many months until a deal was brokered behind closed doors and the German citizen was returned.

Since meeting him almost thirty-two hours ago at the Amsterdam Airport Schiphol, Taber had immediately liked Ambrose. His fondness only grew as the hours passed. Taber could tell Ambrose was a quiet island in a sea of surging noise. That quality shouted volumes about his confidence. He didn't need to plug himself to the world. Men only became like Ambrose after ascertaining a lifetime of knowledge, which they usually parlayed into positions of power.

But after listening to Ambrose's initial criticisms of the lawsuit, which had been transmitted to The Group over a secure satellite connection, they felt Ambrose would continue to be a vocal critic of it. While his critique was exactly what Broederlam and The Group wanted in order to make sure the lawsuit was credible, his nonstop ranting could rip holes in their clandestine plan, exposing it to the light of unwanted scrutiny. The Group also realized that ultimately, as a civil rights lawyer who lived a modest lifestyle, Joseph Ambrose could not be bought.

Taber twisted the doorknob and eased into Ambrose's bedroom. He saw nothing at first. Then a breeze tickled his face. He stalked over to the open door that led out to a small balcony. The drape billowing in the doorway obstructed his view. He ripped through it, confident that his ability to kill could overcome any situation.

He stepped onto the balcony and saw Declan Drake standing over Joseph Ambrose. Blood was still flowing from Ambrose's neck with considerable propulsion.

Taber held up his watch. "One minute thirty-eight seconds."

"It's done, isn't it?" Declan declared, his Irish accent adding to his arrogance. "No sound, no mess. Just like you ordered."

Taber eyed the growing pool of blood. "No mess?"

"Tile floor. Easy cleanup." Declan gazed into the wilderness that encapsulated this wing of the monastery. It, along with eight other sections, had been converted into private suites. "No chance for witnesses either."

"Not the point," Taber reminded him. Taber sized up Declan Drake. The other ICJ guards on this detail had pledged their allegiance long ago to Taber and to The Group. Drake was the only wild card left. "Clean it up then. I've got one more job for you."

Taber pictured Sydney Dumas sitting quietly in her quarters, reflecting over the lawsuit documents. Unlike Ambrose, she wasn't a vocal opponent of the lawsuit; she barely said two words about it during their initial discussions. But she was the one who suggested they table the meeting and go off to think about the lawsuit privately. She hadn't made any calls about it; the only phones that worked here were the satellite phones the guards carried. But The Group knew all about former professor Sydney Dumas. Like Ambrose, they needed her interpretation of the lawsuit while it was still a confidential matter, but they weren't going to risk their ultimate plan for it.

Taber fingered the Glock 9mm stuffed in the back of his waistband. But, instead of giving Drake's gun back to him, he decided against it. This next task would be a much better test to determine Drake's commitment. Women and children proved harder to kill for some men, especially a woman like Sydney. Men had ended careers, given up entire countries, and even summoned their own deaths for women nowhere near her caliber. Killing her without the ease of a gun—a messy, very personal death—would prove Drake's loyalty once and for all.

Chapter 6

It was time to give up.

Danny Cavanaugh had been down here for a week. As he watched the sun fall from the sky each night, he always came to that same conclusion. He examined the only real choice he had left, which was in the gun cabinet before him. The four shots from the bottle of Jim Beam he found underneath the kitchen sink still warmed his gut. They mellowed his pulsing mind, too. *This is what women must go through when they stand in front of an open closet and agonize over the right accessories*, he thought as a dry smile formed on his mouth. Ever the smartass, even now.

He walked away from his task once again, like he had countless other times this past week. He sat down in one of the mismatched chairs that surrounded the kitchen table. As he stared into the deep scratches that scarred the rickety tabletop, his mind replaced it with the table and set of matching chairs that he and his dad had made with their own hands. He surveyed the cabin and replaced each piece of strange furniture with the familiar ones from his memory. The ratty love seat was gone in the blink of an eye and replaced with the Striped Monster, his nickname for the eight-foot long couch that his mother had recovered three different times over the years before sending it off to the cabin, a fate worse than death as she put it. The same went for the flimsy coffee table next to it. Danny closed his eyes for a split second and was rewarded with the sight of the other table that he and his dad had built and decorated with bottle caps from the various beers they would bring down here with them. Another smile crossed Danny's lips. He was nowhere near twenty-one when they started that tradition of Danny taking the first sip of his dad's fresh beer. "You'll have many drunken nights in your life,

14

Danny boy. Might as well have your pop guide you through the first few until you get your sea legs."

Danny trudged back over to the unfamiliar gun cabinet and finally made his selection. He had broken the lock the first day, and now, only a slight tug on the glass door was needed to gain access. He reached inside and grabbed the one rifle he was certain would do the job—the Winchester Model 70. It was dependable, accurate, and could be loaded with 7-millimeter bullets for bigger game. Danny yanked open the drawer below and grabbed a bullet. He loaded the rifle and then buttoned everything on the gun cabinet back up before heading out the door.

Built of treated pine, the front porch was another project that Danny and his dad had successfully completed. It took more than six visits to the cabin over the course of two years to officially finish it with the attached railing and capped support posts. Danny meandered over to the corner post on the west side of the porch. He squatted and stared at the marks that neither time nor a change of ownership could wash away.

Little Danny Cavanaugh was here.

Three small horizontal impressions marked the post. Danny was thirteen when his dad had decided to take on the porch project, and sinking this post was the very first item on their to-do list. After it was secured in three feet of concrete, his dad told him to stand next to the post so they could measure his growth. Danny had grown five inches during the construction time: two between the first three visits to the cabin, one more before the fourth, and two more inches before the porch was finally finished. As Danny relived those memories, he could feel the rigid post as it hugged his equally straight back. He could feel the weight of the pencil his dad would hold firmly against the crown of his head, as he made his mark into the soft pine. He could feel the anticipation in his gut, as he spun around until he saw the tiny mark that was, in that moment, everything in the world to him.

As Danny ran his hand over each tiny notch, he realized how much he had changed. In the past, whenever he pictured this post with its marks, he always pictured himself with his own son, mirroring those few good times with his own father and hopefully avoiding the far too many bad ones. He would simultaneously feel both the joy of hopefully being a father himself one day and sorrow at what had been his relationship with his own dad. But this time there was nothing. There were no imagined scenes with Daniel James Cavanaugh Jr. There was no emotion welling in his soul. He was simply staring at a post with three forgotten scars.

Danny still couldn't believe the situation he had gotten himself into. Scratch that. The situation that had gotten into him. He was a fugitive, a man without a country. Try as he had for the past seven days, he couldn't come up with a better solution than the one he was about to take.

There's no going back.

Danny propped the rifle against his thigh and yanked back its bolt. The chambered bullet ejected into his hand. He stood tall against the post and jabbed the bullet's tip into it at the crown of his head. He turned and examined the mark, rubbing it with his finger.

Danny Cavanaugh was here once more. But not for long.

From the corner of his eye, he saw the date on his wristwatch. His birthday was a couple weeks away, on March 30. Thirty-eight years. It was such a long time. A lifetime. Memories of birthdays past reeled through his head. His father's reserved smiles, handshakes instead of hugs. His mother's story of his birth; how labor pains initially believed to be indigestion caused a last-minute, mad dash to the hospital. Even those thoughts couldn't persuade Danny against giving himself this early birthday gift.

Danny took one last look out over his dad's favorite setting on earth. He was procrastinating now, examining every bit of the nearly untouched valley before him. The official first day of spring was less than a week away, but many of the plants here in northern Mexico had already begun to bloom. But within the uneven quilt of the budding wilderness, Danny noticed something strange in the lone building that occupied the western edge of the valley. He swore he could see lights on inside the monastery.

Suddenly, Danny forgot himself and his morbid task. He ducked back inside the cabin and fetched the Browning 10 × 42 hunting binoculars he found during his initial search of the place. Looking through them, Danny confirmed his suspicions. Not only was the power on, but smoke was rising from one of the monastery's chimneys. There was life inside it, where there shouldn't be.

As Danny saw it, there were two possibilities. The Lake Guerrero valley was less than two hundred miles from the U.S. border. The Mexican cartels were continually expanding their networks all over northern Mexico. They often used secluded structures as transition points to smuggle the big three— drugs, guns, and humans—across the border. Danny had to admit there was no better building to house a host of illegal activities.

On the other hand, the building and surrounding land, which was once and might still be owned by Phoenix Oil, could be occupied by one of the well-heeled groups of American businessmen the Phoenix guys would invite down here during dove and quail season. The problem with that theory was that both seasons were still several months away.

Danny looked to the heavens. Was it a sign? A test? A way to make him stop his awful plan? Then he looked down, trying to gaze past the earth and into hell. Could it be an early birthday gift from dear old Dad? Make the cop, the Texas Ranger, inside Danny take over and save his son's life?

Danny considered this new option. If criminals were using the monastery as a hideout and he got killed raiding it, he would die an honorable death. He would be, as Jon Bon Jovi had so eloquently put it, shot down in a blaze of glory. If harmless American businessmen were there, maybe they could help convince Danny that his life was worth the trouble of living. *A win-win situation if there ever was one,* he thought.

Danny walked back inside the cabin and decided that, for now, he wouldn't take his own life. He would let fate decide.

While he took the next five minutes deciding on what weapons to take along, Danny couldn't keep his eyes off the spot in the kitchen where his father had committed suicide. Without even closing his eyes, he visualized every centimeter of the crime scene photos that he was never supposed to see. He concentrated on the empty bottle of Old Grandad whiskey lying on the floor next to a lake of his father's blood. Although he craved another shot of Jim Beam or several to temporarily lasso his unruly mind, he didn't want anyone to think that he had gone out like his old man.

Though his brain wouldn't let go of the image of his father's dead body, Danny was able to see beyond it as he headed out the door. He concentrated on simply putting one foot in front of the other, as he walked into the wilderness toward his destiny.

Chapter 7

Evan Pruitt left his apartment building at eight o'clock this morning like he had every weekday morning for the past two months. The rationale was simple. Performing tasks that are second nature reinforces confidence. Confidence breeds success. So, Evan Pruitt got up at seven in his drafty one-bedroom apartment in Crystal City. Like every morning, he dressed in a suit, tie, overcoat, and gloves. The black leather briefcase that hung from his right shoulder carried the same forged think tank documents inside the same manila file folders. In his right hand, Evan clutched this morning's copy of the *Washington Post*, which was delivered in the hallway outside his front door. He balled his other hand into a fist and then slowly released the pressure, feeling the glove around his fingers. The weather was beginning to warm in the afternoons, which bothered Evan. But his luck held out. It was still cold enough in the mornings that wearing gloves wouldn't seem strange.

Evan gazed at the empty basketball court in Virginia Highlands Park on the corner of 15th and Hayes streets. Past the court was an open field where he would see the pee-wee football practices on his return this afternoon. Evan crossed 15th Street and joined the flow of commuters shuffling toward the escalators that would carry them to the Metro platform beneath the street. From the corner of his eye, he scanned the faces of these people and imagined what they would soon be telling their coworkers about their close call with catastrophe.

I was just on those very same tracks! That could have been me!

Evan opened his wallet and fingered the Metro card he had paid for in cash. He inserted it into the reader, glided through the open gates, and retrieved the card on the other side. As he walked toward another escalator that would ferry him to the boarding platform, he inspected the dwindling balance recorded on the card. A mere $9.65 remained.

He edged past the other rush-hour subway riders and headed toward the front of the platform. As he waited for the blue-line train that would take him into the heart of D.C., Evan Pruitt nonchalantly thumbed through the wallet that was given to him three months ago. He looked at his fake business cards that were linked to the real think tank, credit cards with real limits, and even a real Virginia driver's license with holograms embedded in the lamination. The name Evan Pruitt was plastered on everything.

But Evan Pruitt was not his real name.

-

The train operator's familiar baritone rolled over the rustled silence that was the unwritten rule of the Metro during rush hour.

"L-L-L-L-L'Enfant Plaza next stop. Transfer station for orange, yellow, and green lines."

The squealing brakes signaled Evan, along with the rest of the standing passengers, to shift toward the train doors. When the train finally stopped, Evan allowed himself to get swept along with the flow of people through the train's open doorway. It was only after he stepped a few feet onto the platform that he broke free from the crowd.

He walked along the platform toward the set of stairs that would take him up to the main level of the L'Enfant Plaza station. Once there, he strode over to the center and plopped his briefcase down on the same empty concrete bench that he used every weekday for the past month. He glanced down toward the other end of the platform and saw the face he expected to be there. They held each other's eyes for only a second—a nanosecond—same today as they had for the past month. But today was no longer just practice.

A new confidence washed over Evan. It worked its way into his shoulders, down his back, and energized his core. He knew that nearly every inch of the station was being watched by cameras, the eyes in the sky. But that still couldn't stop them. Their plan was sheer genius, and it was being carried out with exacting precision, careful patience, and swift timing.

Evan kept his head down as he opened his briefcase. He concentrated on hearing the activity around him: the endless clicking and clacking of hard-soled shoes striking the floor, the occasional voices of people engaged in conversation as they rushed by him, the sliding fabric that covered passersby as it stretched and rubbed against moving skin.

Evan pulled the newspaper out of his briefcase, just like he had done every weekday for the past month. But today, he made sure the device was safely tucked inside it. He had practiced this part of his mission every night in his apartment since he first moved in. *Practice makes perfect.* He closed his briefcase, slung it back over his shoulder, and started down the platform with a death grip on his copy of the *Washington Post.*

Evan saw his colleague coming toward him. He noticed how much they were dressed alike. Both had department store overcoats covering single-breasted, charcoal gray, off-the-rack suits. Underneath that, they both wore white shirts and conservative ties. They clapped toward each other in their polished black cap-toed shoes. The message they were sending spoke loud and clear. Each one was a young man on a budget trying to act the part of a D.C. player: typical $30,000-a-year millionaires. There were thousands of them in this city, and each one just as anonymous as the next.

They passed each other without a word or glance. But Evan couldn't help looking around the platform to quench his insatiable thirst to be in the know. The others would be there, but he wasn't privy to their part of the plan. Would they be wearing disguises? What exactly were they going to do? When would their part of the plan begin?

Evan stopped the guessing game as he continued heading for daylight. On his way out of the station, he sidled over to the recycling bin near the exit, just like he had done every weekday for the past month. Evan waited behind a middle-aged black man to deposit a copy of the *Washington Post* before he did the same.

As he made his way through the exit turnstile, Evan increased his swagger toward the up escalators. When he finally reached the light of day again, crisp wind engulfed his face. Evan had to smile. It really was that easy.

-

Evan Pruitt had just slipped into line to order his usual extra hot, no foam, hazelnut café latte in the Liberty Place Starbucks on 7th Street when he heard the sirens. He looked behind him and saw a fire truck rocket by. Then another. They were followed by an ambulance.

Evan exited the store before ordering and followed several other Starbucks patrons down the block, following the commotion. He could tell what was going through their minds. Ever since 9/11, sirens made people uneasy. Especially in favorite targets like Washington, D.C.

As the street calmed and life in this part of the district returned to normal, Evan could only imagine the chaos ensuing only blocks away; chaos that he and his colleagues had engineered.

Evan turned back toward the Starbucks and thought about adding a hunk of coffee cake to his usual drink order. *What the hell?* he thought. He could deviate from his routine a little now. Call it a reward for a job well done.

Chapter 8

The shower loosened Sydney Dumas's body, but the water wasn't strong enough to break the hold strangling her mind. Sydney always did her best thinking in water. Not this time.

She stared at the stained-glass window that nearly filled the entire back wall of the shower stall. It was a scene of baby Jesus in the manger with a crowd of both man and beast looking on. The glass was exquisite in its detail. The midmorning sun made the three wise men's white robes glow, while it sharpened their faces as they basked in the presence of their infant king.

Sydney gazed at every face in the glass, picturing her godfather's face alongside them. She reeled back to the moment Colin Tanner, whom she had playfully nicknamed Knobby for his pointy, balding head, was sitting in his favorite booth in the Land's End Pub in London, and telling her that he was dying of lung cancer. But that revelation wasn't as shocking as the one that followed.

"Sydney, there's something you need to know about me. Something you need to know about the world."

His explanation had concluded with what seemed like a madman's prophesy. *"There will be a single event, something that might even seem inconsequential at the time. But it will happen within a larger context. If it happens within your lifetime, I hope you will at least recognize it for what it is and tell the world."*

On the surface, the lawsuit that Nathan Broederlam had presented this morning looked normal, highly confidential at this stage, but normal. As members of the ICJ's finance chamber, it was their job to discuss sensitive legal documents and consider the repercussions that could send shockwaves through the relatively fragile international financial system. But ever since joining the ICJ,

Sydney had tempered every case that came before her with Knobby's warning. His prediction had yet to come true. In fact, as time passed, his words seemed more and more foolish, the wild accusations of a conspiracy nut.

But, as she added the implications of this lawsuit into the economic equation created by Japan's recent actions against the United States, she couldn't help thinking the worst. Could this finally be the sign Knobby had foretold?

Sydney pulled back the shower curtain. Hoping to give her anxious mind a break, she tried focusing on items in the gracefully appointed bathroom. She concentrated on the antique mirror that hung on the wall. Noticing the strain in her face, she switched to the pedestal sink below the mirror. She followed the pearl inlay that curled from the front edge to the fixtures. She even traced the lines of caulk that held the hand-painted tiles of the backsplash together. Nothing worked.

Sydney's head began throbbing. *Never a swimming pool around when you need one*, she thought. Then she remembered the explanation from a university colleague about why she always did her best thinking while she swam lap after lap. He had told her that only when the conscious brain was occupied would the unconscious mind be able to run free and find answers. Her eyes caught on the object on the side of the tub. *Maybe that would do the trick.*

Sydney grabbed the can of shaving cream and began lathering her legs. She swiped her razor off the tub's edge and made a few passes along her left leg, hoping her simple task would break something loose in her head. But the only realization she came to after several strokes was that she needed to change blades.

-

Declan Drake hadn't been able to fully keep his mind off of the ravishing woman who he was supposedly protecting down here in the Mexican wilderness. She was tall, his own height in fact. The way she carried herself, it was with subtle confidence. He didn't know her background, but he knew she had to be smart. No one became a judge on the International Court of Justice without being intelligent. But this was the capper for Declan. She was French. That accent was beyond sexy. She spoke English most of the time she was around him, but Broederlam had tried his hand at French with her, a sophomoric attempt to be charming. But when her native tongue flowed from her mouth, shivers actually jolted Declan's spine and everything else in his body. He imagined what her actual tongue could do to him.

He washed away those thoughts and got on with the mission at hand. He knew he was on shaky ground with Stefan Taber; his allegiance to The Group was still being questioned. He grabbed the doorknob of Sydney Dumas's quarters and twisted it. He crept into her room and shut the door behind him. He could hear water running behind the bathroom door. *She's taking a shower.*

Drake visualized her stunning face. Soon he would see it, crowning her taut, naked body. *What a waste*, he thought as he stalked across the room and pulled a blade from his pocket.

Chapter 9

Sydney stepped out of the tub, making sure to stomp off the water that clung to the bottom of her shower shoes onto the towel she had laid on the floor. She walked over to her toiletry bag, which lay on top of another towel underneath the sink. She squatted and searched her bag for a new razor blade to finish the job. That's when she saw the light underneath the door shift. Someone was in her bedroom.

Sydney squeezed her head down to the crack underneath the door. She stared past the mosaic of multicolored tiles that covered the floor and saw a pair of black combat boots closing in on her. She remembered when she met the guards on their security detail. Each one looked menacing dressed entirely in black with their expressionless faces. But it was their boots that were the most intimidating, the heavy sounds they made as they struck the ground.

Sydney was about to yell to the guard when Knobby's voice echoed inside her head.

Guards follow orders. Someone sent this guard here. They realize you know the lawsuit is the sign.

Sydney shot back up. She scoured the bathroom for anything to defend herself. She stared at the hair dryer, envisioning throwing it into the tub and electrocuting her attacker. But that wouldn't work. There was no standing water in the tub. *Yeah, Syd, maybe he'll give you time to fill the damn thing up and then stand quietly while you throw in a working hair dryer,* she thought sarcastically. She considered the razor blade. *What, shave him to death?* There was only one way in and out of the bathroom. She was trapped.

Sydney looked at herself in the mirror and suddenly realized that except for her shower shoes, she was naked. She pulled her bathrobe off the hook on the back of the door and slid it on as quietly as she could.

Then Sydney saw it. A possible weapon. It was dangling from the marble holder that hung on the wall next to the mirror. Her toothbrush. A desperate idea edged into her head. She stalked over to the tub and eased the curtain shut. Then she lifted her toothbrush from the wall just as the doorknob turned.

Sydney crept behind the door and squeezed herself into the corner. She turned the toothbrush around in her hand and stuck it between her ring and middle fingers while she made a fist. The door moved toward her. She pressed her body into the wall, trying to evade detection until the last possible moment. The door kept coming. She sucked in her taut belly and stopped breathing. The door finally stopped just before it hit her shower shoes, and the intruder slipped inside.

The guard crept over to the bathtub and raised one hand to grab the shower curtain. He readied a knife in his other hand. A sudden thought of the parents she never knew entered Sydney's mind. *They want to kill me, just like they killed my parents.*

The guard raised his blade and yanked back the curtain. Just as fast as he had tensed, his body went limp at the sight of an empty bathtub. But he also revealed something else: Sydney's salvation.

The guard stood dumbstruck, staring at the stained-glass window. Sydney turned the toothbrush in her hand so that now she gripped the spine with all four fingers and reinforced the brush end with her thumb. Then she moved, her eyes flashing on baby Jesus while a prayer raced through her mind.

Sydney wrapped her right arm around the guard's neck. As she did, he instinctively looked back toward her, finally revealing his face. She didn't know his name, but she would never forget his face as long as she lived.

Sydney's other arm was already in motion. She only needed to adjust her target a few inches to make solid contact.

She tightened her choke hold and drove the toothbrush into his ear. The guard let out a barbaric wail as his knife clattered into the tub.

As he clawed at his ear, Sydney thrust away from him. But she didn't give him any time to recover. He was still trying to yank the toothbrush from his ear when she used every bit of strength she could muster and shoved him into the brilliant manger.

Sydney turned for her bedroom and saw the only guard whose name she knew standing in her bedroom doorway. Stefan Taber. He actually smiled at her as he raised his gun.

Sydney threw the bathroom door shut and locked it. She grabbed her bra and panties off the toilet seat and then scaled across the motionless guard. She stepped through the hole in the window and climbed out onto the roof just as two bullets blasted through the bathroom door.

Sydney examined her options and chose the best conceivable route. She took a step down the roof when she felt her robe catch on something. She whirled around to see that the guard had a handful of it clenched in his fist.

His cold eyes pierced the veil of blood pulsing on his face. "You're not going anywhere, bitch," he spat at her.

Sydney yanked on her robe, trying to free it from his grip, but he had a firm hold. She saw him reaching for something in his pocket. Another gunshot echoed from the bathroom. Taber would reduce the door to splinters in seconds. She had to get out of there.

Sydney untied her robe and ducked out of it. The guard grabbed her ankle, but Sydney was able to kick free of his grip.

As she stutter-stepped down the tile roof in slippery shower shoes, Knobby's voice once again filled her head.

"Run, Sydney! Run as fast as you can!"

Chapter 10

Danny heard the sound of shattering glass followed by two gunshots and then one more. His instincts took over. He shouldered the Browning BAR Safari rifle while he intensified his gaze.

He was nearing the perimeter where wild brush and untamed trees met the monastery's purposeful landscaping. Through the wild mesquite trees, he could see the northeastern corner of the guest quarters that had been added to the monastery's main structure thirty years ago. He stepped past the property line, ducking under an oversized saguaro cactus. As he did, he saw the remains of a shattered window refract sunlight in a hundred different directions.

Danny pictured bored drug runners firing off rounds and trashing the joint, including the beautiful stained-glass window of baby Jesus in the manger that he remembered. *They have no respect.* He kept the rifle squarely against his shoulder as he came upon the walking trail that wound around the base of the hill. It would take him up to the rear of the monastery compound and hopefully to its current occupants. As he started toward it, he heard footsteps behind him.

Danny fought his instincts to leap for cover and slowly turned to face his adversary, letting fate decide whether he lived or died. One emotion overpowered the rest. It was regret and it cried out to him.

Don't let this happen! Don't let your life end!

Danny completed his turn and couldn't believe his eyes. *I must already be dead*, he thought. Standing before him was a breathtaking sight.

It was a statuesque brunette clad only in a bra and panties.

Danny almost didn't notice she was holding a log above her head. She was thirty steps away and heading toward him fast. She froze as soon as she saw him take aim at her.

"Hold it right there!" Danny commanded.

Her arms shook under the weight of the stout log, but she kept it perched where it was as she spoke. "You're American," she said, her wild eyes everywhere.

Danny could tell that she had an accent, although he would need to hear her speak again to confirm her nationality. "Yes, I am," he replied. He considered the best way to explain himself. "My name's Danny Cavanaugh. I'm a police officer."

She didn't relax after he declared his name and occupation. "What are you doing here?"

Her accent was French. *Matches her panties*, Danny thought. She had to be a dream or a mirage, something brought on by the constant stress he was under for the past week. He tried reasoning with his senses. *There's no way this was happening. A six-foot tall French beauty wearing only underwear does not live in the Mexican wilderness.*

"I have a cabin nearby," Danny replied. "And you?"

Her eyes hadn't slowed. She remained on high alert, scanning the woods in every direction.

"Ma'am, is someone chasing you?" Danny asked.

She finally glared at him. "Show me your identification."

Although Danny had the more powerful weapon, he didn't want to do anything to scare her. She might run off, or simply disappear in a cloud of pixie dust. "I'm going to reach into my pocket and get it."

He reached for his back pocket and produced his wallet. Thank God he had the second thought of bringing it along. He had totally forgotten about it back at the cabin until he considered how his body would be identified.

He opened his wallet, revealing his Texas Ranger badge. She leaned forward and studied it. Then she looked back up at him. Satisfied, she lowered the log but held it firm in front of her chest.

Danny couldn't help but look her over again. A jagged band of blood stained her ankle. There were no cuts or abrasions on her skin.

"That your blood?" he asked, pointing to her ankle.

She examined her ankle. "No."

"Then whose is it?"

She stared at Danny without answering. He took a few moments to analyze her body language. She was standing there, her toned appendages tensed with adrenaline. She tried looking tough, but Danny read her eyes. She was scared shitless.

"Look," he continued, "I'm here to help you. But you need to be straight with me."

The French goddess filled her lungs and opened her mouth. Danny was about to get his confession when her molten eyes darted beyond him and flashed with terror.

Chapter 11

Look out!

Sydney opened her mouth to scream, but the words didn't come. Fortunately, she didn't have to warn Danny. He reacted to the horrified look on her face by rolling forward. He ended up in a crouched position with his rifle aimed at the guard from Sydney's bathroom.

Danny ordered the guard to freeze, which he did. His face still leaked blood from the gashes he sustained from the stained-glass window. Although the toothbrush was gone, the guard's ear and half his head were soaked in darkened blood. His eyes finally swung over to her.

If looks could kill, Sydney thought, *the guard would have murdered me several times over and used my carcass for numerous unspeakable acts.*

"Drop your weapon," Danny said. The guard stared at him again, but the knife stayed in his hand.

"Drop the knife," Danny repeated.

The guard didn't move.

"*Gota tu arma*," Danny ordered in Spanish, no doubt mistaking the guard's black Irish looks for Hispanic. The guard still didn't budge.

Sydney tried to help. She pointed at Danny and told the guard, "Are you fucking crazy? The guy's a mercenary. Do as he says or he'll shoot you where you stand."

Danny eyed her. Sydney suddenly remembered how she was dressed, but modesty wasn't something she was prone to. After all, she'd performed in front of hundreds of people in swimsuits just as skimpy.

Sydney tightened her grip on the log, willing herself confidence. She wanted to tell Danny that others were no doubt coming for her, and fast. They didn't have time for whatever was transpiring here in the woods. Her legs were brimming with nervous energy. She wanted them to carry her far away from this place.

"Drop the fucking knife!" Danny snapped. Sydney watched both men's eyes. Each sighted the other's stare. Out of the corner of her eye, she saw Danny's body tense. She dare not shift her head for fear of the guard figuring out what he was doing.

Then it happened.

Chapter 12

Danny lunged at the man and used his rifle like a bat, knocking the knife from the man's grip. The impact sent it flying into the bushes. Danny then swept his legs out from underneath him, knocking the man to the dirt. Danny pounced on top of him and wrapped his arm around the man's throat. He had used this hold only a half dozen times over his career. He had subdued a father who nearly beat his six-year-old son to death, he kept a husband holding his wife hostage from blowing off her head with a shotgun, and he had used it to restrain a few violent drunks. He learned the highly illegal hold at the police academy in Houston. While it walked all over the rights of the suspect, it was the most effective way to gain control of a situation without the use of lethal force.

"Did you kill him?" the woman asked.

"No," Danny answered as he guided the man's limp body to the ground. "I made him pass out."

She edged over to the man. "How long will he be unconscious?"

"Long enough." Danny retrieved the knife from the bushes. It was a Junglee Extreme Forces model, a favorite weapon of military types. Although a weapon like this one could slice through rope or saw through a small tree limb in seconds, it was intended for only one use: close combat.

Danny glanced at the woman. She was still studying the motionless body at her feet. Suddenly, she held the log away from her chest and let it drop. It landed with a *thud* on the guard's chest. He didn't move an inch. *She's thorough,* Danny thought. *I'll give her that.*

Danny walked toward her. "I take it this isn't the first run-in you've had with our friend."

"We must get out of here now." She strode past Danny and clipped away from the monastery.

"Listen, lady, I don't know who you are, and I don't know what's going on here. Until I do, I'm not going anywhere. Neither are you."

She stopped and turned toward him. Danny tried putting her mind at ease. "Look," he started, holding up the knife, "this guy's a professional. There's only one reason why he's carrying a knife like this. It's to kill in silence. He didn't want to alert anyone to his actions. He's working alone—"

"He's not working alone! His captain fired a gun at me!"

Explains the shots I heard, Danny thought. He looked around in all directions at the quiet terrain. There was no one in sight. "Still, I think we're safe for the moment." He closed the knife and jammed it into his pocket. "I can help you. But I need to know why this guy and his captain are after you."

Sydney took in a huge breath, let it out, and walked back to him. Danny had to fight the very male urge to leer as her toned muscles worked underneath her butterscotch tan.

"I'm Sydney Dumas." She glanced toward the monastery. "I was meeting with two other members from our group here at the monastery."

"What group?"

"The International Court of Justice."

International Court of Justice? Danny had never heard of it, but then again he had never heard of half the clandestine groups that he learned about during his short tenure with the Texas Rangers. *There's a whole big world out there, Danny boy. A world about which you know damn little.*

"What're you meeting about?" he asked.

"We're here to discuss the implications of a lawsuit."

"So, you're a judge?"

She huffed. "Even out in the middle of nowhere people are surprised to learn that."

It's just that I've never seen a judge make underwear look that good, Danny thought. He motioned toward their assailant. "Who's this guy? A military officer?"

"He's one of the guards assigned to our security detail. I don't even know his name."

"And his captain? The one who shot at you?"

"He's the head of the guards. His name I do know. It's Stefan Taber."

"How many guards on your detail?"

"Including this one and Taber, five."

"So, eight people total? Three judges and five on the security detail?"

Sydney nodded. *Five guards,* Danny thought. *A group named the International Court of Justice must be flush with resources. That meant their security detail was well equipped.* Danny eyed their surroundings again. His confidence that they were safe for the moment was no longer high.

Danny picked up the guard's arms. Then he motioned for Sydney to pick up his feet. "Let's get him out of sight." They carried him off the path a few yards and dumped him behind a dense patch of prickly-pear cactus.

"Let's get his clothes off. You can wear them." Danny squatted, taking cover behind the cactus. Sydney followed his lead. He started working on one of the guard's boots. Sydney went to work on the other one. "So what's this lawsuit about?" he whispered.

"Japan is suing the United States."

"On what grounds?"

"They want to redeem their U.S. treasury notes."

"Redeem? You mean cash them in?"

"Yes."

"How much?" Danny asked.

"All of them," Sydney replied.

"All of them? How much money are we talking?"

"A little over $1 trillion."

Danny whistled. "No wonder we don't want to pay up."

Sydney nodded. "America has been living well beyond its means for the last twenty-five years. Why start paying your bills now?"

Danny let that one go. He was aware of the mind-boggling amount of debt that America had racked up, something in the neighborhood of $13 trillion, which easily made the United States the world's largest debtor nation.

"A few months ago," he started, remembering, "didn't China and Japan stop buying our debt?"

Sydney nodded. "Three months ago, yes."

"Does this lawsuit have something to do with that?"

"It has everything to do with that."

Danny waited a moment for Sydney to continue with an explanation. "You don't like giving away too much, do you?"

"I think there is something else, something more."

"You think the lawsuit's a cover?"

"Yes."

Danny pulled off the boot and stared at her. Again, she balked at an explanation. "Why?"

She yanked off the other boot. "Beyond the fact that I was almost killed for trying to interpret it?"

"Good point. But countries are no different than people, right? No matter how badly they want to get paid, Japan would exhaust every other option first. Litigation is a last resort."

"More or less."

Danny waited a moment for her to continue. He asked, "Can you be a little more specific?" when she didn't.

Sydney narrowed her eyes. "Japan thinks they are out of all other options."

"Why's that?"

"Because the United States isn't going to be around much longer."

Chapter 13

"You're gonna have to explain that one," Danny said.

Sydney had already said too much. She kept silent, choosing to begin unbuttoning the guard's shirt. She shucked it off his torso and slid into it. It was a few sizes too big, but at least it covered her. Moments later, Danny was helping her remove the guard's pants.

Sydney had never been in the business of trusting other people, especially after hearing Knobby's tale, which appeared as if it were finally coming true. But there was something about this man, this Texas Ranger, this policeman. Although his eyes were beyond weary, kindness glowed inside them. It also didn't hurt that he was gorgeous. His dark hair provided the perfect backdrop to a tanned face framed with a few days' worth of stubble. He resembled a rugged adventurer dressed in a tattered long-sleeved T-shirt, cargo pants, and hiking boots. Women would want to trust this man as soon as they met him, including Sydney.

"Japan also stipulates that dollars won't be accepted as payment," she finally said, choosing her words carefully.

"They can't not accept dollars. It's currency, the most accepted currency across the planet."

So, he isn't just another pretty face, Sydney thought. "That's exactly what I thought when I read what they want as payment."

"What?"

"Gold."

Danny stopped fooling with the guard's pants. "Gold? I'm pretty sure our government doesn't have a trillion dollars worth of gold just lying around. And even if they did, they wouldn't want to part with it."

Danny probably had no idea how close he was to the truth. But Sydney couldn't disclose it. Not here anyway. Still, she felt she had to give him something more. "My theory is that they want gold because they believe the dollar will soon be worthless."

"Worthless? What makes the dollar worthless?"

Sydney looked around. "We don't have the time—"

"Then give me the short version." He scanned the area. "We're okay for a quick story."

Sydney sighed. "The debt that China and Japan regularly purchased represented 20 percent of the revenue for the U.S. operating budget."

"Which means they were subsidizing our daily operations," Danny concluded.

Sydney nodded. "In the three months since Japan and China have stopped buying that debt, which caused the rest of the world to play follow the leader and do the same, the Federal Reserve has had no choice but to print more money to make up the difference."

"Which has devalued the dollar and caused the huge jump in inflation everyone's been griping about, right?"

"I'm glad to see you're up to date on fiscal policy, Sergeant."

"I like keeping current. But the Fed can't just keep printing more money, right? If they do, won't there come a point when inflation spirals out of control and a loaf of bread costs like $15,000?"

"There is another tool the Fed can use well before it gets to that point. They can raise interest rates so other countries will start buying your debt again."

"And the problem with that is?"

"The higher the interest rate, the more you have to pay in interest to your investors."

"I got that part, but how does that apply to the U.S. budget?"

"To date, you've accumulated just over $13 trillion in debt. Interest payments on that debt represent the third largest expense in your federal budget. To make your debt attractive again, the Fed will need to increase the interest rate at least three, most likely five, percentage points. When that happens, America will not be able to afford to do much else but pay the interest on that debt."

Danny jumped ahead. "Which our government can't do because we need to pay for essential services like our military and Medicare."

Sydney nodded. "And when America can't pay—"

"We'll be bankrupt." Danny exhaled. "Jesus."

Hearing herself tell the story made doubt creep into Sydney's mind. *It does sound fou,* she thought. *Crazy.* But then she thought back to the monastery's conference room only hours ago, where she sat staring at the two sentences in the lawsuit that stood out from the rest.

Payment in U.S. dollars will not be accepted. Payment must be made in gold.

Sydney had considered the possibilities. With the price of gold already at all time highs, a handful of countries—including Italy, France, Holland, and Germany—had recently sold off small portions of their gold reserves to pay down their national debts. But not since the world abandoned the gold standard had any country demanded gold for any type of payment. And no country had ever parted with all or even close to the majority of their gold reserves.

Then Knobby's warning had exploded in Sydney's head.

"There will be a single event, something that might even seem inconsequential at the time. But it will happen within a larger context."

Danny tugged off the guard's pants and handed them to Sydney. She finished buttoning up the guard's shirt. Then she kicked off her shower shoes, unfurled the guard's pants, and stepped into each pant leg. She buttoned the pants around her waist, and they slid down to her hips. She bent over and began rolling up each pant leg above her ankles.

"So, let me get this straight. You're meeting about the lawsuit and then the guards just turn on you and started shooting?"

"No. I knew the lawsuit didn't look right. I tabled the meeting so the three of us could consider it by ourselves until the afternoon."

"That's when they tried to kill you."

"When I was back in my room, yes."

"What about the other two judges?"

"What about them?"

"What did they think about the lawsuit?"

"Joseph Ambrose was as shocked as I was when he saw it. Nathan Broederlam, who headed our meeting, he was the only one who knew …" Suddenly, Sydney stared off into the woods.

Danny aimed his rifle in the same direction. "What?"

Sydney continued eyeing the woods, as she recalled the strange turn of events. "Nathan must have sent the guards to my room." She finally returned her gaze to Danny. "He was the one that presented the lawsuit to us. He was the only one who knew about it beforehand."

Danny relaxed. "No offense, Sydney, but all this sounds very circumstantial. I mean, the notion that this lawsuit means the coming collapse of America, that's just your theory, right?"

She stood over the guard's feet and pulled off his socks. She again considered giving Danny the full story. And again, she decided against it. "Is it also my theory that this asshole is trying to kill me? Do you have his theoretical knife in your pocket? Did you hear imaginary gunshots coming from the monastery?"

"Okay, okay. Just keep your voice down." Danny surveyed their surroundings again. "You want to explain why you were in your underwear?"

Sydney already had one foot in one of the socks. "I was in the shower when the guard came into my room. I hid behind the bathroom door, and when he came in, I pushed him through the window and escaped."

Danny sighed. "You're in a meeting to decide the fate of the United States, and you decide to break and take a shower?"

"I needed to think everything through. I think better in water. There wasn't a pool so, yes, I took a shower."

"Oookay," Danny replied, drawing out his reply in a smug American tone.

She had the guard's boots in her hand and glared at him. "You don't believe me!"

"Quiet!" Danny whispered through clenched teeth. Again, he looked around to see if anyone heard her.

Sydney tried reading Danny's eyes. *Does he really believe me?* She thought again about Knobby's stories on that late spring afternoon in the Land's End Pub. Her thoughts began to betray her. Had those conspiracy tales infected her perception of what was really happening?

What were the odds that she uncovered some unbelievable plot to alter the world as she knew it? Her eyes fell on the guard. She wished that he was conscious so she could get the truth from him.

What is really going on here?

"I won't even attempt to understand the intricacies of international economics," Danny said as he surveyed their surroundings again, "but wouldn't the Supreme Court be involved with something like this? Or the International Monetary Fund? Plus, something like this is huge. Wouldn't it be all over the six o'clock news?"

Sydney shoved her left foot into the guard's boot. It was at least two sizes too big, but she hoped by the time she had it laced up around her ankles, it would fit better.

"The ICJ is the legal arm of the United Nations. The whole idea behind its creation was to manage disputes between countries as efficiently and as quietly as possible. The three of us are members of a special financial chamber formed to try cases in secret that could have enormous impacts on the global economy, a system that could be described as a schizophrenic suffering from massive panic attacks and constant paranoia."

Danny chuckled. "You certainly paint a distinct picture."

"Our chamber operates under a strict gag order. We take extreme measures to meet in communication dead zones all over the world to ensure our discussions remain secret. Not even the other judges know what we're deliberating. That's why the three of us are out here in the middle of nowhere. At least that's why I thought we were here."

Sydney could tell from the look on his face that Danny was processing everything. "So, what do you do now?" he asked.

Knobby's urgent command pulsed through her head and she repeated it to him. "I have to tell the world what's going on."

"You just said that you can't."

"That was before people were trying to kill me. I have to tell someone."

"Okay, who?"

Exactly. Tell who? Sydney hadn't thought that far ahead. She looked around at the endless woods, as she finished tying on the left boot and began working on the right one. Plants and trees reached out to her from every direction. She looked toward the monastery and could barely make out its shape beyond the foliage.

Tell who? And how do I get to them?

Sydney's head began throbbing under the weight of the possibilities, which all seemed to lead nowhere. She looked over at Danny and did something that was foreign to her.

"I need your help, Sergeant."

"It's Danny. And I can see that you might."

"So? Will you help me, Danny?"

"You're in luck. I didn't have much else going on today."

Her shoulders eased as she smiled. She always had a feeling of relief after she asked for assistance, but still, it was just so damn hard to do.

"What do you think we should do?" she asked as she finished tying up the right boot. Out of the corner of her eye, she saw Danny eyeing the monastery.

Sydney heard his answer, but couldn't believe it. She had to ask him to repeat himself.

"I said we need to go back to the monastery," Danny repeated.

Il est fou. He is crazy, she thought. "We can't," Sydney declared. "I don't know who's involved. I don't know why this is happening. I don't know anything. We need to get to the border and into the United States. You're a police officer. You must know people who could help me."

He hesitated. "I agree 100 percent. But we need something first."

"What's that?"

"Proof. I've been a cop long enough to know that spoken accusations are nothing without hard evidence to back it up."

Sydney had to admit that Danny had a point. She stood tall and wiggled both feet inside her new boots. They slid around in all directions, and she winced at the thought of the blisters that would soon form on them. But it was better than tromping around the forest in shower sandals.

"The lawsuit you saw is on paper, right?" Danny asked.

Sydney pictured the three copies of the lawsuit that Nathan Broederlam had taken out of his briefcase earlier that day. "Yes. To my knowledge there are three copies."

"We need to get at least one of those copies. Do you know where one would be?"

"I left my copy in my bedroom. But I'm sure they took it back by now."

"Where was it discussed? Where did this Broederlam set up shop?"

"The conference room."

"Okay. The conference room it is."

"Wait. How do we get in there?" Sydney asked. "They'll be watching for me."

A cocksure look materialized on Danny's face. "Simple," he replied. Then he let her in on his plan.

Sydney had to laugh.

Il est fou. There is no doubt.

Chapter 14

Seeing Vanessa Dempsey enter whatever White House venue where President Jack Butcher was holding court before he was scheduled to leave could only mean one thing. Something unplanned had arisen; rather, something *else* unplanned had arisen. The attack on the L'Enfant Plaza Metro station was certainly news to the world that morning. Jack thought about canceling the rest of his day and then decided against it. He had already given an impromptu briefing from the White House Press Room less than an hour after it happened. It was now two hours later, and he was confident that the right people were in place, doing what they did best to find out what exactly was going on. Plus, his visitors had traveled a long way for their moment with the president, and Jack was not about to disappoint them.

Vanessa was a fifty-five-year-old mother of two. She wasn't an especially attractive woman, but she was catching some of the eyes in the Diplomatic Reception Room as she clipped along the back wall in a bright red dress. Jack nodded to her, recognizing his need to wrap up things. She perched herself in a shadowy corner and waited.

President Butcher was hosting a short reception to congratulate Boy Scout Troop 30 from Little Rock, Arkansas, on being named Troop of the Year. Being a former Boy Scout himself, Jack picked this room when Vanessa approached him with the idea for the meet and greet nearly a month ago. He knew the story that unfolded on the walls of this room better than any other venue in the White House.

"Gentlemen," Jack addressed the young men over the continuous sound of clicking cameras. "The thirty-two scenes you see before you are based on engravings of American landscapes from the 1820s.

Here we have the Natural Bridge of Virginia, Niagara Falls, New York Bay, West Point, and Boston Harbor." Jack paused to let the Scouts admire the artwork. It reminded him to astonish them with another tidbit of knowledge that had remained in his brain after his own initial tour of this room. "If we ever need to make repairs to this room, we can take these scenes down." Jack encouraged the Scouts to get closer to the wall. "You'd never know it, but this is all just wallpaper. The artists used wooden blocks to print on the wallpaper panels. A pretty good idea for 1834, huh?"

"Mr. President?"

Jack turned to the pudgy, freckle-faced boy at the end of the line. "Yes, sir?"

"Can I ask you a question, sir?"

"Well, since you're one of my bosses, sure you can." Jack made sure not to take his eyes off the boy, even though he heard chuckles coming from the reporters and cameramen. He never just played to the crowd.

"Are we safe?"

The question caught Jack off guard. He was expecting something about the room or the mural on the wall. But he never flinched, never stammered, never showed for one second that Jack Butcher wasn't prepared to handle anything that came his way.

"Of course, son. The White House is actually a working military fort. It is the safest place in the nation, probably in the entire world."

"No sir," the boy continued nervously. He was gripping his pant legs so tight that the cuffs had risen two inches off the tops of his sneakers. His cheeks were burning red. "I mean the country. I-Is the country safe?"

A new wave of camera snaps crashed in Jack's ears. He pictured Brian Williams on *NBC Nightly News* talking about the president's reaction to this little boy's question. The consensus among his advisers was to scrap the Scout meeting and concentrate on the attack. But Jack wouldn't do it. He had to set an example for the country. But was this the right example? Holding court for a small group of over-privileged kids while Washington, D.C. was on high alert and the rest of the country was anxiously watching?

Are we safe?

"What's your name, son?" Jack asked the boy.

"Connor, sir."

"Connor, do you know the old saying safety in numbers?" Connor nodded. "That's something that each one of us needs to remember. To ensure the safety of this country, you, me, all these reporters in here, your mom and dad, my so ..." Jack stumbled for only a moment. He quelled the emotion welling in his gut and continued. "Your teachers, our friends, your scoutmaster, my colleagues, your aunts and uncles and grandparents and all of the citizens of the United States need to make awareness a part of our daily routine. If something doesn't look right, tell someone. If someone is doing something that we know is wrong, report it. We can't sit back and expect our government, with its ignored color-code terror alert system and bloated bureaucracy, to keep an entire country of more than three hundred million people constantly safe. We must depend on each other." Jack paused to let his words sink into every person in the room. "Does that seem like a reasonable request, Connor?"

The boy was stunned. He remained silent, as the cameras continued snapping away. Jack was about to continue when Connor broke from his daze.

"Yes, sir. I totally agree."

Jack walked over to him, squatted, and lowered his voice. "I know you're scared, Connor. We all get scared sometimes. Even presidents. But we can't stop living. Because that's what the terrorists want. They want us to stop living. They want us to seize up with fear. We can't do that, Connor. We need to continue to spend time with our families, to hang out with our friends, and to work hard at school and at our jobs. We need to watch each other's back harder than ever, Connor. But we need to keep living our lives." Out of the corner of his eye, he saw Vanessa approaching him. Apparently whatever she had come in to tell him couldn't wait any longer. He stood up and edged a few steps away from Connor to receive her.

"They found the sources of the gas at L'Enfant Plaza," Vanessa whispered in his ear.

"And?" Jack whispered back to her.

Vanessa rolled her eyes back and forth, suggesting that this may not be the right time for this information.

Jack stared at her. She leaned into his ear again.

"Recycling bins on each level. We got confirmation that it was sarin with traces of hydrogen and cyanide. So far, no deaths. Just injuries from the panic."

They made eye contact once again, and Jack nodded at her. She continued. "Simon's waiting for you in the Oval. Harry Tharp's with him."

Harry Tharp. No one was close enough to hear them, but Jack was paranoid about the devices reporters had these days that could pick up hushed conversations. He bit his lip to keep from making a comment.

Jack nodded at her once more, and Vanessa left the room. He spent another two minutes for a couple group shots with the Scouts and then he was off to the next task on his never-ending to-do list.

Chapter 15

"Gentlemen, long time no see," Jack said as he entered the Oval Office. It may have sounded like a joke, but the president was not in a joking mood. It had been less than an hour since Simon Shilling, Harry Tharp, and the president were seated around the Situation Room conference table surrounded by the joint chiefs and other military and anti-terrorist strategists. He shook their hands and motioned for both men to sit. They sat on the opposite couches that flanked the coffee table. Jack took his usual spot in the JFK rocker.

"Sorry for the delay. I had a photo op with some Boy Scouts who have been waiting for months to meet their new president."

"No worries, Mr. President. You need to spend some time with your own kind once in a while," Simon said, grinning.

Jack eyed Simon. If Jack Butcher was the all-American boy, the good-looking, gregarious, high school quarterback, then Simon Shilling was his complete antithesis. Although Simon wore his signature bowties and owlish horn-rim glasses every day, he was Bill Gates geeky. Middle age and what seemed like a new nationwide respect for eggheads had finally allowed Simon's concave body and pensive features to appear cool. Simon had taken the liberty to remember everything about Jack's life like it was his own. He also took the liberty to remind Jack of it every so often.

Jack crossed his legs and eased back in the rocker. "Spending time with the kids sends the message to the nation and to whoever attacked us that we are not going to be deterred from living our lives because of a—"

"Disruption?" Harry Tharp finished. Harry was the current secretary of homeland security and the former director of FEMA.

He was a numbers guy, whose personality reflected his love of math over his fellow man.

"I was going to say 'an unmitigated act of barbarism,' but disruption may work," Jack replied. He glanced at Simon, who was scribbling some notes on a legal pad.

"Vanessa said that it was sarin gas but that it was mixed with hydrogen and cyanide. Accurate?" Jack asked Harry.

"Yes, sir," Harry replied. He took out a piece of paper from his portfolio and handed it to Jack. It was a schematic of the L'Enfant Plaza Metro station. "Sarin's a nerve agent. It's odorless and colorless. But when it's mixed with other agents, it turns a faint yellow. An FBI biologics team recovered the gassing devices from three recycling bins, one on each level of the station." Harry pointed to the circled items on the diagram. "A CDC emergency response team then took samples from each device."

"Why would they mix the three agents?" Jack asked.

"They figure if the sarin doesn't kill the victim straight away, then the hydrogen and cyanide would finish the job. Terrorists like these kinds of weapons because they're low tech and fairly easy to assemble. The dumbasses that rigged these up though, got them all wrong. CDC confirms that the amount of chemicals inside them was non-lethal. Lucky break for us."

"Do we have any idea which terrorist group is responsible?"

"This type of weapon is a favorite of numerous groups, mostly Middle Eastern. We're having every available staffer scour the Internet for individuals or groups taking responsibility. There's nothing so far. There was no abnormal chatter leading up to this event and none since. I don't want to even suggest any groups at this point, Mr. President. All we can say for sure is that the biologics team is combing through every newspaper in those bins for fingerprints. Hopefully, we'll get a good match to a bad person or two."

"Anything on video?" the president asked.

Harry shook his head. "Thirty-eight cameras watch that station, Mr. President. The recycling bins are located in areas the cameras don't cover."

Simon huffed. "They knew where the goddamned blind spots were."

Harry eyed Simon Shilling before reassuring the president. "We're reviewing previous tape, Mr. President. We're also questioning anyone who has ever worked with those cameras since they were installed. If anyone so much as gave the cameras a second look, or if they bribed a current or former camera company employee for information, we'll find them. We'll get whoever did this, sir."

"When will we have the full report?" Simon asked Harry.

"It'll be sometime tonight at the earliest," Harry replied.

Simon gave his famous look of confusion. *Why can't it be faster?* He was a master at it. He could plaster those distinct lines in his forehead that rested on those memorable eyeglasses and stare for an eternity at anyone—a reporter, a staffer, a member of Congress—making them fill the silence, like it was their job to explain the look off his face.

Although Simon had asked the question, Harry addressed the president with the standard bureaucratic answer. "I'll get more people on it, Mr. President. We'll have answers for you as soon as possible."

Jack nodded. "Tell me more about the devices."

"Like I said, they're fairly crude actually," Harry started. He dove into his portfolio once again and retrieved an eight by ten close-up of one of the devices. He handed it to the president and began pointing to its various parts with his pen. "It's really just a sixteen-ounce aluminum canister with a timer and a radio transmitter backup."

Jack looked at the photo intently, picturing it doing its job inside the recycling bins. He tried to put himself in the shoes of the first Metro commuters who saw gas emanating from the bins.

What an awful feeling to think that you're going to die at any moment, actually seeing your death slowly blowing toward you. A thought of his son cracked across his brain. *But isn't it better to see a quick death coming than to be slowly murdered by a hidden killer?*

"Even if they hadn't screwed up the mixture, how much coverage are you going to get out of three sixteen-ounce canisters? Can't be much, can it?"

"No, sir. Each one had the capacity to only cover about a thousand square feet," Harry replied. "Whoever did it obviously didn't give much thought to the size of the station."

"Do we know if the device was triggered by the timer or by the radio control?" Jack asked.

"Why does that matter?" Simon asked.

Harry breathed deeply. Jack could tell that his Homeland Security secretary was about to educate them with one of his long-winded explanations. Jack beat him to the punch.

He said, "Because if they set them off using the radio transmitters, they would have to be present when the gassing started." He looked at Harry. "Why don't you have your people check the tapes for anyone acting suspicious near the recycling bins. We may not have gotten them planting the bombs, but maybe we can see them activating them."

Harry arched his eyebrow.

Yeah, Harry, I'm a smart guy. Don't underestimate me. Jack still couldn't believe that he had to put Harry Tharp in as Homeland Security chief. Harry was a blowhard, a know-it-all who had worked his way up through FEMA. He still didn't think that "skirts" should be in any positions of power. But during his watch at FEMA, he had led an impressive response to Hurricane Karen in Florida. His leadership proved to be so successful that most Floridians even started calling him "Hurricane Harry." If he wanted a leg up on securing Florida's twenty-seven juicy electoral votes for his reelection campaign, Jack had no other choice than to promote him.

Damn the politics.

"What's the current status of the Metro system?" Jack asked him.

"Whole thing's still shut down, sir. As of this minute, no other stations or buses have been affected."

Jack tried rubbing the stress out of his neck and then looked over at his chief of staff. "Any thoughts, Simon?"

"Just my usual. Stay on message. Vigilance and caution are the words. Remember the London underground bombings in '05. They were a hell of a lot more severe than this, and things got back to normal pretty quick. We are in a new age, Mr. President." Simon glanced at Harry before continuing. "These *disruptions* are part of it. We address them but then move forward—with vigilance and caution."

Vigilance and caution. Jack repeated the words in his mind several times. He would be repeating them endlessly to the media over the next few days.

There was a familiar knock on the door that led to the foyer.

"Come in," Jack yelled.

Vanessa Dempsey entered in red blur. She glided over to the president and handed him a note. Jack unfolded it and read the message.

"Tell the networks to hang tight. We go forward as planned."

"Yes, sir." Vanessa tapped her watch. "You've got the Mazoka meet and greet in ten." Jack nodded, and Vanessa was back at her post in the foyer in a matter of seconds.

"The TV honchos worried about the State of the Union?" Simon guessed.

"They want to know if I'm still planning on delivering it Sunday night."

Harry huffed. "They want to know if they can run *Titanic* for the hundredth time or something?"

Simon cleared his throat, signaling to Jack that he had this one. "Actually, they're fishing for a scoop. News of the president canceling the State of the Union would get them licking their chops for more information on what we're thinking about this event and terrorism in general." Harry pursed his lips as he nodded. He didn't think like Simon and Jack did. Inside the White House, it was all about the message, working the words. That's why Jack had instructed Vanessa even before he took office to interrupt whatever he was doing when any of the news outlets had their panties in a twist.

"Maybe we need to start some folks thinking about the consequences of moving the State of the Union," Simon said. "This attack is awfully close, Mr. President."

"Absolutely not. There are too many important items on the docket. The American people have waited long enough for their new leader to tell them what the hell their government will do to earn its keep for the foreseeable future. Increase security if you have to, have the skies over the district filled with F-16s, ring the greater metro area with the National Guard for all I care, but the State of the Union will proceed as planned—with caution and vigilance."

Jack looked at both of them. He realized that he had subconsciously ratcheted his volume up more than a few notches. "Okay," Jack stood, signaling the end to their meeting. "Obviously this attack is top priority. Feel free to yank me from anything whenever we get something new."

"Don't you think we need to increase the terror alert, sir?" Harry responded as he stood.

Jack hated that useless thing. It reminded him that their government treated its citizens like two-year-olds. "Americans are intelligent, Harry. They don't need someone to change a color to know that they need to stay on their toes. Oh, sorry. Let me rephrase. To proceed with caution and vigilance."

Simon smiled at his boss getting comfortable with the message he had crafted. Both men responded according to White House protocol. "Yes, Mr. President."

As Jack went for the door, Harry stopped him.

"Who are you off to charm next?"

Jack looked at him. Was he being sarcastic? The words came out flatly, but Jack had to wonder. It was obvious Harry didn't agree with his blatant indifference to the terror alert system. Damn Harry Tharp and his twenty-seven votes.

"It's the anniversary of the Kabwe massacre in Zambia. I invited President Mazoka here to talk about what we can do to inspire peace in their homeland. I think we need to do more than offer them some handouts with terror swatches on it. Wouldn't you agree, Harry?"

Harry ducked his chin into his chest. "Of course, Mr. President."

Jack went for the door again, but this time he stood there, holding it open. Harry glanced at Simon, who offered only a cocked eyebrow. Harry practically ran out the open door.

Jack closed the door behind him and returned to his seat at the head of the sitting area. Simon stood still. He waited the requisite thirty seconds that he always did after someone left the Oval before speaking candidly.

"What an asshole," Simon said on his way back to his seat on the couch. "If it wasn't for Florida ..."

Jack smirked, but then his expression quickly dissolved from his face. "What's our friend's status with his project?" The coded language about how a National Archives conservator was proceeding with his examination of the lost Constitution article and the accompanying letter, which was running past six hours now, sounded like Tony Soprano talking over a public phone line. But Jack didn't yet know if the walls in the Oval Office had ears or not.

"He's finished and taking full advantage of being sequestered in the residence, sir."

Jack didn't know what Simon meant by 'taking full advantage', and right now he didn't care. "What's his conclusion?"

Simon's face remained as rigid as the lifeless memorials scattered across the D.C. landscape while he delivered the shocking news. "He examined the ink; iron gall with traces of gum arabic and logwood colorant. The ink make-up exactly matches the ink on the Constitution. The handwriting also matches letter for letter. The documents themselves are parchment. There are several rough areas on both documents, as there are on the Constitution. He said they were undoubtedly made by the scribe using a penknife to erase his mistakes. As you may already know, parchment is an unforgiving medium, and was very expensive at the time. Scribes had only one shot when working with parchment. The documents have also been damaged by years of humidity and moisture, not to mention that insects have nibbled away at their edges over the years. There was also random ink splatter—"

The president held up his hand. "Just tell me if he thinks they're authentic."

Simon cleared his throat. "He says they're authentic, Mr. President. There's no doubt in his mind."

Chapter 16

Anthony Fantroy heard his private line ringing from across his study. Two staccato shrieks followed by a full second of silence. Then another two shrieks. He picked it up on the fourth round of rings. Before he put the phone to his ear, Fantroy prepared himself for the news. Even though their phone lines were completely secured, they all knew the rules. Communications are halted during missions, except for emergencies. Fantroy could only assume things were not proceeding as planned.

It was Nathan Broederlam, and yes, the news was as bad as it could get.

Anthony Fantroy continued listening to Nathan Broederlam, but he had already heard the most important words.

Sydney Dumas has escaped.

"Have you heard back from Taber?" Fantroy asked.

"Not yet, sir," Nathan replied. "But Mr. Taber and his men are professionals. It shouldn't take long to find her."

Fantroy sat back in his antique leather chair, its wood frame creaking under his unassuming weight. He began formulating his wishes to deal with the situation. He had been the one who made sure Nathan used the monastery for this exact reason. Without suitable transportation, there was nowhere to run. There was little chance that Ms. Dumas would last for more than a day or two in the Mexican wilderness without food, water, a cell phone, or money. Still, Fantroy couldn't take any chances. He was listening to the meeting when Sydney Dumas had tabled the discussions. It was before Broederlam made her and Joseph Ambrose the offers they couldn't refuse. Something in the lawsuit must have tipped her off. Fantroy had reviewed the lawsuit ad nauseum. One could read whatever they wanted into it, but ICJ judges were not armchair conspiracy theorists. Sydney Dumas must have known something else that pertained to the case. But what?

Nathan was convinced that Sydney didn't see or hear Ambrose's murder, but Fantroy had another theory. He thought about what he knew of Sydney Dumas. She was the adopted daughter of a French professor who decided to follow in her father's footsteps before being selected for the ICJ. It was assumed that she didn't know of The Group's existence. Fantroy had to now assume differently. He also had to assume that she knew what The Group was planning.

Fantroy reeled back to The Group's meeting at the Schloss Velden hotel in Austria. Hideo Akimoto, a Bank of Japan official and foot soldier for The Group, insisted on the Schloss Velden for his disclosure. He also insisted that The Group rent out the entire hotel. Hideo was sure what he had to tell them needed the utmost privacy.

Usually when The Group met, they rented entire floors of suites, even several floors of suites, to accommodate their numbers. That was standard protocol for groups attending large meetings and conferences. They had only commandeered an entire hotel once before during Fantroy's tenure. It was a year to the day before the American dot com bust. The Group's financiers had helped engineer it. They wanted to make sure everyone in The Group would benefit from it and reap their fair share.

Fantroy remembered the breathtaking views of the Austrian Alps that the Schloss Velden offered. He remembered the gentle sounds of Lake Worthersee's waters rolling into the rocky beach he walked along every morning during his visit. Even now, he could taste the crisp air. The hotel's soothing experience was the perfect contradiction to Hideo's staggering idea.

Fantroy imagined the scenario at the time. Being able bring the United States, and consequently the world, to its knees without firing a single shot. Extraordinary. It was the instrument of change for which The Group had been waiting all these years. But to use it to their advantage would require careful planning and perfect timing. Their plans could not be leaked. Their actions could not be discovered.

Fantroy had begun popping both Zanax and Zantac soon after his initiation into The Group. He swallowed a cocktail of the two and choked them down without a chaser while he thought of the consequences if Ms. Dumas reached civilization. If The Group's actions were uncovered, the anonymous financiers and those born into the wealth and power of the world's monarchies could simply deny accusations and continue living their privileged lives. But Fantroy was a political animal. He lived and died by headlines and public support. If their plan was exposed, he might as well be dead. But that's why he was involved with The Group. He wanted to be above such pettiness. He wanted what his birthright did not give him.

While the effects of the two pills couldn't have taken effect so quickly, the mere act of ingesting them brought a sense of peace to Fantroy's mind. He reminded himself that regardless of why Sydney Dumas was running, she had to be silenced before she reached anyone. Fortunately, Nathan Broederlam had been trained well enough to confirm out loud what Fantroy was thinking.

"We will take every precaution necessary to hunt her down and ..."

Nathan stopped talking.

"Nathan? Are you there?" Fantroy asked. But there was no answer. He looked at the phone on his eighteenth-century writing desk. The call timer continued ticking away. The connection with Nathan was still intact.

"Nathan? Hello? Nathan?"

Another voice came on the line, a woman's voice. "Who is this?"

It was Sydney Dumas. Fantroy slapped the phone down. Sydney Dumas was back in the monastery. She had overtaken Nathan. "What the hell is going on?" Fantroy said as if someone might suddenly appear in the room with all the answers. He stared into the darkness of a crystal clear London night as his brain immediately began dissecting the situation.

He jammed his hand into his jacket pocket and retrieved a list of hastily scribbled phone numbers. He dialed the one at the bottom and anxiously waited.

After six rings, a panting voice answered.

"Taber here."

Even though they used secure phones, Fantroy didn't want to say his name. Besides, his number would appear on Stefan Taber's phone, a number that Taber had been required to memorize.

"Talk to me," Fantroy said.

"Sydney Dumas is back, and she has company."

Chapter 17

Nathan Broederlam wanted to jump out of his chair and wipe the smug look off of Sydney Dumas's face. *How dare she jerk the phone from my hand!* But there was no doing that anytime soon. Not with Sydney's accomplice pointing a hunting rifle at him.

"What's going on here, Nathan?" Sydney asked. Nathan didn't answer her. Instead, he watched her accomplice scour the room. *He's comfortable with the weapon*, Nathan thought. *He has the movements of a professional.* The man's stare stopped once he saw the closed door on the far side of the room. Then he squared himself so that Nathan was on his left side and the door was on his right.

Nathan focused his attention back on Sydney. He noticed that she was dressed in Declan Drake's clothes. Did that mean that Drake was dead? Did Sydney really have it in her to kill the son-of-a-bitch? Nathan eyed her accomplice again. His weapon remained aimed squarely at Nathan's heart. *No*, he thought. *If Drake is dead, this is the guy who did it. By the looks of him, he could probably kill anyone without a hint of remorse.*

Nathan wanted to stall for as long as possible. He hoped that after hearing the commotion on the phone, Anthony Fantroy had enough sense to try and contact Taber. Nathan wished that he had yelled when he first saw them and that one of the guards was on the grounds close by, but they had surprised him from behind. If he tried anything now, Sydney's friend probably wouldn't hesitate to put a bullet in his chest.

"What are you doing, Sydney? Who is this man?" Nathan asked.

Sydney ignored him. "I heard you on the phone, Nathan. Who were you talking to?" Nathan kept his mouth shut. Sydney grabbed the lapels of his shirt and glared at him, her eyes only inches from his. "Why in the hell are you trying to kill me, Nathan?"

Again, Nathan tried stalling. He sighed and looked down at his useless legs, lying like dead snakes underneath him. He always wanted to explain his actions to someone. He wanted to tell Sydney that his motives were altruistic, that The Group meant well for the entire planet, for the future of mankind. If he did, would she embrace their cause?

We are the only ones who have the power, Sydney. If you only knew. If you only had the slightest clue. Your entire view of the world, of your life as you know it, would be forever different. Could you handle something so big? Could any one person beyond The Group handle the truth?

Sydney's eyes flashed at Nathan's silence. "Where's Joseph? What have you done with him?" Sydney yanked on his shirt so hard that she lifted him from his wheelchair. "Damn it, Nathan! I want answers, and I'm not asking again!"

Nathan looked up. It seemed to take forever for his eyes to travel up her elegant body until he met her stare. Her face was brimming with anger. Maybe Sydney Dumas did have it in her to cause another human being significant pain.

She let go of Nathan's shirt and looked over at her accomplice. His eyes and his gun were firmly aimed at the conference room door. Then she turned back to Nathan and moved even closer to him. She gripped his wheelchair armrests and whispered. "I know what the lawsuit is really about, Nathan. I know who you really work for."

He instantly tried to wipe away the shock that registered in his face, but he could see it in her hardened glare. His reaction had confirmed her guess about his loyalties.

Nathan's eyes sagged in defeat. As his sight fell, he naturally focused on Sydney's working legs. Even in Drake's bulky cargo pants, Nathan saw the strength in those limber appendages. Those glorious legs that could take her anywhere she wanted to go.

"You don't have to worry about Joseph any longer," he whispered. He may not have had power in his body, but Nathan knew his words packed a punch.

Before Nathan could look back up to savor Sydney's reaction, a faint noise echoed from outside the conference room door. He glanced toward it and saw the curved doorknob begin turning.

Sydney's accomplice noticed it as well. He leveled his rifle at the door and, before saying a word, blasted two shots through it. Nathan instinctively flung himself underneath the conference table.

"Move! Back the way we came!" the man barked at Sydney.

He's American, Nathan deduced from hearing his accent. Nathan remained on his stomach, but from his angle, he could see the lower half of Sydney's body move. Her feet sped to the edge of the table and momentarily stopped before they changed directions. In an instant, she and the American were gone.

After a few dizzying moments, Nathan pulled himself out from under the table. He was panting as he fought to get himself up on his forearms. He flashed back to the moment when, on the day before his fourteenth birthday, he lost the use of his legs. He had just jumped a traffic light in downtown Amsterdam and was blindsided by a delivery truck, his spine crushed underneath its tires. Just like he struggled now, he had tried to pull his useless body out from underneath the truck. But it was no use, and eventually he had blacked out from the pain. But while pain gripped his body once more, Nathan would not succumb to it.

He finally shimmied back into his wheelchair and glanced toward the double doors at the far side of the room. Two armed guards were now bookending them.

Moments later, Taber and another guard were standing over him with their SIG Sauer 550 assault rifles at the ready.

"Are you okay, sir?" Taber asked.

Nathan silently thrust a finger toward the double doors that Sydney and the American had used for their escape. He envisioned the library that stood beyond them for what it was: a dead end.

As Taber approached the doors, he only needed to nod. The two guards grabbed the doorknobs and yanked both doors open wide. A split-second later, all four guards, including Taber, plunged into the doorway. They yelled "Drop your weapons!" simultaneously in their various accents.

Nathan edged up behind Taber. In his haste to see what was happening, his hands slipped on his wheels and he nearly fell over forward.

Damn this chair! Damn this body!

Nathan regained his composure and peeked around Taber. He saw the same books, tables, and accented leather furniture that he had before. But no Sydney and no American.

"The chimney!" Nathan whispered through gritted teeth. "Check the chimney!"

The four soldiers moved as one. Their backs were to each other with each gun barrel pointed in a different direction. They raced over to the fireplace. Taber yanked on the chest pocket of his utility vest. He extracted a small, square mirror and shoved it into the fireplace. A few seconds ticked by as he examined the chimney. Then he stuck his head in the fireplace and looked up.

Nathan could tell from Taber's reaction they were not there. But that wasn't possible. They couldn't have disappeared into thin air.

Move! Back the way we came!

The American's words repeated in Nathan's head as he slowly turned his wheelchair in a circle, studying the room. The library was a dead end, or was it? Suddenly, Nathan's eyes caught the view beyond the open double doors. The memory of Sydney approaching the conference table and then sprinting away flashed in his head.

No. Please God, no.

Nathan used every bit of strength he had to power his way back into the meeting room. He could see what he feared was true from fifteen feet away.

His panic swelled as he got closer.

Ten feet, then five.

Nathan collapsed on the table, his hands frantically shuffling the pages in front of him. He found two copies of the lawsuit, his and Joseph Ambrose's. The third copy, the one he had retrieved from Sydney's room, was gone.

Chapter 18

As he sprinted through the darkness of the monastery's underground passageway, Danny glanced behind him. He expected Sydney to be several yards back and struggling to keep up, but she was right on his heels. He figured that if the tunnel hadn't been so narrow, she would be leading them right now and he would be the one struggling to catch her.

Who was this woman?

When they first ducked into the tunnel to gain access to the monastery, Danny had regaled Sydney with the story of how he found it. "I discovered it when I was kid. The monks who lived here three hundred years ago built it as an escape route when the Spanish were trying to exterminate the population."

Her response allowed him to label her as a confirmed smartass. "So, you were a kid once. Hard to believe." Of course, it took one to know one.

Danny hoped his pocket Mag-Lite flashlight had enough juice left in it to keep their path lit. The stench of dampened earth seemed to intensify with each breath he took, forcing memories of his childhood adventures in this tunnel to materialize. Although he couldn't remember if he had imagined a scenario where he was being chased by bad guys back then, it was actually happening now.

When they reached the end of the tunnel, Danny shined the flashlight on Sydney. She wasn't even breathing hard.

Danny handed her the flashlight and swung the rifle onto his sweaty back.

"You ready?" he asked her, still trying to catch his breath.

"Yes," she replied calmly and aimed the light on the ancient wooden ladder that would carry them up into daylight.

Danny popped his head up first. Seeing that the coast was clear, he hopped out of the hole and helped Sydney up behind him.

"You okay?" Danny asked her.

"Yes." She lifted up her shirt and took out the documents that she had tucked into her waistband. As she began scanning through the pages, Danny eyed the woods around them once more. He thought again about his childhood. He remembered that there was one man who was always at the monastery whenever Danny and his father visited. Booker Halsey. If Phoenix Oil still owned the monastery, was it possible he might be involved in all this? Danny took his thinking one step further.

If Booker is involved, was Dad involved, too?

If Sydney's theory about some kind of conspiracy to bring down the United States was even a remote possibility, such a plot would place anyone involved under tremendous pressure. That kind of pressure would inevitably make some people crack.

Is that the real reason why Dad killed himself?

Suddenly, Danny found new momentum. Since meeting Sydney, his desire to help her was fueled by a deep altruism that was the main reason he became a cop in the first place. More important, by helping her, Danny could possibly clear his name. But now, this woman was much more than a way to a better future. Sydney Dumas could hold the key that unlocked the secrets to his past.

It wouldn't be smart to share any of this speculation with Sydney just yet. Not until he got a chance to talk to Booker. Danny stopped examining the woods and turned to Sydney.

"You got everything we need?" he asked.

She tucked the papers back into her waistband. "It's all here."

"Good. Now let's get out of here."

"Where are we going?"

"Houston, Texas. I know someone who might be able to help us."

Chapter 19

Despite the combination of rage and paranoia that pulsed through him, Nathan Broederlam had a revelation about the library. *There must be a secret passageway.*

He had ordered two guards to stomp on the floors and listen for hollow spots. The other two he ordered to tear apart the bookshelves. Taber found what they were looking for after several long minutes of searching. After clearing the bookcase that bordered the left side of the fireplace, Taber beat on the back wall with his forearm and heard an empty *thwock.*

Taber stepped back and leveled his rifle at the wall. He opened fire. The other guards joined in. In less than six seconds, they had torn the wall to splinters. Nathan couldn't believe it. The darkened passageway in front of him looked like it had been carved out by hand.

Taber extracted a flashlight from his utility vest and examined the empty passageway. He sent his men into it with orders to shoot to kill. Taber stayed behind.

"You're not going with them?" Nathan questioned.

"My men don't need me with them. Besides, Sydney came back once. She may come back again. We need to be ready for any contingency."

Taber loped back into the conference room. Nathan sat at the tunnel's mouth. He noticed two large hinges on the right side and then saw a cable attached to a clasp in the upper left corner.

Nathan angled his chair back and forth until he was as close as he could get to it. He reached for it in vain, his body giving up after only a few attempts.

Goddamn this body!

He wheeled over to the set of fireplace tools and picked up the poker. He rolled back to the tunnel's entrance and was able to hook the poker around the cable. He had to rest for a few seconds before giving the cable a good tug. When he did, Nathan heard a scraping noise in the fireplace. He rolled over to it and saw that the grate had moved. *The grate was the secret doorknob*. Sydney couldn't have known that detail, Nathan thought. It must have been the American. But there was no way he found it in the few moments they had in the library before the guards opened the doors. The American had to already know about the passageway's existence.

Nathan remembered how the American acted in the meeting room. He knew how to handle a gun. Was he a soldier? An FBI agent? A mercenary? Nathan's mind was all over the place as he entertained every possibility.

Who was the man helping Sydney Dumas?

Chapter 20

Declan Drake's heavy boots had taken their toll on Sydney's ankles. They were killing her by the time they reached Danny's cabin.

Danny performed a slow lap around the wraparound porch, watching the woods the entire time. After he was done, he noticed Sydney limping.

"You okay?" he asked.

Sydney took a seat on the first step of the porch and grabbed at her bootlaces. "It's these boots; they're too heavy."

"There are some women's clothes and shoes inside. Maybe something will fit."

Danny turned and walked into the cabin. Sydney slid both boots off and held her legs out in front of her. She rolled her feet around in the air and then focused on the woods beyond them. The wilderness was foreign and endless. With Danny no longer there, she suddenly felt alone. It was a feeling she knew all too well.

Sydney carried the boots with her as she padded up the porch steps and into the cabin. She could tell it was a man's place. Several dead animals, deer heads and fish, were mounted on the walls. Two mismatched couches formed a sitting area in the living room, each with its own plaid blanket thrown over it. An oversized stone fireplace crowded the far corner.

The gun cabinet across the room caught Sydney's attention. She crossed to it and eyed each gun through the glass doors. She wasn't scared of guns, but the sight of them had always made her uneasy, aware that the power to kill was within reach.

"Try these on for size," Danny said from behind her. Sydney jumped, dropping the boots and nearly knocking the clothes out of Danny's hands. "A little jumpy, are we?"

"I usually don't act like a frightened mouse."

"It's okay. I don't think you usually have people trying to kill you either. Or do you?"

Sydney smiled at him. "Not every day." Silence fell between them, the kind of awkward pause that happened on a first date where the guy tried to decide if it was the right time to move in for the kiss.

"Your family likes killing, yes?" Sydney finally asked him.

"Excuse me?" Danny snapped.

"I'm sorry; my English still fails me at times. It's just all these guns, here inside your home. The French do not display the power to kill so—"

"Obnoxiously?" Danny finished. "I never thought hunting was fair. I mean, what did the animals ever do to us, right?"

"So then, it's only fair when your opponent is also armed? Is that the idea?"

Danny gave her an odd look. "Something like that." He handed her the clothes along with a pair of white sneakers with socks rolled up and stuffed in them.

"Thank you," she said as she balanced everything in her arms. "Is that why you got into police work? For the thrill?"

"I got into it strictly to rescue damsels in distress."

"Is that what you think I am?"

"You tell me."

"I can take care of myself. But I'm not stupid enough to, what do Americans call it, look a horse in the eye?"

Danny chuckled. "In the mouth. Look a gift horse in the mouth."

"Right. I'll accept a gift horse or a gift … what did your badge read, ranger?"

"Texas Ranger, yes ma'am."

"Are the Texas Rangers like cowboys?" Sydney asked.

"Some folks think we're nothing more than that." Sydney didn't get the joke and scrunched her face. Danny continued. "Are you familiar with the American FBI?"

She nodded. "The Federal Bureau of Investigations."

"We're similar to them, only we serve the state of Texas."

"So what are you doing down here in Mexico?" Sydney asked.

Danny hesitated. "Vacation."

"By yourself?"

Another hesitation. "Sometimes, I like being alone. Don't you?"

"Not really," she replied, her honesty surprising her.

Danny motioned toward the bedroom. "You can go in there to try on your new threads."

Sydney smiled at him and headed for the bedroom. As she tried on each item, she could hear Danny shuffling around the cabin. Drawers and cabinets were opened and shut, zippers unzipped and then zipped closed again.

Sydney was back out in the living room in less than ten minutes. Except for the well-worn sneakers on her feet, she was still dressed in the guard's outfit. Everything was folded back up the way it was given to her.

A backpack and two canvas bags were on the kitchen table. Danny looked up from the backpack, his hands still buried inside it. "Let me guess, too small?"

"Way too small. But the sneakers fit almost perfectly."

Danny held out a box of large Ziploc bags. "I found these underneath the sink. We can use one to protect the documents."

Sydney took out the papers that she had stuffed back in her waistband, put them in a bag, and sealed it up. She handed the bag to Danny, who put it in the backpack. She took another bag and stuffed it in her pocket. "Just in case."

"Good idea," Danny said and dropped the box into the backpack.

"Who are we seeing in Houston?" Sydney asked. "Your parents perhaps?"

Danny stopped organizing their luggage and looked up. "My parents? No. Mom lives in Houston, but I don't want to get her involved in any of this. My father ... he's deceased."

Sydney clutched her chest. "I'm sorry, Danny. Was it recent?"

"No. It happened many years ago." Danny tapped the floor where he stood. "In fact, it happened right here."

"Here? Was he killed?"

Danny didn't hesitate answering. "Sort of. Dad shot himself."

Sydney's gut immediately ached with guilt. "Oh Danny, I'm so sorry for prying."

"No. It's no big ... like I said, it happened a while ago. I was sixteen at the time. A lot of time has passed, so it's okay." Danny paused and then smirked. "I guess my dad liked killing so much he had to do it to himself."

Once again, an uneasy silence hung in the room. Sydney felt incredibly small. How could she have said that about his family? She should have known better. *Never assume about families. Especially after having the one you did, or rather didn't have.*

"Danny, I am very sorry for saying—"

Danny held up his hand. "Forget it. You didn't know." He checked his watch. "Come on. We need to pack the truck and get going. They may have found the passageway by now. They could be on to us."

"Right. May I use the bathroom?" Sydney asked.

Danny pointed at the back door. "Do you know what an outhouse is?"

"Out ... house? No."

Danny explained it to her; Sydney cringed.

"There should be a roll of toilet paper out there," he added.

Danny slung the backpack over one shoulder, grabbed the duffle bags, and headed for the front door. "One word of advice. Check the toilet before you sit down."

"Why?"

"There are all sorts of animals around here. They'll get into anything."

Sydney shuddered. She walked to the back door and peeked through the window. The outhouse was fifty feet from the cabin. The grimy white toilet glowed against the three walls that surrounded it. *Wait. It doesn't have a door!*

Sydney was about to say something just as gunshots ripped across the air.

Chapter 21

The force of the bullet knocked Danny back through the cabin's front door. Shaken, he was still able to roll out of the doorway, pull Sydney in behind him, and slam the door shut.

Danny felt pain in his shoulder. He checked it. No gaping hole, no blood. The pain had been from landing on it. Then he felt the brunt of the bullet's impact against his right hip. He checked it. Again, nothing. He looked at the duffle bag that was now lying on the floor next to him. He had filled it with the hunting rifles from the gun cabinet. The bag had a quarter-sized hole on one side. One of the rifles had stopped the bullet.

He unzipped the bag and pulled out the Browning BAR Safari rifle, the only semi-automatic of the bunch. He had refilled its three-shot magazine, but three shots wouldn't nearly be enough. He had to assume all five guards were out there. Judging from the fleeting glance he got of the assault rifles they were carrying back in the meeting room, he was severely out-gunned.

Danny shifted around on the floor until he could look at the back door. Sydney was on her stomach. She was looking at him with the fear of God in her eyes. It was obvious that she had been in enough life-and-death situations for one day and one lifetime.

He pointed toward the bedroom. Sydney nodded and began crawling for it.

One of the windowpanes in the front door had been shattered. Danny got to his knees and leaned the rifle's barrel against the door. He was about to raise it up into the window and fire a cover shot when he had a second thought.

They probably think I'm dead.

He pressed his ear to the sliver of space between the door and the doorframe. He heard a man's voice outside but couldn't make out his words. *What's he saying? Who's he talking to?* Danny closed his eyes, willing all of his energy to his ears.

What the hell is he saying?

His eyes shot open after a few seconds. He wasn't able to recognize any words, but he could distinguish the squelch from a radio. *Whoever's out there is getting orders before proceeding,* he thought. That meant they had some time. He grabbed the backpack and strapped it to his back. Then he found the box of bullets in the duffle bag and stuffed it into his pocket. He looked across the living room at the kitchen, where his other duffel bag lay on the table. Inside it, underneath several clean shirts and pants, was a small paper bag filled with a few hundred in cash. He wanted it more than anything, but the kitchen featured a full-length window through which he could be easily seen. He silently twisted the deadbolt on the front door and slithered in the opposite direction to the bedroom.

Sydney was huddled in a ball up against the foot of the bed.

"You okay?" Danny whispered.

She nodded. "What do we do now?"

"We get out of here."

Sydney's face fell. "How?"

Danny pointed to the closet. "Monasteries aren't the only buildings that have secrets."

Danny took the lead and crawled into the closet. As soon as Sydney was in behind him, he closed the door. He grabbed the mini Mag-Lite from his pocket and turned it on. He scooted over to the back of the closet and hoped that the new owner had the common sense not to change one small but important detail.

Danny stopped moving the flashlight as soon as he saw what he was looking for gleaming in its beam. He grabbed the eye-ring and yanked. The trapdoor squeaked open. He propped it open and latched onto Sydney's arm.

"Ladies first," he whispered as he shined the light on the hole in the floor. "It's safe down there. Just watch out for the plumbing pipes." Sydney disappeared into the hole. Danny wriggled off the backpack and followed her. He stood on the ground underneath the cabin and was chest-high in the hole. He grabbed the backpack and then the rifle and shoved them down into the crawlspace. Then he pulled whatever clothes he could find hanging above him off their hangers. He threw some of them on the closet floor in front of him, and the rest he tucked up behind the trapdoor. As he sunk down into the crawlspace and pulled the door closed above him, he hoped the clothes would hide the access door his dad had installed to service the plumbing pipes that snaked underneath the cabin.

As Danny took the lead and crawled through the web of pipes, an alarm exploded in his brain. *What have I done?* He may have bought them some time, but now they were trapped underneath the cabin. Once the guards found it empty, it wouldn't take long for them to figure out where they were hiding.

Danny stopped. He was about to whisper to Sydney that they needed to go back when he heard the sound of boots crunching through the brushy perimeter no more than fifty feet from the cabin's edge.

Chapter 22

Nathan Broederlam was at the head of the conference table, frantically trying to regroup. He had read through every word of the lawsuit and had started over again, weighing the possibilities that could have set off Sydney.

I know what the lawsuit is really about, Nathan.

The Group took immense measures to ensure their secrecy. Nathan had helped create the lawsuit and was the only one who had copies of it, until now anyway. How did she know?

I know who you really work for.

But she didn't actually say who it was. Was she just guessing, trying to get him to talk? Whether she knew Nathan was an agent for The Group or she was just pulling at straws, Sydney Dumas was a smart woman. Before serving on the ICJ, she was an international business law professor at the International University of Monaco. She was not afraid to speak her mind. Now she had risked her life, not once but twice. She had to be dealt with.

Then there was the American. Nathan had no idea who he was. But then he remembered how Sydney positioned herself before she floated her theory. *I know who you really work for.* She made sure to whisper so the American couldn't hear her words. Could Nathan contact the American and make him question her motivation? Could he make the American turn on her?

Nathan didn't know those answers, but what he did know was that Sydney and the American had come back specifically for the lawsuit. That meant they had a plan, a purpose. Maybe they had someone in mind to tell about its existence, maybe a news reporter or a U.S. government official. Whether anyone else believed them was now a moot point. There was now a story with evidence, a story that would need to be investigated.

And it's all my fault.

Nathan shuddered at the possibilities his error would cause. He had to contain this situation. But how? Could he count on Stefan Taber to help him massage the truth? Could Taber be bribed if it came to that? As if reading his mind, Taber appeared in the doorway. Nathan jumped in his chair but tried not to dwell on the fact that Taber startled him.

Nathan had known Stefan Taber personally for two years and had known of Taber's reputation for over six years. He was a ruthless operative who made sure nothing could be linked to The Group, an ability that both intrigued and scared Nathan at the same time.

"Any news from your guards?" Nathan asked as Taber approached.

"Declan Drake radioed." Taber had informed Nathan about what Sydney did to Drake in her bathroom. After sending all his guards, including Drake, out in the woods after her, Taber hadn't heard from him until moments after they discovered the escape tunnel behind the library. Drake had been incapacitated by the American. But, ever the professional, he was able to continue the hunt. "They're tracking them due north as we speak."

As if on cue, the Motorola Talkabout T7400 radio lying on the conference table burst to life. It spewed out static followed by a short, inaudible sentence. Nathan was about to grab it off the table but Taber swiped it first.

"Repeat," Taber blurted into the radio and turned up the volume.

"We've tracked them to a cabin almost two clicks due north of the monastery," Drake replied in his calm Irish brogue. "I had a clean shot at the man and took it."

A glimmer of hope rose from Nathan's gut. "Is he dead?" he asked. Taber repeated the question into the radio and waited for a reply.

"Nothing's affirmative yet, sir. We have the cabin surrounded and are waiting further instruction."

Taber stared at Nathan for instructions. The guards had the cabin under control, and the American was, in all likelihood, dead. Nathan was about to give the order to move in and kill Sydney when he stopped himself. The lawsuit was a highly unusual and controversial document. Still, as a seasoned ICJ judge, Sydney Dumas was bound by her duty to adjudicate it without passion or prejudice. Nathan couldn't get past her initial reaction to it in the conference room. It was as if someone had just told her an unbelievable secret, like she knew the real story behind the lawsuit and it was just proved true.

The questions that had been lurking in Nathan's mind for the past few hours were now peppering the forefront of his brain. Was Sydney that sophisticated to see beyond the words in the lawsuit? Was she some sort of spy sent to infiltrate The Group? If so, who sent her? Nathan's questions needed answers, and Sydney Dumas was the only one who could answer them.

"Do not kill her," Nathan said. "At all costs I need her alive."

Chapter 23

Sheets of wooden lattice surrounded the cabin's border, providing a barrier between the porch and the sloped earth underneath it. Beyond it, Danny saw a pair of bare legs emerge from the brush. *The guard from the monastery grounds.* He wasn't giving up.

Danny heard the guard's voice and then the squelch from a radio, but couldn't make out what he was saying. Danny and Sydney were still frozen, waiting for the guards to make their move. There was one more pulse of radio noise and then the feet began to move toward the cabin's front steps. In seconds, the guards would see that Danny's body wasn't there.

"Let's go," he mouthed to Sydney. He began crawling again and hoped Sydney had enough will left in her to follow.

They made it to the cabin's western edge just as turmoil erupted above their heads. Wood splintered as the front door was kicked in; glass shattered as windows were broken. The floorboards shook, jolting Danny as he reached through the lattice panel and twisted the wing nuts that held it in place. He pulled the panel aside. His truck was parked in front of a clump of mesquite trees a little over forty feet away. Sydney was next to him now, waiting to hear the next part of his plan. The sounds in the cabin had changed. Danny could tell that the men were nearing the closed bedroom door. They took slow and cautious steps. Soon they would realize the cabin was empty. It was now or never.

"I'm going for the truck," Danny whispered as he strapped on the backpack. "Look for my signal when I get there. Then get moving. Don't stop. Don't look around. Don't do anything but run. I'll cover you."

Sydney hesitated. Danny shined the light in her face. "Sydney!" he hissed in a whisper. "It's either that or die. Hear me?"

"Okay," she whispered back.

"I need you to drive so I can shoot if I have to," he said. Sydney hesitated again. But then she nodded.

"The keys are in the ignition." Danny touched her hand. "Wish me luck."

"Good luck," she replied.

Danny crouched on his feet, took a deep breath, and gripped the rifle across his chest. Then he burst out from underneath the cabin. He was running flat out, waiting for the rain of bullets he was sure was seconds away.

Chapter 24

Sydney's heart was in her throat as she watched Danny cross the wide-open field between the cabin and his truck. *This was a bad idea*, she thought. He had no cover, nothing to hide behind. All it would take was for one of the guards to look out the window and see him. With the tick of each second, Sydney kept waiting to hear a gunshot. She kept imagining Danny falling dead on the ground. When he finally made it to the rear passenger side of the truck, she breathed a sigh of relief. He turned around, and his eyes were instantly on the cabin windows. Then they fell on her and he motioned.

Sydney remembered back to her days on the starting blocks, thinking more about keeping her muscles loose than the competition around her. Those ancient thoughts propelled her relaxed movements once again as she exploded forward.

She made it to the driver's door and looked back at the cabin. The guards still hadn't detected their activity. Danny eased open the back door, and Sydney followed suit, opening the driver's door. She slid into the driver's seat and saw the keys dangling in the ignition.

I can do this.

Sydney looked back over her shoulder. Danny had twisted around backward in his seat. He was staring out the back window, his gun idling in his hands. He was ready to protect them at any cost. The least she could do was put her foot on a gas pedal and keep both hands on the steering wheel.

Sydney had driven a car before, but it was only once, when she was a teenager. The result wasn't good. She had plowed head-on into the only tree in the barren field her foster father had selected to teach her how to drive. Sydney's fear of cars instantly transform to hatred and remained that way for several years after Knobby informed her of how her own parents had died. It was a car accident, or rather a murder that was planned to look like a car accident. Sydney didn't get the chance to say good-bye, or even hello for that matter.

As she sat in the driver's seat, staring at all of the components that would allow her to control this metal beast, panic sparked in her gut.

I can't do this.

She heard Danny whisper over her shoulder. "Get us out of here, Sydney."

Her hands trembled as she gripped the keys. She looked in the rearview mirror and saw a body pass by the window inside the cabin. Seeing the guards, men who were out to kill her, men who were controlled by the same people who ordered the death of her parents, steeled her resolve.

I must do this!

She turned the key and the engine roared to life. She dropped the shifter into reverse and tromped on the gas.

The truck immediately got away from her. Her body lunged forward, her chest slamming into the steering wheel. She didn't know what happened. She looked up in the rearview mirror again and saw that they were headed straight for the cabin. She slammed on the brakes. Danny screamed from the backseat. "Drive Sydney! Get us out of here now!"

Sydney turned around and looked at him. He had been thrown to the floorboard between the seats and was struggling to get up when Sydney saw the guards, including Declan Drake's still-bloodied face, crowd into the window. They took only a split second to assess the situation. They all raised their guns to fire.

"Get down, Danny!" Sydney yelled at him. She ducked down in her seat and yanked the transmission into drive. She heard gunfire strike the back windshield, shattering it to pieces as she floored the gas pedal. The truck rifled forward, heading straight for the mesquite trees in front of them. Sydney grasped the wheel and yanked it to the right. The truck tilted violently. Danny cursed at her several times from the backseat, but at least he was still alive.

Sydney kept the gas on the floor even though there were more trees coming up fast. She yanked on the steering wheel even harder, shoving the truck to the right as far as it would go. But it wasn't far enough. The glancing impact sent her into the steering wheel again, knocking the wind out of her.

As Sydney frantically tried to catch her breath, movement in the passenger door mirror caught her eye. One of the guards had jumped through the cabin window and was now sprinting toward them.

Chapter 25

Danny was wedged down between the seats. His hands were useless. His right arm was pinned underneath him, and his left hand had a death grip on the rifle, their only defense weapon. He had seen four guards, including the one he had incapacitated, through the cabin window. He also caught a glimpse of their firepower. Each had an assault rifle strapped to his chest. They would be out of the cabin any moment. Sydney and he were sitting ducks.

Danny willed all of his energy into getting up. He let go of the rifle and grabbed for the center console. He pushed up on it and pried loose his body. He shifted himself up on the backseat and spun around for the rifle. He heard sounds behind him and then felt the truck wiggle. He glanced out the rear windshield that was now merely a jagged hole in the back of the cab only to see one of the guards standing over him.

The guard grinned as he leveled his weapon at Danny's head. Danny did the only thing he could think of in this situation. He closed his eyes and prayed for his soul. But instead of his soul being saved, Danny was granted a miracle.

The truck shot forward, sending the guard reeling back. He tried balancing his feet under him, but it was no use. The truck's tailgate undercut his legs and the guard was sent spinning to the ground.

Danny stared at the guards as Sydney finally drove them away from the cabin. They didn't have vehicles of their own and weren't making movements to chase them.

They were a good hundred yards down the dirt road before Danny finally turned to Sydney. Her face was still stained with terror.

"What the hell was that? Can't you drive?" he asked her.

"It takes me no more than twenty minutes to jog from one end of my entire country to the other! There is no need for me to drive!" she snapped. "But I can! Not well, but I *can*!"

Danny felt her spirit in her words. It was that spirit that kept her alive to this point. Hopefully, it would continue to be her greatest asset through this situation.

"Whoa! Eyes on the road Evel Knievel," Danny instructed as he lunged at the steering wheel, righting the truck back on the road.

Sydney turned back around and stared out the front windshield. "Who?"

"Nobody. Listen, you did really good back there. But now we have a little problem."

"What's that?"

"We need to get across the border, but we won't be able to use any of the major checkpoints with my truck looking like this."

"Why can't we just go to the authorities?"

Because I'm a fugitive. Danny didn't want to divulge his problems right now. Fortunately, he had a ready answer. "Corruption is widespread among the authorities in this part of the world, Sydney. We can't trust them."

"So?"

"So, fortunately crossing the border is as easy as driving in a straight line." Danny managed a smile. "For most people that is."

Sydney didn't reply. But she didn't slap him either, so Danny took this as a good sign. Then he glanced into the rearview mirror and saw Sydney's perfect white teeth gleaming behind her smile. *This*, he thought, *is an amazing and beautiful woman.*

Then he reminded himself that they probably wouldn't live through the day, so maybe he should keep his mind on the business at hand.

Chapter 26

Stefan Taber leisurely paced back and forth behind Nathan's wheelchair. As he did, he tossed his combat knife up in the air, letting it flip several times before catching it by the blade between his palms.

"Could you not do that?" Nathan quipped.

Taber shot Nathan a look and then stopped pacing. He returned his knife to the holster on his belt.

"Your guards should have reported back by now," Nathan surmised.

Taber kept quiet. He had been trained to read situations. He knew when not to give up information, even to the people that he served. Nathan eyed the radio lying on the table. He reached for it, but once again, Taber got to it first.

"We do not speak until spoken too, sir," Taber hissed. Nathan was well aware of the rule. Any attempt to contact the guards could give up their position.

The radio squelched while still in Taber's claw. Declan Drake came on and filled their ears with troublesome news.

Nathan was wild. "They're gone! Fucking gone! How in the hell could those fucking idiots lose them?" The news of Sydney getting away, this time by vehicle, meant it was his ass. Now she and the American could go anywhere.

"I thought the American was dead," Nathan said.

Taber relayed Nathan's concern over the radio. The answer instantly came back.

"He got lucky." Drake explained about the duffle bag filled with rifles and the apparent ricochet. "But we got lucky, too. As Stavros was falling off the truck, he managed to drop his weapon in the truck bed."

Nathan snapped at Taber. "He shot the bag the American was carrying? I thought that you people were supposed to be expert marksmen! Tell me they at least got the vehicle's license plate number."

Taber relayed the question through the radio.

"I already had it run, sir," Drake replied. "The truck was reported stolen four months ago in Laredo, Texas, by a Carlos Martinez. The description of Martinez doesn't come close to Ms. Dumas's accomplice."

"Jesus fucking Christ!" Nathan hollered. *Please God, give me two minutes of use in my legs! Let me show the incompetent bastards what I think of them!* What infuriated Nathan most was that Taber was simply standing there with his arms calmly crossed on his chest like he didn't have a care in the world.

"Sir, you need to stay calm," Taber advised. "All of our rifles are equipped with GPS tracking chips."

Nathan offered Taber a strange look and then he remembered what Drake had just reported: *As Stavros was falling off the truck, he managed to drop his weapon in the truck bed.*

Nathan motioned to a laptop at the end of the meeting table. Taber had been using it on and off since this madness began. "Do we track it with that?"

"No, sir." Taber reached in his pocket and extracted an odd-looking PDA device. "*I* use this."

Nathan nodded and tried to at least look relaxed as questions seemed to bombard his brain from every direction. Where would they go? Being that they were so close to the United States and that Sydney was with an American, they would no doubt head for the border. The closest checkpoint was Hidalgo, Texas, just south of McAllen. But would they use a major checkpoint? No. Not with a bullet-riddled vehicle. They would get interrogated for sure. They would need to find one of the lesser-used crossing points.

Would Sydney show the lawsuit to the border authorities? Nathan was fairly certain she wouldn't. She would seek people higher up on the food chain, people she thought she could trust.

Trust.

Sydney Dumas's strength and weakness was that she didn't trust people. But what about the American? Why did she trust him? Could she have known him? Certainly not. Nathan pictured Sydney with her striking features and her perfect body. Then he pictured the American, gazing on her with desire in his eyes.

Of course.

He had been so focused on Sydney, he wasn't thinking about the American. The American knew the monastery, he knew about the secret passageway. He had a cabin here, which meant he either lived here or, more likely, it was a vacation home. They could be traveling to his other home in the states. But where was that?

Nathan eyed Taber. "Tell your men to turn the cabin inside out. I want the American's name."

Chapter 27

Danny took over behind the wheel as soon as he could. Now, almost three hours later, he was worn out from steering his battered truck over the fractured oil-tops that snaked across the Mexican wilderness. When they stopped to change drivers after their messy escape, Danny noticed that the guard who almost killed him had dropped his assault rifle in the truck bed as he was thrown out. He stared at it now, lying idle in the backseat. He finally had a surprise on his side.

Sydney had fallen asleep in the passenger seat, which was an incredible feat considering the amount of jarring the truck was putting them through. Danny wanted to sleep as well, especially now that day was bleeding into night. But while his body was tired, his mind was brimming, feasting on a new buffet of details.

After forty-five minutes into their trip, the two of them finally felt safe enough to talk. Sydney had filled Danny in on Nathan Broederlam. Originally from Amsterdam, Nathan was not only the presiding member of their chamber, but he was the current ICJ vice president. Danny looked at Sydney's mouth as she slept. He pictured it moving, forming the words that made him cringe.

Nathan is a powerful man with powerful friends. All he has to do is reach for the phone to speak with almost any world leader.

An avalanche of imaginary scenes, each more vivid than the previous one, plummeted through Danny's head. He watched helplessly as both his and Sydney's throats were cut by unknown assailants. Then he saw them both get hanged. Then shot in the face. The last horrific vision had them both drawn and quartered by unrecognized men speaking in foreign tongues. But these scenarios were not just fantasy. For Danny, every scene was experienced, each sense sending information to his extraordinary brain as if he was actually living it. He felt the knife slice across his skin, catching on his Adam's apple and then ripping it in half. He saw Sydney's eyes bulge beyond comprehension as the hangman's noose applied terrific pressure to her head. He smelled the gunpowder and then the cooking flesh of the gunshot wounds. He finally heard his own bones crack, as cables pulled his limbs in different directions. *Goddamn my fucking mind*, he thought.

Danny finally crested the hill at the edge of San Miguel Camargo. Not wanting to arouse anyone's suspicion by driving a vehicle that, thanks to the guards and their automatic rifles, resembled a giant block of Swiss cheese, he pulled off the main road at the first side street. He was careful to avoid hitting the goats and chickens that littered the street and parked next to what looked like an abandoned mill house.

He gently nudged Sydney's shoulder. Her eyelids rolled up like sagging garage doors, revealing her piercing green eyes. Seconds later, those eyes hardened along with the rest of her body. She bolted upright in her seat, her torso catching against the seat belt.

"Hey, it's okay. We're okay, Sydney," Danny said calmly as he touched her arm. "Don't freak. We're almost home."

The fog of sleep cleared away from her mind and her face eased. "I'm sorry," Sydney offered as her head fell back against the headrest. "For a moment there I thought I had dreamed all of this."

Danny produced an understanding smile. "It's easy for your mind to play tricks on you?" *Believe me*, Danny thought. *I know.*

"Where are we?" she asked, looking around.

"We're at the border," he replied. Sydney stared out of the cracked windshield at the ramshackle adobe buildings around them. "Actually, we're about three miles away from it. Welcome to beautiful San Miguel Camargo. It's a village just outside the city of Díaz Ordaz. I figure we can get a bite to eat and stretch our legs before we cross."

Sydney nodded and got out of the truck. Moments later, three little boys appeared from nowhere and immediately besieged her.

"*Chicle! Chicle!*" they chanted as they held up tiny packs of gum in their filthy hands. Before Danny could tell her not to, she took one of the packs, thinking that a simple "*gracias*" would suffice.

Danny came to her rescue with change stashed in the truck's ashtray. "These kids are born salesmen." He handed two quarters to the boy who had just unloaded his gum on Sydney. As soon as the other two realized who had the money, they surrounded Danny and shoved their wares in his face.

"Chicle! Chicle!"

"Oh. I'm sorry. I thought it was a gift," Sydney replied.

"Don't worry about it." Danny took a package of gum from the two other boys and handed them each fifty cents. He was rewarded with smiles and many "graciases." Then, as quickly as they came, the children tore off to find their next marks.

Danny looked back at his busted-up truck. He yearned for his gleaming black Chevy Avalanche. He missed the hell out of that truck, but he had to get rid of it. Too many eyes were watching for it. He had traded down instead to a dark green 1993 Silverado Crew Cab. It, and a thousand in cash, was what the chop shop guys in Laredo traded him for his baby. But he had to look on the bright side. The Silverado fit in much better down here, until now.

He started walking down the street and Sydney followed. "Hungry?"

She stuck her nose in the air and sniffed. "Whatever's making that smell, I want it."

They turned onto the mangled dirt street that bisected the center of the town. Smoke wafted out from a jagged hole in the side of the second-closest building on the left.

"They're cooking tamales, another well-known tourist attraction."

Sydney sounded out each syllable. "Ta-ma-le?"

Danny nodded. "Tamales are rolls of cornbread filled with spicy pork and then steamed inside a corn husk."

By the reaction on Sydney's face, Danny could tell that his description needed work. He smiled. "Actually, they're very good. Two tamales and a cerveza always does the trick. Come on. My treat."

"I'm sorry for getting you involved in my problems, Danny."

Danny stopped and faced her. "You don't have to apologize, Sydney. If your theory holds water, then this isn't just your problem. If America really is on the verge of collapse, it's my problem, too."

"Yes, but your family's cabin. The guards are probably tearing it to pieces as we speak."

Danny knew she was right. They would be looking for anything they could to find out who was helping Sydney. They would find out who owned the place. But could they find out who the previous owner was? If they did, then it wouldn't take long before they found out about his dad and how his business dealings had been tied in with the monastery. They would find out about his dad's suicide, too.

Danny remembered contemplating his choices when he first got to the cabin. It was, in fact, the best place for him to hide. It was out of the country but close enough so that he could investigate the turn of events that had put him on the run. It was a place he knew very well but was no longer tied to his family. Danny had always felt drawn to the cabin because of what his dad had done there. He thought that by being there, he could get some answers as to Dad's desperation. Was it stress that broke him? Pressure from his business? Danny pictured his parents. They were a happy couple. Didn't Dad even consider what Mom would …

Oh God.

The thought nearly drove him to his knees.

"Danny." Sydney gripped his shoulder. "Danny, what is it?"

"My mom. Those bastards will find out who I am. They'll find out who my family is. And when they do, they'll find out where Mom lives."

A second later, they were both sprinting for the truck.

Chapter 28

The monastery's facade was the only part of it that hadn't been upgraded over the years since Phoenix Oil practically stole it from the Catholic church. From the installation of indoor plumbing and electricity to outfitting each guest suite with its own bathroom and air-conditioning unit, the monks who built the monastery would have never guessed that their humble building could have been transformed into an opulent resort pulsing with all the modern conveniences.

Nathan Broederlam was utilizing the most recent upgrade to the building: the satellite Internet connection. It allowed him to access The Group's secure network and download the encrypted e-mail that contained the urgent message for which he had been waiting.

The Group had maintained a small administrative support staff of two dozen since its inception. These were lifetime positions, and over the years, staffers only had to be replaced due to death. These staffers had been picked for their expertise in fields such as computer hacking, money laundering, and covert communications. Despite an exhaustive search, the guards found nothing about the American at the cabin. So, Nathan turned to a particular staffer who was an expert in research. It was the same staffer who had given him an impressive dossier on Sydney Dumas before she was invited to join the ICJ. Thanks to The Group, her biological parents were dead. Thanks to Father Time and cancer, her foster parents were also gone. Sydney had no other family members and only a short list of boyfriends whom she grew tired of long before anything serious could develop.

Nathan opened the e-mail and began reading. The cabin's financial history listed six different owners, but only one leaped up and slapped Nathan in the face. James Cavanaugh had owned an oil company called Venture Pipeline, Inc. headquartered in Houston, Texas. The researcher included old press releases and dated quarterly reports proving the ties between Venture and Phoenix Oil. But the connection between the two companies wasn't the reason that stopped him cold. It was the personal information regarding James Cavanaugh, or rather, his only son.

Danny Cavanaugh is a sergeant with the Texas Rangers. So that's how he could handle himself so well.

The personal section of the report began with information about James Cavanaugh's suicide. It happened twenty-one years ago. His body was found down at the same cabin Taber and his men just tore apart. Nathan considered this new information. Suicide was a favorite explanation of death The Group used. Could they have killed James Cavanaugh? Nathan tucked that question in the back of his brain and continued reading the report.

Maureen Cavanaugh, James's wife, was a retired social worker. Her mailing address was listed. She still lived in Houston. Would big, bad Sergeant Cavanaugh run to his mommy? Again, Nathan tucked that possibility away and focused on the next section, which contained two links to newspaper articles on the sergeant.

Nathan clicked on the first one and read through it. By the time he started reading the second article, hope was brewing in his gut.

Danny Cavanaugh has fallen on the wrong side of the law.

Nathan continued on and read the researcher's summary of Danny Cavanaugh's life. He concentrated on each detail, careful not to miss one word.

DC began his career in law enforcement in Houston, Texas, and quickly rose to the rank of detective. He left the Houston Police Department for a detective position with the Dallas, Texas, Police Department. He was lead detective on one controversial case that involved the death of the Dallas police chief. DC left the Dallas Police Department shortly thereafter to join the Texas Rangers, the investigative arm of the Texas Department of Public Safety, with the rank of Sergeant. DC led a human smuggling sting operation at the Nuevo Laredo, Mexico, border station two weeks ago that resulted in planted explosions being detonated and the deaths of several dozen people. *DC is allegedly linked to Rafael Espinoza, a reputed Mexican drug lord, and is wanted for killing FBI Special Agent Crayton Ripley.* He is considered armed and extremely dangerous. His whereabouts are currently unknown.

Armed and extremely dangerous, Nathan thought. Danny Cavanaugh is a police officer with all the requisite physical and mental training. But that still didn't explain why he was helping Sydney.

Questions snowballed in Nathan's mind. *Sydney's a beautiful woman, but is that enough for a man on the run to get involved with her? Does Sydney know about Cavanaugh's past? Could I somehow contact her and tell her that she's with a killer? Would that warning be enough to make her stop running?*

Nathan didn't have any answers, but he would soon. He clicked on the reply button and typed out the next set of orders for his staffer.

Need more information on JC's ties with Phoenix Oil and possible links to Group.

Need detailed background of border incident. Need more info on Espinoza.

Confirm mother's current address.

Nathan considered his reply and then had a thought. *Danny Cavanaugh's whereabouts are currently unknown. Unknown to everyone except him.* In Nathan's experience, that kind of exclusive information would prove to be very useful to him in the future.

Nathan included the "EYES ONLY" icon at the bottom of the e-mail, which let the staffer know that this request was of utmost privacy and was not to be discussed with any other staffer or any other member of The Group for now. He was confident that the staffer would comply with the order. Her life appointment as a staffer, and her life itself, depended on her discretion.

Nathan was about to hit "send" when the satellite phone sitting on the table next to him beeped. He clawed it off the desk and answered it. The distinctly calm timbre of Stefan Taber's voice purred in Nathan's ear.

"We have them."

"Where?"

"I can almost hit them with a rock," Taber said. "They're trying to cross the Rio Grande on a ferry. It's a hand-powered job. I don't know if they'll even make it."

"What do you mean hand-powered?" Nathan asked.

"They are pulling themselves and their piece of shit truck across the river on a rope line along with six or seven other suckers."

Nathan couldn't even begin to envision the scene. He glanced out the window and considered the sun. It had already begun its descent in the untamed sky.

"Do you have a clear shot at them?"

The reply was instantaneous. "Yes."

Nathan's thirst for information reared its head. *You need to pick Sydney's brain. She may have told others about what she knows. You need to figure out why Cavanaugh is involved. You need to investigate his father's death.* But this time, Nathan was able to ignore his inner voice. He wasn't going to take any chances again. He closed the window containing his e-mail message without sending it and then spoke flatly into the phone.

"Take them both out."

Chapter 29

"Shit!" Danny exclaimed as he ripped the cell phone away from his ear.

Sydney continued tugging on the rope line. "Still no service?"

"No," Danny snapped. He stared at her and then jammed the phone back into his pocket. He grabbed the rope line and began yanking on it as hard as he could.

Sydney eyed the border checkpoint station on the U.S. side. "I'm sure they have phones in the station house. Once we get across, you can talk to the border patrol agents and use their phone."

Danny grimaced. "No, I can't."

Sydney stopped tugging, reading his face. "Why not? You're a police officer. Aren't you?"

"They can't know who I am."

"Who? The border patrol? Why not?"

Danny couldn't look at her. Instead, he channeled his frustration into tugging even harder on the line. "Now isn't the time, Sydney. Once we're safely in Texas and past the border, I'll fill you in on my problems. Okay?"

"It's not okay. No more mysteries." She locked eyes with him. "Are you a goddamn officer or not?"

"I am."

"And?"

"It's a long story, too long to get into now. You've got to trust me, Sydney. Like I've been trusting you. Once I know Mom's safe, I'll tell you everything. Deal?"

Sydney sighed. "Okay." She grabbed the rope again and starting pulling.

There was nothing else they could do for the moment besides get across the river. She focused her concentration on the physical goal in front of her. She replaced thoughts of international conspiracies with the much simpler thoughts of gripping a rope to move the ferry.

As she worked, Sydney felt eyes on her. She turned around and saw two Mexican men dressed in grungy farming clothes. They were staring at her with misshapen grins. Sydney turned back around and continued her task. She was used to men staring at her. Living in such an international city as Monte Carlo, she was also used to being analyzed in different languages. As Sydney pulled, she heard them speak to each other and then chuckle back and forth, only recognizing the word *senorita* a few times.

Sydney's anger rose, and her heart began to beat faster. She had to will herself to ignore them. But Danny didn't. He stopped pulling on the rope line and leaned past her.

"*Hablo español, puto,*" Danny growled. "*Sé lo que usted dice acerca de ella. Discúlpese a la dama.*"

Sydney kept right on pulling, only recognizing, "hablo español." I speak Spanish.

Danny tapped her on the shoulder. Sydney turned and noticed a change in the men's demeanor. They were now staring down at their feet.

"These men were speaking badly of you, Sydney. But they realize their mistake and want to apologize." Danny turned to the men. "*Discúlpese ahora.*"

The one man rattled off something in Spanish and then his buddy repeated him. They never looked up at Sydney, who towered over them.

"Gracias," she replied as soon as they were finished.

The men nodded. The man on the left finally glanced up at her. She caught his eyes for a moment and smiled. Then her smile collapsed as she looked beyond him.

There's no way.

"Gracias, mi amigos. Ahora permita—"

Sydney grabbed Danny before he could finish and tugged him down just as a bullet struck the car next to them. Two more bullets splintered a wooden plank near them. The sound of gunfire sent everyone on the ferry scrambling for cover behind the vehicles.

Danny peeked out from behind his truck. "Bastards! How the hell did they find us?"

More gunfire pelted the ferry and the vehicles. Suddenly, Sydney remembered what was lying on the backseat of the truck. Before she allowed fear to stop her, Sydney was on all fours crawling along the ferry's edge.

Chapter 30

Danny wasn't paying attention until it was too late.

"Sydney? Goddamn it! What are you doing?" She was leaning into the backseat of the truck, an open target if there ever was one. Suddenly she whirled around, holding both the assault rifle and Danny's hunting rifle. *Brave girl*, Danny thought.

Sydney hunched down and scurried back to him. "I thought these would help," she said, handing him the guns.

Danny checked both weapons' magazines and handed the hunting rifle back to her. "You know how to handle a rifle?" he asked.

Sydney nodded. "Much better than I handle a truck."

"It's a semi-automatic. All you do is pull the trigger. You've only got three rounds, so use them sparingly."

Danny needed to see exactly what they were up against. He rolled onto his stomach to scan the Mexican side of the river when another flurry of bullets ended in an enormous blast that cut through their eardrums. The car behind them burst into flames, and the entire ferry shuddered.

"Stay down!" he told Sydney. He rolled over and looked behind him. The third vehicle at the other end of the ferry, a broken-down Pontiac Firebird, was now a ball of fire. That meant there was a new danger they had to handle. The wooden ferry itself would no doubt catch on fire soon.

Danny looked at the U.S. side. The checkpoint station was a hundred yards away from the river's edge. A border patrol jeep was speeding from it toward the river.

Danny gawked back at the fire. A wall of flames stretched fifteen feet into the air and then transformed into black smoke that coated the sky. The sound of gunfire had ceased for the moment. He could use the fire and smoke as cover to do something. But what? He scanned the ferry and focused on the rope line. A plan materialized in his brain. He ran toward it and yanked the Junglee Extreme Forces knife out of his pocket.

The rope line sagged a good three feet away from the ferry. The wooden safety railing creaked as Danny stretched out over it. He grabbed the rope line and sawed halfway through it before two bullets struck the railing near him. He slammed down on the deck. Bullets kept coming. He scrambled back to the crawl space that existed between his truck and the car behind it.

The gunfire intensified but also became more concentrated. It seemed that every bullet was hitting the car behind him. Danny figured out the guards' new strategy. *They're aiming for the gas tank. Why aim for people when you can take out the entire ferry itself?*

Danny stared at the rope where he made his cut. Despite the fact that it was nearly severed, it held strong. Cutting the ferry loose was their only chance to get away down the river. But there was no way he could risk standing out in the open at the rope line any longer.

He whipped the assault rifle off his back and aimed at the rope. It was next to impossible that a bullet would hit the rope exactly where he had cut it. Plus, there were less than fifty rounds left. Better save those rounds for the guards anyway.

Pop! Pop! Pop! Bing! Bing Bing! The guards' bullets continued hammering the car. Sooner or later, one would reach the gas tank.

Fire! Of course!

Danny dropped the rifle and tore off his shirt. He scrambled on all fours toward the flaming Firebird. He held out his shirt to the flames. As soon as it caught fire, he sprinted back behind his truck. He lunged at the rope line and flung the flaming shirt. It clung to the line, wrapping itself around Danny's incision.

Danny scurried back behind his truck and grabbed the rifle. *Burn baby! Burn!* He was so caught up watching the rope line burn that it took him a few moments to realize that Sydney was gone.

Danny feverishly searched the ferry's deck. There, at the opposite side of the ferry. There she was! It took only milliseconds for Danny to figure out what she was doing.

"No Syd ..."

But it was too late. She had already disappeared into the turbid water.

Chapter 31

Sydney's fingers sank deep in the muddy river bottom. She stopped herself in midstroke but stayed underneath the water. Her heartbeat echoed around her. Even if she opened her eyes, she wouldn't be able to see anything in the filthy water.

Sydney swallowed the remaining air trapped in her mouth so her hungry lungs could feed on the oxygen. She untied the ferry's tow cable from her ankle. She had seen it snaked in a heap on the front edge of the ferry when she grabbed the rifles from Danny's truck. As soon as she saw the border patrol jeep racing down to the shoreline, she knew their only chance was to use it to tow the ferry to shore. She also knew that if she explained her risky plan to Danny, he wouldn't let her try it. Sydney didn't know any police officers personally, but she was familiar with enough men to know that they always wanted to play the hero. Police officers had to be even worse.

Sydney hung onto the tow cable with both hands as she tucked her feet up underneath her and broke the water's surface with maximum thrust. She didn't dare relinquish her hold on the cable to wipe the water from her eyes. Instead, she blinked furiously until she saw the Jeep. It was less than thirty feet away. She churned through the water, climbing up the gummy slope until she hit hard surface. It was the ferry's concrete landing dock. She tried not to think about the fact that now she was out in the open, an easy target for the guards. She concentrated on the Jeep as she charged forward.

Just get to the Jeep.

Suddenly the ground slipped out from under her. She crashed down, both knees hammering the concrete beneath her. Sydney stuck both palms out to brace the rest of her body against the impact. As she did, she let go of the tow cable. Her hands struck the slimy concrete and slid a few inches before they dug in, finally bringing her body to a stop.

The cable!

Sydney remained still as she frantically searched the ground and water around her. She found nothing. She looked behind her and saw the ferry. While the huge wall of fire had completely engulfed the last car, both of the other vehicles were still intact. But where was Danny?

She finally saw him in front of his truck, crouched behind one of the two guide-on ramps that had been set in the upright position as safety blocks so cars wouldn't slide off. Danny spotted her and signaled. Sydney held out her damaged hands in the air and shook her head back and forth.

"I don't know what you want," she mouthed, hoping he could read her lips.

Danny pointed again, more furiously this time. *He wants me to look at the shore for something.* But before Sydney could turn her head, she felt a hand grip her shoulder. She looked up and saw a border patrol agent standing over her. In his other hand, he held the tow cable.

"Get to my Jeep," the pudgy agent said as he grabbed her arm and helped her to her feet.

A wave of adrenaline revived Sydney's legs. The pain in her knees subsided as she ran for the Jeep. Using her speed, she broke free of the agent and got to it before he did.

"Shit!"

Hearing the agent's plea, Sydney whipped around. The ferry had broken free of the rope line and was now floating sideways down the river. The agent was still holding onto the cable, but he was being dragged back toward the water.

Sydney dashed over to the driver's side of the Jeep and climbed in. Whatever confidence she had mustered after driving Danny's truck was immediately wiped away. Sticking up from the floorboard next to her throbbing knee was a manual transmission gearshift.

Chapter 32

"She can't drive!" Danny wanted to shout at the border patrol agent as soon as Sydney climbed into the Jeep. As he watched Sydney's plan disintegrate before his eyes, he had to formulate a plan B. Although the ferry was moving toward the U.S. shore, it was also drifting down the river. He predicted their landing spot. It was a flat, sandy spot but had steep cliffs looming above it. Even if he could get his truck off the ferry, there was nowhere to drive. He would have to escape on foot. Or he could dive into the river and swim to shore. But the curtain of fire and smoke from the ferry that blocked the guards' view of the U.S. shore was creeping aside. They would soon have a clear shot at the border agent, the Jeep, and Sydney. They would also have a clear shot at Danny in the water. Their only hope was to get the ferry to the landing and hope the fire continued to provide them cover.

Danny heard gears gnash together. He looked over and saw the Jeep lunge forward.

It's stick shift, Danny thought. He felt helpless as he heard the gears grind several more times. After each time, the Jeep would lunge forward and stall. He shut his eyes and concentrated, willing Sydney the ability to drive the Jeep. He opened his eyes and saw the Jeep sliding toward the river's edge.

She can't stop it!

But instead of plunging into the river, the Jeep turned and headed over to the agent, who had dug himself into the shoreline and leaned against the ferry like an anchorman in a tug-a-war. Maybe she couldn't drive the Jeep, but she could still steer it in neutral with the engine off.

Sydney coasted to a stop only a few feet from the border agent. She hopped out and ran over to him. She grabbed onto the tow cable and the two of them were able to pull enough slack in it to wrap it around the Jeep's tow hook and tie it off.

The agent ran to the driver's door and jumped in. Sydney hopped back in as well, this time in the passenger side.

The Jeep reversed, and the ferry jerked as the slack ran out of the rope. It listed more toward the shore, and Danny knew that the guards would be able to see the Jeep any second. He needed to do something to cover Sydney and the agent as they towed the ferry to land.

Danny turned toward the Mexican shoreline and sprayed it with bullets until the gun was empty. He felt another jerk and looked toward the U.S. shore. The ferry had careened into its dock.

Danny hopped in his truck, started it, and hit the gas. His front bumper hit the guide-on ramps. They were still in the up position. He stepped harder on the gas pedal, and the back wheels started spinning. He stopped and shoved the truck in reverse. He backed up a few feet, dropped the transmission into drive, and floored the gas. He heard a *crack,* as the truck slammed into the ramps. But they still didn't give way.

"Come on you son of a bitch! Move!" Danny backed up and slammed into the ramps again. This time the truck kept moving. It bounced over the ramp remains and onto the concrete landing. He was on terra firma once more.

Danny caught up to the Jeep seconds later. Sydney was already out of the passenger seat and running away from it while the border agent yelled at her to stop. She hopped into Danny's truck, and he flew past the border station, shattering the wooden arm that barricaded the entrance into the United States.

Danny looked over Sydney. "You okay?"

"I've been better," she replied, wincing. She wiped mud off on her thighs, revealing her injuries. Dirty blood oozed from several slices in each palm.

He motioned to the glove compartment. "There's a first-aid kit in there."

"Thanks," she replied as she took it out.

"You know, we've got to get you enrolled in a driver's education class."

Sydney smirked as she began caring for her wounds. "That's the first thing on my to-do list when I get back home."

Home. Danny was back inside the United States, back in Texas, back home. He glanced in the rearview mirror at the bedlam behind them. Then he stared out at the open road through the windshield. He had a bad feeling that this was only the beginning. Much more chaos was in store for them.

Welcome home, Danny boy.

Chapter 33

Nathan Broederlam felt as if he couldn't breathe. He was doubled over in his wheelchair, his pulse beating in his forehead. He had been screaming at Stefan Taber nonstop ever since he delivered the bad news.

"Why couldn't you kill them? Why couldn't you dive into the river, climb onto the ferry and shoot them dead at point-blank range? Why didn't you chase them into the United States?"

Taber had calm, collected answers for all of Nathan's questions.

"We were spotted before we could plan an attack. They had taken cover; we were unable to get clean shots. I decided that we should try and blow up the ferry by shooting the gas tanks of the cars on board. We couldn't chase them into the U.S. because, besides not having a way across the river, authorities would be converging on that area within minutes. We did not want to get caught. Secrecy is The Group's top priority, Mr. Broederlam."

Nathan glared at Taber. He was sitting at the head of the conference table, staring at his PDA and casually flicking its stylus in between his fingers.

Incompetent idiot, Nathan thought. He wanted so badly to jump out of his chair, run over to the muscled guard, and physically show him just how much contempt was brewing in his soul.

I am surrounded by fools! By second-rate hacks!

Nathan mashed the armrests on his chair as he again imagined what he could do with a healthy body. His heart beat faster, and he imagined that whatever amount of adrenaline inside his worthless legs was surging now.

"Are you tracking them?" Nathan asked Taber.

"They are on Highway 83. They have passed through McAllen, Texas. I believe that they are probably headed for—"

"Houston," Nathan interrupted. "They're heading to Houston. Not only does Cavanaugh's mother live there, but it's the hometown of someone else that his father undoubtedly knew well."

Taber didn't ask who. He simply stared at Nathan, waiting for him to fill in the blank.

Nathan wheeled over to his laptop. He hit the mouse key to wake up the screen and then turned the computer toward Taber.

"Senator Booker Halsey is the reason why we're here. Phoenix Oil owns him as well as this place. One of my people found out that Phoenix Oil had ties with Venture Pipeline. Danny Cavanaugh's father was Venture's founder and CEO."

Taber walked over to Nathan. He sat down next to him and analyzed the data on the screen.

Nathan continued. "Cavanaugh knew about the passageway in the library. It's obvious that he spent time here in the past. He must know Senator Halsey is tied to the monastery. There is little doubt in my mind that Cavanaugh will make every effort to confront Halsey ASAP."

Taber pointed to the information at the bottom of the screen. "It says here that Halsey will be in Houston this weekend."

Nathan looked over Taber's shoulder. The Group's administrators always knew where their members were at all times. Their researcher had gone to the liberty of providing Nathan with Booker Halsey's information. He explained the senator's current schedule to Taber.

"He's got meetings with some of his benefactors before the president's State of the Union address this Sunday. I'm guessing that he will want to quote some of them when he issues the opposing party's rebuttal after the president's speech."

Taber looked at Nathan like he was speaking a different language. Nathan didn't have the time or the patience to explain how American politics worked to a military grunt.

"You're sure that Cavanaugh and Sydney are on their way to Houston?" Taber asked.

Nathan nodded. "There's no doubt. Cavanaugh's a cop. He wants answers. If he knows that Booker's in Houston, he'll want to talk to him. I'd bet my life on it."

"Then I've got to get to Houston." Taber shut Nathan's laptop. He began stacking all of the papers on the conference table. "My men will stay here to take care of the bodies."

"What the hell are you doing?" Nathan asked. He grabbed at the papers in Taber's hand, but Taber snatched his wrist. Suddenly, Taber's last words registered in his brain.

Take care of the bodies.

Taber moved around behind Nathan and gripped the wheelchair's handles. "Your services are no longer needed, Mr. Broederlam."

Nathan spun back and forth wildly in his chair. "What are you doing?"

Taber gently backed Nathan away from the table. Nathan tried gripping the wheels to stop him, but Taber was too strong.

Your services are no longer needed.

Nathan knew what that really meant. The Group no longer needed him. For the first time in years, he felt an overwhelming force surge throughout his entire body. It was unrelenting fear.

Taber capsized the chair, spilling Nathan's body out on the floor. Nathan immediately tried willing his legs to work, to carry him away from Taber as fast as they could. But they wouldn't. He channeled all his energy into his arms, as he scraped himself along the floor toward the conference room door.

Don't look back! Don't give up!

Nathan managed to pull his handicapped carcass only a few feet before he felt Stefan Taber grab a handful of his hair. Taber yanked back Nathan's head and put a blade to his throat.

"Being a cripple sucks doesn't it, Nathan?" Taber lulled into Nathan's ear.

As Taber swiped the blade across his throat, Nathan prayed that, like in his legs, there would be no feeling. But Nathan Broederlam was not that lucky.

Chapter 34

Sydney stretched the sleep out of her body. Her eyelids cracked open. She first saw only darkness and felt the familiar aloneness trying to engulf her. She turned her stiff neck and saw Danny next to her. He was in the exact same sitting position that he was when she fell asleep, with one hand draped over the steering wheel of the Toyota Camry he stole outside of McAllen, Texas. But instead of being topless, like he was when she fell asleep, he was now dressed in a long-sleeved plaid shirt.

Sydney sighed as she lifted her arms above her head. Danny noticed that she had come back to life.

"Good morning, sleepyhead," he said.

"I'm sorry. It is very easy for me to fall asleep in moving vehicles."

"No worries. I wish I had that same ability."

"What time is it, anyway?" Sydney asked as she grabbed for the guard's clothes that she had laid out on the backseat behind her. They were still damp and cold. She decided to let them dry out a little longer and then hunted for the lever on the side of the seat that raised the seatback.

"A little after twelve."

"That's not morning. That's the beginning of the night where I come from. I'm either still up or out for another four or five hours."

"You're a night owl, then?"

"Just on my days off." She found the seatback lever and pulled it. After grinding through the gears in the seat, she finally raised it to the same position as Danny's.

"You and machines don't like each other, do you?" he asked her.

"Excuse me?"

"Never mind."

"Where are we?"

"About halfway to Houston."

"Did you ever get in touch with your mother?"

"Yes. She's going to stay at a friend's for a while."

Sydney touched his arm. "It's good to hear that she's safe."

Danny smiled his reply. The dashboard's faint glow highlighted his worn face in the darkness.

"You look tired, Danny. Don't you want to stop for a while and rest?"

Danny shook his head. "I'd rather get to where we're going before I worry about resting. But now that you're up, you can help me stay awake by talking to me."

"What shall we talk about?"

"Not anything about conspiracies or the people hunting us, okay?"

Sydney chuckled. "Agreed."

"How about you? How does a French girl get the name Sydney anyway?"

When Sydney met people, the conversation would eventually roll around to her past, as normal conversations tended to do. That was where the conversation usually ended. But she would probably be dead right now if it wasn't for Danny, so she at least owed him the short answer.

"I'm an orphan. A French couple took me in when I was still a baby. They were great fans of the American actor Sidney Poitier."

"Makes sense. Guy's French. At least his name is."

"He's actually from the Bahamas and moved to Miami when he was still a teenager."

"Are you trying to wow me with facts about American actors, or do you just want to keep the topic of conversation off your past?"

Sydney cocked her head. "Only one experienced in trying to hide their past can readily recognize it when it happens."

"Touché, Ms. Dumas." Danny offered her a funny look and then grinned. "By the way, that's about all the French I know."

"I'd be happy to teach you a few lines to keep you out of trouble."

"Well, I do know one line, "*Voulez-vous coucher avec moi, ce soir?*""

Sydney clapped. "*Très bon.* Very good. But we just met, and you are already asking me to sleep with you?"

Danny stammered. "No ... I ... I was just ..." Sydney chuckled again. "Having some fun with me, Ms. Dumas?"

She offered him a flirty grin. "*Absolument.*"

Sydney was sure that he felt their shared look as much as she did. "I'm sorry we got off topic," Danny finally said. "You were telling me your life story."

"Yes, well, I graduated high school and enrolled in the Toulouse School of Management. I had a knack for numbers, for economics specifically, and went away to study international business law at Cambridge. In a nutshell."

"So, in addition to being an ICJ judge, you're a Cambridge-educated lawyer specializing in international business law?"

"My foster father was a business law professor at Toulouse. I guess I just picked it up over the years."

"Like father like daughter, huh?"

You have no idea, Sydney thought. "Yes."

"So what kind of cases did you handle?"

Sydney shook her head. "I never tried a case. I only went to law school because I wanted to teach. Having two areas of expertise gives a woman in Europe a much greater chance to become a professor."

"So, you're a professor, too?"

"Until my election to the ICJ, I was the head of the international law department at the University of Monaco."

"You mean the Monaco in Monte Carlo, the playpen of the rich and famous?"

"One and the same."

"Wow. So how did you wind up serving on something called the International Court of Justice? Pretty lofty stuff."

"My boyfriend at the time nominated me."

"Who was your boyfriend?"

"The prince," Sydney replied flatly.

Danny's eyes whipped off of the road. "Your boyfriend was the prince of Monaco?"

"Yes. Does it seem that hard to believe?"

Danny looked back into the dark void beyond the windshield. "No. But I imagine the next guy is gonna have it a little rough living up to the prince of Monaco."

"Ever hear the story of the frog that is really a prince, Danny?"

"Yeah, Sydney. Even I've heard that one," Danny said with a trace of sarcasm.

"Sometimes it's the other way around. The prince is just a frog in disguise." Sydney could tell that he was contemplating her rather honest comment as he flipped through a couple stations on the radio before finally settling on one.

"I see we have the same taste in music," Sydney said as Eric Clapton broke into his classic rendition of "After Midnight."

"You're a Clapton fan? Outstanding!" Danny replied. "Plus, the song seems appropriate, don't you think?"

Sydney grinned. "Absolument." But her smile quickly faded as she recalled the secret Danny had been keeping from her. "I can assume from our conversation on the ferry that you were not at your family's cabin on holiday." As soon as the words crossed her lips, she knew she had struck a nerve. Danny shifted in his seat. It took him several seconds before he answered her.

"I did say that I'd tell you why we can't go to the authorities with your story, didn't I?"

Sydney nodded. "I think we have some time to kill here."

Danny sighed. "It's not my family's cabin anymore. We sold it a long time ago."

"So why were you there?"

"I was hiding."

"Hiding from whom?"

Danny glanced at her. "That's not altogether true." He gripped the steering wheel with both hands and stared straight ahead. "Here goes … I was about sixty seconds from putting a bullet in my head before I saw that the monastery was occupied."

"What?" Suicide? Did she hear him right? "But why? Why would you want to kill yourself, Danny?"

"Because I'm a man without a country."

"I'm sorry, Danny. I don't understand."

"I'm a wanted man, Sydney. I took a chance that no one would be using the cabin, so I went down there. My plan was to hide out. But while I was planning a way to exonerate myself, I got to thinking about everything, and it was just too much. So I thought I would end it all, just like my old man did."

"You mean your father?"

"Yup."

"Why did he kill himself?"

"I don't know. No one does. He just went there one weekend and shot himself. He didn't even leave a note."

"Oh Danny, that's awful. I'm so sorry." Sydney touched his clenched hand on the steering wheel. "But then why would you want to do the same?"

"Like I said, I'm a wanted man."

"But you're a police officer."

"It doesn't matter. I've been framed by some seriously powerful people. The kind who won't stop until they get what they want."

"Framed? You mean for a crime?"

Danny nodded. "I've been accused of being involved with a very bad man named Rafael Espinoza. He's head of a Mexican drug cartel, the largest cartel. I've also been blamed for the deaths of many people." Danny paused. Sydney could see the conflict raging inside him. She wisely kept her mouth shut, offering the space he needed to continue. "We had intelligence about an eighteen-wheeler that was being used to smuggle illegals across the border. I was the lead on the operation, and it literally blew up in my face. The truck was booby-trapped with explosives. In the ensuing confusion, a dirty FBI agent tried to kill me. But I got the drop on him. I had to kill him in self-defense."

"What do you mean, he was dirty?"

"He, along with many other FBI and border patrol agents, was the one working for Espinoza."

"How do you know there are others?"

"Because it's like the Wild West down here. There are too many drugs going one way and too much money and guns going the other."

"And you thought you could stop it all? All by yourself?"

"Call me an idealist, but yes, I believe one person can make a difference." He offered her a look. "I'd say you'd agree or else you wouldn't be doing this."

"I'm just glad you've decided to help me, Danny."

"The only reason I'm helping you is that I might be able to clear my name after we get to the bottom of whatever the hell is going on here." Danny set his eyes firmly back on the road. "Well, that's not the only reason," he continued after a moment. "How could I say no to a naked woman lost in the middle of the woods?"

"I don't recall being naked."

He smiled. "Nearly naked."

"If nothing else, you're an open book, Danny."

"I don't want there to be any surprises, Sydney. I wanted you to know just who is helping you."

Sydney squeezed his hand again. "I appreciate your honesty, Danny. Honesty with ourselves and others is the best policy, no?"

He nodded in agreement. "You're right."

Sydney quickly shifted her eyes to the road. While she sensed that Danny was uncomfortable with his reply, she didn't want him to read her face and realize that she didn't believe her last statement for a second either.

Chapter 35

"Mr. Speaker, Vice President Mulroney, members of Congress, fellow citizens: I stand before you tonight in awe of America's opportunity. Great philosophers and political experts throughout the ages have stated that a democracy cannot exist as a permanent form of government. What starts as a republic of free people eventually evolves into a dictatorship under the weight of increased corruption within government and carelessness among the ranks of the citizenry. My fellow Americans, whether you agree with this statement or not, whether you believe that America is still sheltered underneath the umbrella of liberty or you feel that your government has long been infected by the temptations of fraud and dishonesty, I am here to tell you that America is on the brink of greatness …"

A commotion at the back of the room caused President Jack Butcher to stop. He looked up from the teleprompter that was feeding him his State of the Union speech to see his Secret Service detail rushing toward him.

There was no time for questions, and the Secret Service agents offered no words. They each grabbed a handful of Jack's suit and vaulted back up the aisle of the White House Family Theater. Within the cocoon of rigid arms and solid torsos, Jack heard gasps coming from the sparse audience of speechwriters and his inner circle who had gathered to review his speech.

Simon Shilling yelled, "What's happening? Pete? For Christ's sake, tell us what's going on!"

But Peter Devon would not answer the chief of staff. Devon had only one directive: protect the president at all costs. No explanations, no chances for second guessing, no answers needed to be provided, even to the president of the United States himself.

Jack understood what was happening. A security risk had been discovered. It was big enough and close enough to warrant the president's immediate protection.

Jack's toes finally touched the ground once he was inside the Presidential Emergency Operations Center. His Secret Service detail placed him at the head of the conference table and backed away, finally giving him room to breathe.

"Are you okay, Mr. President?" Peter Devon asked. His head was cocked to the side, revealing the corkscrew wire that ran up the side of his shorn skull and into his ear.

"If you're going to carry me for that long, Pete, could you maybe have some peanuts and a Coke to offer next time?"

Peter Devon's face remained an unwavering hunk of stone. Jack smoothed his rumpled suit. "I'm fine, Peter. Thank you." Peter Devon and the rest of his team all turned at once and left the room.

Jack eyed the people that had followed them down to the PEOC. They had run two PEOC drills since Jack had taken office, and now, like in the practice runs, the usual suspects were present. Simon was sitting to Jack's left, the same spot he commanded in the Situation Room. Next to Simon was Charlie Jacoby. Charlie was Jack's National Security Council adviser and one tough lady. She neither accepted nor dealt in pleasantries or bullshit. Jack had never met a more direct person on the planet, which made her perfect for her job. Especially since Harry Tharp was seated next to her. Jack stared at him for a moment. *What the hell is Harry doing in here?*

As if he read Jack's mind, Harry explained his presence. "I was in the building, Mr. President, and thought you could use my expertise."

Jack nodded at him and moved on. To Harry's left was Rita Rodriguez, Jack's senior White House counselor. Rita was second only to Charlie when it came to pulling punches. She called them like she saw them and played with the cards with which she was dealt. But right now, she needed to work on her poker face. She had no time for Harry Tharp and had confided to Jack during more than one of their Oval strategy sessions her thoughts on Harry's incompetence.

Seated on Jack's right was Blake Conway. Blake was Jack's press secretary and was the complete opposite of Charlie and Rita. Blake came from a wealthy African American family in Baltimore. A true Gemini, Jack had seen Blake transform himself many times from one of the most well-spoken bullshit artists in the D.C. game to one of the boys in the hood and pull both sides of his personality off with astounding sincerity. Underneath the suave demeanor and impeccable wardrobe that cost much more than even Jack spent on clothes, Blake Conway was a Baltimore kid who had the golden ticket. He was going to make good for his community, his family, and most of all for himself. During one of the usual late nights that Blake remained working in his office, Jack had asked him how he had come to work so hard. He was a trust fund kid; why not spend his nights partying and his days sleeping in? Blake had given an answer that Jack would never forget.

"Because the idea of America is too important, Mr. President."

From that point on, Jack would have bet money with any takers on Blake Conway becoming a future president of the United States.

The final occupant in the room was Benjamin Speakes. As director of the White House Military Office, he managed several items, one of which was the nuclear football. He sat in one of the chairs that ringed the room's perimeter, firmly aware of his position. Just like in the practice runs, the unassuming briefcase that contained the nuclear launch codes was handcuffed to his wrist. In the two practice sessions, it had remained on the floor next to Speakes's chair. Now, however, it had the more visible perch in his lap. White House protocol stated that anytime the president went to the PEOC, the nuclear football went in with him. Jack's gut tightened as he realized the power to end much of the life on the planet rested only a few feet away.

Jack settled his eyes on Blake. "What's going on?"

"One of the ring sensors went off near the Washington Monument. A NEST team is investigating as we speak."

A natural feeling of dread penetrated Jack as soon as the acronym for the Nuclear Emergency Search Team registered in his brain.

"Have they cleared the monument?" Jack asked.

"Yes, sir," Blake responded.

"How?"

"Gas leak story, sir."

Jack didn't like the fact that his administration had been reduced to lying to the American people to cover the possible discovery of a nuclear device. But with six situations where suspicious packages had been discovered on American soil since taking office, and all of them being false alarms, Jack knew that America would see him as the boy who cried wolf if he disclosed them all. It was always better to cover evacuations of public places with alternate stories, like natural gas leaks. NEST even carried with them a machine that spewed natural gas vapors into the air to back up their story.

Jack visualized Blake Conway standing behind the White House Press Room podium in his Joseph Abboud suit, the spotlights highlighting the conviction in his cool, brown eyes as he delivered the gas leak story. But of course, this time was different. This was the first time a report had come from inside the Beltway, on District of Columbia soil, let alone on the grounds of one of America's most coveted memorials.

"Wait a second," Jack peered over at Simon. "Ring sensor? You mean the ring around Washington?" Simon nodded. They were referring to the grid of radiation detection devices that had been secretly placed around the entire district in 2001. The system was a complete failure. Not only could it not ascertain unique signatures from various types of radiation, it was constantly picking up false readings from medical waste, hazardous materials, and even emissions from the granite monuments and buildings that speckled the D.C. landscape.

"I thought the ring was offline?" Jack asked.

Harry took the liberty of fielding this question. "The original system was, Mr. President. But after a few years of tinkering with it, we have a new grid. It's in perfect working order." A look of satisfaction appeared on Harry's face. He knew something that the president did not.

Jack stared at Harry. "I'll believe that when I get human confirmation. Where exactly is the NEST team searching?"

"They're searching the monument itself and any conceivable structure on the grounds that could contain a nuclear device: porta-potties, trash cans, things like that."

"How sensitive are these new ring sensors?" Jack paused and then reworded his question. "Can they tell us how long ago a device was put there, if there's a device there at all?"

Harry cleared his throat before responding. "That time window isn't a factor of the sensor, Mr. President. It's a factor of the device. It depends on the material used and if the device is shielded or not. If it isn't shielded then radiation could leak from it and reach the sensor fairly quickly; we're talking seconds to just a few minutes. If it was shielded, the leakage could take hours or even days to reach the sensor."

Jack looked over at Simon. Even in this situation, Jack was able to read Simon's thoughts, and vice versa.

The monument. How would it look on the news? What would they tell the American people?

"When will we know what's there?" Jack asked.

Just then the phone in front of Jack rang. Simon stared at him as it fell silent and then rang again. "I think we'll know as soon as you pick up that phone, sir."

The ringing phone wasn't a good sign. If it was a false alarm, the NEST leader would have called Harry Tharp and given him the all-clear. Any questions that Jack had about the harmless package could be fielded by Harry or answered at a later time. But this call was coming into the direct PEOC line. Bad news for sure.

Jack picked up after the third ring. "Jack Butcher," he said.

"Mr. President, Clarence Warner here. I'm in charge of the NEST team investigating the Washington Monument incident, sir."

"Just a moment, Clarence." Jack replied. "I'm at PEOC. I'm going to put you on speaker."

Jack pressed the speaker button and hung up the phone's handset. "Clarence, you still with us?"

"Yes, sir."

"Why don't we get down to brass tacks, son," Harry quipped. "What'd you find?"

There was a pause during which Jack stared at Harry. *This is my show, Harry.*

"We found a suitcase in a trash can on the eastern edge of the monument grounds twenty yards north of the 15th Street Jefferson Drive intersection."

Blake Conway had a street map up on his PDA. Jack looked over his shoulder as he pointed to the location with his stylus.

"Is it nuclear, Clarence?" Jack asked.

"Yes, sir," Clarence replied. "It's a dirty bomb."

Chapter 36

Danny was still feeling the effects of only getting an hour's sleep at a rest stop as he pulled into the parking lot of the Houston Racquet Club. He hadn't been there since the days of his youth, when his dad would help him hone his tennis skills. But everything remained the same. The same soaring pine trees bordered the parking lot; the same flawless landscaping, bursting with azaleas and monkey grass, filled out the clubhouse's façade, wrapping its way around the sides of the building. *That's what money does*, Danny thought. *It insulates against the passage of time.*

Rather than passing through the main parking lot and parking alongside the tennis courts, Danny made a sharp left and pulled back into the corner furthest away from the clubhouse. He considered the guns on the floorboard in the Camry's back seat and decided against taking them. It was just common sense. He didn't want anyone alerting the police. He was already nervous about driving a stolen vehicle, which couldn't be helped. Any American cop would have pulled him over in his truck, complete with its newly acquired bullet hole design job. Besides, he still had the combat knife. That, along with some serious attitude, would hopefully get Booker Halsey to spill his guts.

Although he could tell she was hesitant, Sydney was already climbing back into the guard's outfit. Danny waited outside the car until she was done. Like a gentleman, he made sure to keep his eyes off of her, although he had spent the last eight hours sitting next to her in her underwear. She finally cracked open the door, and they began walking across the parking lot. As they did, Danny examined her. Her clothes were still damp, and they stunk of Rio Grande water, but she remained drop dead gorgeous. He could only imagine what she looked like if she had a hot shower and a little time to freshen up.

They strode past the club's front door and walked down the side driveway to the tennis courts. Before Danny could see the courts, he heard them. They were the tennis tarts, as his mom used to call them, ladies having their morning lessons before they gathered in the clubhouse grill for lunches comprising of the club's signature southwestern salads and stout Bloody Marys. He heard shoes pounding against the court surface, hard breaths puncturing the air, and the accented commands of the foreign tennis pros who had found their meal tickets in America. The sounds brought back years of memories in a matter of seconds. The menagerie included both the games when his dad used to beat him, when Danny was a young kid just learning the game, to set after set in his early teenage years, when the old man complained when he couldn't return any of Danny's fierce, left-handed serves. Of course, everyone complained about playing a left-handed tennis player. The balls always spun the wrong way. It was the same way Danny felt about his mind. Thoughts just spun differently inside it.

"I'm doing all the talking, agreed?" Danny reminded Sydney as he led her to the group of clay courts at the back corner of the tennis area. Besides confessing the real reason he was at the cabin, Danny had also confessed to Sydney that Booker was the reason he knew so much about the monastery. Booker was heavily connected to Phoenix Oil, the corporation that had purchased both the monastery and a sizeable piece of Booker's Senate seat.

Sydney nodded. "Yes. I'll just stand there and look pretty."

"I'm sure these guys will be drooling over you," Danny gave her the once over, "even in your current … condition."

Sydney pretended to swoon. "Oh Danny, I bet you get all the girls with compliments like that."

Danny could hear Senator Booker Halsey's grief-spewing drawl before he spotted him.

"Damn it, Brick! The way you move, we should be playing fucking triples instead of doubles!"

Danny stopped outside the far corner of the court and crouched down to see underneath the windscreen. He recognized all four players, their aged feet shuffling across the scratchy clay surface. Booker and Brick Burdett of Phoenix Oil were in the near court. In the far court were Skeeter Coburn and Jimmy Trotter. Skeeter owned an oil-refining company, and Trotter was the one they called Garage Sale Jimmy. He made his money in oil early, still in his forties, by hauling in a mammoth gusher after nearly a decade of drilling one dry hole after another. Since making his initial fortune, he had tripled it by buying up troubled oil and natural gas companies all around Houston and then selling off the pieces. Jimmy was the one who bought Danny's father's company shortly after his death at a cut rate and had sold off everything within a year: the pipelines, the land, the machinery, everything.

Danny stood back up and walked toward the courtside bleachers. Sydney followed him. With the combined net worth of the men on the court close to a hundred million dollars, Danny was expecting bodyguards perched on them. But the bleachers were empty, as were the rest of the courts around them. Only men of this stature could get away with a friendly game at eight o'clock on a workday morning.

Booker was about to serve when he stopped and looked over at Danny. The other three men followed his lead, but it was Jimmy Trotter who first broke the silence.

"Holy shit. Is that little Danny Cavanaugh?"

Danny had no idea how much these men knew about the recent events in his life. And he had no idea how much they knew about the events of the last twenty-four hours. But he had only one play, and so he played it. "Sorry to interrupt your game, gentlemen." Danny stared at Garage Sale Jimmy. "And Jimmy." The old man smirked a "fuck you" look back at him, but Danny was already focused on Booker. "Booker, we need to talk."

The senator huffed. "I've got a game going on here, Danny."

"We need to talk right now, Senator," Danny said quietly. "Trust me. It's more important than playing for the breakfast tab."

Minutes later, Booker and Danny were strolling along the wooded jogging trail that snaked throughout the Houston Racquet Club grounds. Booker was sipping from a water bottle filled with an energy drink the color of cherry Kool-Aid.

"How'd you know I'd be here?"

"Human beings are creatures of habit, Booker. You've flown back to Houston every third week of the month for constituent meetings and donor dinners for how many years now? Twenty?"

Booker grinned. "Twenty-three."

"Over those twenty-three years, how many times have you missed Thursday morning tennis with the boys?"

Booker chuckled. "I always thought you were smart, Danny." He sipped his drink. "Well, except for getting mixed up with Rafael Espinoza. Not a wise move, kid."

Danny ignored his jab. "I see that Garage Sale Jimmy took over Dad's spot in tennis, too. Thanks for being so loyal to his memory."

Booker's face sunk. He would have never let that look materialize if a camera was near. "What can I do for you, Danny?"

"I need to know everything about your relationship with Phoenix Oil and the monastery down at Lake Guerrero."

The look of confusion on Booker's face could have won awards. "What the hell are you talking about?"

Danny grabbed Booker's elbow and applied generous pressure. "Booker, this is not the time to pull any of your bullshit doubletalk. The woman I'm with was at a meeting down there and was almost killed for this." Danny let go of him and pulled out the Ziploc bag from his waistband. He extracted the lawsuit papers and shoved them in Booker's face. He allowed the politician a few moments to digest the information. "I want some fucking answers, Booker. Now."

Booker drew his eyes off of the documents and scowled at Danny. "Son, let me tell you something. I don't know what the hell this is, and I don't know what the hell you're talking about. You shouldn't have come here. Last I heard, you were wanted for killing a federal agent."

"It was self-defense. He was the one with Espinoza."

"Uh-huh. Listen, you need to concern yourself with your own problems before you take up with some crazy girl who's whacked out of her goddamn mind. Hell, I should call the cops right now and tell them that you're here."

Danny was about to speak when he heard footsteps and a female voice.

"Senator Halsey, my name is Sydney Dumas. I am a member of the International Court of Justice, and I serve in its international finances chamber," she said, taking a position at Danny's side. "The other two chamber members and I were meeting at a monastery in Mexico with which you have ties. Our proceedings are not the illusions of a crazy girl. They are facts, facts that I believe warrant serious attention from the United States government as well as an explanation as to your dealings with the group involved with the monastery."

Over the years, Danny had witnessed Booker's deft handling of accusations about his questionable practices both on TV and in person. Danny's dad had said that even though Booker was as crooked as a mesquite tree branch, he could make things happen for the boys in the oil patch. That's why he was blessed with being one of the longest reigning senators in American history.

"Ms. Dumas, if what Danny has told me is true and that you were in a life-threatening situation down in Mexico, you have my deepest sympathies. Danny's daddy and I go way back. Yes, I, like Danny's daddy, visited the Lake Guerrero monastery many times over my life but always as a guest of Phoenix Oil. And yes, it is true that Phoenix owns the monastery. However, whatever Phoenix Oil has to do with any kind of situation that involves the International Court of Justice is news to me. I can assure you of that."

As Booker took another swig of his concoction, Sydney hit him with another bombshell. She tugged open her shirt, revealing a Ziploc bag tucked in her waistband. Inside it was a single piece of paper.

Danny could tell that Sydney was about to launch into another allegation of Booker's involvement with the lawsuit when he stopped her. Even though Booker may be guilty, he could easily talk his way out of any accusation Sydney made against him. Then he wouldn't offer up any more information. He had to get Sydney out of there.

Danny stepped between them and got in Sydney's face. He whispered to her, "What the hell are you doing? I told you I'd handle this. Get out of here now."

But Sydney sidestepped him. She took out the paper from the bag, unfolded it, and shoved it in Booker's face. "Sir, isn't that your name and your signature?"

Danny stepped over to take a look. He saw Booker's name in both printed letters and as the signature that he had seen only a few times in his life, but nevertheless recognized it on sight. The huge B and H were followed by pulse-like bumps along a heart-monitor readout.

Sydney continued. "Senator Halsey, per ICJ guidelines, whenever a lawsuit is brought before the ICJ or any chamber therein, it must first be recognized by agents of both parties."

For the first time since Danny had known him, Senator Booker Halsey was speechless. Danny stepped toward him and leveled his eyes.

"All right BH. Let's cut the BS."

Chapter 37

Anthony Fantroy was in his car when his cell phone, his *other* cell phone, rang. He caught his driver's sidelong glance in the rearview mirror, but the glance was gone as fast as it had come.

Fantroy studied the Caller ID. His driver was no doubt familiar with the various rings of Fantroy's phones and knew that this was his personal line. He thought about raising the divide that would turn the backseat of the limousine into a soundproof booth, but he decided against it. Leaks can happen anywhere at anytime by anyone. He didn't need to raise suspicions of his activities when they were so close to the finish line; well, not the finish line exactly, rather the starting point to their long-awaited goal.

"Yes," he uttered into the phone.

"Sir, it's Stefan Taber. I hope my call hasn't put you in a compromising position."

"Of course not. How can I be of service?"

"Sir, I have tracked the targets to their next destination. I have them in my sights, and I await further instruction."

Fantroy could hardly believe the events of the last twenty-four hours. He didn't like it when things got out of control, and Nathan Broederlam had done more than let things get out of control. Now Sydney Dumas was making waves with a Texas Ranger wanted for murder. Of all the people for Sydney to run into. Was it fate? Luck? Chance? All three? Who knew?

"Sir?" Taber said after the long silence.

"You may proceed."

"Proceed with termination?"

Fantroy paused to analyze his choices one last time, but he had already made up his mind. "Yes."

Fantroy flipped shut the cell phone, ending the call. *We are so close*, he thought. *Now is the time for absolutes.* There was nothing more absolute than death.

Chapter 38

Sydney let Booker Halsey study the document, but she kept it firmly in her hands and firmly out of his reach. She finally snatched it back to her chest, which seemed to wake a dazed Senator Halsey back to reality.

Booker turned to Danny. "Danny, we need to talk." He was still sweating from the tennis match, but his perspiration seemed to drip down his face with greater velocity now. His eyes rolled to Sydney. The edges of his mouth curled like a cornered dog ready to bite. "Alone."

Danny knew Booker wouldn't make another sound until Sydney left their presence. He turned to her. "Sydney, you heard the senator. Go back to the tennis courts. I'll meet you there."

Sydney was about to argue when Danny intensified his stare. He whispered through his clenched jaw, "If you don't do as I say, I'm done with you. You're on your own."

Sydney stood there for a moment, every inch of her six-foot plus frame preaching her outrage. She finally relented and trudged back along the jogging trial.

Danny turned back to the senator. "Okay, Booker. Talk."

Booker looked as if Danny had just slapped his flushed jowl. "Don't order me around, Danny. You are not in control here. I only need to make a phone call, and I can have you arrested on the spot. Or have you forgotten that you're a fugitive? If anything, I'm doing you a favor by even agreeing to stand here and talk to you."

"Is that right?" Danny grabbed Booker by the neck and shoved him against a tree. He yanked out the Junglee knife and thrust the blade against the senator's throat. Despite Danny's outrage, Booker remained calm and stayed silent.

"Now I'm doing you a favor by letting you live," Danny growled. "You are going to tell me everything you know about this lawsuit, the monastery, and your relationship with Phoenix Oil. But most important, you will tell me everything you know about my father's death. I never bought the suicide story."

"Danny, I told you ..."

Danny pulled Booker off the tree and slammed him against it again. "You will tell me everything, Booker. Like you said, I killed an FBI agent. What makes you think that I won't add a senator to that list?"

—

Sydney had retreated far enough away from Danny and the senator to be sure she could neither be seen nor heard. She wandered off the jogging path and carefully picked her way through Asian jasmine and ruellia plants that swallowed her feet to the ankles. She ducked from pine tree to pine tree until she had flanked the two men, approximately twenty yards away. She stopped behind one towering pine and stood tall. She edged one eye out to see Danny holding the senator up against a tree. She also saw the shiny blade up against Halsey's throat.

Pain suddenly flared in both of Sydney's ankles. She looked down to see that she was standing in a fire ant bed. Several ants had already made their way up her sneakers and were attacking her bare skin. She took a few steps back to a bald patch of dirt and bent down to swipe away the ants. As she did, she heard a strange sound. She looked up just in time to see the senator's body spill down the tree trunk and collapse in the dirt.

Chapter 39

Danny sprinted for cover. He found it behind the root ball of a fallen pine tree. He didn't know where the shot came from, but he knew it was meant for him. If Booker hadn't shoved back against him, the bullet would have been in him instead of in Booker right now.

His mind raced. *Was it Booker's bodyguards? If he had any, they were nowhere to be found at the tennis court. Did Jimmy or one of the others call them? Could it be the police? No way. Cops wouldn't fire without warning first.*

Danny looked at Booker, who was doubled over on the ground. He wasn't moving. There was no activity in the woods around him. If the shot had come from a bodyguard then he would have been administering aid to Booker by now.

It had to be the guards from the monastery.

Danny squinted through the endless sea of trees around him. *Military men are prepared,* he thought. Besides using silencers, they would be camouflaged among the trees. They also had another advantage. They knew where Danny was. He had to move.

He churned through ten yards of thick brush toward the jogging path. He could not only hear the words of his police training officers in his ear, but he could see the absoluteness in their faces as they drilled their commands into his head.

During flight, do not look around for your opponent's position. That will only slow you down. Keep your eyes on the prize and haul ass.

Danny couldn't help himself. He searched the woods in every direction. But he wasn't looking for his opponents. Instead, he was searching for Sydney.

He found her as his feet hit the jogging trail. He ran through it and found cover behind a soaring pine tree. He eased one eye around it and spotted her. She was to his left, a good fifteen yards away, squatting behind another pine tree. She jumped as soon as she saw Danny notice her. He could instantly read her thoughts.

Why did you kill the senator?

Danny wanted to scream his innocence to her, but another gunshot did it for him. Slivers of bark flew into his eye, as the bullet bored into the tree he used for cover. As he tried blinking out the shards, the whispered hiss from the gun's silencer replayed in his head. It was close. Too close.

He rolled toward Sydney and held up three fingers. "We move on three," he mouthed. Danny pointed toward the jogging trail and then in the direction of the exit. Sydney nodded.

Danny looked in the direction of the sound he heard from the gun. He saw nothing. *Fuck it*, he thought and jabbed each finger in the air.

One.

Two.

Three.

He rolled off the tree and ran. He kept his injured eye shut as he sped along the jogging trial. By now, Sydney was well out ahead of him, and there was no way that she would know where to stop. Danny's adrenaline surged. He kicked his legs faster. He tore through the S curves that switched back and forth through the trees. He finally caught up to Sydney just as she reached the wall he remembered from his past visits.

Danny grabbed her shoulder. "Stop!" Sydney threw on the brakes. "Over the wall!" he yelled as he grabbed her hips and boosted her up. She scaled over it and disappeared on the other side. Danny followed suit and jumped over it into the dry creek bed that curved underneath the back porch of the club's restaurant. They scrambled up the embankment on the other side and ran into the parking lot. While it was half-filled with cars, no people were around.

As they ran toward the Camry, Danny blinked the bits of wood from his eye. They were twenty feet from it when he grabbed hold of Sydney's arm. She stopped in her tracks. He held out his hand, ordering her to stay back. He readied the knife to strike and examined the car. It was clear. He motioned for Sydney to get in.

Thirty seconds later, they were past the club's front entrance gates and cruising down the road.

Danny stayed silent as he examined his eye in the rearview mirror. He imagined the scene as Brick, Skeeter, and Garage Sale Jimmy discovered Booker. Was he even still alive? It didn't matter. It wouldn't take long for the shooting of Senator Booker Halsey to be all over the news. There was little doubt that Danny Cavanaugh would again be the prime suspect.

For the next fifteen minutes, as they wound through the privileged boulevards of Houston's Memorial area and then weaved their way toward downtown, Danny and Sydney remained silent.

Once they reached the congested downtown area, Danny drove down several streets, making random turns along the way, before finding a parking garage. He pulled into it and screeched through seven levels. The eighth floor was nearly empty. He steered the Camry into a corner spot and shut off the engine.

Danny was fuming. He jerked toward Sydney. "Come clean, Sydney."

"I don't—"

"Quit lying to me, Sydney! There's more to all this than what you're telling me!"

Sydney's eyes flashed. "I didn't lie to you, Danny. I just didn't think it was the right time to get into all this."

"Well, there's no time like the present, is there? I want to know why you didn't show me the page of the lawsuit with Booker's signature. Why didn't you tell me that he was the one representing the U.S. in the suit? And how the hell do these guards of yours keep finding us?" Danny slammed his fist against the steering wheel. "What the fuck is going on?"

Sydney sighed and kept her voice even. "I don't know how the guards keep finding us. I wanted to keep the signature page and the representation information to myself until we found the proper authorities. I was going to tell you about it, but after you told me the reason why you were at your cabin, I decided it was too much for you. I thought I could handle this without getting you involved any more than you already were. I was only trying to protect you, Danny."

"Protect me," he said with absolute cynicism. "That's terrific. You're doing a great job. And what would it be that you're protecting me from, Sydney?"

"From the truth."

Danny's frustration spiked. "Goddamn it, Sydney! I am sick and tired of all the mystery! Tell me the fucking truth!"

Sydney flared back at him. "You didn't want to tell me about that FBI agent you killed did you? There are some things that we would rather not reveal."

Their eyes remained locked until Danny finally relented. "Okay," he uttered as calmly as he could. "But I need to know, Sydney. I can't go on unless I know everything."

Sydney looked out the windshield and stared at the concrete wall in front of them. She remained silent for a long time.

"Sydney?" Danny urged.

"I need a few moments," she replied without moving her eyes.

"For what?"

"To determine the best way to unravel the world as you know it."

Chapter 40

Considering their situation, Sydney was surprised Danny allowed her the time to gather her thoughts. *How can I tell him? How do I not sound like a lunatic?*

Sydney once again flashed back to the moment when Knobby enlightened her in his booth at the Land's End Pub. The light streaming in from the window made his eyes glow. She could tell from the look on his face that he was so proud of her, his protégé's only child. She was there to tell him that the University of Monaco had offered her a teaching position. She was going to follow in the footsteps of the three men in her life: Knobby, her foster father, and her real father.

As Sydney sat there, she felt her unwavering affection for her godfather. Knobby was the one who had Jacques and Claire Dumas adopt her. Jacques had been a visiting professor at Oxford for a semester when he met Knobby. The two became squash opponents at first and then fast friends. Jacques and Claire were such loving parents, more than any child could ask for. Knobby had made the perfect choice.

Knobby's voice caught as he explained the truth about her biological parents' death. "Your parents ... their car accident was planned."

"What do you mean planned?"

"It was planned to look like an accident, but it was a carefully orchestrated event."

Whenever she visited London, Sydney had traveled to the spot along the River Thames where her parents' car plunged into the water and they drowned. But now, she envisioned a faceless killer stalking them, waiting to strike.

"You mean they were murdered?"

"Yes," Knobby answered.

How could you lie to me? Sydney thought as she stared at him. Her affection for her godfather, along with the trust of her fellow man, immediately began to erode away. But she forced herself to hear the rest of the story. "Who killed them?"

Sydney listened intently as Knobby explained not only the who but the why. Now, she would use his same words to explain herself to Danny.

"History is not accidental, Danny. Events are not part of some chaos theory in which God or luck determines the outcome. There are powerful people behind the scenes who have conspired to manage the events of history. They truly rule the world. They are part of a secret faction that runs our lives. Since this faction was created, they have been determined to extinguish freedom and democracy once and for all." Sydney added her own words to Knobby's dire revelation. "The lawsuit is the signal, Danny. They are nearing the point when they will begin their undisputed reign over the entire planet."

Danny chuckled. "If I was anywhere else but here, I'd ask you if we were on *Candid Camera.* Come on, Sydney. A secret group runs the world? Something like that could never happen."

"Why not?"

"Because I'm not James Bond, and this isn't a movie."

Sydney expected Danny's reaction. She had reacted the same way, as she sat listening to Knobby's crazy words. But then Knobby continued with proof. Now Sydney would, too.

"I know this is a lot to take, Danny. But it's best if I start at the beginning."

Danny's face was stained with doubt, but he nodded anyway. "Be my guest."

"In 1940, a pro-Marxist student group was formed at Oxford University. It was their view that the blossoming industrialized countries, which would no doubt become the leading nations of the world, should be taken over by Marxist regimes for the betterment of the entire planet."

Danny raised his finger. "I'm sorry to interrupt. But I'm a little fuzzy on Marxism since my college days. I know it's like communism but …"

Sydney continued. "Marxism and communism are one and the same, and yet they are completely different. The communism that most Americans think of, the one associated with the old Soviet Union, isn't true communism. It was a bastardized version of it based on Joseph Stalin's tyrannical regime. True communism, the type that Karl Marx promoted, creates a classless society of abundance in which all people enjoy equal social and economic status. However, Marx believed, as did the Oxford students, that true communism would only work in highly developed countries like Germany, Britain, and the United States. In Russia, which was largely agrarian with an autocratic political system at the time, communism was doomed from the start."

"Thank you for clearing that up, Professor Dumas."

Sydney ignored his snide comment and continued. "At one of this group's meetings, they hosted a guest speaker who regaled them with tales of a secret society that concocted a Marxist plot to take over the world. He explained how he was a member of this group and further explained how they were building in both numbers and power by operating as political moderates instead of the usual left-wing extremists. He concluded his speech by declaring that he had been chosen to head their operations in Britain, and he further boasted that he would one day become prime minister."

Sydney paused. Even though Danny was staring at her, she wanted to make sure he was listening. Because this was only the very tip of an enormous iceberg.

"So did he?" Danny asked.

"His name was Harold Wilson. He was the prime minister of the United Kingdom from 1964 to 1970 and again from 1974 to 1976."

"What makes you believe that this meeting happened or these groups even existed?"

"Because my godfather, Colin Tanner, was the professor who organized that student group. He was a sociology professor at

Oxford University. He also knew while this group's intentions may have been honorable, they were doomed from the start."

"Because?"

"Because basic human nature would never allow communism to blossom into what it was supposed to be."

"Which is?"

"A vehicle for people of every race, sex, and nationality to flourish."

"You're saying we humans prefer the survival of the fittest mentality? Dog eat dog and all that?"

"Exactly."

Danny's eyes danced for a few moments. "So, Wilson's group was a bunch of Marxists that became infected by their own human nature?"

Sydney nodded. "And over time, like any untreated infection, it has only gotten worse."

"So, they're the ones behind all of this world domination nonsense?"

Sydney nodded again. "Have you ever heard of the Bilderbergers?"

"No."

"The group Wilson belonged to has never had an official name. It's one of the rather elementary yet brilliant ways they have kept outsiders from proving they actually exist. They came to be known as the Bilderbergers, because they first became identified by the media during their meeting at the Bilderberg Hotel in Oosterbeek, Holland, in 1954. The group is comprised of people who define power. They are European royalty, politicians, international bankers, CEOs of multinational companies, and the heads of media empires all around the globe. Members of two American banking families are on that list."

"You're going to make me guess?"

"Aren't you dying to?"

"I have no idea."

"The Rockefellers and the Morgans."

"You might as well have said the Washingtons and the Lincolns. Those two families helped build America, why would they want to destroy it?"

"Because they were after something larger from the start, Danny. They wanted to rule the world."

A laugh escaped Danny's lips. "You can't just destroy a country. There has to be a war, or an invasion, or at least—"

"Someone on the inside," Sydney finished.

"Do you have a name?"

A knowing look appeared in Sydney's blazing eyes. "Does the name Dexter Walsh ring a bell?"

Chapter 41

Stefan Taber checked his PDA device. He had used it to track Stavros's assault rifle during his entire journey from the McAllen, Texas, airport to Houston's Hobby Airport. The private Gulfstream V was the same jet the ICJ group had used to fly from the Amsterdam Airport Schiphol to Texas. Little did Sydney Dumas and Joseph Ambrose know that the jet was owned by The Group.

As he cruised around the concrete jungle behind the wheel of a rented Volvo S60, Taber's PDA still performed brilliantly. After zigzagging throughout the city's downtown streets, the tracking device's signal had finally come to a stop for over ten minutes now.

Taber had to assume that Sydney told Cavanaugh the real reason why she was running from him and the other guards. He put himself in Danny Cavanaugh's shoes. Cavanaugh had to know he would be the prime suspect in the shooting of Senator Halsey. He was already a man on the run, and now the noose had tightened around his neck. Cavanaugh couldn't go to the police; he couldn't go to any officials. So what would he do next? What do desperate men do? Was Cavanaugh even still just desperate? Or had he turned the corner toward hopelessness?

Taber stopped the car at a red light. He tapped the PDA screen, accessing the zoom feature. He studied the tracking signal's coordinates from his present location. A right, a left, and then another right.

Taber continued on his way, examining the skyscrapers around him. People were everywhere. The streets were choked with vehicles of every size, shape, and color. Cavanaugh had been smart enough to ditch the truck that Taber and his men had turned into Swiss cheese back at the cabin. It was nowhere to be found outside Booker

Halsey's racquet club. Taber figured Cavanaugh must have stolen another car. But while there had been numerous cars parked in the club lot, most were high dollar jobs with car alarms. At the back of the lot, however, was where the help undoubtedly parked. There had been a dozen vehicles parked there. But as Taber left the club lot, he had noticed that the gold Toyota Camry in the middle of them was missing. The fresh tread marks left behind indicated that someone had driven off in a hurry.

Taber kept his eyes peeled for the Camry as he tried thinking like a fugitive cop. *I would need somewhere to go to think of my next steps,* Taber thought. *Somewhere private.* Where would Cavanaugh go for private shelter? Where would he go to avoid detection until he could think his way out of the mess he had made for himself?

Taber turned the wheel at the next intersection and was somewhat disappointed in himself as he stared at the parking garage before him.

Of course.

Taber pulled up into the garage's entrance. Seeing no one in the attendant's booth, he put the PDA on the dashboard and grabbed the parking ticket as it spit out from the machine. He rolled past the wooden arm as it rose above the car's roof. His eyes were everywhere, as he grabbed for his SIG Sauer assault rifle from the floorboard behind his seat. The muzzle and silencer were still warm from the shot Taber had taken at Senator Booker Halsey. Taber kept his hand on the muzzle for a bit, reliving every detail of the moment. He could see the explosion of blood on Booker's chest and the almost comical way the senator's body crumpled to the ground. Exquisite.

Taber was still savoring the moment when he positioned the gun in his lap and switched off the safety.

Come out, come out, wherever you are.

Chapter 42

Disbelief registered in Danny's face. "Dexter Walsh. You mean the chairman of the Federal Reserve?"

Sydney nodded. "The one and the same."

"So tell me about Mr. Wonderful."

"I will. But first, do you know the history of the Federal Reserve?"

Danny shook his head. "I was too busy staring at Stacey Jacobs back in Economics class."

"Don't you now wish you were paying attention instead of letting your penis rule your mind?"

"Yeah, yeah ..." Danny rolled his hand, wanting her to keep going.

"On the night of November 22, 1910, a group of seven very upstanding men," Sydney couldn't keep the sarcasm out of her voice, "held a secret meeting on Jekyll Island off the coast of Georgia. Six of them represented the international banking families—the Rockefellers, the Morgans, the Rothschild family, the Schiffs, the Warburgs, and the Kahns, nearly a quarter of the entire world's wealth. A seventh man was Rhode Island senator Nelson Aldrich, who was the chairman of the National Monetary Commission. The island was owned by none other than J. P. Morgan himself. These men wanted to devise a plan for banking reform in light of several negative events that showed the weaknesses in America's banking system at the time."

"Negative events?"

"Panics that caused runs on banks in 1873, 1893, and the big one in 1907."

"You're going to tell me that these panics were engineered by these very guys, aren't you?"

Sydney nodded. "The panics were started as rumors of certain banks' insolvencies by agents of the international bankers. Wouldn't you agree that even today the best way to advertise is still word-of-mouth?"

Danny sighed. "Okay, so they start rumors about banks going under, which causes panics, thus making the public scream for banking reform. These bankers then turn around and offer the perfect solution: the Federal Reserve."

"The Federal Reserve Act was signed on December 23, 1913."

Danny did the math. "That would make President Woodrow Wilson the signer."

"A darling of the international bankers, along with several other U.S. presidents over the years. It seems you know your history better than your economics, Danny."

"Stacey Jacobs wasn't in my American History class." He looked in the rearview mirror again. It was still clear. "But why would an organization that's part of America want to bankrupt it?"

"That's where you're wrong, Danny. The Federal Reserve is not part of the U.S. government. It's a private network of banks, which have evolved into multinational corporations, whose major stockholders include a very short list of powerful families."

"Let me guess. The Rothschilds, the Morgans, the Rockefellers, and their fellow jet-setting, polo-playing, world-dominating friends."

"They not only have their tentacles in the Federal Reserve, they control many of the banking systems across the globe."

Danny remembered back to their initial conversation outside the monastery. "Like the aforementioned Bank of Japan."

Sydney nodded again. "Which, by not buying America's debt any longer, is supposedly forcing Walsh's hand to print more money and then raise interest rates."

"What about the Chinese?"

"What about them?"

"Why did they stop buying our debt? Are these Bilderbergers in with the Chinese as well?"

"No. Although it is the more powerful, bigger brother, China has always shadowed Japan's financial movements. They just assume that the Bank of Japan is wired in better to the international financial markets and follow their lead."

"And since they've always done it, the Bank of Japan knew China would play follow the leader again here."

"Correct."

"So, if the Bank of Japan is just a front for the Bilderbergers, they're the ones who want America's gold."

"You're thinking like a detective, Danny. Now think like an economist."

He wasn't in the mood to be a student. "Just tell me how the gold fits in, professor."

"I told you that our ICJ chamber meets in secret to prevent any information that we discuss from affecting the markets."

"I'm sensing that was a big, fat lie."

Sydney shook her head. "Not a lie, just not the entire truth. While we do meet in secret, information concerning our deliberations invariably gets out before we want it to."

Danny knew where she was going. "Plausible deniability."

"I'm sorry?"

"Bank of Japan officials will leak the story about wanting payment in gold, which will make the rest of our creditors want the same thing, no matter the outcome of your deliberations. That news will not only send the price of gold through the stratosphere, it will ensure that the dollar completely tanks. But if anyone tries to call Japan on it, all they have to do is point to the ICJ and say they tried to keep it hush hush. Plausible deniability."

Sydney nodded. "The Bilderbergers have undoubtedly purchased much of the gold on the world market to take advantage when the dollar collapses and the price of gold skyrockets to unprecedented levels. While your economic analysis was top notch, Danny, you forgot one important thing."

"Which is?"

"The values of all paper currencies across the planet are inextricably linked, with the dollar being the most powerful one. If it becomes worthless, it sends the whole global fiat money system into freefall. The only currency that will have any value left will be gold. And while most countries still maintain a small gold reserve, those reserves won't last long, especially during a global financial crisis."

"If the Bilderbergers have most of the gold and none of the expenses that countries do, they'll be sitting pretty," Danny surmised.

"Correct."

"And he who has the gold, makes the rules."

"And in this case, rules the world," Sydney added.

"Why can't we track those purchases and put the screws to the buyers for information?"

"The Bilderbergers do not make big movements, Danny. Theirs are fractional actions over time. They would have made small purchases of gold over a period of several years and spread them through their various businesses and interests. The last thing they would want is for their activities to be found out."

Danny looked out the back window. It still framed a motionless scene. "So what makes you think Walsh is their puppet?"

"The summer after my sophomore year in college, I was part of a research team that was sent to the island of Trinidad and Tobago. The island's economy was almost solely dependent on its oil reserves. We were there to perform research into diversifying their economy so that fluctuations in oil prices, which had recently bottomed out, wouldn't have such a detrimental effect. The research group was led by Dr. Walsh. I fell in love with his assistant, Alex." Sydney smiled as her eyes lulled into a pleasant memory. "Alex was several years older than I. He had a mop of wavy black hair that never looked the same two days in a row. And what a smile. Like one you'd see on a Ralph Lauren model." She laughed. "The clincher was his wardrobe. He had a different gaudy Hawaiian shirt for every day of the week."

"Sounds like you were real fond of him."

"He was my first love."

"What happened to him?"

"He and I could never be together. Our personalities were too similar. There we were not only living in paradise but trying to save it. We both knew that if we lived together under normal circumstances, with rent and utility bills to worry about, wondering if the other was straying during our times apart, we knew it wouldn't work. So we left each other with gorgeous memories of a two-month long affair."

Although it was an interesting story, which was giving Danny insider information on what made Sydney Dumas tick, he needed to get her back on track. "You were saying about how you knew Dr. Walsh?"

"Oh yes, sorry. One night Alex told me the real reason why Dr. Walsh had us crunching numbers all summer. He wasn't there to save the country. He was there to make sure that the island was forever in debt to the United States."

"Why?"

"To ensure a long-term source of oil. It was the same reason why Dr. Walsh was called in to Saudi Arabia in the 1970s. The 1973 OPEC oil embargo nearly crippled the United States. To inoculate themselves from future embargos, the U.S. needed to forever link itself with the Middle East. They realized that Middle Eastern countries like Saudi Arabia desperately needed to upgrade their infrastructure in order to maximize their oil extraction capability. Saudis had also been exposed to the Western world and had acquired a thirst for things that world had to offer."

"Like?"

"Jet fighter planes, giant skyscrapers, Bentley convertibles, and beautiful women."

"And here I thought you were going to say baseball gloves and apple pie."

Sydney let that one go. "The U.S. formed JECOR, the United States-Saudi Arabian Joint Economic Commission. Through JECOR, the Saudis agreed to hire American engineering, construction, and defense companies to provide the infrastructure needed. But there was one problem. The Saudis had enough money to pay for it all and then walk away from the U.S. Walsh devised what he called the Markov Monte Carlo model, where he used statistics and probability methods to show that future economic conditions are independent from past or even current conditions. Basically, he used Double MC to persuade the Saudis that because their wealth comes from oil, a commodity the world needs in perpetuity, they could afford to finance their massive infrastructure expansion while using monies on hand to pay for their new, lavish lifestyles."

"And the financing naturally came from the U.S. government."

"Naturally."

"So who did Walsh work for when he devised all this?"

"Both he and Alex worked for the Central Intelligence Agency."

"It always comes back to the CIA," Danny mused. "Did Alex tell you that?"

"Yes."

"Was it pillow talk?"

Surprise formed in Sydney's eyes. "Does that mean you think he was lying to me?"

Danny shook his head. "The complete opposite, in fact. That's when the truth usually comes out."

"Looking back, I'm sure Walsh was already involved with the Bilderbergers back then."

"This Double MC model, it sounds like he used it to sell us down the river with all of the recent bailouts and our government's spending spree."

Sydney smiled. "I'll make an economist of you yet, Danny. Walsh blessed the bailouts and the massive deficit-spending programs. He said America could spend her way out of the recession. I tried contacting U.S. Treasury officials and called every American I knew to sound the alarm. But nobody would listen."

Danny blew out a nervous chuckle and looked off in the distance. "So why can't anyone figure Walsh out?"

"It's not a question of figuring him out, Danny. Walsh is a very charismatic fellow, and he proved, on paper at least, that Double MC would work. There are numerous schools of economic thought, many of which contradict one another. It is only after they are put into use that they are lauded or ridiculed. But by that time, the damage is already done."

"But several decades have passed since 1973. Why hasn't Walsh's model been rejected?"

"Because the Saudis' wealth has, in fact, allowed them to keep on spending without a care in the world."

"What about Trinidad and Tobago?" Danny asked.

"Because the world doesn't care about the economics of a tiny third world island," Sydney answered flatly.

"Why can't we just go to the authorities, like some kind of world economic police, and show them the lawsuit?"

"World economic police? There is no such thing."

"What about the IMF? Or the UN? Or even your ICJ?"

"You've worked within a bureaucracy, Danny. You know it would take too much time to go through all the hurdles. Besides, I have no idea who's involved. I had no idea Nathan Broederlam was involved, and I worked with him on a daily basis. Like you said before, we need proof.

"Danny, I know I sound like I've gone completely mad, but I've studied these events. The United States is finally in a position with its unimaginable debt load for the Bilderbergers to strike and send your country, and the world, reeling into a financial freefall from which there is no recovery. If you must, check everything I have told you about Harold Wilson, Colin Tanner, the history of your Federal Reserve, and the U.S. financial records. Recorded history verifies everything. Like I said, history is not accidental. Everything is ..."

The look on Danny's face made Sydney stop.

"What? What is it, Danny?"

Nothing's accidental.

It hit him like a kick in the face. He looked at the assault rifle in the backseat, the one the guard had dropped in the back of his truck at the cabin. He grabbed it and began disassembling it in record time. He started with the clip. Nothing. Then he moved on to the scope. He unhooked it from the gun and peered into the scope mounts. Nothing.

Sydney stared at him like he was a madman. "What are you doing?"

"A tracking bug. That's how the guards keep finding us. There must be a bug in this gun."

Danny ripped the shoulder pad from the rifle's butt. Still no bug. He eyed the two screws that held the butt together. Inside it would be the safest place for any foreign objects. Especially tiny sensors that needed to transmit a signal.

"The toolbox I found underneath your seat. I need it," Danny ordered.

Sydney retrieved it and handed it to him. He cracked it open and found a flat-head screwdriver.

Danny had the screws out in seconds. He pried the screwdriver into the butt's seam and twisted. It popped open with a *crack* to reveal the treasure he was seeking.

The tracking bug itself was no bigger than a nickel. Two wires led away from it to a lithium ion battery that resembled a credit card. Danny learned about these devices during his surveillance classes with the Texas Rangers. The bug was GPS enabled. It could be tracked via satellite anywhere in the world. The battery was the most advanced available and, once activated, could power the tiny bug for over a month. More than enough time to find the weapon and the person using it.

Icy panic leaked into Danny's body. They had been in this parking garage for at least ten minutes; plenty of time for their stalkers from the racquet club to find them here. The frigid feeling then flooded through him as his next thought entered his mind.

The parking garage has no way out other than the way in. They were trapped.

Chapter 43

Taber looked up and saw that there were only a few floors left before the top. *I'm getting warmer*, he thought as his grip tightened on the rifle. He slowed the vehicle to a crawl before approaching the turn that would take him to the seventh level of parked cars. As he did on the previous levels, Taber looked into the fish-eye mirror fixed high on the garage's outer wall. No cars were coming down the ramp toward him. There were no bodies in motion either. Still, he made sure the tip of his gun barrel was secured on the driver's windowsill before stepping on the gas and ascending another floor.

Taber spotted a gold Toyota Camry backed in between a Lexus sedan and an immense concrete support pillar. His stomach tightened, and he turned the rifle over so that the barrel was now facing the passenger door. He was ready, but the license plate wasn't the same one that Taber remembered seeing at the club. He kept his foot on the gas and returned the rifle barrel to his windowsill.

Taber rounded the next turn and began ascending the ramp to the eighth floor. *They must be up here.* His thoughts were confirmed as he gazed into the fish-eye mirror at the end of the ramp and he saw another gold Camry parked at the far end of the garage.

As soon as he rounded the corner, he studied the license plate. It matched. There were only two other cars on the entire floor, and they were both parked next to the elevator.

Taber pulled in between the two cars, turned in his seat, and stared at the Camry. If there was anyone inside it, he couldn't see them through the tinted glass. He reached behind his seat again and felt his Glock 24 pistol. He quietly chambered a bullet and then stuffed the pistol into his shoulder holster. He double-checked the clip in his rifle. It was full.

Once he was out of the Volvo, he didn't hesitate. Taber charged the Camry straight on. As he came upon it with his rifle ready to spray it with bullets, he could finally see inside the back window. The cabin looked empty. He came around the driver's side and looked inside it. Although the tinted glass obscured his view, it was obvious that no one was there. But then he noticed something shining on the floorboard near the gas pedal. It was a tiny device connected to a slim battery.

I've been hoodwinked, Taber thought. He vaulted over to the nearby stairwell. He threw open the door and stepped inside. He lunged down a few steps when the sound of screeching tires several floors below made him stop.

Taber sprinted back to the Volvo and dove into it. Seconds later, he slashed around the corner of the eighth floor. He careened the car down to the seventh floor as he opened his window. He still didn't see any movement, but he could hear tires continue to screech beneath him. His frustration surged as he spun the car through the next corner. He came only inches away from the parked cars, as he alternated between flooring the gas on the short straightaways and mashing the brakes on the U-turns.

He ripped around the corner between the fifth and fourth floors and had to slam on the brakes with both feet. His car smashed into the side of an empty pick-up truck. It was parked across the middle of lane. There was no getting by it.

Taber bolted from his car to the garage's edge. He peered down to the street. He was on the opposite side from the exit. He sprinted the length of the garage to the stairwell and flung open the door. He flew down the stairs with rage fueling his steps.

He reached the bottom and raced out onto the ground floor by the attendant booth with the now smashed exit arm. He ran out into the street and looked in all directions. He didn't see them anywhere. Once again, Stefan Taber had lost Danny Cavanaugh and Sydney Dumas.

Chapter 44

"I still don't see him," Sydney said. She was staring out the rear windshield of the late model Lincoln Town Car that Danny had stolen from the parking garage. "I think we're safe."

Danny glanced in the rearview mirror, as he continued weaving through the grid of downtown streets. "For now," he said as he tossed the straightened coat hanger and screwdriver into the backseat. They were the same tools he had used to break into and then start the Camry back in McAllen, as well as the pick-up truck and the Town Car from the parking garage.

Sydney faced forward in her seat. "Where did you learn to steal cars?"

"The police academy."

Her brow furrowed. "The police taught you how to steal?"

Danny came to the intersection of Walker and Bagby. He turned the corner and headed for the on-ramp to Interstate 45. "Sometimes you have to think like a criminal to catch one. Other times, you do what you can to save your ass. I'd be happy to teach you how sometime."

A chuckle escaped Sydney's lips. "Don't you think I should practice my driving first?"

"Definitely. But with the way you drive, the only way to practice is to steal a car. No one in their right mind should let you borrow one."

He flashed an irresistible smile. She returned one of equal measure.

"I should slap you for saying such things."

"Then why don't you?"

"And deface such a gorgeous façade? It would be like spray painting the Mona Lisa."

Danny blushed. His only comeback was, "right back at ya," but he wisely decided to keep that winner locked up tight behind his teeth.

"Finally, the smart mouth is trumped by a compliment," Sydney continued.

Again, all Danny could do was stare at the beautiful, intelligent, and sassy creature in breathtaking silence.

"So what now?" she asked.

"We need to get the hell out of Dodge."

Sydney frowned. "Dodge? I don't understand."

"It's an expression. It means that as we speak, three very influential men are probably giving their statements to the Houston police concerning the last two people they saw with Senator Booker Halsey before he was shot. We need to get out of Houston ASAP."

Concern flooded Sydney's face. "The police are not the only people we have to worry about."

Danny nodded. "The Bilderbergers."

"Stefan Taber won't stop, Danny."

"I figured asking him pretty please wouldn't do it. At least he can't track us anymore."

"They can track us other ways, Danny. Through financial transactions, finding our family and friends and intimidating them."

"Plus they'll send others, reinforcements."

Sydney nodded. "They will never stop."

The two fell silent for a long moment. The only sound came from the thumping of car tires as they crossed over the on-ramp's concrete sections.

Danny remembered back to the last moments of his conversation with Senator Halsey just before he was shot. Halsey hadn't given him anything that wasn't already known about his public service record and his private life. Booker tried changing the subject by questioning Sydney's motives.

"How much do you know about this girl, Danny? Who is she really working for? Christ boy, for all you know she's in bed with the same bastards who pulled off the attack on the D.C. Metro system."

"We have to get to Washington, D.C," Danny blurted.

"Why Washington?"

"Because during my little chat in the woods with Senator Halsey, he told me about a sarin gas attack on the D.C. Metro system. I don't believe in coincidences. It has to be related to your Bilderberger plot."

Sydney gasped. "Oh God. Was anyone hurt?"

Danny hunched his shoulders. "Don't know. But it only confirms that we need to go straight to the top with what we know."

"The top of what, Danny?"

"I wouldn't be a very good American citizen if I didn't try to warn my president of a possible threat, now would I?"

Chapter 45

President Jack Butcher remained sequestered inside the Presidential Emergency Operations Center while the NEST team completed their investigation of the remaining National Mall monuments.

So far, the NEST team hadn't found anything. The only good news was that their trigger expert had been able to deactivate the bomb at the Washington Monument.

Jack didn't like playing the waiting game. He clamored to his feet, ignoring every piece of state-of-the-art communication technology surrounding him, and went straight for the dry-erase board on the wall. He scribbled three notes in blue marker.

Wait for material confirmation
Contact leader of nation of origin
Begin negotiations for identities of terrorists

Jack clicked the marker cap several times. "What's the consensus on the material being Russian?"

Jack looked at Simon, who was about to answer when he heard Harry Tharp clear his throat.

"High, Mr. President. Damn high. The Russians have little to zero security of their nuclear material. I'm sure you've read my reports on the efforts of Al Qaeda, Hamas, and even the Irish Republican Army. They're always on the lookout for lost Russian nukes."

"I agree with Harry," Simon continued. "I'm sure most of us caught that story on *Dateline NBC*, where the producers gained access to a Russian nuclear laboratory with fake credentials they made with Photoshop." All the heads in the room nodded. "But I wouldn't count out our friends in North Korea or China either. With all the whining Iran's doing about their need to be a recognized nuclear power, I wouldn't be surprised if Ahmadinejad doesn't already have some weapons-grade plutonium stuffed somewhere."

"And I can guarantee that we're not on any one of their Christmas card lists," Charlie Jacoby chimed in.

Jack looked around the room and saw the rest of the group nodding. He was about to ask the next logical question when the PEOC phone rang.

Jack strode back to his post and picked up the phone. "Jack Butcher."

"Mr. President, I have some news for you, sir."

It was Vanessa Dempsey. "What is it?" Jack answered.

"Senator Booker Halsey's been shot."

"Shot?" Even though they couldn't hear Vanessa, the word made everyone in the room stiffen. "Where?"

"He was playing tennis at his club in Houston, sir."

"Jesus. Who shot him?"

"The alleged suspect is a Texas Ranger named Danny Cavanaugh, sir."

"Danny Cavanaugh?" The name sounded familiar to Jack. He only needed to flash his eyes at Simon Shilling to jog his memory.

As usual, Simon didn't disappoint. "He's that Texas Ranger who's on the run for killing an FBI agent, Mr. President."

"Right," Jack replied to Simon, "the Espinoza debacle." He put the receiver back to his mouth. "How's Booker doing?"

"He was transported to Ben Taub Hospital. He's in surgery right now."

"What about Cavanaugh?"

"He escaped, sir," Vanessa replied.

Just then, the phone beeped and a red light appeared on the Line 2 button. "I've got another call, Vanessa."

"I'll keep you posted, Mr. President," Vanessa said and then hung up.

Jack hit the Line 2 button. "This is President Butcher."

"Mr. President, it's Clarence Warner again, sir. I have news."

"Hold on, Clarence. Let me put you on speaker." Jack pressed the speakerphone button and hung up the handset.

"Clarence?"

"Yes, sir."

"Give us what you've got."

"We've checked every building along the mall, sir. They're all clear except for the Lincoln Monument. We're getting low-level radiation readings from it. My team has cleared the area and is performing a full-scale search as we speak."

"Hold on, Clarence." Jack put the phone on mute and turned to Simon. "Another gas leak story?"

Simon nodded. "NEST knows how to handle it, Mr. President."

Jack nodded and depressed the mute button again. "Okay, Clarence, we're back."

"Mr. President?"

"Yes, Clarence."

"Sir, are you familiar with how nuclear material is fingerprinted to its country of origin?"

"Keep talking, Clarence."

"Sir, we have the plutonium's source country."

Clarence paused, and Jack felt his blood pressure rising. "Would you like to tell us, Clarence, or should we play twenty questions?"

"Mr. President, the material inside the Washington Monument bomb is from Great Britain."

Jack forced himself to keep his face clear of any expression. He read the other faces in the room. Shock was pretty much the prevailing emotion. No surprise there.

"Clarence, the plutonium identification has been verified, correct?"

Clarence Warner's answer was instantaneous. "Yes, Mr. President. Our SOP is to travel with both electronic and hard copies of the global nuclear materials list. This list is managed by the NNSA and is crosschecked with the DOD's nuclear materials database, sir. It's as accurate as accurate can be."

NNSA? Jack squinted at the brainstorming list on the dry-erase board and began clicking the marker cap again. After only a couple months in office, he was still green with all of the federal government acronyms. But he didn't dare ask Simon what NNSA stood for in front of others, especially Harry Tharp. That mental lapse would definitely make it out of the room.

"Clarence, Simon Shilling here. Remind me who's directing the National Nuclear Security Administration again?"

"Sam Ashworth, sir."

Thanks, Jack thought as he eyed Simon.

Simon continued. "Mr. President, I think that we need to get Ashworth over here ASAP to get his take on the situation."

Before Jack could agree, Clarence came back on the line. "Mr. President, may I put you on hold for a moment? One of my guys has some information for me."

"Of course, Clarence." Jack hit the mute button once again. He addressed the group. "Thoughts?"

Simon followed up with another question. "Anyone know who's in charge of Britain's nuclear security?"

All eyes turned to the one person in the room who should know. As Jack's National Security Adviser, Charlie Jacoby didn't disappoint. "They have a director of civil nuclear security in their Department of Trade and Industry. I think his name is Nottingham, but don't quote me. I haven't had the pleasure to meet him yet, but I'm sure I can get him on the horn to verify that some of their nuclear material is missing."

"Do we really think this Nottingham's going to admit that they lost some of their nuclear material?" Blake Conway asked the group.

"Or if it was stolen, tell us who stole it?" Rita Rodriguez added.

Harry Tharp hacked a few times to get the floor. "How do we know it's not intentional?"

Harry's statement did more to silence the room than any amount of his throat clearing could.

Jack couldn't help his eyes crossing over the room to meet Simon's. *Does Harry know about what really happened at the Library of Congress and at Monticello?*

Blake outright laughed at Harry's suggestion. "You're suggesting that the British government planted dirty bombs inside the United States? That's ludicrous."

Harry leaned forward in his chair and stared at Blake. "That's exactly why they would do it, son. Nothing's impossible in love and politics. 'Course you're too young to have much of a track record in either."

Jack could feel the tension pulsing inside his press secretary. *What an asshole Harry is,* Jack thought. He didn't know if calling a black man "son" was as bad as calling him "boy," but from the look on Blake's face, it was. Jack took back control of the room.

"Okay folks. Let's stick to task here." He looked to Charlie and Rita for answers to his next question. "Let's entertain Harry's notion if nothing else but to get it off the table. If it's intentional, why?"

Charlie went first. "Extortion. Someone in Parliament might be making a deal with terrorists. Maybe there was a kidnapping, and they bargained a son or daughter of a prominent Parliament member in exchange for nuclear material."

Rita played off of Charlie's theory. "You know, the Saudis do a hell of a business with the London banks. Maybe they were threatening to go somewhere else unless they got their hands on some nukes."

"They could still be pissed off at us for that little difference of opinion we had back in 1776."

Harry Tharp's mouth had once again silenced the room. This time, Jack forced himself to look anywhere but at Simon.

Clarence Warner's nervous voice crept into the phone. "Mr. President, sir?"

Jack depressed the mute button. "Yes, Clarence?"

"Sir, we found another suitcase device here at the Lincoln. Same brand and color. Black American Tourister. Same guts, too. I'd say it was made by the same people who are responsible for the monument bomb."

"Jesus. So it's another dirty bomb?" Jack asked.

"Yes, sir," Clarence replied.

"Have you checked the material yet?"

"Yes, sir. I was just talking to our analyst when I got off the phone before."

"And?"

"This bomb's plutonium is also from Great Britain, sir."

"Son of a bitch," Jack replied.

"Sir, there's more."

"Go ahead, Clarence."

"I need to tell you exactly where this bomb was found."

Chapter 46

As soon as Clarence was done telling the PEOC group about the unnerving location, Jack hit the button to end the call. "Any thoughts?" he asked his staff. He had to ask the question twice in order for it to actually sink into their obviously dumbfounded minds. Initially, no one had any ideas. Even Harry Tharp had nothing to say about the location of the suitcase.

"Mr. President, whoever is doing this is sending us a message," Blake Conway offered.

"You mean besides the message of 'I don't care for you guys very much'?"

Jack crossed back to the dry-erase board. He wrote:

Location #1—Monument, trash can

Location #2—Lincoln Memorial, sub-basement

"Sir, the locations of the bombs are telling us that they can go virtually anywhere at anytime," Blake replied.

Simon and Jack stared at each other. "Mr. President," Simon finally uttered, "it's time to call Tony."

Jack made eye contact with every other person in the room, one-by-one. "Could you all excuse us for a minute?"

They did as they were told. Blake Conway was the last to leave, and he closed the door behind him. Jack sat back down in his chair as Simon waited the requisite thirty seconds before he spoke. He hitched his thumb toward the door. "It's also time to tell them about Monticello and the library, sir. But call Tony first." Jack did a double take, wondering if these walls had ears. "I know, Mr. President," Simon continued as he took his seat. "But it'll be a hell of a lot better to talk strategy about this thing with everyone in the know. Plus,

I'd like to get the monkey off our backs and let some others carry it around for a while. Wouldn't you?"

Jack nodded reluctantly. "You think Harry already knows about the documents from the break-ins? What if one of our experts leaked it?"

Simon shook his head. "It's only God's sense of humor that Harry is continuing to make his comments without realizing he's pretty much hitting the nail on the head every time. Harry's not subtle and definitely not that clever. He's a square peg continually ramming a round hole. If he had something on you or me, he wouldn't be smart enough to use it for political leverage. He'd grandstand it so he could get his fifteen minutes in front of a national audience."

Relief trickled into Jack's system. "You're right. By the way, what are your thoughts on Booker?"

Simon huffed. "Son of a bitch got what was coming to him."

"Seriously."

Simon shifted in his chair. "I'd love to be the governor of Texas right now. Just think of all the perks the oil patch boys must be throwing at him to pick a warm body that's pro oil to fill Booker's seat." He held up his hands, a fake look of concern on his face. "Should he die, God forbid."

Jack sighed. He picked up the blue marker and began clicking it again. "What's your gut reaction on Danny Cavanaugh? What the hell would make him go after Booker?"

"Hard to say. But it looks as if he's a wild card. I think we need to get to know his story a little bit better."

Chapter 47

Anthony Fantroy sipped tea at his desk. He reveled in his hour-long respite from the daily onslaught of pressures and tensions that constantly tugged at him. Where many Londoners regarded high tea as a traditional time for socializing with others, high tea for him was reserved for one man alone with his thoughts. As he eased back in his chair, keeping his exceptionally British feet on the ground, Fantroy stared out through the window of his office at the shapeless gray blanket that covered the sky.

Taber must have lost them for good.

Fantroy hadn't heard a word from Stefan Taber for several hours. The only thing he knew for sure was Taber had screwed up again. Fantroy had heard the news about Booker Halsey being shot. *How the hell could Taber have let this happen?* Fantroy knew how The Group dealt with failure. The Group didn't fire people; they wiped them off the face of the earth and replaced them with someone equally as expendable. Simple.

Taber was well aware of the consequences for his incompetence. Fantroy was chiding himself for allowing Taber to pursue Sydney Dumas into America by himself, but there was nothing else that could be done. The rest of the team was cleaning up the mess at the monastery. The idea was to make it look like the place had been raided by a Mexican drug gang and that Joseph Ambrose and Nathan Broederlam were in the wrong place at the wrong time. For now, Sydney Dumas's disappearance could be explained as a kidnapping.

Fantroy thought about Taber's situation. Would he go to the authorities with what he knew? Was he still on the job? Still tracking them? Doubtful. The bastard was no doubt on the run by now. Fantroy had received the tracking report an hour ago. Both the tracking unit in the gun that Sydney Dumas and her police officer friend were using and the one in Taber's assault rifle were at the same coordinates in Houston, Texas. They had been at that location for the past few hours. It must have been a point of confrontation. But what happened? And why were both weapons still there?

Two twenty-inch flat panel monitors were hooked into Fantroy's desktop computer. One screen showed the contents of Stefan Taber's dossier. The other displayed information on Sydney Dumas's new partner in crime. Fantroy looked over Taber's information as he pictured Taber prying the surveillance bug out of his gun and leaving it wherever he had found the other assault rifle and then pursuing them on his own. Taber was the kind of bloke who wouldn't stop a mission just because of the threat of his own demise. He would still go after his target, no matter what. But if Taber had lost them now, he no longer had the upper hand, and he was no longer theirs. He was now another liability, like Sydney Dumas and her American friend, Sergeant Danny Cavanaugh of the Texas Rangers.

Fantroy thought about his other options, really his other only option. The Group's agents were watching Cavanaugh's mother's house in Houston. She wasn't home. Her email account was being hacked and so were her phone records to determine who she knew and where she might have gone. Hopefully, they could find her and use her as leverage against the policeman.

Fantroy looked at his watch. The Group would be meeting in less than five hours. There would be many questions about Ms. Dumas and Sergeant Cavanaugh. Fantroy needed to concentrate on them for a while. He sipped his tea while his thoughts turned to Sydney Dumas.

Sydney Dumas was a smart woman. Fantroy assumed for the moment that she had somehow figured out The Group's plan. Where would she turn next? Would she go to the authorities? *Normally yes*, Fantroy thought. But Ms. Dumas had taken on a partner who wouldn't allow her to make that choice. So now what? Fantroy closed his eyes.

I am Sydney Dumas. I am being helped by a police officer who has talents and abilities, but who cannot go to his brethren for help. He is a wanted man, a fugitive. What do I do next?

Brinngg! Brinngg!

The phone yanked Fantroy from his tea-induced trance. He glared at it and then at the door, past which his secretary was stationed. She knew very well that this was his hour. There were to be no interruptions unless another country was declaring war on England or the King himself had dropped dead.

Fantroy pressed the speakerphone button. "What is it?" he hissed.

His secretary offered no apologies but replied with the one phrase that reminded him of his unrelenting duties.

"Mr. Prime Minister, the president of the United States is holding on line one."

Chapter 48

Simon Shilling cracked open the PEOC conference room door. Charlie Jacoby and Rita Rodriguez each had somehow managed to smuggle fresh Starbucks coffees into the secured area. They were both in mid-sip when the door opened. Blake Conway was writing notes on his legal pad while he spun a bottle of water in his hand. Harry Tharp leaned against the wall in the corner, eating sunflower seeds and spitting the shells into a nearby trash can. Benjamin Speakes sat as he had inside the PEOC, motionless with the power of God resting on his lap.

"He's ready for you guys to come back in," Simon informed them. He looked at Speakes. "Ben, could you wait out here for a little while longer?"

Speakes cleared his throat and nodded. "Yes sir, Mr. Shilling."

As soon as everyone had taken their old seats around the conference table, Jack stood up from his chair and tried to sound as official as possible.

"I just got off the phone with Tony Fantroy. I informed him that we have discovered two suitcase nuclear devices within the District of Columbia and that the plutonium contained within these devices has been traced back to Great Britain. Prime Minister Fantroy has denied any knowledge of these devices but has pledged to conduct a full investigation into the matter."

Harry Tharp warmed his vocal cords with an obnoxious grunt. "Mr. President, did you disclose the exact locations of the bombs?"

"No, Harry. I just ballparked them for him. If Tony does know something about these bombs, he might slip and say something about their locations."

Blake interjected. "Mr. President, why would Prime Minister Fantroy have any knowledge of the bombs?"

Jack turned to Simon and nodded. He sat down and let his chief of staff take over.

Simon swiveled to face his audience. "You all remember the attempted robbery at the Library of Congress and the break-in at Monticello?" They all nodded. "What you do not know is that the library attempt was not about the rare book that got reported in the news."

"The Henry Harrisse manuscript," Blake clarified. Simon nodded. "Then what were they after?"

"That's what we need to talk about—"

A knock on the door interrupted Simon. Jack stood up and answered it. He opened the door just enough to retrieve the folder that he had sent Agent Peter Devon to the Oval Office to retrieve. Jack closed the door and turned around, clutching an oversized, army-green file folder in his hand. It was sealed shut with three thick bands, each embossed with the presidential seal. Jack returned to his seat and began tearing through each seal.

Simon waited his thirty seconds after the door was shut and continued, saying, "The thief at the Library of Congress attempted to steal documents originally drafted by the Founding Fathers. We believe the thieves at Monticello stole copies of those same documents."

Jack placed the folder on the table and rested his hands on top of it. He eyed every person before speaking. "Let me be crystal clear here, folks. What I am about to show you has been verified by Director of National Intelligence Howard Fielding as pertinent to our national security and is therefore classified information. You are forbidden by law to disclose any part of this conversation to any persons. If you do, be ready to spend the rest of your days confined to a prison cell."

Jack went back over everyone in the room. They each gave their own look of understanding. He opened the folder and retrieved the two documents sealed in separate plastic sheets. "Simon and I have met with several experts, including a conservator from the National

Archives, who put the documents through a thorough examination. They have all concluded that they are the real deal."

He passed both documents to Blake Conway, who couldn't wait to read them. Jack watched Blake's eyes meticulously hike across the page. Blake's confused look exploded into shock.

"My God," he choked out. "Is this really ... It can't be real."

Jack nodded at the second document. "Read the letter."

Blake slid the first document over to Charlie, who began devouring every word with Rita hovering over her shoulder.

Blake finished reading the letter a minute later. "This is incredible." He passed the letter on to Charlie and Rita, who were still going over the first document. Harry Tharp continued to stay seated, not showing any anxiousness or even a hint of excitement. He just kept popping his sunflower seeds and spitting the shells into a wastebasket next to him.

Spit one more goddamn seed and you and I will go a few rounds out in the Rose Garden, Jack wanted to growl at him. He managed to corral his anger and concentrated on the reactions of the others as they digested this unimaginable information.

Simon waited until Charlie and Rita were done reading the letter before he spoke.

"Now you know why we think Tony has a vested interest in the demise of the United States of America."

Chapter 49

Anthony Fantroy was hosting the event but would be the last attendee to arrive. As he navigated the foggy rain that settled over London earlier that evening, he couldn't help but worry about President Butcher's phone call and his blunt admission of what they had discovered. The president's words still echoed inside Fantroy's head.

"Prime Minister Fantroy, let me get right to it. We have found two dirty bombs on American soil that can be traced back to Great Britain."

Fantroy tried to get a moment's peace from the rollicking thoughts pounding his brain. He looked out from underneath the brim of his black Burberry bucket hat that resembled those strapped on several other pedestrians. No one gave him a second look as they scurried around the sidewalks in the rain. Still, to avoid recognition, he pulled his umbrella in tighter to his head as he turned onto Regent Street. He walked to Conduit Street and then finally onto Bond Street. He continued eyeing the people around him, making sure no one recognized him. The rain didn't deter women from crowding into Versace and Tiffany's. Men of means were no less deterred by the rain from heading into Armani and Burberry. Seeing these people made Fantroy remember the words of American philosopher Henry David Thoreau.

> Most of the luxuries and many of the so-called comforts of life are not only not indispensable, but positive hindrances to the elevation of mankind.

He had read several of Thoreau's works shortly after his induction into The Group. The passages had reminded him about the ironic fact that man's quest for prosperity was in itself a descent into slavery.

But it was this quest that allowed people like Fantroy and the others he would soon be sitting across from to stay in power. Another one of Thoreau's lines, perhaps his most famous, came to mind: "Most men live lives of quiet desperation."

How The Group reacted to their current situation, as well as their next moves, would ultimately determine if that quote would continue to stand the test of time.

Fantroy came upon the façade of the Westbury Hotel. But instead of heading for the front door to be properly received by an overzealous manager and a franticly doting staff, he ducked into the alley that ran alongside it. The Westbury was on a short list of locations across the globe that The Group used for emergency meetings. Fantroy himself had traveled to and helped select each destination on that list. He was confident that The Group could meet at these locations without worrying about their proceedings, or even their presence, being leaked to the press.

Fantroy stepped down a flight of stairs and opened a flimsy door marked "Deliveries." He walked along a series of dank hallways he was sure that no guest of the Westbury ever saw. He stepped through a door that read "Private, No Admittance." He turned several corners and came to a second door stamped with the same foreboding words. He tapped their secret beat on it. The door opened, and Fantroy was greeted by the people that truly ruled the planet.

The minute Fantroy passed the threshold, the room was effectively sealed. As he began peeling his rain gear from his body, Fantroy couldn't help twisting Thoreau's words around for a better fit that described the world's current situation.

Most men live lives of blissful ignorance, and then thought, *I'll buy that.*

The other members of The Group continued milling about the room in clusters of twos and threes. Fantroy didn't bother with greetings. He didn't need to call the meeting to order. When the others noticed him heading toward his spot at the front table, they assembled themselves in their usual seats. While the settings for their meetings may have changed, their seats never did.

Fantroy didn't waste any time. He said, "Ladies and gentlemen, I have an update on the situation in Mexico. But first, let me inform you of something new that needs our utmost attention. I received a phone call from the president of the United States earlier this afternoon. He informed me that his Nuclear Emergency Search Team has found two nuclear suitcase devices, dirty bombs, inside the District of Columbia. The president also informed me that the nuclear material inside these devices can be traced back to Great Britain."

There were no gasps from this socially refined and politically savvy group. Instead, eyeballs all over the room shifted almost unnoticeably. Fantroy knew what each person was thinking.

Could one of us be behind this?

He continued. "President Butcher said that he will inform the American public about the bombs in a special address tomorrow evening. I will need to be there in order to show our support for America and to let the public know that our government has no involvement in this plot. It goes without saying that conspiracy theories will be thrown around like confetti at a party. It is the policy of The Group that we be proactive in order to maintain our privacy. That means we have only a few hours to find out who is behind this plot." Fantroy glanced at his watch. "I recommend we take an hour break to give each of us some time to gather whatever information we may have concerning this incident."

Fantroy looked around the room as he considered his speech. While his people were still checking their plutonium deposits, he opted not to deny having anything to do with the bombs. In fact, it was a more powerful message that he simply ignored that possibility altogether.

He remained standing for another long moment to field any objections to his suggestion. There were none, and he cued the room by taking his seat. As if choreographed, the rest of the members broke apart. Some jettisoned to the four corners of the meeting room before cracking open their cell phones. Others, like Fantroy, kept their seats and began punching messages into their secured BlackBerries. Fantroy took in the scene with a sense of superiority.

If only they knew what I know.

For a moment before addressing the room, Anthony Fantroy thought about revealing the other part of his conversation with the president, the part concerning the attempted robbery of secret documents from the Library of Congress. President Butcher wouldn't elaborate as to their exact contents, but he did mention it concerned the relationship between Great Britain and the United States. That was the real reason Fantroy was anxious about getting to Washington, D.C. as quickly as possible. If he had revealed that part of his conversation with President Butcher to The Group, each member would surely throw their suspicions firmly on his back. Fantroy couldn't have that. He needed to have each Group member struggling, almost panicking to get him information about themselves and hopefully about each other.

Every Group member in the room was of a different nationality. They followed various customs, they practiced diverse religions. But they were all unified by one common goal: the bottom line. It was the overwhelming force behind everything they did. But while they had caused some of the biggest economic incidents in history, the actions of The Group were slow and methodical, taking years to craft and months to execute. Fantroy was well aware that this philosophy pained some members of The Group. They wanted things done quicker, with bigger payoffs. But while they stood at the brink of the biggest economic catastrophe in history, one that would ensure their reign over the entire planet, Fantroy couldn't help but think that someone in this room didn't have faith in their plan.

One of Anthony Fantroy's strong suits, in fact it was his single biggest attribute, was his ability to see a few steps ahead. It was what his American acquaintances called, "seeing the forest for the trees." He knew very well the one thing that could generate massive amounts of revenue, the kind of revenue that would spark the interest of any Group member.

War.

Wars always boosted—no, fully engorged—the bottom line of those who engineered and supported the conflict.

Fantroy sat quietly in his chair while his innards burned with one question. Did someone in this room want the United States and Great Britain to go to war?

Chapter 50

Sydney felt tension grip her chest as she woke. She clawed at it, realizing it was only the seat belt when she opened her eyes.

"Hey. Hey. You're okay."

Sydney turned in the direction of the calming voice to see Danny, the kindness in his face highlighted by the dashboard lights.

Although sleep had given her the gift of temporary amnesia, Sydney's situation immediately flew back to her.

I'm on the run.

She looked beyond the windshield into the darkness. "Where are we?"

"Just west of Knoxville, Tennessee."

"What time is it?"

Danny eyed his watch. "5:10." Then he grinned. "In the morning, in case you were wondering."

Sydney opened the glove compartment and pulled out the first aid kit. She loosened the bandages on her palms and used an alcohol swab to clean out specks of dirt that remained embedded in the cuts.

She winced in pain. "Ouch."

"Can I help?"

"No. It's just a little stinging." Sydney looked away from her hand and thought that talking to Danny would get her mind off the pain. "I'm sorry that I fell asleep while we were talking. How rude of me."

"It's okay. You were tired."

"What was the name of the city we were passing through at the time?"

"Tuscaloosa, Alabama."

172

"Right. Tus-ca-loos-a." Sydney finished with her left palm and reattached the bandage. She ripped open another alcohol swab package and grimaced as she prepared for the next round of pain. "I believe you were about to tell me why you wanted to kill yourself."

"I already told you. Because I'm on the run."

"Bullshit, Danny. You're a fighter. I can see that in the short time I've known you. You wouldn't end your life just because you're a fugitive. Tell me the real reason."

Danny sighed. "You don't pull any punches do you?"

"*La vie est trop courte.*" It was obvious Danny needed the translation. "Life is too short."

Danny stared into her eyes for a long moment. She barely heard his next words. "Some other time."

Sydney wanted more from him. She knew she had to give more to get more. "You asked me before if my life is about revenge for my father's death. I am who I am because I want to change the world, Danny. It is unforgivable that millions starve to death because they don't have enough money to eat or even have access to clean water. The international financial system is broken. It is built on greed, nothing more. I am repulsed by it, but the only way to make changes is from the inside. That's why I jumped at the chance to be on the ICJ. I am what you would call a crusader. I would say the same about you, no?"

Danny didn't answer. He was silent for a while but then he gave up his secret. "I have a photographic memory."

"A photographic memory?"

"The official term for it is eidetic memory. I can look at something for only a few seconds—a map, sheet music, a diagram—and I can recall everything about that same image hours or days later."

"That is quite useful for your profession, no?"

"It can be. But ..."

"But?"

"There's more to it than just memorizing maps and charts. My mind also recalls things I never experienced: strange, awful things."

"Like nightmares?"

"More like hallucinations. They started shortly after my father died."

"Are they about him?"

"Some. The worst part is, I can't control them. What I see and hear … it feels as real as you are sitting there."

"My God, Danny. I couldn't even imagine."

"Dealing with my mind has made me abuse drugs and alcohol my whole life. It's the real reason why I was at the cabin to, you know, end it all. Being on the run just gave me a final excuse." Danny stared out through the windshield. "I never told anyone that before."

Sydney touched his arm. "Thank you for trusting me with your story, Danny."

He smiled at her. "It's easier to talk to a stranger about who you really are."

Sydney's face caught. "You're absolutely right, Danny. I guess it's time for me to tell you who I am, or more specifically what I am."

Chapter 51

What else could there be?

Danny could tell from the look in her eyes Sydney was about to blow his mind. Again.

"Have you ever heard of the eugenics movement?" she asked him.

Danny thought for a moment. Movements were political. He thought back to his freshman year in college, to Political Science 101. He could recall everything: seeing his professor at the front of the room, hearing the ancient air-conditioning unit cranking out mildewed air near the windows, smelling Becky Johnson's hairspray and wanting to feel every curve beneath the tight sweaters she wore. But his photographic memory could not recall any of the lessons to which he didn't care to remember. He broke down the word eugenics and took a shot at an answer. "It's got something to do with genetics, right?"

Sydney nodded. Then something Danny wasn't ready for happened. A lone tear crept down her cheek.

Danny reached out to her. "Hey," he whispered. He touched her shoulder, and she embraced him in an awkward sideways hug constrained by seat belts and rattled nerves. "It's okay."

Sydney straightened and wiped away the tear. "I'm sorry. It's just …" She stared into Danny's eyes and didn't need to finish.

"I know, Sydney. All this … I know it's hard. Take your time."

Sydney stared out of the windshield for a long moment and then sighed. "A British scientist named Sir Francis Galton was obsessed with human characteristics, more specifically how to perfect human characteristics. He studied the bloodlines of prominent members of Victorian-era British society, including members of the royal family.

175

He concluded that he could manipulate the genes that gave them their higher than average intelligence and physical qualities such as their above-average height and empirically attractive features. He believed that if he could manipulate genes from a relatively small group, genes from whole populations could be altered as well."

Sydney paused. Her eyes swelled again, and she looked away from Danny. He knew where she was going.

"Who I am, or more specifically what I am."

Danny only needed to look at her to confirm her explanation. Sydney Dumas was over six feet tall and had used her brilliant mind to ascertain a high station in life. Then there were her "attractive features." Her skin glowed with unblemished perfection, her teeth resembled navy officers standing at attention in their perfect dress whites. Her green eyes loomed with a quiet confidence that could only be backed up by her superior intellect. As Danny analyzed each part of Sydney and then wrapped her up into a whole person, it was easy for him to see that the creation of Sydney Dumas hadn't been left up to random chance. She had been a science experiment.

"My biological father was Knobby's ... that was my nickname for Colin, Knobby. He was Knobby's assistant before becoming a full professor himself. Years later, they both were initiated into the Bilderbergers as academic advisers. At that time, my father was asked to take part in one of their experiments, which was eugenics. He agreed, and a woman handpicked by a Bilderberger doctor was inseminated with his sperm. My father was never told who would be the mother of his child, but his curiosity got the better of him. He was able to track her down. She was also a professor, at Cambridge. She taught English there after she graduated on a full athletic scholarship."

"Let me guess," Danny interjected, "swimming."

Sydney nodded. "It was the seventies, and women's liberation was in full swing. My mother wanted a baby and didn't feel she needed a man to help her raise it."

"So what happened after they met?"

"My father had already begun having ill thoughts about the Bilderberger agenda. He and my mother became friends, and he told my mother about his feelings. She persuaded him to tell the world what he knew. But he never got the chance. They were killed in a car crash made to look like an accident ..."

Her voice trailed off. It didn't take a cop to figure out the obvious. "The Bilderbergers."

Sydney nodded again as a second tear plunged down her cheek. "Knobby was also concerned with what the Bilderbergers were doing, but he wasn't in a position to go against them. If he did, he would have suffered my parents' same fate."

Danny touched her arm with an understanding hand. "Sydney, I'm so sorry."

She sniffled. "I've never shared that with anyone."

"Feels good to get it off your chest, doesn't it?"

She nodded. "Yes." She stared deep into Danny's eyes. Then she leaned over and kissed him on the cheek. "Thank you for listening."

"Thank you for listening too, Sydney."

Minutes later they pulled into a gas station on the outskirts of Knoxville. Danny rolled down his window and got out. He didn't see the cashier behind the counter or anywhere inside the store. He chose the cash payment option and started the gas pump. Then he used the driver's windowsill to stretch.

"By the way, I heard a news report on the radio while you were asleep," he said.

"Is it about us?" Sydney asked.

"Could be. The president has suddenly canceled most of his schedule until the State of the Union."

She offered an explanation. "They've probably got him under close wraps after that gas attack at the subway station."

"Jack Butcher doesn't seem like that kind of leader. He was in the marines. Marines don't hide behind security." Danny paused and then continued. "That brings me to something else that's been bothering me."

"Yes?"

"How do we know for sure that Jack Butcher isn't a Bilderberger? You said that other presidents besides Woodrow Wilson have been members."

"It's a possibility," Sydney replied.

"It's a possibility?" Danny repeated. "That's not the answer I was hoping for, Sydney."

"He doesn't seem to fit their typical mold, but as president of the United States, he'd be a prime candidate to join their ranks."

"Perfect." The bad dream that had started with Danny's decision not to swallow a bullet back at the cabin was getting almost unbearable. Military-trained assassins supported by people with unlimited resources were chasing him. A woman he didn't totally trust continued to reveal new information at every turn that further doomed their mission. Now, to top everything off, she was telling him that they could be heading straight into the lion's den.

What the hell am I doing? We're attempting the impossible.

Danny's head was throbbing. He glanced up at the neon signs that hung in the convenience store windows. *Miller. Bud Light. Coors.* God, how he could use a drink right now. Just one beer. Or six. He wiped away his thirst by concentrating on things he could control.

I can operate a gas pump. I can get a Coke and an energy bar. I can take cash out of my wallet to pay the cashier.

Danny finally saw the cashier emerge from the back of the store carrying a large cardboard box. He reached down and grabbed the Junglee Extreme Forces knife from the floorboard. He noticed Sydney watching him. "Better safe than sorry."

Sydney glanced at the tubby, middle-aged woman stocking the cigarette shelves behind the front counter. "Oh yes, she looks like she could take you."

Danny shoved the knife under the back of his waistband, underneath his shirt. "Want anything?"

A glimmer of hope danced in Sydney's eyes. "How about some fresh clothes?"

Sure, the women's clothing section is right between the Slurpee machine and the beef jerky, Danny thought. "I'm pretty sure they don't sell women's clothes here, Sydney. But I'll check."

"What about a bottle of water?"

"That I know they have."

Danny straightened, finished pumping the gas, and walked inside the store. The cowbell above the door jolted the cashier, who had her back to him.

"Morning," he said to her.

"Morning," she replied as she stopped stocking the cigarettes. She slid onto her stool behind the cash register and watched him as he loped through the aisles.

Danny checked his wallet. He had two twenties, two tens, and three ones left. God how he wished he grabbed the bag that contained his money from the cabin's kitchen. Using a credit card was out of the question; it was the easiest way to track someone. But he had an unnerving feeling that the people chasing them had already figured out where they were going.

They know who I am. They know I have nowhere to turn. They think I will go for broke, which is exactly what I'm doing.

Once again, the bottom fell out of his gut. Once again, he tried to concentrate on the little things he could control for the moment.

Open the cooler door. Grasp the Coke can. Close the cooler door.

Danny repeated the procedure as he got Sydney a bottle of water. He stepped down the candy bar aisle and picked out two protein bars from a box at the end of the aisle. He approached the cashier as she hung up the phone.

"Coffee fresh?" he asked, setting his items on the counter.

The cashier nodded and then forced a grin on her scared face. As Danny looked into her shifting eyes, his stomach tightened with anxiety. He noticed the back of a small TV on the counter to his left. The sound was muted, but he could see the TV screen's reflection in the window behind the cashier. One half of the screen showed a reporter standing in front of a scene that had never changed over the years: the soaring pine trees, the bursting azaleas, the seamless rows of monkey grass. The other half held the head shot taken on his first day as a Texas Ranger.

Across the bottom of the screen were words that made Danny's heart shudder.

SENATOR BOOKER HALSEY PRONOUNCED DEAD

The cashier's hands were trembling as she reached for the Coke can. She could barely type its price into her register.

Danny had his wallet halfway out of his pocket. He pushed it back down and slid his hand toward the knife in his waistband.

The cashier grabbed the bottle of water. She was trying to input its price into her register when Danny ordered her to stop.

"Keep both hands on the counter where I can see them."

The cashier's eyes were glued on the blade in Danny's outstretched hand. She jumped back from the counter, knocking over her stool. Then her eyes fell and focused on something behind the counter. Danny instantly knew what it was. He reached around the back of the counter and felt cold steel underneath it. He grabbed the Smith and Wesson .45 and pointed it at her.

"Please don't kill me!" she screamed, her whole body shaking.

Danny didn't bother asking her if she had called the cops. He grabbed the phone's receiver and pressed redial. He put the receiver to his ear in time to hear three familiar tones in his ear.

Danny dropped the receiver, and it clattered on the counter. As he calmly tucked the knife back in his waistband, grabbed his items off the counter, and turned to run away, he could hear a woman's voice spill out of the receiver.

"911. What's your emergency?"

Chapter 52

Prime Minister Anthony Fantroy's breakfast at his 10 Downing Street residence consisted of eggs Florentine with roasted mushrooms, herb-filled sausages and a strong cup of Earl Grey tea. Afterward, he reviewed appointment changes for the next few days with his scheduling assistant. Fortunately, there was nothing major he would be missing.

He used the open hour before an early lunch meeting with his two senior economic advisers to pack for his trip. He stood in the doorway of his spacious walk-in closet, staring at his collection of ties. He pictured himself standing at the podium in the White House in his favorite Maurice Sedwell suit as he sent his message to the American people and the world.

The United Kingdom and all of her provinces give our full support to the United States in clearing up this unsettling matter.

"Lost in a thought, Tony?"

Even though he recognized the booming voice, it startled him. Fantroy turned to see Lars Karlsson leaning against the open bedroom door. Even though he had just celebrated his eighty-seventh birthday and a shock of wild, white hair cascaded down from his sunspot-speckled head, the sight of the six-foot six-inch Lars Karlsson in a perfectly tailored pinstriped suit demanded respect. That respect was intensified by the fact that Lars was head of The Group's intelligence committee. It was rumored that, although he was just a young man at the time, Lars had served in Swiss military intelligence during WWII and was instrumental in building the secret channel of communication between Swiss military officials and the Nazis. While the details of these relations remained fuzzy, rumors had always circled inside The Group that Lars's extensive knowledge of obtaining information from people relied heavily on methods he observed the Nazis use. Fantroy himself had been in Group meetings where Lars had informed members about certain individuals who were getting too close for comfort. However, each one of those people had unfortunate accidents that resulted in their untimely deaths. It was no secret that Lars had them killed or did the dirty work himself. Fantroy always wondered just how the old man orchestrated those events and, if he did it himself, had he enjoyed it.

Fantroy opened his mouth to ask how Lars got inside his house but then remembered who was guarding the back door. It was a British military guard who had been initiated into The Group's service core. His standing orders of granting access to any Group member at any time allowed members to meet with their political director knowing that their conversations would remain private inside the secure walls of the prime minister's residence.

"I received a call from James Trotter late last night," Lars declared.

Fantroy crossed the closet and grabbed four different colored ties as he tried to kick start his memory. *James Trotter ... James Trotter ...*

"You mean Jimmy Trotter? Booker Halsey's ... protégé?"

"Correct," Lars replied, his heavy Swiss accent echoing across the bedroom and into the closet.

Fantroy stepped toward the open suitcase on his bed. He rolled each tie in tight circles and then placed them inside the suitcase. He recalled the time when Senator Booker Halsey approached The Group over two decades ago with a new method of selecting their foot soldiers. At the time, Booker was the vice chairman of the U.S. Senate's Select Committee on Intelligence. He was given a copy of a new testing procedure that both the NSA and the CIA were using for new spy recruits. The tests were basically personality tests with one exception: they focused on the person's individual frustrations. If they didn't trust authority figures, if they weren't satisfied with the status quo, if they had unbridled ambition, if they were easily seduced by women or money—all of these factors would make them excellent spies. They would do anything for the people who gave them what they wanted.

The Group immediately made those tests the center of the admission procedure for their own spies inside various industries. One of the first guinea pigs for these tests was Jimmy Trotter. He was a failed Texas oilman who was nearly bankrupt when Senator Booker Halsey sat him down for a conversation and to take a few simple tests that would change his life forever.

"What did he want?" Fantroy asked Lars.

"He wanted to relay some disturbing information." Fantroy stopped packing his suitcase and stared at Lars. Lars finally stood up straight, his frame eclipsing the entire doorway. "Booker Halsey is dead."

Fantroy felt his knees buckling, but he willed all of his energy into steadying his legs. Thoughts of damage control blurred in Fantroy's mind. What would this mean for The Group? Most important, how could they sever all ties to Senator Halsey?

"Who's being blamed?" Fantroy asked.

Lars walked toward Fantroy and dug into his jacket pocket. He pulled out a folded piece of paper and handed it to him.

"I believe you know of the suspect," Lars replied.

Fantroy unfurled the paper and stared at the news article that Lars had printed off the *Times* website.

U.S. Senator Dead. Fugitive Texas Ranger Suspect.

Fantroy scanned through the half page of information. The *Times* had ascertained the same information about Danny Cavanaugh that Stefan Taber had relayed to him. Cavanaugh was a lawman on the run for murder. Make that two murders now.

"Have you heard anything from your boy Taber?" Fantroy asked.

Lars shook his head. "Not a word."

Fantroy stared at the article, while he reflected on the events The Group had engineered to get to this point. He was the one who had worked Hideo Akimoto's theory about bankrupting the United States and thus the world, while cornering the global gold market, into a doable plan. Fantroy had initially suggested the lawsuit idea after Dexter Walsh was appointed Fed chairman. After he was Booker Halsey's guest for an impossibly successful quail hunting trip down at the Mexican monastery, Fantroy was also the one who convinced Nathan Broederlam to take his chamber down there for unmatched privacy to try and convince the other chamber members of the lawsuit's viability. Now Halsey was dead. Sydney Dumas was still on the loose, and no one had a clue what she knew. Plus, none of the other Group members knew who planted the nuclear bombs in Washington, D.C., at least none who were willing to confess at the Westbury Hotel meeting.

"Do you think Taber's a lost cause?" Fantroy asked.

"Taber's a solid chap," Lars replied. "There must be a good reason why he's maintaining his silence for the time being. Trotter described a woman who showed up at the club with Cavanaugh. The description matches Ms. Dumas. I'm very sure that the two of them are still together."

Lars dove into his jacket pocket again and produced another *Times* article printed off of the Internet. Fantroy unfolded it and stared at the title.

Fugitive Spotted at Knoxville, Tennessee Gas Station

Again, Fantroy read through the article. The gas station attendant on duty stated that Cavanaugh was driving a late-model Lincoln Town Car and that there was a woman in the passenger side.

Fantroy asked a rhetorical question. "Why would they be in Tennessee? That's a long way from Houston, Texas."

Lars took the liberty of answering it. "Do you know what city is in an almost direct line with Houston, Texas, and Knoxville, Tennessee?" Fantroy shook his head. Lars continued. "The same city for which you are headed, my dear Prime Minister."

Fantroy's heart pounded in the back of his throat. He stared at the last paragraph of the article.

"Cavanaugh and his unidentified accomplice managed to escape the gas station before authorities arrived. Their current whereabouts are unknown."

"What does this mean for us, Lars?" Fantroy asked handing back the papers.

Lars folded them up and slid them back inside his flawless jacket. "It means that I have already contacted our White House man. He will be keeping extra close attention to the course of events during the next few days."

Chapter 53

One lone knock vibrated through the door leading to Simon Shilling's office.

"Come in," Jack yelled across the Oval. The door swung open and Simon appeared with four men dressed in similar dark suits and blue ties on his heels. Simon veered out of the way to let them greet the president.

George Connelly, Jack's pick to head up the Department of Energy, was first. The media had given Connelly the nickname Gorgeous George. He was in his mid-sixties but still made the women that worked in the White House swoon whenever he visited. He had a year-round tan and thick salt and pepper hair. But most importantly, Gorgeous George was charming; he was a smooth talker but an even better listener.

"Mr. President," George said shaking hands. "This is Sam Ashworth, NNSA administrator."

Sam Ashworth was what Jack's predecessor would have called a, "tall drink of water." He had to duck underneath the doorway that led from Simon's office into the Oval, a doorway constructed for the much shorter people of the nineteenth century. His hand engulfed Jack's as he gripped it.

"Mr. President," Ashworth started and then turned to introduce the next man down the food chain. "I believe you've been talking with Clarence Warner, sir."

Clarence, a black man whose body angled sharply from wide shoulders into an almost childlike waist, was noticeably intimidated by his surroundings. Jack smiled at him and held out his hand. Clarence shook it with a sweaty palm. "Mr. President."

"First time in the Oval, Clarence?"

He adjusted his glasses. "Yes, sir."

"Thanks for coming on such short notice."

"Of course, sir. It's an honor to be here."

Jack eyed the last man to enter the Oval. "Admiral," he said as they shook hands.

"Mr. President," Howard Fielding replied. Although Fielding had retired from the navy to become Jack's director of National Intelligence and no longer wore his dress uniform, he still cut an impressive jib in an off-the-rack suit.

Jack glanced at the item tucked under Fielding's arm. It was a document rolled up in a tight cylinder and stamped with a blood red "CLASSIFIED" designation.

"Gentlemen," Simon called to them. He was already sitting in his usual chair. He motioned for the men to take seats around him on the couches.

Jack threw the bureaucratic rules aside as he sat down and asked the lowest man on the totem pole for answers.

"Clarence, please bring us up to speed on NEST's activities during the night."

Clarence looked at his boss, who then looked at his boss. Shock stained both their faces, like Daddy just said he didn't love them anymore.

"Clarence?" the president pressed.

"Yes, sir. I'm sorry. Four Pave Hawk helicopters surveyed the District and the metropolitan areas in Virginia and Maryland. Those surveys all came back negative, sir. The mobile—"

"Excuse me one second, Clarence," Jack interrupted.

"Yes, sir?"

"What do these helicopters use to detect for nuclear material?"

"Radiological sensing equipment, sir."

"These are NEST choppers?"

"Sir?"

"Are the Pave Hawks the property of NEST, or did you borrow them?"

"We borrowed them, sir. From the air force."

"From Andrews?"

"Yes, sir. As soon as the NEST incident team found the second suitcase bomb under the Lincoln Memorial, NEST airplanes were scrambled from Nellis Air Force Base in Las Vegas. They flew to Andrews Air Force Base, where they were stripped of their radiological sensing equipment. That equipment was then placed on the Pave Hawks."

"Thanks for clearing that up, Clarence. Sorry for the interruption. Please continue."

Clarence gulped down a mouthful of nerves. It took him a moment to find where he left off. "We also performed ground searches. Our mobile ground units consist of eight vans specially outfitted with radiation detection equipment. Those vans are our property, sir."

Jack nodded. "Got it."

"They started crisscrossing the District at ten o'clock last night, and they traced every street by dawn. All reports came back negative."

Clarence waited a few moments to field any questions Jack might have before he continued. "Our incident team completed their second inspection of the National Mall at 5:35 this morning. It was all clear."

"Except for the bomb found outside the Washington Monument and the one found in the Lincoln sub-basement?" Jack asked.

"Correct, sir," Clarence replied.

"Does the incident team use the same kind of equipment that's used on the choppers and in the vans?"

"Yes, sir. It's all gamma ray and neutron detection equipment, sir."

"Is it fair to say that the equipment used out in the open is a smaller version, handheld, something of that nature?"

"Yes, sir. But—"

Sam Ashworth piped in. "Mr. President, the equipment is—"

Jack cut him off. "Thank you, Sam. But I like getting the facts straight from the horse's mouth. In my experience, it's the best insurance against using tainted information that could make me look like a horse's ass."

"Yes, Mr. President," Ashworth replied.

Jack turned back to Clarence. "We concocted stories about natural gas leaks, Clarence. A gas leak is the reason why people were evacuated from the Washington Monument yesterday. A second gas leak is the reason why people were evacuated from the Lincoln Memorial. I am tired of lying to the American people, Clarence. I am about to address them with the truth, and I need specific details that will corroborate my explanation. As they say, the devil's in the details."

Four silent seconds staggered to their death before Clarence continued.

"Sir, the equipment is disguised in backpacks and briefcases. Our people are trained to search urban areas without compromising the security of their mission or arousing suspicion."

"Good," Jack replied. "The device was delivered through a utility access door. Is that still your assessment, Clarence?"

"It's a fact, Mr. President."

Jack smiled. "A good man is one who deals in absolutes." He turned to Sam Ashworth. "You agree with Clarence, Sam?"

"Yes, sir," Ashworth responded and then added, "100 percent."

"Okay," Jack started and then rose to his feet. The other men followed the president's lead. "Clarence, Sam, George, thank you for your time. We'll need you to stay on-call in case the White House needs updates."

The three men responded simultaneously. "Yes, Mr. President," and then headed for the door.

Jack sat back down in the JFK rocker. The remaining two men, Simon Shilling and Howard Fielding, also took their seats. Jack eyed Simon, adhering to Simon's thirty-second rule before speaking. Simon nodded when time was up.

Jack eyed Fielding. "Howard, how close did they get to the Capitol tunnels?"

The admiral shifted to the edge of his seat and unfurled the map of the Capitol escape tunnels still clenched in his hand. "The bomb was placed thirty feet from the opening, sir."

Jack huffed. "Jesus. How? How does something like this ..." He stopped, shaking his head.

"Sir, we've had teams sweeping the tunnel system all night. There's no evidence of recent usage."

"What about evidence from the Lincoln basement? Is there anything in there that can tell us the names of the bastards responsible for this?"

"We haven't found anything so far."

"Come on, Howard. No DNA or fingerprints? Not even a goddamn cigarette butt to process?"

"There's DNA and cigarette butts everywhere, sir. But that's the problem. Exhaust grates are right on top of the basement. Seventy years' worth of cigarette butts, gum wrappers, and other scraps of garbage have slipped through those grates and into the basement. To test all that, you're talking needle in a haystack. Besides, these guys wouldn't make these specific deliveries and then leave traces of themselves behind. They aren't that stupid."

Simon piped up. "They're deliberate."

Fielding nodded in agreement. "Agents are checking with District officials to determine if there's been any activity with the city's archived blueprints for the Mall infrastructure or any of the surrounding area. We're also reviewing every second of surveillance tape we can get our hands on from every security camera within a ten-block radius of the Lincoln."

Jack sighed. "When will we know things?"

"ASAP, Mr. President."

Jack gazed off in the distance and his voice fell. "Thirty feet, Howard." He shifted his stare to Fielding. "They got within thirty goddamn feet."

"I'm sure that was just luck, sir."

"Luck?"

"We're confident the suspects don't know about the tunnels. Their choosing the Lincoln basement, it was just—"

"Coincidence?"

"Yes, sir."

"You really believe that?"

"I believe what the evidence tells me."

"The evidence tells me that they delivered a dirty bomb out in the open, to a very public place, to ensure maximum body count. The second bomb was found in a place that's supposedly off limits thirty feet away from the entrance to a tunnel system that accesses the United States Capitol."

"Exactly, Mr. President. Why abandon it under the Lincoln if that's just your starting point?"

"You think the Lincoln was their target? Blow it up and make it radioactive, to leave a blemish on the National Mall as a constant reminder?"

"That's exactly what I believe, Mr. President."

"You ready to bet your job on that?" Simon asked.

Fielding shot him an angry look. "I would."

"What about your life, Howard?" Jack asked. "Would you bet your life?"

Fielding paused. "We will find out who did this, Mr. President."

Silence marinated the room for several seconds, a rarity in an Oval Office meeting. Jack finally rose from his seat. "I think we're done here, gentlemen. Howard, thanks for coming in." As if on cue, Vanessa Dempsey knocked once and, not hearing any objections, strode into the Oval with Jack's stylist in her wake.

Fifteen minutes later, Jack ordered everyone out of the Oval Office. His collar was still ringed with tissue paper that his stylist used to keep the finishing touches of makeup off his shirt.

Jack stood next to the door that led out to the portico. Beyond Peter Devon's mountainous shoulder, he could see the beams from the klieg lights that would be focused on him in a matter of minutes. This was the first time he would have to do some backpedaling, explaining why they used gas leak stories to cover up terrorist attacks. But Jack was sure it wouldn't be the last.

Communication is your specialty, Jack. It's time to put the country at ease.

Jack noticed the tissues in his collar in the window's reflection. He fished them out from his shirt and cracked the Oval's seal.

Peter Devon didn't flinch. He merely moved his wrist to his mouth.

"Devon has POTUS outside the Oval, en route to Rose Garden."

Jack walked a few steps to where Simon Shilling was standing. Simon turned to receive the president of the United States.

"Are you ready, Mr. President?" Simon asked. Jack nodded. "Blake wanted me to remind you to stay on message. I told him that you were going to come out wearing a gas mask for effect. The kid nearly had a heart attack."

Jack chuckled, which quelled the butterflies in his stomach. Jack and his chief of staff walked shoulder to shoulder along the portico with Peter Devon and two other members of the Secret Service a few paces behind them. As the flashbulbs began popping in the early morning light, Jack wondered what clever euphemisms the White House press core would use to tie the attacks in with his name.

Butcher cuts deep with nuclear device announcement.

Has the Butcher administration's cuts in homeland security slashed The District's ability to thwart terrorism?

Is Butcher cutting off D.C.'s nose to spite the nation's face?

As his black, cap-toe Peal & Company dress shoes tapped down the steps and then carried him purposely toward the podium, Jack thought about the best advice he had ever received during his political career. It was from the outgoing senator of Pennsylvania on the day that Jack was taking his job away from him.

"Never answer the question asked. Answer the question you wish had been asked."

Jack stood tall behind the podium, cleared his throat, and began reassuring the country that it is, and will always be, the safest nation on the planet.

Chapter 54

Signs, signs,
Everywhere signs.
Fucking up the scenery,
Breaking my mind.

Tesla's acoustical rendition of the song *Signs* entered Danny's mind as one billboard after another led him to McGhee Tyson Airport's sole terminal. One in particular caught his eye. It read:

SEA-RAY BOATS THANKS FEDEX AND THE LATEST ADDITION TO THEIR FLEET, THE BOEING 747-400 FREIGHTER, FOR THEIR SUPPORT.

Danny read the sign a second time and then pulled the truck over in the passenger drop-off area where he spotted a newspaper dispenser. He felt his pockets in vain.

"You wouldn't happen to have any change would you?" he asked Sydney.

"Sorry," she replied.

Danny yanked open the center console of the late-model Chevy pickup he stole minutes after they escaped the gas station. He found nothing but CDs, some pens, and a tire pressure gauge. He finally found pay dirt when he opened the ashtray. Four quarters were rolled up inside a dollar bill. He used the change to grab a newspaper from the dispenser and then he wheeled the truck toward the arrivals parking lot. He found an empty spot near the rear of the lot and tore into the front page section.

"I figured you for a sports page first and comics second kind of guy," Sydney said with a wry smile.

"So much for woman's intuition," Danny scowled. He found the article he was after at the top of the fourth page.

"Do you remember hearing the president's address on the radio this morning?"

"Hard to miss when the guy starts talking about finding dirty bombs inside Washington, D.C.," Sydney replied.

"He also said that even though the area has been checked by the Nuclear Emergency Support Team and they've given the all clear, he is going to raise the homeland security threat level to red."

Sydney looked confused. "So what does that mean?"

"Three things, actually."

"The first being that the dirty bombs are tied to the Bilderbergers?"

"How'd you guess?"

"Woman's intuition."

"It's not broken after all."

Sydney smirked. "But that's not their style. Remember what I said—"

Danny cut her off. "Just follow me for a second."

Sydney sighed. "Okay. Continue."

"Second, Butcher's State of the Union speech is coming up. Most of the movers and shakers will be there."

"You're suggesting the Bilderbergers would try an attack there? During the president's speech?"

Danny nodded. "They have the resources to not only buy nuclear bombs but smuggle them into the U.S."

"But bombs and killing aren't what they do, Danny."

"I seem to recall they wanted you dead."

"Touché, Danny. But with nuclear bombs there would be an unprecedented hunt for answers. It just ... it doesn't fit."

"Maybe they chose a different method this time. All these events are taking place too close together to not be linked, Sydney."

"You don't believe in coincidences."

"Exactly."

"Neither do I, but if they want to blow up the Capitol during the State of the Union, why would they be planting these other bombs? Look what happened. The American government is now on high alert. If the Bilderbergers are planning to blow another bomb, their job just got much harder to pull off. It doesn't make sense."

"Which brings me to point three. By raising the threat level, the government has surrounded D.C. in a tight security bubble ..."

"Which will make it that much harder for us to get inside."

"Bingo. The president mentioned checkpoints set up at all roads leading into the city. If we attempt to drive into it, we'll get caught for sure. All forms of public transportation will be heavily monitored. That includes buses and trains." Danny tilted the newspaper toward her and pointed at the headline on page four.

FedEx to Ship Replica Just in Time for America's Regatta

"This is our only feasible way in." He watched for Sydney's reaction as she began reading the article. Her eyes bulged and then slammed into him.

"What are you suggesting, Danny?"

"That we become stowaways on the U.S.S. *Monitor*."

Chapter 55

The FedEx distribution center on the northeast corner of the airport was decorated with signs trumpeting FedEx's latest triumph. The company was just a few hours away from attempting the most important delivery in its history. Two sets of bleachers were being erected in front of a ten-foot high chain-link fence. Between the bleachers was a stage with five folding chairs on either side of a podium. On the far side of the fence sat a massive 747 jet. Its hinged jaw was open wide, the top half of its mouth folded up toward the sky. The bottom part was split in half, and a ramp protruded out like a giant steel tongue. Sydney gazed into its belly. The darkness inside it seemed to go on forever.

"You ready?" Danny asked her as he strapped on the backpack containing the lawsuit documents. She was sure he could probably see the nerves pulsing under her skin. He put a hand on her shoulder. "You'll do fine. You look stunning."

Sydney took a deep breath and let it out. "Thank you, Danny."

"No one would ever guess you showered and dressed at a truck stop."

Sydney laughed. As she did, the tension in her body eased. Then she steeled herself and started toward the hangar's office in a confident stride. Danny played his part perfectly, as he trudged along on her heels. Other than the handful of workers who were putting the final touches on the public relations event, the place was empty. Sydney hoped that Danny's plan would work. It required her to perform a fair share of acting, and she hoped she would be up to the task. She remembered the American movies she had seen over the years. The actors would typically use their bloated muscles and an unnecessary amount of guns and bombs to gain access to secured areas. Sydney was only armed with a form-fitting suit she purchased a little over an hour ago, a single pen, and a used notepad.

She knocked on the office door as Danny pulled down on the John Deere baseball cap he found in the back of the stolen truck. The doorknob jerked, and the door swung open. They were greeted by a burly, mustached man in a purple and white FedEx uniform, whose demeanor immediately changed on looking up and into a set of gorgeous emerald eyes.

"Hello," Sydney smiled as she emphasized her French accent. "My name is Simone La Rouche. I am a reporter with *Le Monde*. I was told to meet Dean Feldman here to cover this event."

The man's moustache trembled, as he tried to speak to the most beautiful woman he would ever meet. "I-I'm sorry, ma'am, but Mr. Feldman won't be here for another few hours."

Sydney curled her lips into a pout for a few seconds before turning them up into a smile. "That is actually better." The man's face screwed up in confusion. "I'm sorry, my English sometimes fails me. What I mean is that my cameraman and I can look over the area to determine the best shots before Mr. Feldman gets here." Sydney pleaded her case for open access to the hangar by latching onto the man's arm. "Maybe you can show me around?"

Chapter 56

Danny couldn't blame Ed the hangar manager for getting lost in Sydney Dumas as he led her around the hangar like an excited puppy. With the money that Danny had taken out of the ATM on the eastern edge of the city, Sydney had entered an Ann Taylor store and purchased a spectacular cream-colored suit with matching shoes. The skirt came down just above her kneecaps, giving Danny the opportunity to watch her toned calves work underneath her olive skin. The bottom of the jacket caressed the top of her backside, as the skirt clung to each cheek with every step. Nope, Danny couldn't blame old Ed at all.

Danny was still worried about having to use the ATM machine, but he had no other choice. The FBI hadn't frozen his checking account, which didn't surprise him. Most law enforcement agencies learned years ago that monitoring account usage made it easier to track suspects. Plus, forcing a suspect to engage in clandestine activities or even commit more crimes to finance their time on the lam didn't go over so well in the PR department anymore. Danny just hoped that by using an ATM on the east side of Knoxville, the police and the people hunting them would figure that they were headed east out of town. In reality, he had parked the stolen truck in the airport's remote parking lot, and seeing as it could be classified as a piece of shit, it wouldn't have a vehicle locater system on it. Danny was confident that it wouldn't be found for days, maybe weeks.

"How come your cameraman doesn't have a camera?" he heard Ed ask Sydney.

Sydney huffed. "He keeps all his equipment in his pack until the last moment he needs it. He doesn't want to feel, how do you say, *tenu en arrière*, held back."

"You mean constricted?" Ed guessed.

Sydney's eyes flashed. "Yes. Yes. He doesn't want to feel *constricted* by the camera's viewfinder. Luke is an artist first and a cameraman second. He must attain a feel for the space before he shoots." She once again showed a smile that made Ed lose all concern over Danny's lack of proper equipment. "Believe me, he is sometimes hard to work with, but he is one of the best."

After Ed gave Sydney the extended tour, which included going over every forklift, gas truck, and tool chest, he was ready to show off the main attraction.

He led them to an enormous set of closed double doors. Then he shuffled off to a control panel on the side wall and pressed a button. The doors crept open, receding accordion-style into the walls. Ed scurried back to Sydney's side and stretched his arms wide. "Here it is. The *piece de resistance.*"

Ed beamed at Sydney, waiting for her approval. She gave him a polite golf-clap. "Très bon. Very good."

The newspaper article that Danny and Sydney read over in the airport parking lot described the replica of the U.S.S. *Monitor* as, "a monument to both modern-day engineering and a salute to America's history." Seeing the boat in its iron flesh didn't disappoint one bit.

Ed strutted like a peacock past the bow, as he filled them in on the history of the original U.S.S. *Monitor.*

"The *Monitor* was an ironclad boat used by the Union to help defeat the Confederates at the Battle of Hampton Roads. Hampton Roads was a strategic harbor at the mouth of the James River that the two sides fought over for control of the Virginia coastline."

Sydney examined the boat. "It looks more like a submarine than a ship."

"Her design is why she's important enough to be in the regatta. When she's in the water, the deck's only eighteen inches above the water line, which made it hard for enemy boats to target her." Ed pointed to the circular turret in the center of the ship. "That is the first revolving turret ever used in battle. It allowed the *Monitor* to use its two guns to shoot in a full three hundred and sixty degree circle. She could take on much bigger ships with that ability."

"You certainly know a lot about this boat, Ed," Sydney purred.

"Boats are my hobby," he said with a twinkle in his eye as he gazed at the *Monitor*. "She's been here for over a week getting ready for shipment, so I've had time to study her. The Sea-Ray folks did a bang-up job replicating the original *Monitor*. I sure am going to miss her."

Sydney's next question was one that she and Danny spent the most time tweaking. "So, there are no delays in the shipment due to the security threat in Washington?"

"You didn't see the president's speech this morning?"

"No," Sydney replied.

Ed actually puffed out his chest before continuing. "This is America. Like a good marine, President Butcher ain't gonna run and hide from threats. We're not gonna hide under rocks being scared of those damn towelheads. We will live our lives, and this regatta will happen."

Sydney grinned. "The show must go on."

"Exactly. Say, shouldn't you be writing some of this stuff down?"

Danny bit his lip, wondering what Sydney would say. He forgot to tell her to act like she was taking notes during Ed's tour.

"I have an eidetic memory," Sydney said.

"A what?" Ed replied.

"I'm sorry," Sydney said, like the foreign word to Ed was a French one. "A photographic memory. I can remember things very well."

"Oh, wow. It must be cool to have such a great memory."

Sydney glanced at Danny before responding. "You have no idea."

The two of them moved past the boat, but Danny stayed behind, confident that Sydney would have Ed's full attention as they headed out to the plane. He circled in behind the boat and found what he was looking for. An airplane gangplank had been rolled up beside it to allow access to its deck. Danny put one foot on the first step but then heard Sydney's voice echo across the hangar.

"Luke? Luke? *Où vous sont?*"

Ed was no doubt concerned about Danny's whereabouts. Danny stepped around the side of the boat. He saw Sydney and Ed standing at the edge of the hangar's immense mouth. He turned around and framed a picture with his outstretched hands, backing away as he did so.

"*Où vous étaient?*" Sydney asked him.

Danny could only assume that she asked where he was. Under pressure, he only remembered a few of the words that Sydney had taught him in the parking lot.

"*Bateau papiers l'avion l'autorisation,*" Danny replied.

Sydney turned to Ed, who had no clue what Danny said. "He said he was lost in a thought." She rolled her eyes. "Artists."

Ed chuckled. "Let me show you our new baby."

By this time, Sydney was laying it on thick. She clung onto Ed's arm as they strolled out past the hanger and pretended to hang onto his every word.

Ed unfurled his arms in front of the plane. "This is the Boeing 747-400 Freighter. We just purchased five of them to help move larger freight orders." He pointed back at the *Monitor*. "When we successfully put that boat in this plane and then ship it up to President Butcher himself, we will show our customers we're ready for those orders."

Ed led Sydney over to the plane's mouth. They walked up the ramp, and he flipped a switch on the plane's interior wall. Light erupted throughout the fuselage. Danny stood at the bottom of the ramp and his jaw dropped. He wasn't pretending. He meandered up the ramp as his eyes adjusted to the grand canyon in front of him.

"The 747-400 can hold up to 135 tons of cargo. Its wide-mouth design allows for several different schematics when loading her." Ed turned to Sydney. "I'm sorry, ma'am. Do you know the word 'schematics'?"

Danny laughed to himself. If poor Ed only knew the extent of Sydney Dumas's knowledge.

"It is like design or map, no?"

"You got it."

Just then, Ed's cell phone chirped.

"Ed? You there?" a gnarled voice shot through the speaker just as Ed pulled it off his belt.

Though he didn't show it, panic jolted Danny as he imagined the worst-case scenario. *We're busted.* His eyes raced around, as he tried to visualize their best escape route.

Ed clicked the button on the side of his phone. "Yeah. Go ahead."

"One of the guys assembling the grandstands has a question, and I can't answer it."

"Okay, so put him on."

"Actually, he backed his truck into one of the support beams and bent the sucker. You need to come see it to figure out how we can fix it real quick."

Ed sighed and looked at Sydney. "If it's not one thing, it's another." She nodded politely. Ed clicked his phone. "Okay, Phil. I'll be there in a minute." He clipped the phone back on his belt. "Well, there goes the rest of my tour."

"That's okay. I think you showed us enough for some good background to my story." Sydney turned to Danny. "Luke, *vous faire a assez pour vos coups?*"

Danny nodded to her and framed a few shots of the plane with his hands. Sydney turned back to Ed. She shook his hand and kissed both of his cheeks.

"Thank you for your time. If it's okay, I'd like to stay here for a few minutes and go over some things with Luke about getting some appropriate shots of the plane."

A gorgeous woman was asking the bloated working stiff for a favor. There was nothing Ed could do but say yes.

As soon as Ed was out of earshot, Sydney turned to Danny.

"How did I do?" she asked him.

"If they ever give an Oscar for fugitives, you'd win hands down."

Sydney squeezed Danny's arm and kissed him on the cheek.

"By the way," Danny continued, "back in the hangar, when I answered you in French. What did I say?"

"You said, 'I want your body.'"

Danny felt his cheeks flush. "I did? I'm sorry. I didn't …"

Sydney chuckled and squeezed his arm again. "You said 'boat, papers, plane, authorization.'"

"Having a little fun at my expense again, are we?"

Sydney flashed the type of wicked grin that had been turning men into putty since the dawn of time. "Just because the fate of the world rests on our shoulders doesn't mean that we can't have a good time with each other, right?"

Chapter 57

"Mr. Karlsson?" The girl's voice whined in the telephone speaker on Lars's desk. Unlike The Group's support staff, members of the administrative support team that worked at Credit Suisse First Boston's London office were always changing. Lars Karlsson could only imagine what life would be like if he worked for the kind of slave wages that were paid to these people. Lars had been born not only with the spoon, but the entire silver service in his mouth. But, as he no longer had to remind himself, he was part of the world's elite, the true ruling class that ensured the very survival of the planet. That responsibility warranted his considerable wealth.

Lars answered her pithy whimper with an abrupt, "Yes?"

"Excuse me sir, but there is a Mr. Barrett Bradbury on the phone for you."

Lars knew no man named Barrett Bradbury. But he did know the initials. BB. It was The Group's coded language.

Bilderberger.

Lars had written the name of his latest executive assistant down on a legal pad, and he glanced at it now. Then he said, "Thank you, Bridget. Put him through."

He heard a series of clicks. Lars didn't know or care if Bridget or anyone else was listening in; all members of The Group knew the protocol for using unsecured lines.

"Mr. Karlsson?"

Even though he was disguising his voice with an American accent, it took only those two words for Lars to recognize the voice of one of his trainees. It was Stefan Taber.

"Yes?" Lars replied.

"Mr. Karlsson this is Barrett Bradbury. I don't know if you remember me, but I am one of the consultants your company hired to analyze fraudulent activity as it pertains to the executive accounts."

Lars needed only seconds to break down each chunk of the message. Taber was well aware of the situation he was in. He was AWOL from The Group. But it seemed that he had a good reason and wanted desperately to clear his name. Lars Karlsson had only one soft spot in the thick armor that he had developed over his lifetime, and it was for Stefan Taber, the captain of The Group's security force. Taber had come into The Group's fold after four years with MI-6 in England. His young wife had complications during the delivery of their daughter. Both mother and baby died on the delivery table, which sent Lawrence Stilson into a tailspin. The same had happened to Lars Karlsson; his wife had died while giving birth to their stillborn son decades before the day he offered a new existence to Lawrence, complete with the new name of Stefan Taber.

"Refresh the memory of an old man," Lars started. "Which company are you with?"

"Kemper Turlington, sir."

K.T. Taber had already disclosed that he was in the United States by using the accent. Now, he narrowed it down further. Lars assumed that Taber had heard about the news report on Danny Cavanaugh and had probably flown on the first available flight to Knoxville, Tennessee.

Lars was very aware of The Group's policy on failure. He wrote it himself. Failure met with expulsion from The Group, and expulsion meant death. No exceptions. Still, Lars's heart outweighed his head for the son he never had. He refreshed his computer screen. He was linked into the Bank of America checking account page of Daniel James Cavanaugh. The link had been provided by one of The Group's associates, the president of Bank of America's European Division.

Lars squinted as he read the last line one more time.

Withdrawal—$500.00. ATM—2217
BROADWAY, KNOXVILLE, TN 37917

"Yes, of course. Kemper Turlington. I was mistaken for a moment, but now I remember. I trust you have all the information you need to carry out your next task."

Lars was now sending his own code: *You made a mistake, but I trust you, Stefan. I'll tell you what you need to finish your job.*

"Actually, sir, that is the reason for my call. We've finished reviewing all the existing accounts to date, but I need to know if any new accounts have been opened and by whom?"

"Yes, in fact, there has. A new account was recently opened by an American executive by the name of Weldon Donald Chapman. His is a special case and needs to be handled with the utmost sensitivity. I don't have the time now, but let me make an appointment to talk with you further about this situation."

When they had settled on a time, they would both be on secure phones in secure locations and would be able to speak freely. But at least his coded message would get Taber moving in the right direction. Weldon Donald Chapman stood for Washington, D.C.

Lars hung up the phone and got up from behind his desk. He opened his office door and spent a moment chatting with the young lady named Bridget. This one was pretty. Very pretty. Too bad the odds of her occupying that chair the next time Lars Karlsson showed his face in the London office were practically none.

Chapter 58

Danny checked his watch. It had been four hours since they snuck onto the U.S.S. *Monitor*. Their hiding place, a cramped sleeping compartment that contained a bare, double mattress on top of a plywood platform, had forced the two of them to lie as still as possible next to each other. Their only communication was in the form of smiles, playful touching of arms, and pats of reassurance on each other's shoulders. Danny would have given anything for four more hours of that interaction with Sydney in this claustrophobic space but then reality invaded their tiny world. The boat was finally being loaded on the plane.

They were still moving twenty minutes later. From the time the transfer started, Danny had heard nearly constant cheering, garbled words echoing from a loudspeaker, and even music blasting from a marching band. He looked beyond the open doorway that separated the sleeping compartment from a larger storage room. Their only light source had been a small, opaque skylight in the storage room's ceiling. But now, as the ship edged further into the 747's belly, the light grew dimmer until it was completely extinguished.

They finally came to a stop. Danny felt whatever machines they used to move the *Monitor* unhook from the ship's hull. The drivers gunned the engines to move the machines out of the plane. More muffled words from the loudspeaker were followed by a wave of enthusiastic cheers. A heavy hum emanated from the plane, followed by the whine of working hydraulics. Danny pictured the plane's nose closing, like some futuristic whale swallowing the ship in one gulp. *A Moby Dick quote would work well here*, he thought. Unfortunately, he had never taken the time to pick up the classic tale of man against beast that, from what his dad had told him one time, was really a story of man against himself.

Suddenly, Danny felt Sydney's hand on his thigh. He was going to say something but then held his tongue as she began moving her hand higher. The message she was sending made Danny's body reply. His muscles tightened, he began to bulge inside his pants. The shady thoughts stirring in the back of his mind since meeting Sydney Dumas were about to become sweaty reality. *Yes*, he thought. *They didn't find us. We're safe. It's okay that this happens now. She wants it to happen now.*

Danny put his hand on her shoulder. He was about to pull Sydney to him when she grabbed what she was looking for. His flashlight. She pulled it from his pocket, switched it on, and angled it toward her face.

"Is it okay to talk now?" she whispered.

Danny went limp all over. The bland words reminded him that his male fantasy had almost got the better of him. He chuckled to himself about how bad he and the rest of his gender were at reading women's minds.

"I think so," he whispered back.

"So what now?" Sydney asked.

Danny pictured the heavy police presence at Reagan National Airport. He would be surprised if they even let a cargo plane approach the terminal without being searched first.

"Now we have to figure out a way to get off this plane without getting caught."

"Easier said than done."

"Much," Danny replied. As the jet engines fired, a wave of nausea crashed into Danny's gut.

"What's wrong?" Sydney said, reading his face.

Danny sighed. He had given a fleeting thought about it as he concocted their plan, but he was able to distract himself with the mountain of other details. But now, Danny's fear grew, as the noise from the jet engines got louder.

"There's something I forgot to tell you, Sydney."

"What is it?"

"I have a huge fear of flying."

Chapter 59

Stefan Taber exited the jetway and fell into stride with the rest of the passengers headed toward the baggage claim area. The plane's stale atmosphere slowly flushed out of his lungs as he breathed the humid terminal air. Taber had only to worry about a black carry-on packed with the normal accessories for a businessman on a trip to Washington, D.C. He felt the tension of the increased security presence before he actually saw them. But as he came upon the mouth of the terminal, several figures in military fatigues milling around the security checkpoint confirmed his suspicions.

He noticed the weapons strapped to their chests. They were standard issue American military M-16s. Taber's mouth watered. He felt naked as he walked through Reagan National Airport without any weapons. He shifted his path to get closer to the military personnel, if only for a closer look at their rifles, if only to hear a sliver of their conversations. But he stopped himself and remained hidden in the middle of the crowd.

Soon, Stefan. Soon you will be back in your comfort zone.

Lars Karlsson thought that Danny Cavanaugh and Sydney Dumas were headed toward Washington, D.C. As he continued walking, Taber reviewed his second phone conversation with Lars Karlsson, the one they held over a secure phone line.

"Sir, Sydney and Cavanaugh are wanted for the death of Senator Halsey. Why would they go to the head of American government?" Taber had asked.

Taber remembered the vagueness of Karlsson's answer. "They have information, and they feel that information needs to be heard."

Taber had pressed him. "Heard by whom?"

"They haven't gone to local authorities or the media yet, which means they could be headed straight to the top."

"The president of the United States."

"Correct, Mr. Taber. But that is not your concern. Your concern is the directive I have for you."

Taber reached the baggage claim area and threaded his way through the crowd until he found the exit signs. Once outside, the attendant at the taxicab stand took one look at him and hailed the next cab in line. None of these people, from the self-absorbed travelers to the minimum wage workers, knew what The Group had in store for them. Who had said that line about ignorance being bliss?

Taber was in the backseat of the vehicle within seconds. The cab was already in motion before the cabbie asked for his intended destination.

"Where to, sir?"

Taber contemplated Karlsson's marching orders. He was to find Sydney Dumas and Danny Cavanaugh and stop them by any means necessary. Then he focused on his *other* orders, the same ones that had included his last minute directive to shoot and kill Senator Booker Halsey. He considered the fading sunlight that flirted with the Potomac River's choppy waters and then gave the cabbie his answer.

"The Georgetown waterfront, please."

Chapter 60

Standing outside the 747's landing gear compartment, Sydney stared at Danny with horror staining her face. She had spent the entire trip helping him to calm down. She used meditation techniques such as breathing exercises while she rubbed his temples. She even sang him a French lullaby during a long stretch of turbulence. Now though, it was Sydney who needed to calm down. Danny was sure she wanted to climb back into the *Monitor* and take her chances hiding from the police.

Her eyes fell on the inflatable life raft once more. "No. Not this. There has to be another way, Danny. You might want to commit suicide, but I don't."

"Sydney, there's no other way. Federal agents will be swarming this plane the minute we land. If we stay in the plane, we'll get caught for sure."

A gasp of impossibility coughed out of Sydney's body. "But Danny, it's insane. I mean, it's insane enough that we are jumping out of an airplane in a life raft, but now you're telling me that we can't even inflate it until we're already out? We'll never make it alive."

"It takes no more than five seconds for this thing to fully inflate," Danny assured her. "Figure we'll be falling at ten feet or so a second. So, it should fully inflate by the time we hit the water."

"*Should* is not the same as *guaranteed to,* Danny," Sydney replied.

Before he had a chance to answer, the sound of hydraulics overpowered them. They both jumped and stared into the window of the access door. The plane shuddered underneath their feet as air exploded into the landing gear compartment.

The landing gear began to lower. Danny caught a glimpse of the night sky, and his body instantly reacted to being thousands of feet in the air. The backpack suddenly felt like it was getting tighter on his back, the straps digging deeper into his shoulders. His breathing accelerated as it caught in the shallows of his lungs.

He shut his eyes, turned away from the door, and cursed his mind. "Not now, goddamn it!"

"Danny, look at me!" Sydney shouted over the deafening sound of air continually blasting into the plane only steps from them. She grabbed his head. "Open your eyes and concentrate on me!" He did as he was told. "If we're going to do this, I need you at 100 percent! Do you understand?"

Danny whittled his vision down to only Sydney's eyes. He willed every thought to be about only her.

It worked. His breathing eased, his lungs opened up. The panic attack passed.

"Thank you," he said to her.

She smiled. "Anytime."

Danny turned and gazed into the access door window for a long moment. "I'm going to open this door. When I do, expect a shitload of air to come rushing at us. You see that ledge?" He pointed to the thin ridge of metal on the left side of the gaping hole in the night sky.

"Yes," Sydney replied.

"We need to get over to that ledge with the raft. Once we're there, you need to be ready to jump."

"Okay."

Danny held up the slim cable that ran along the raft's edge. "I want you to hold onto this cable like your life depends on it. It's the only way to make sure you stay with the raft. Got it?"

"Got it."

He grabbed the inflation ring. "Whatever you do, don't pull this. That's my job. Okay?" Sydney nodded. "You ready to do this?"

Sydney gripped the raft's cable. "Yes."

"Okay." He offered a weak smile. "Good luck."

Sydney let go of the raft, grabbed Danny's face, and kissed his mouth hard. "We don't need luck, Danny! We are going to do this!"

The fear that had nearly paralyzed Danny only moments ago all but vanished with the fleeting taste of her lips. Sydney gripped the raft again and waited for Danny to open the door.

Chapter 61

Danny yanked open the door, and a huge rush of air sent Sydney tumbling backward. She scrambled on all fours until she made it back to the doorway. She grabbed onto the life raft again just as Danny started for the ledge. Sydney shuffled behind him until he stopped. He turned toward her and pointed where he wanted her to stand. She scooted over until her feet were only inches from the open sky. Danny cautiously leaned down and stared out into the darkness. He had told her that they would approach Reagan over the Potomac River. But as Sydney looked out past him into the shapeless night, fear overwhelmed her.

How the hell can he tell where the water is?

Danny turned to her. "We jump on three!"

She nodded, and he turned back to watch the sky.

"One!"

"Two!"

"Three!"

Sydney's mind went blank. She shut her eyes tight and lunged forward.

Seconds later, she figured they were well past the landing gear, but the raft remained limp in her grip.

Oh God! We're going to die!

She pictured the look of disappointment on Knobby's face. *"You failed, Sydney. You failed us all."*

Sydney yelled at the top of her lungs, but she couldn't hear anything. She squeezed her eyelids even tighter, but hot tears still stung her face.

She was still falling ...

falling ...

falling.

Suddenly, the wind ripped the raft out of her grip. She wanted to look, but her eyes wouldn't open. Was she thrown from the raft? Was she falling free through the air?

I don't feel the wind anymore.

Sydney willed herself to open her eyes. Beneath her, she saw black. But it wasn't the darkness of night. The raft had inflated around her!

Sydney was about to cheer for them when her body slammed hard into something. Her head snapped back, and her world went black.

Chapter 62

Danny heard the sounds of the jet engines whine off in the distance. He opened his eyes and saw Sydney lying next to him. She wasn't moving.

Danny heard himself screaming. "Sydney! Sydney! Come on, Sydney! Talk to me!" He cradled her in his arms and put his head on her chest. He could hear a heartbeat. He fumbled for the flashlight in his pocket. The pain that consumed his own body from the fall ceased to exist now. All he cared about was making sure Sydney was okay.

He flashed light in Sydney's one eye and then the other. She finally came to, immediately thrashing around in his grip.

"Sydney!"

"I'd appreciate you getting that blasted light out of my face, Danny."

"Are you okay?"

She felt various parts of her body. "I'll live."

He helped her sit up. "Thank you," she said, holding her head with both hands. "Is that water I hear?"

Danny felt the easy tug of the river's current. Then he listened to the waves slapping up against the raft. He looked up and saw the Potomac's black water shimmer under the light of a new moon. "It is."

"We landed in the river?"

He nodded. "Did you ever doubt me?"

"Of course not. It just felt like we hit a concrete wall is all." Sydney looked off in the distance. "Where exactly are we?"

Danny stared out in the same direction. The first thing he saw was the District's lights in the distance. He could make out the familiar shapes: the Lincoln Memorial, the Washington Monument, the Capitol's dome. Then he scanned the rest of their surroundings to see if they had been spotted. He saw no witnesses.

"We're right by the monuments, exactly where we need to be."

"Très bon," Sydney said. She attempted to clap and winced as pain stung her traumatized body.

"Can you paddle?" Danny asked her.

She lifted her arms over her head, gritting her teeth as she tried to rotate her arms in circles. "I can."

"No you can't."

She looked at him like he just slapped her in the face. It was obvious she didn't like being told she couldn't do something. "I'll be fine." She knelt over the side of the raft and began paddling toward the monuments. A perfect stare of determination, something she no doubt honed over the years in her swim meets, forced any sign of weakness to abandon her face.

I'd hate to see that staring at me from the next starting block, Danny thought. He checked his watch and then began paddling next to her. It was nearing eight o'clock. He wondered how long it would take them to reach dry land.

Three nervous minutes passed. Danny kept one eye on the skies above them and the other on the District. It was hard to tell at night, but he figured they had made some headway. He heard the sound of an approaching plane and watched it on its final descent. Although they were a good distance away from it, the plane's ferocious jet engines throbbed inside every inch of his body. He stopped paddling and motioned to Sydney.

"Let's take a break."

"What?" she asked.

Danny edged closer to her, figuring she couldn't hear over the plane's noise. He prepared to yell the same four words when a familiar sound reached his ears over the jet noise.

Danny had heard that same noise before during training exercises. The whine of a shoulder-fired missile screamed through the air above their heads. Danny instantly realized its intended target. He grabbed Sydney's arm and yelled in her ear.

"Get in the water! Now!"

The missile struck the plane just as Danny and Sydney hit the water. Sound blasted through the water, as the river erupted in an orange glow around them. Danny let go of Sydney's arm to claw his way down further and further underneath the water. The backpack was making it difficult for him to make any headway, but he dare not shed it and lose their evidence.

Soon though, he felt Sydney's hand around his wrist. Danny swam down through the water as fast as he could, but Sydney was still pulling him along. He felt the strong turbulence as her powerful legs kicked beside his body. She was dragging him further and further. Down, down. Pressure intensified inside his head with every passing second. He couldn't go down any more; his ears were about to explode. He pulled against Sydney's grip. She stopped and came over to him. Danny opened his eyes, and although he could feel Sydney right next to him, he couldn't see a thing.

Suddenly, Danny had a new problem. His lungs were out of air. He grabbed Sydney's hand and hit his chest, then his mouth, hoping she knew what he meant.

I need to go up!

Danny kicked his feet and started to gain altitude under the water. But then he felt Sydney's hand tugging him back down.

What is she doing? Is she trying to kill me?

Danny felt Sydney's body wrap around him. Then he felt her lips lock onto his as she pushed air into his mouth. He finally realized what she was dong. She was giving him her air so he could stay under the safety of the water a little while longer.

Sydney pulled on him again, but this time instead of going down, she cut across the water in what Danny hoped was away from falling airplane debris.

Nearly a minute passed, and Danny was out of air again. He turned loose of Sydney's grip and shot toward the surface. He pierced the surface of the Potomac, hungrily feeding on the scorched air around him. Although he only traveled what he figured was the length of a swimming pool, Danny couldn't see their raft anywhere. Instead, he stared at pools of fire burning on the river and scattered pieces of airplane bobbing up and down. He also noticed the last thing he saw just before he and Sydney escaped the raft. It was the boat at the end of the missile's smoky tail.

Danny took a few strokes toward it but then remembered the person who had just saved his life. Where was Sydney?

He frantically splashed around in every direction. He was about to yell for her when he noticed a familiar body once again clad only in a bra and panties. She was slicing through the water like a torpedo, heading for his same intended target.

Chapter 63

Sydney pumped out twenty fierce strokes before taking a breath. As she did, she caught a glimpse of the boat in front of her. The fires that continued to burn on the water behind her cast a menacing glow around it. She was only thirty feet away when she slipped underneath the water. Plagued by zero visibility, Sydney stiffened her arms out in front of her and scissor-kicked toward the boat's hull. She started toward the surface when something brushed alongside of her. She realized she made an awful mistake when she grabbed for what she thought was Danny only to feel a wetsuit and then a scuba tank.

It's the person who launched the missile!

Sydney clamped her hand on the diver's wrist. Then she swiveled her legs forward and locked them around his waist. He clawed at her legs, trying to escape. He dug his fingers into her thighs, but Sydney wouldn't let go. She reached out through the black water, felt his mask, and ripped it from his head. He let go of her thighs, and she gripped his waist even harder. She was about to reach for his regulator when she felt a sharp blade against her throat.

Sydney instantly released her legs, and like a caught fish now being released, her assailant wriggled free of her and swam away.

Sydney shot to the surface as fast as she could. She was only feet away from the boat's swim platform. She lunged for it, hoping she could spot Danny and warn him of the diver.

She scurried up the swim platform and scrambled to every corner of the boat, searching the water for Danny. "Danny! Danny!"

"Over here!"

The sound came from beyond the bow of the boat. Sydney dashed to it and finally noticed Danny waving at her. He was treading water a good thirty yards away. She was about to yell at him to get out of the water when she looked past him at strange lights in the sky. They hovered where they were for a moment and then spread apart into three different clusters. As they approached her, the unmistakable chopping of helicopter blades quickly drowned out every other noise.

Chapter 64

Danny turned as soon as he heard the helicopters. *Gunships!*

They had to get out of there. The only option was to try and swim away from the boat as fast as possible. There was little chance they could outswim three helicopters, but they had to at least try.

He looked back at the boat. Where was Sydney? An instant later, he saw her. She was climbing down to the swim platform, dragging an oxygen tank behind her. She hugged it as she splashed into the water.

Danny didn't think twice. He swam as fast as he could for her. The water around him was trembling from the helicopter noise, but he figured that as long as he wasn't in their direct light, they couldn't see him.

The burning sensation in his shoulders from the surge of lactic acid was finally too much to handle. Danny stopped swimming and wiped the water from his eyes. He was now only five feet away from the boat's swim platform. He looked up in the sky, the blinding curtain of light nearly on top of him.

"Danny!"

He looked at the boat's port side and saw Sydney's head bobbing in the water. He dove under the water and headed in her direction just as the boat was awash in the choppers' floodlights.

Danny surfaced next to Sydney. She grabbed him, pressing him into the sliver of darkness that hung underneath the boat's deck.

"We've got to get out of here," he told her. "They'll have people in the water any second!"

He barely spoke the last word before an object materialized from the water in front of his face. It was the scuba tank's regulator.

"Let's just hope there's enough air to get us both to shore," she said.

Sydney shoved the mouthpiece in his mouth, and they both dove under the water. Danny tried to keep his breathing as calm as possible as he swam away from the boat. What seemed like an eternity ticked by before he felt a tap on his shoulder. Sydney finally needed air.

Danny pulled the regulator's mouthpiece from his lips and felt around in the murky blackness for her face. He hovered under the water, as he heard the faint sound of her inhaling a breath. She tapped his shoulder again, and he returned the mouthpiece to his lips. They kept up that same routine until his feet finally struck the Potomac's muddy shoreline.

Chapter 65

President Jack Butcher ended his phone call with the First Lady. Instead of focusing on the events transpiring in D.C., Jack needed a break from it. He wanted to hear every detail of his wife's trip.

Monica Butcher was halfway through her tour of the Middle East to promote women's rights within those countries. She regaled her husband with detailed accounts of interacting with everyday people of other cultures. She listed the food and drinks that were considered haute cuisine in far-off lands. She also offered her innermost thoughts on foreign dignitaries that, if the press ever got a hold of them, would be fodder for the talking heads for weeks and would certainly taint his administration's foreign policy efforts. But that's why Jack loved Monica. She called them like she saw them. She was his island of reality in an unrelenting ocean of bullshit.

Jack also reveled in his wife's toughness. Monica was stronger than Jack when it came to their emotions. The only time Jack ever saw his wife lose it was when their little boy's body finally gave up on his incredible will to live.

Jack swiveled over to the credenza and grabbed the lone photo of his son, Simon, that adorned the Oval Office. He wanted more photos of their only child surrounding him at work, but Monica thought that some visitors might think he was parading their dead son around to gain political leverage. Although that was the furthest thing from the truth, Jack had agreed with his wife and left her to decorate the private areas of the residence with the solemn reminders of their little boy.

Jack was immediately consumed by the photo of him crouching over Simon's deathbed. He noticed the way he had purposefully bent down so he and Simon were equals. He had posed that way for a selfish reason. He wanted it to seem that Simon was in better shape than he actually was, that he didn't require the hours of attention that Jack simply could not provide in the last weeks of his son's life.

As tears invaded the corners of his eyes, Jack also noticed the way Simon held his father's hand so tightly, like even death itself couldn't sever their bond. But it had. An agonizing and, worst of all, patient death had waited for Simon to expire slowly. The last weeks had been the most painful of his short life. His disease, dysautonomic mitochondrial myopathy, its name so clinical and clerical, seemed like it couldn't be the cause for Simon's demise.

Jack spent as much time as he could during those final weeks with Simon, even taking days at a time away from his senatorial campaign. Seeing their hands gripped together in the photo reminded Jack of one particular night only days before Simon's death.

Simon Butcher gazed into his father's eyes. "You're falling back in the polls, Dad," he coughed out through what seemed like a solid wall of phlegm.

Sitting here, alone in the Oval Office, Jack could almost feel his son's sweat-soaked hair as he remembered stroking it.

"Don't worry about that, Simon. The only thing you need to worry about is getting better."

Simon's glassy eyes squinted as he smiled at his father. There had been many times in the past when Simon had been hospitalized and had bounced back. But this time was different. Jack knew it. More important, Simon also knew it. They both knew that there was little else they could do than to watch the body of an eleven-year-old boy slowly wither away.

Jack noticed his son was struggling to speak again. He nearly shushed him when three words crept out of Simon's mouth.

"Simon says win."

Ever since Jack taught the 'Simon says' game to his son, Simon used it to emphasize things he wanted his dad to remember.

Simon says pick me up at three o'clock after school. Simon says play hoops with me. Simon says you're the best dad ever.

Simon says win.

Jack returned to the campaign trail the next day. Two days later, he and Monica buried their only child at the family plot at Finch

Hill Corners, near the small coal-mining town of Carbondale, Pennsylvania, where they met in high school and never looked back.

Jack closed his eyes. He could read the special inscription that he had added to the bottom of the epitaph on Simon's gravestone.

Dad says you're my hero.

A soft knock at the door startled Jack back from memory lane. Before swiveling back around in his chair, he wiped the tears staining his cheeks and returned the photo to his credenza.

"Mr. President."

The man for whom President Butcher's son was named stood in the doorway that separated their two offices. Behind Simon Shilling, Jack could see Harry Tharp champing at the bit. Something was up.

Jack swallowed hard, hoping to dislodge the lump in his throat. "Just finishing up a call with Monica."

Simon approached the antique desk that once belonged to Benjamin Franklin. It had been part of Jack's office in the Pennsylvania capitol, and it too was on loan for the duration of his term in the White House.

"How is the First Lady?" Simon asked, his voice that of a longtime friend.

It still sounded awkward to Jack that Simon rarely ever called Monica or him by anything other than their official titles, not even in the residence or when they were visiting with each other socially, away from the glare of political life. When Jack asked about it a few weeks after he took office, Simon had told him that every time they speak, the formal title is a gentle reminder that Jack was the president 24/7, 365 for hopefully 8 full years.

"She's fine. Not only will she have democracy instilled in every Middle Eastern country by next Tuesday, but I'm sure some of those nations will have female presidents."

Instead of even nervous laughter that Jack had come to depend on when he assumed his comedian in chief role, Simon remained silent with a hollow look etched in his face.

"What is it?"

"Mr. President, we have a situation. A plane has crashed at Reagan National."

Due to the tight security surrounding the nation's capital, Dulles had been closed to the public. All flights, both private and commercial, were being diverted to Reagan and were being screened by both NEST and FBI personnel before they taxied to the terminals. Because Andrews Air Force Base couldn't manage the influx of military aircraft that both delivered troops to help seal off the District and the ones that flew in to help monitor the airspace over D.C and the surrounding metropolitan area, Dulles had been converted into a secondary military airstrip for the time being.

"Crashed? Do we know how? Was it private or commercial?"

Simon's thin eyebrows vanished behind his glasses as his eyes hardened. "Mr. President, it was Prime Minister Fantroy's plane. We are certain that it was shot out of the sky."

Chapter 66

Lars Karlsson was feeling the weight of a full bladder after three cups of tea. It was almost two in the morning and he was no longer hungry but, having a mother who chided him as a child for not clearing his plate, Lars sunk his fork into the remaining half of his third scone with Devonshire cream. He finished reading the *London Financial Times*, folded the paper, and laid it on the table. Then he soaked up what was left of the raspberry jam puddle on his plate with the scone and popped it into his mouth. He remembered his mother's stern commands as he chewed.

"Chew slowly, Lars. Food is to be enjoyed. Think about what you are tasting."

Lars closed his eyes and savored his last bite, as the starchy pastry mixed with the sweet tang of the jam. He opened them in time to notice a young woman sauntering down the tight aisle of the New Piccadilly Café. Her clothes were French couture; Lars appreciated fine clothing and kept up with the latest in both men's and women's fashions. The dingy light that hovered inside the café picked up each brilliant speck of mini-pearl embroidery woven in the cashmere fabric of the woman's black Chanel dress. Her square-toed heels tickled the dull vinyl floor. As she squeezed past him, a calfskin tote clutched between her elbow and ribcage, her wake smelled of cigarette smoke and a hint of citrusy perfume that left her admirers wanting more.

Lars figured she was stopping in for a snack or a visit to the water closet after a night on the town. He didn't make the obvious move to swivel his broad, arthritic body around in his chair for a second glance. Instead, he watched her reflection in the side of the chrome napkin dispenser on the edge of his table until she disappeared at the back of the café.

Lars jammed his hand in his jacket and fished out a pack of cigarettes. He stuck one between his lips and set it ablaze. Lars had been coming to the New Piccadilly Café for over twenty years. In that time, he never knew if he sat in the smoking section or if the buffoons in Parliament even allowed smoking in restaurants anymore. Either way, Lars Karlsson could not give a damn.

As he waited to get a second glimpse of the woman strolling out from the bathroom, Lars's cell phone vibrated inside his jacket. He pulled it out and looked at the caller ID. It was an international area code. He pressed the "send" button, put the phone to his ear, and waited for the person on the other end to do the talking.

"Hello? Are you there?"

Lars recognized Stefan Taber's voice but would not use his name on an open line. "Go ahead."

Stefan lobbed the fairly obvious coded message into Lars's phone. "Have you seen anything good on TV lately?"

"No, I haven't."

The line went dead. Lars took one last drag before crumpling the cigarette in the middle of his empty plate. He jammed his phone back in his pocket and was about to get up when he heard the rhythmic clapping of heels on the floor behind him. Seconds later, Lars captured the sight of the Chanel-wrapped beauty as she exited the café. It was a defining moment if there ever was one. If he were thirty years younger, he would have chased after her. But at his ripe old age, Lars was wise enough to know that women like that were impossible to keep. It was better to admire them from afar and savor their image, for that's all they were anyway.

Lars threw down enough money to cover his tab as well as a generous tip and sauntered out into the night. He took a left and clipped up the street, walking straight into a brisk breeze. Lars's imagination threw possibilities into his consciousness as Taber's cold words echoed in his head.

"Have you seen anything good on TV lately?"

Lars wrestled with his thoughts as he gathered his suit jacket tighter around his body, fighting the stiffening wind. Things were not proceeding as planned. Now something else had gone wrong. Someone was peeing in their pond, and they damn well had better find out who it was and fast.

Lars saw a group of people huddled in front of a storefront window, their eyes glued to the TV screens inside it. His steps grew quicker as his mind raced. Just what the hell had happened in Washington, D.C.?

Chapter 67

While the Bull Run Pub was located on M Street near the heart of Washington, D.C., it wasn't anything close to being in the best part of town. In fact, its closest neighbor was a strip joint called Baby Dolls. On top of that, Sydney was barefoot and wearing Danny's soggy shirt over panties and a bra. Danny was now shirtless, with the backpack slung over his shoulder. He was shocked that a cab had even stopped to give them a ride from a lonely side street near the National Mall. But this was his only chance to see his solitary friend in Washington, D.C., and the word "friend" was a stretch. Danny could only hope that he could trust him, for they had nowhere else to turn.

Danny eyed the scene through the bar's bay window. It was mobbed with people, just like it had been when he visited it a decade ago during a trip to D.C. for a cybercrimes convention. He scoured the wall-to-wall faces and tangled body parts, hoping to recognize his friend sitting, hopefully still halfway sober, at the bar. He did see Big Gay Fred, who wasn't really a homosexual but was six-four and over three hundred pounds. Just like before, Fred was tending more to the sports highlights that dangled on the TV above his head than to the bar that he manned. Rocco still worked there as well. The self-proclaimed Italian Stallion was in the same pose in which Danny remembered him: one foot up on a shelf, leaning across the bar into two girls who probably got in to the place on fake IDs.

Three college guys swung past Danny and Sydney down the short flight of stairs and threw open the front door. As they did, Danny heard Joe Cocker's "You Can Leave Your Hat On" start up with the DJ's voice talking over it.

"Okay ladies, we're giving away two tickets to tomorrow night's John Mayer concert. But it's gonna take skin to win!"

Same song, same DJ, same challenge to get the girls stripping and the heated men around them drinking more. Danny remembered reading a passage from a forgotten book that home is the place that never changes. *No wonder this place is packed with people*, he thought. Time stood still in this cramped space tucked deep in a city that seemed to change by the day. But then he recognized something that had, in fact, changed.

"Holy shit," he muttered, staring at the Shiner Bock tap handle behind the bar.

"What is it?" Sydney asked him.

He grabbed Sydney's hand. "Come on."

"Where are we going?"

"Back door." Danny was already pulling Sydney down to the corner at 19th Street. "We're going to go see the new owner."

Chapter 68

Danny led Sydney around the corner of M Street and then up 19th Street. As they passed couples and small packs of yuppies fully engaged in their own private pub crawls, the bittersweet smell of cigarette smoke tried in vain to mask the grungy street odor. Halfway up the block, Danny turned down a familiar alleyway. He remembered it like he had been there only last night. Before Sydney could object, he grabbed her and picked her up.

"What are you doing, Danny?"

"There's no telling what's on the ground down here," he replied as he began walking into the darkened alley. "The last thing we need is for you to cut your foot and get an infection. Just sit back and enjoy the ride."

The grimy city smell grew more pungent the deeper Danny plunged into the alley. Sydney seemed to melt into his chest more and more with every step. She leaned her head against his for just a moment. Danny smelled her hair. It was still damp from the Potomac, but it reminded him of past girlfriends, both the ones he merely liked and the only one that he truly loved. He wanted Sydney to turn her head. He wanted their eyes to meet. He wanted to kiss her as he held her in his arms.

Danny stopped next to an unmarked, metal door. Two college guys were using a Dumpster just a few feet away as cover while they pissed.

"Dude," the one said as he tucked himself away and stumbled toward Danny, "you guys just get married or something?"

"Yeah, chief," Danny replied. "We just got hitched at the White House. You mind opening the door, so I can take my new bride over the threshold?"

The guy didn't move. "What'd you call me, asshole?"

The second guy moved past his friend. "Don't be a prick, Tom," he said in a thick Virginia accent. He opened the door for Danny. "After y'all."

"Thanks, man," Danny replied. He carried Sydney into the back of the Bull Run. The long hallway that led from the packed upstairs bar back to the men's restroom looked exactly the same. The two guys edged past them. "Chief" stared at Danny with bloodshot eyes the entire time. He knocked against the corner of the wall as the two ambled back into the chaos.

Danny placed Sydney down as gently as he could. She kissed him on the cheek and said, "Merci."

"My pleasure," he replied. He clamped his hand on hers and thread his way past several twentysomethings, both men and women, standing in line to use the men's room. They all gave him looks that said, "Who's the shirtless asshole who smells like shit?"

The odor of sweat, alcohol, and smoke punched him in the face as Danny emerged into the bar. Bulging DJ speakers hung in each corner of the area that was no bigger than Danny's living room back in his old house in Dallas. Two bartenders he didn't recognize were working feverishly, with half-drunk smiles hanging on their faces as they served the impossibly packed room. They simultaneously tilted two and three second pours into their concoctions as they ogled several college coeds in halter tops and young Hill staffers in designer outfits that they couldn't afford. The bench that extended along the back wall provided an impromptu stage for the girls as they bumped and grinded to the throbbing music. If anyone in the place knew or cared about the plane crash, Danny sure couldn't tell it by the party going on.

He led Sydney past the bar and stepped down a short hallway to a closed door that read, "Private." He knocked. There was no answer. He knocked again. Still nothing. He tried the knob and it turned. He pushed his way into the room and saw a framed photo on top of a four-drawer metal cabinet. It was of a man hugging his mother. It confirmed his guess after seeing the Shiner Bock tap handle through the bay window on M Street.

Just like he said he would one day, Carver Sutton had bought the bar.

Danny eyed the top of the blond head cresting the high back of the chair in front of him. "You know, it's a cliché that a cop retires to open a bar, don't you?"

The reply was instantaneous. "Almost as much of a cliché as it is for a fugitive to take up with a beautiful stranger."

The chair swiveled around, and Danny's smile turned to a shocked expression. "My God, Chip. What happened to your eye?"

Carver Sutton sported a black eye patch over his right eye. He rolled to his feet, all five feet six inches of him. He hitched his thumb at Danny and looked at Sydney. "He'll look for any excuse to take his shirt off." Sydney giggled, which made Chip beam.

"Seriously Chip, what happened …"

Chip waved Danny off. "Forget the eye. Check out the hair. Or what's left of it." Carver Sutton pulled his thinning hair back to expose a sizeable forehead. "It's running away from my face."

"But what about—"

"Permanently and totally disabled. All in the line of duty, of course."

"But you were a desk jockey, a cybercop," Danny reminded him.

"You don't want to hear my sad story, really you don't." Chip barely made eye contact with Danny. He was awash in Sydney's presence. He stuck out his hand to her. "Carver Sutton. My friends and lovers call me Chip." As soon as their hands made contact, Chip turned Sydney's hand over and kissed it. His one eye rolled over to Danny. "I trust you are only in his company due to some heinous circumstance?"

Sydney was obviously charmed. There were few people in the world that could resist Carver Sutton.

"On the contrary. Danny has saved my life several times since I met him."

"Ah!" Chip exclaimed. "*Vous êtes français. Que est votre nom, bel étranger?*"

Sydney giggled. Danny was about to ask Chip what he asked when Sydney answered him.

"Sydney Dumas."

Chip continued his French inquisition. "*Quelle part de France vous son?*"

"*Toulouse. J'habite en Monte Carlo maintenant.*"

"Ah, Monte Carlo." Chip finally let her hand go. He swung his full attention over to Danny, put his arm around Danny's shoulder, and stomped the floor with his heel. "That little spit of land is almost as much fun as this little spit here. Isn't that right, Sergeant?"

Sergeant. Danny hadn't talked to Chip since becoming a Texas Ranger, but it seemed that Chip had kept up with his career.

"I saw the Shiner tap at the downstairs bar."

Chip laughed. "I bet you about shit a brick when you saw it." He turned to Sydney. "I had the unfortunate luck to meet this son of a gun almost, how long has it been, Cavanaugh?"

"Ten years."

"You're kidding?" Chip eyed the ceiling as he double-checked the math in his head. "Right. Ten years. Anyway, I was presenting the session on cyberstalking at a conference here in D.C.—"

"Cyberstalking?" Sydney's accent made the potentially horrific subject sound not only tolerable but pleasant. Danny took the liberty of answering her.

"Pedophiles, adults who prey on children, they go online and surf chat rooms and sites like Facebook for young girls and boys. Acting like kids themselves, they strike up chats with these kids. Before you know it, they try to get the kids to meet them in person. You can only imagine what happens next."

Sydney grimaced. "That's horrible."

Danny motioned to Chip. "Chip here learned how these guys worked. He would go online disguised as a child to lure these guys to him. They put away a lot of perverts thanks to Carver Sutton."

Chip grinned. "Now that you've stunk up the air with undeserved accolades, Sergeant Cavanaugh, let me get back to the meat of our story." He offered his chair to Sydney, and she sat down. Danny expected drool to begin dripping from Chip's mouth as he watched Sydney get comfortable in his chair and cross her long legs.

Chip leaned up against the desk next to her. "Our young hero here, who had just become a detective at the time, was such an inquisitive fellow. He had question after question for me. I decided to take the lad to my favorite watering hole. I mean, he could at least buy me drinks while I gave him such valuable information for free, right?"

Sydney playfully nodded. "Absolument."

Chip shook his head back and forth. "God I have already fallen in love with you, Ms. Dumas." Sydney giggled again. This time she blushed, and it made her even more beautiful, something Danny thought couldn't happen. "Anyway, we sat at the downstairs bar for a couple hours, as I explained everything I knew about cyberstalking. For the next few hours after that, Danny boy and I took turns entertaining the nubile, young beauties who come to Washington, D.C., seeking fortune and fame."

Danny continued the story. "Chip always said that he wanted to buy this place. He promised me that if he ever did, he would install a Shiner Bock beer tap and have it flowing."

"As long as there is blood flowing through my veins, there will be Shiner Bock flowing in this bar. Besides our young crusader here, it's the only good thing to ever come out of Texas."

"So you've been watching the news?" Danny asked.

"I have. Your adventures are a big story. But there's a new story giving you some competition, I'm afraid." Chip grabbed the TV remote from his desk and pointed it at the twenty-inch LCD TV hanging on the wall behind his office door. The first thing Danny noticed was the familiar CNN logo at the bottom of the screen. An image of dark water consumed the rest of it, with only small patches lit up from helicopter spotlights.

Danny recognized the boat in the center of the shot. He had been swimming near it a short time ago. As he read each word in large block print at the bottom of the screen, anguish pulsed in his soul.

Prime Minister Fantroy's Plane Destroyed

Chapter 69

As Lars Karlsson stared out the window of his usual suite at the Marriott County Hall Hotel, he didn't see one car move on Westminster Bridge. No one was walking up and down the sidewalk beneath him. It was as if the entire city had slipped into a coma.

It was an awkwardly clear morning. The rising sun illuminated Big Ben and Parliament, attempting to warm their stoic façades with a pink sky. This sight would have normally warmed Lars as well, but not this morning. He felt like the rest of London did, for both similar and different reasons.

Lars skulked away from the window and returned to the bathroom. He was half dressed in his Chester Barrie suit when the announcement on the television yanked him from his routine.

"We will hear from King Edward shortly."

He glanced at the TV. The newscast broke to a commercial. Lars returned to his perch at the window, as he contemplated The Group's options. Fantroy's position as England's prime minister certainly allowed The Group to massage certain geopolitical events in their favor, but it was Fantroy's mind that would be the greatest loss. He was a brilliant strategist, and as a wave of sadness crashed into Lars Karlsson's heart, he was also reminded of the fact that Anthony Fantroy was a good friend.

"Fellow countrymen, I address you today with a sad heart ..."

The beginning of King Edward's address snapped Lars from his daze. He sat down on the bed and turned up the volume on the remote control.

"We have confirmation from President Butcher that Prime Minister Fantroy's airplane was indeed attacked. The source of this attack was a shoulder-fired missile launched from a small craft in the Potomac River. I have dispatched a team of top MI-6 specialists to Washington to assist with the investigation."

King Edward paused from reading his prepared statement and looked directly into the camera. Lars couldn't believe it. The normally reserved monarch was on the verge of tears. "Let me say this to those responsible for this tragedy. As commander in chief of Great Britain's military forces, I can assure you that I am putting the full weight of the Crown behind our mission to bring you to justice. Whether you are part of a cowardly terrorist cell or are carrying out orders from even the most powerful government on the planet, it does not matter. Know this: Anthony Fantroy was a good man, a man of honor and courage. I will stop at nothing to avenge his death by destroying you and all that you stand for."

With that, King Edward collected his papers and stepped down from the podium. The House of Parliament had been the setting for strong sentiments over the years, but Lars Karlsson was sure that no man had ever declared his thoughts more clearly and with more conviction that King Edward just had.

The King has just thrown down the gauntlet.

Although the scene on TV erupted into a shouting match between the reporters trying to get the King's attention as he left the room, Lars shut off the TV. He didn't want to cloud his own judgment with the rambling analysis regarding the King's words that would be broadcast for the next few hours.

Lars paced around the room as questions stung his mind. *Had Fantroy informed the King about the presence of British nuclear material in the bombs found inside Washington, D.C.?*

"Whether you are part of a cowardly terrorist cell or are carrying out orders from even the most powerful government on the planet, it does not matter."

Was the King's threat directed at President Butcher? Did King Edward think the United States was behind Fantroy's death?

There was no doubt that the rest of The Group's members had heard King Edward's address. Lars had to get their thoughts.

He grabbed his cell phone off the nightstand and punched in a number.

"Yes," the baritone voice on the other end answered.

Lars cleared away the morning mucus from his lungs. "We need to get everyone together. Now."

Chapter 70

A lesser man would be paranoid by now. A lesser man would be worrying about someone having seen him emerge from the Potomac and scramble to the waiting Jeep Grand Cherokee parked in the Kennedy Center's parking garage. A lesser man would have considered taking the scuba gear in with him to his room at the Willard Hotel instead of stowing it in the Cherokee. A lesser man would even go as far as visualizing the police finding the gear and obtaining DNA samples from it.

But Stefan Taber's mind didn't work like that. He strolled into the hotel lobby confident that his mission was completed flawlessly. He was certain that after spending most of his adult life completing impossible missions his DNA was on file somewhere in the world, but not in any databases used by law enforcement organizations or intelligence agencies inside the United States. Plus, in the off chance that the Cherokee was actually searched while it was tucked safely inside the parking garage of one of the most prestigious hotels in the world, Stefan Taber had no ties to it. He was also sure that the boat he had used to carry out his mission, the one that had been waiting for him at the Georgetown Marina and was now probably being examined by teams of experts, would not divulge any information about his real identity.

As he approached his room on the fifth floor clothed in black Brooks Brothers slacks and a black mock turtleneck, he passed an elderly couple dressed to the nines. The man was trying to open their room door with a keycard. Taber saw the pair of opera glasses clutched in the woman's liver-spotted hand.

"Back from the opera?" Taber guessed, using an American accent.

The woman turned toward him. "They canceled it because of the news."

Taber gave his best blank stare. "News?"

"You didn't hear? The prime minister of Great Britain…his plane was shot down by a missile."

"Shot down?" Taber replied, an Oscar-worthy look of shock on his face. "Where?"

"Here," the woman answered. "Just before it landed at Reagan National."

Taber shook his head. "My God. What's this world coming to?"

The old man swerved his eyes at Taber. "Fortunately, we won't have to worry about that much longer."

Taber smiled politely. He motioned at the keycard. "Need some help with that?"

"Yes, would you?" the old woman replied. "Walter, let him try." She gave her husband a nudge, and he stepped aside.

Taber slid the keycard in and out of the lock in one swift motion. It beeped, and a green light came on. Taber twisted the handle and the door opened. "There you are."

"Thank you, young man," the woman said.

"My pleasure. Have a good night."

Taber stopped down the hall in front of his own suite. He used his keycard to open the door. By the time it was halfway open, he realized his room was already occupied.

While Taber recognized the scent of his guest's cologne, his body still reacted to the unexpected surprise. He clenched his fists and stepped through the doorway on the balls of ready feet. He used the closet's mirrored doors to see into the suite's sitting room.

Taber unclenched his fists and dropped his hands to his side as soon as his eyes confirmed the identity of the unassuming man seated on the couch along the back wall. But instead of heading straight for his guest, Taber loafed into the bathroom. Although he was Stefan Taber's temporary employer, Taber wanted to show this man who was really in control.

Taber smelled his hands. Whether it was imagined or real, the odor of burned gunpowder was still on them. He washed them vigorously, swallowed two handfuls of tap water, and then finally strolled into the sitting room.

"How'd it go?" the man asked, keeping his voice low.

"You of all people must have access to a TV. You tell me."

"Did anyone see you?"

Taber grinned. "No one saw me." The grin slipped from his lips a moment later, but in his mind, he was still smiling.

No one saw me. But someone felt me.

Although he didn't want to, Taber entertained his guest for exactly thirty minutes. It was the least he could do for the man who was paying his rather exorbitant fee. They discussed the next steps of Taber's mission, something Taber had already committed to memory. After his guest left, Taber fixed himself a tap water on ice and sat next to the open bedroom window. As he looked over the Washington skyline that was both receptive and intimidating, he replayed the moment when he engaged Sydney Dumas in a little fun and games underneath the Potomac River. He had to will himself to stop thinking about what he would have done to Ms. Dumas if he was still under The Group's orders.

Not only had Danny Cavanaugh and she survived the fantastic fall he saw them take from the enormous Federal Express plane, but at least Sydney had enough stamina to pursue her goal.

Taber grabbed his PDA and, in seconds, was scrolling through the information regarding Sydney Dumas he had scanned into it from Nathan Broederlam's computer one more time. She was like that blasted Energizer bunny; she kept going and going and going. Stefan Taber needed to know what exactly would make her want to quit.

Chapter 71

"Do you believe me?"

Chip glanced up at Danny and then went right back to work. Danny was dressed in Chip's bathrobe, while his clothes were spinning in the dryer in the nearby locker room. News of the incredible act of terrorism still spewed out of the TV behind them, but it couldn't hold a candle to Danny's story of what happened at the border with the Espinoza bust and why he was on the run in the first place. Danny felt the weight of the Junglee knife in the robe's pocket. Although his only option was to trust Carver Sutton, which he prayed was the right move, his head still throbbed with doubt about Chip's motivations.

"I do," Chip replied. Armed with two spatulas, he was standing over the sizzling grill, cooking two different piles of ground chicken and thinly sliced onion. Although the last employee had left an hour ago and Sydney was showering in the employee locker room that Chip had installed shortly after he bought the bar, Danny was thankful that the grill's hiss camouflaged their intimate conversation.

"I saw the news coverage of what happened in Nuevo Laredo," Chip continued. "Right away I knew you were the scapegoat."

"How's that?"

"Informants were always coming to us way back when I was still with Naval Intelligence. All they talked about were all the dirty Fibbies mixed up with smugglers along the Mexican border. I can only think how much worse it's gotten over the years."

"The navy used to investigate smuggling at the border?"

"Christ, Danny. Every federal outfit at one time or another has had a border case going. They knew whoever could curtail the Wild West shit down there for good would be eternal heroes."

"What do you think I should do?" Danny asked.

"I'll see if I can set up a meeting with some old friends." Chip took the side of one spatula and ran it through each pile, chopping up the mounds of meat and onion. Then he used both spatulas to mix them. "What kind of evidence do you have?"

"Just my word."

"You got names, dates, places?"

Danny tapped his head. "All up here."

Chip snorted. "Ah yes, that supercomputer in your skull."

"Thanks for believing me, Chip."

"Think nothing of it, especially after you brought such a beautiful creature into my otherwise mundane world."

Danny made sure the shower was still running before he continued.

"Speaking of, what are your thoughts on her?" He was dying to know what a fellow law enforcement veteran thought of Sydney's fantastic revelation that tied her story to the bombed plane.

"Prime Minister Fantroy is a Bilderberger."

That simple yet shocking statement was the segue Sydney had used to share her story with Chip. As Danny listened to it a second time, he made sure to gauge Chip's reaction. He had none. He simply sat still and listened to her, only reaching up every few minutes to dab a tissue underneath his eye patch.

"I really am in love with her," Chip replied. "Did you know that love at first sight is the strongest love there is? It's based on gut reaction, something we both know well." Chip touched his eye patch. "It's even stronger when it's all concentrated in one eye."

"I was talking about her story and about Fantroy."

Chip grabbed an oversized spice bottle off the rack above his head and dusted the chicken concoction with what he referred to as his "Essence de Sutton." He slid over to the refrigerator and came back with several slices of American cheese, carefully topping each pile. He covered both mounds with a giant metal wok that looked like it had been used as target practice by a hockey team and then stepped over to the butcher's block where Sydney's evidence rested. He looked over the lawsuit one more time and then answered Danny's question with charming vagueness.

"I've heard a lot of stories in my life, Danny. None, however, stack up to hers."

Danny sighed. "Is she telling the truth or not?"

Before answering, Chip moved on to the next stage of preparation for his guests' meal. He spun around, dove under a counter, and came back with a bag full of foot-long bread rolls.

"It makes sense. China and Japan have stopped buying our debt, which has totally fucked us. Chairman Walsh has been printing money ever since like a mad Monopoly banker."

"And you agree with her that that's a bad thing."

"History is literally littered with examples of how creating fiat money has failed. The Chinese first tried using paper money in the tenth century, and then again in the twelfth century. Both times they printed too much and the country nearly flat lined. In Germany after World War I, the German mark was so devalued that people used stacks upon stacks of them to heat their furnaces. Even today, you only need to look to Zimbabwe, where the economy has completely collapsed. President Mugabe just printed more and more money to pay for things he wanted. If you tried to buy a roll of toilet paper there, it'd cost you around $150,000."

"Look at you, Mr. History."

"I don't just pour drinks and break hearts, Danny boy. History has proven time after time after time that you can't just create money out of nothing."

"Which brings us to the part about the gold. I'd love to hear your analysis."

Chip extracted two rolls from the bag. Then he twisted it shut and returned it underneath the counter. "The international financial markets are as jumpy as a sober virgin on Spring Break."

"Nice analogy."

"It's actually a simile."

"Great. Now I've got two professors on my ass."

Chip shrugged. "I've heard about these Bilderbergers, mostly from nut jobs on the Internet spouting conspiracy theories. But if they really do own most of the world's gold, leaking a story about Japan wanting gold instead of dollars creates one hell of a self-fulfilling prophecy. The price of gold will go supernova."

"While the dollar, and confidence in it as an investment, falls into a black hole."

"Walsh then uses his magic chalkboard to convince the powers that be that dramatically raising interest rates is the only viable option to get countries buying our debt again. Sooner or later, we will have to choose between paying our creditors or paying for grandma to keep receiving her Social Security checks. But by then, it really doesn't matter what decisions are made up on the Hill, because all roads lead to the same place."

"America going broke," Danny said. Chip nodded. Danny was simultaneously relieved and anxious that he and Chip had reached the same conclusion after hearing Sydney's story.

"And if America goes broke, so does the world. Well, everyone who isn't heavily invested in gold that is. As my pappy always said, whoever has the gold—"

"Makes the rules," Danny finished, thinking about his same reaction to Sydney back in the parking garage in Houston.

"It sounds unbelievable, I know. But the way Sydney explained it, it could happen. This could be the starting point, Danny boy. And I can't see any way to stop it." Chip whipped over to a knife block and extracted a ten-inch serrated blade. He cut the rolls in half, sliced them along their spines, and placed them open-faced on the grill. He suddenly stopped working on their food and looked over at Danny for a few seconds. "You want me to check her out, don't you?"

"You think you could?" Danny asked. "I mean, even though you're officially retired, you still know how to get information about her kind of people, don't you?"

Chip stared at Danny with a look that no person with two fully functioning eyes could ever achieve. "I'll use my special talents to check out the lovely Ms. Dumas and her fascinating story, even down to her old lovers. I want to know if I'll have any competition."

"I know of one."

A spark ignited in Chip's eye. "Do tell."

"The prince of Monaco."

Chip was silent for a long moment, but the spark never left his eye. "I said competition Cavanaugh, not no-contests."

Danny heard the shower water squeak off. Both Chip and he looked in the direction of the locker room. A subject change was needed.

"So, what happened to your eye? Seriously, no bullshit," Danny asked, changing the subject. He downed the last bit of Shiner Bock from his thick pint glass etched with the Bull Run emblem.

Chip bent over the grill and lifted the rolls with his spatula. "Just a bit longer," he said, eyeing them. Then he stood tall and answered Danny's question. "My retina used to spontaneously split in half."

Danny winced. "Sounds painful."

"No shit. Over my lifetime it split, for no apparent reason mind you, a total of sixty-three times."

"What exactly would happen?"

Chip balled his fists, stuck them together, and then broke them apart. "The retina would be one piece and then split in two." Then he banged his fists together again. "Over the course of several minutes to several days, the two halves would then fuse together again."

Danny couldn't help wincing again. "I've never heard of such a thing. Is it rare?"

Chip nodded. "One in ten million people have this condition. I was documented in the AMJA. I was flown to clinics in Boston and New York to be poked and prodded like a fucking lab rat. About four years ago, I was informed that my number had come up for a retinal transplant." He tapped the eye patch. "Needless to say, the operation was not a success."

"That's what got you out of the police business?"

Chip nodded.

"What'd you do, sue the doctor and buy the bar?"

Chip chuckled. "Ah, the American Dream. Go under the knife and hope the doc botches the operation so you can make millions." Chip checked the rolls again and decided they were done. He extracted two plates off the rack above the grill and placed them on top of the lawsuit documents. He continued his story as he plated the sandwiches.

"I was well informed of the chances that the surgery wouldn't take. I made my money the really old-fashioned way, Danny. I inherited it.

My grandfather was a boat builder and patented a polymer coating used in fiberglass boats to make hulls stronger yet lighter."

"No shit?"

"No shit. He sold the patent and made millions."

"Sounds like almost as fantastic a story as Sydney's."

Chip shrugged as he handed Danny a plate. "And yet they both tell the same tale."

"How do you mean?"

"They both illustrate that most of the world's money is in the hands of a relative few. As it gets passed down from one generation to the next, it builds wider and stronger divisions between the haves and have-nots. Like Einstein said, the greatest force in the universe is compound interest. Until changes are made to that phenomenon, there will always be Bilderbergers trying to take over the world and retired, one-eyed cops who are able to open up bars and act like eighteen-year-old boys forever."

Danny decided to wait for Sydney to eat, which wasn't very long. He was on his way back from refilling his glass with a second beer when Sydney appeared in the locker room doorway on the far side of the kitchen.

Danny studied Sydney's new outfit. It had been left in one of the waitresses' lockers after her untimely dismissal. The black pants, which were not meant to stop at her calves, nevertheless fit the rest of her body. They matched the pair of black Crocs sandals on her feet. Danny almost laughed at the pink T-shirt with the word "Princess" stretched tightly across her chest in glittery swirls.

"My dear, you are absolutely breathtaking," Chip gushed. He offered the sandwich to her.

"Thank you, Chip." Sydney studied the food while still drying her damp hair with a towel. "What is it?"

"Chicken cheesesteak. A recipe from a dear old friend and a Bull Run favorite." He offered her a ketchup bottle. "Here. Put a little of this on it, and prepare to go to heaven."

Sydney finished with her hair and the two of them doused their chicken cheesesteaks with ketchup. Then they followed Chip back out to the bar, where he poured Sydney a glass of Pinot Grigio. Danny finished his second Shiner with the first half of his sandwich.

He was halfway through a third by the time he was done eating, as he listened to bar stories from their host. Even though the beer was beyond delicious, he dumped the rest of the glass in the kitchen sink. He couldn't allow himself to slide. Not now.

It was almost four in the morning by the time Danny showered. He put his underwear back on and lay down next to Sydney on the inflatable mattress that Chip had set up for them in the locker room.

Sydney was already asleep. Danny set the alarm on his watch. He didn't even have time to contemplate the connection between Prime Minister Fantroy's death and the plot against America before his body's thirst for sleep overcame him.

Chapter 72

Danny woke up eighteen minutes before his watch alarm was set to go off. He tried to slip off the air mattress as stealthily as possible, but he ended up feeling like a blind elephant in quicksand. Fortunately, Sydney was a sound sleeper and stayed asleep as he clamored to his feet.

He stumbled down the steep staircase to the bar's first floor. Only the one rail light behind the liquor bottles lit his way.

The weak sting of bleach rose up from the floor. The bar stools were turned upside down on the bar, their legs reaching for the ceiling. The chairs at the tables on the other side of the narrow room were positioned the same way. It gave the bar an even tighter feel, like it was a claustrophobic submarine waging war against sobriety.

Danny reached the front of the bar and gazed out the bay window. His eyes were at street level. Parked cars lined both sides of the street. Suddenly, he saw a head move in the white Nissan Maxima to his left. He watched it for ten full seconds. Nothing else happened. Then he looked to the gold Toyota Prius on his right. He saw another head there, but this time it stayed completely still. He blinked several times as he continued watching it. The head never moved. Across the street, he saw four figures in all black. They held what looked to be guns in their hands.

Icy panic raced throughout Danny's body, but he forced himself to stay put to determine just what was happening. From the corner of his eye, he saw weak light fill the inside of the Prius. Danny saw the face of the person sitting inside. It was his father.

The panic released its grip from his body as Danny cursed his broken mind. "Goddamn my fucking head."

Then he felt a hand on his shoulder. Danny whipped around and grabbed a handful of shirt that was really there. He raised his fist and caught himself before striking Chip in the face.

"Easy there, cowboy."

Danny let him go. "Sorry, Chip."

"I shouldn't have snuck up on you like that. My bad."

"I thought I saw someone outside." Danny returned his gaze to the bar's bay window. The same cars were there that he had seen before now. Except this time, no one was inside them. He didn't see anyone walking around the street either.

Chip patted him on the shoulder. "Relax, Danny. No one knows you and I are friends."

Danny leaned up against the corner of the bar and looked Chip over. He was dressed in a black T-shirt with his bar's logo on the chest. His skinny, pale legs jutted out from boxer shorts decorated with a pair of giant kissing lips that glowed in the dark.

"Nice boxers," Danny said.

Chip spun around once, modeling his fashion statement. "They drive the women wild."

"You're the original pimp," Danny replied. His eyes dropped to the papers in Chip's hand. "What's that?"

"Proof."

"Proof of what?"

Chip handed the printouts to Danny. "Proof that Sydney Dumas isn't just another pretty face. She's got quite the piece of gray matter tucked inside that gorgeous head of hers. And her story checks out. Even the part about dating the prince."

Danny stared at the detailed documents for over a minute in complete silence. The last page was a copy of a French tabloid cover. It showed a picture of Sydney sunning herself on the Prince of Monaco's yacht. "How did you …"

Chip put his finger to his lips. "I don't kiss and tell, Sergeant."

Danny and Sydney were ready to leave an hour later. Wanting to at least partially throw off his description on the news, Danny had borrowed one of Chip's golf shirts. Chip had fueled them up with his "Eggs Carver," scrambled eggs mixed with chorizo served on a bed of Cajun-spiced hash browns. Chip washed his down with chocolate milk. Sydney had chosen a can of V-8 juice. Danny had filled a pint glass with Shiner and drained it before he filled it back up with water and guzzled that down as well.

Carver hugged both of them at the back door of the bar. He held onto Danny for an extra long time and then handed him a disposable cell phone. Danny checked it and then put it in his pocket.

"You know my number, right?" Chip asked.

Danny tapped the side of his head. "Right up here."

"You've got your documents?"

"Yes, Mom," Danny replied as he felt them tucked against his back.

Chip looked down at Danny's stomach, noticing the bulge under his shirt. "That's quite the package. No wonder the ladies like you so much."

Sydney giggled. Danny looked down and shoved the gun he took from the Knoxville gas station a little further down in his waistband so it wouldn't be so noticeable.

"You sure you want to go there packing?" Chip asked.

"It's insurance."

"Suit yourself," Chip sighed. "Of all the gin joints in all the world, you had to walk into mine, Cavanaugh."

"I'm a son of a bitch, I know. But seriously, thanks for everything Chip. There's no way I can ever repay you."

"Yes there is," Chip replied as he turned to Sydney. "Keep telling this lovely creature what a great husband I would make someday."

Sydney stared into Chip's eye. She traced the lines of his face with her fingertips and then gently pulled him to her. She kissed him softly on the mouth and then whispered into his ear.

"*Vous êtes véritablement homme parmi les hommes.*"

Chip came away from her starstruck. There was no hint of sarcasm in his voice. "I will treasure this moment for the rest of my life, mon cher."

Sydney smiled. "Thank you for believing me, Carver Sutton."

The chilly D.C. morning blasted them in their faces as they stepped out from the bar's stale warmth. Like the two homeless people scrounging in the alley Dumpsters, Sydney and Danny stepped back into their pungent reality.

"What did you tell Chip back there?" Danny asked as he led Sydney back out to 19th Street.

"I told him he was a man among men," she replied.

"Ain't that the truth."

Danny turned left and figured out the distance. They were six blocks from their destination, and he still had no clue how to infiltrate the most heavily guarded military fort on the planet. All they could do was walk toward it and enjoy a relatively quiet morning.

Chapter 73

Three green pup tents were arranged in a U formation at the edge of Lafayette Park, across the street from the White House. Greenpeace protest signs were plastered all over each one. Stacks of propaganda were arranged next to the openings.

Even though no traffic endangered their passage, Danny grabbed Sydney's hand as they passed the tents and neared the curb. It reminded her of how her foster father, Jacques Dumas, would do the same at intersections as they crossed busy streets. He always told her that French drivers were careless, even reckless, and that crossing a street in France was one of the most dangerous jobs in the world. Danny's gesture spoke volumes to her. He cared about her. He trusted her. Sydney wanted to do the same. She wanted to tell him about her encounter with the diver under the Potomac. But she couldn't. She didn't know why he held a blade to her throat and didn't finish the job. There was no way she was going to burden Danny with that information. Not now. Not when he needed to concentrate on the task at hand.

The threat of terrorist attacks on the National Mall, combined with Fantroy's plane getting blown out of the sky, had increased both the paranoia and the number of White House security personnel. Dozens of uniformed police officers and soldiers in military fatigues were lined up along the White House fence. Besides the massive concrete barriers that blocked vehicles from getting beyond the guard booths at each end of the street, temporary steel gates had been erected twenty feet in front of each barrier. Both gates were guarded by a dozen armed soldiers.

Beyond the gates, Sydney counted eighteen news vans with their phallic transmitters reaching high into the air. Besides the security personnel and news teams, a sea of people, both demonstrators and tourists, took the opportunity that Prime Minister Fantroy's tragic death had given to be a part of the circus outside the White House's front yard.

Both Sydney and Danny had outfitted themselves with sunglasses and black Bull Run baseball caps as part of their disguises. Danny continued holding her hand as he led her through the pulsing throngs of people. Sydney could hear British accents among the shouts being hurled toward the White House. Some people held signs and pumped them up and down in the air.

Avenge Anthony!

God Save the King and PM Fantroy's Legacy!

Butcher the Bloody Bastards Who Took Anthony From Us!

If they only knew what Anthony Fantroy really was, Sydney thought. Just like she had last night as she learned of Fantroy's fate, Sydney relived the moment when Knobby had told her about the first time he met Anthony Fantroy. He had come to visit Knobby in his university office. He wore a seersucker suit to come ask what most would consider a morbid question. Fantroy needed to make sure that Knobby had chosen a replacement for himself after he passed on, someone who could be groomed over time to ensure a smooth transition. Fantroy had the perfect candidate in mind. It was Sydney's biological father. Sydney's own eyes welled as she pictured Knobby, sobbing during his explanation to Sydney about the fateful meeting when he introduced her father to The Group, an act that ultimately signed his death warrant.

Sydney looked at a few of the Brits in the crowd. She felt like grabbing each one and shaking them while she yelled the truth into their ears.

Fantroy is not a martyr! He wanted to enslave you all!

Danny led her down East Executive Avenue along the White House's outer perimeter. The long chain of police officers and soldiers continued all the way around it. Danny stopped next to another crowd of people who were gathered at the southern-most point of the White House grounds. Sydney had never been here before. She looked beyond the fence to a lawn so unspoiled that every blade of grass was perfectly symmetrical. Every flower was planted with purpose. The starch-white columns that held up the south rotunda seemed regal, like nothing could ever keep them from doing their job.

Sydney squinted into the cloudless sky and counted at least a dozen men dressed in bulky black outfits roaming the White House roof. She pulled her eyes back to a small, grayed sign that quietly reminded her of the impossibility of their task.

> These grounds are monitored. Do not climb on the fence.
> Do not attempt to gain access to the grounds.
> Violators will be prosecuted to the fullest extent of the law.

How on earth are we going to see the president of the United States under these conditions?

Danny tugged on her hand, and Sydney pulled herself away from the fence. They were on the move again, picking their way through the crowd. Sydney didn't like being in the dark. She didn't like the fact that Danny was dragging her around by the hand when, in fact, she wanted to shout, "Where are we going now?" But Sydney was smart enough to stay silent. The sign told her the grounds were monitored. An audio recording system would be part of the White House security team's surveillance package.

Sydney kept her eyes on Danny's head. It tilted back and forth every few moments. She didn't know anyone before Danny who had a photographic memory. Was he taking pictures of all the scenes around them? Committing them to memory? Would they go somewhere and evaluate their situation based on these detailed recollections?

Sydney looked around and then closed her eyes as they continued walking up West Executive Avenue. She tried to recall what she had just seen.

A tree, but what kind? Green leaves, crinkly branches. Twenty feet away is a man in a blue warm-up suit. A woman with red hair is standing next to him. They're looking at something. At what? A map? A book? Past them are parked cars: a red one and a black one. Past that is another government building. It is also white—or gray—and is made of marble. Or is it granite?

Sydney opened her eyes again. The tree was there, and so was the bland government building. But the man in the blue warm-up suit was really a man in T-shirt and blue jeans. The redhead was really a brunette, and they were examining their video camera, not a book or map. The car colors were both wrong, too. So much for her memory. She was immediately jealous of and intimidated by Danny's ability for perfect recollection.

Minutes later they were back where they started in Lafayette Park. Danny sat down on a nearby bench. Sydney sat down next to him.

"What now?" she asked him.

He never took his eyes off the White House. "I've got an idea."

"Are you going to share it with me?"

Danny tried to ignore her. He extracted the Ziploc bag that contained Sydney's documents from his waistband. He thumbed through them and then stopped on the last page. He produced a black pen from his back pocket, flipped the page over, and began writing on it. He angled the page away from her so she couldn't see what he was writing.

"Danny, please tell me what you're writing." Danny said nothing, but continued writing. "Danny, I appreciate all you've done to help me, but this isn't just about you. Now, if you've got a plan that has to do with my lawsuit, let's hear it. Otherwise, put away your pen and hand it over."

Danny stopped and capped the pen. "Listen, I'm not trying to be a hero here. But it's better if you don't know what's about to happen. It'll make your act seem more real."

Sydney gripped Danny's wrist so hard that she hurt her own fingers. "So I'm acting again. Is that your plan?"

"Sydney, I am asking you to trust me one more time. I know what I'm doing."

Sydney stared at him for a long moment. She sighed and let go of his arm. "Yeah, I guess you do. We've only escaped violent death a half dozen times or so since I met you," she said sarcastically. But then she leaned into him and kissed his cheek. As she did, her cap pushed up on her head. She came away from him and tried to adjust it back on her head. Danny stopped her and removed her hat. Then he kissed her on the mouth, letting his lips hang on hers.

He pulled himself away from her after a few seconds. "For luck," he breathed. Sydney nodded. Danny took off her sunglasses. Then he took off his own disguise and threw both hats and both pairs of sunglasses in a nearby trash can.

"Wait right here," he told her as he stuffed the disposable cell phone Chip had given him into her pocket. He bolted over to the Greenpeace tents and ducked into the middle one.

Fireworks immediately went off in Sydney's mind. *Now what?* She walked over to the tents. As she did, she read the signs that decorated them.

Stop Butcher-ing the Planet!

Smog Sucks! Ratify Kyoto!

One of the smaller signs caught her eye. It was plastered with a collage of the names of well-known foods as well as the logos of not so familiar agricultural companies. Below the collage, there was a phrase in large black letters:

Say No to GMOs!

Below that was an explanation of the GMO acronym: genetically modified organisms. Reading the words made Sydney stop in her tracks. *She* had been genetically modified. The wind was sucked from her lungs. Standing there in front of the White House, she was reminded that she was a socially engineered experiment. She might have dwelled on the subject except for Danny reemerging from the tent. As soon as she saw him, Sydney's jaw dropped wide open.

He stuffed the Ziploc bag containing the lawsuit down the front of her pants. Then he jammed the one page that he had written on into her hand.

"When I tell you to, drop this piece of paper. Got it?" Sydney stared blankly at him. "Sydney! Do you understand what I said?"

Sydney blinked, and Danny's instructions registered. "Yes."

"Okay. Let's move." Danny grabbed her by the arm and pulled her along as they ran in a clumsy mix of pumping legs and arms toward the White House.

Chapter 74

Jack Butcher had been in the Situation Room since waking up at five this morning. He was lost in half-baked theories and impromptu excuses about how someone was able to launch a shoulder-fired missile at Anthony Fantroy's plane inside what should have been the most patrolled section of the entire planet. He was confident that the residents of D.C., its surrounding suburbs, and the rest of the American people would remain cautious and vigilant after hearing about the attack. So far, he had guessed correctly.

Jack was sick of hearing the voices of the people in the room. Fortunately, he caught a glimpse of one of the monitors on the wall. It was a CNN feed, and it was focused on the section of Pennsylvania Avenue right outside the White House.

Jack pointed at the monitor and spoke, his words cutting off General Seth Meyers in mid-sentence.

"Can we get that CNN feed on the big screen?"

A man in uniform went over to the monitors and pressed a few buttons to make Jack's wish come true.

"What in God's name?" Simon Shilling said as he squinted at the screen. "Is that happening right now?"

"Can we get some volume on that screen, please?" Jack asked the soldier. He gave his commander in chief a brisk, "Yes, sir," and made Jack's second wish come true.

The voice of Grace Styles, the senior White House reporter for CNN, was instantly piped in through all eight ceiling speakers and the speakerphone unit on the table.

"We don't know what this guy wants or why he's undressed for that matter. The only thing we know right now is that he is armed and is apparently holding this woman hostage."

Suddenly, the camera zoomed in on the man and his hostage. "Okay, okay, what's he doing? Now he's lying down on the ground, and he's ordering the woman to lie on top of him. Wait now, his hostage just threw what looks to be a piece of paper on the ground. Now the gunman is yelling something. Do we know what he's yelling? Do we know what he just said? Ladies and gentlemen, we're trying to figure out what this guy wants. Do we know if the president is in fact inside the White House?" Grace paused as she received answers in her earpiece. "Yes, o ... okay. The president is inside the White House, but we're not sure if he knows what's going on outside, just steps away. All I can say is that I've never seen anything like this before in my life."

Just then, Jack heard the commotion outside of the Sit Room and knew what was coming. The doors exploded open. Peter Drake and his men instantly huddled around him. They grabbed underneath his armpits and lifted him out of his chair. The rest of room was standing now, taken aback at the force by which the president of the United States was being handled. Jack let his body go limp again, knowing it was the best way to handle this onslaught. But as he was being pulled out of the room, he kept his eyes on the CNN feed. The camera captured a Secret Service agent running over to grab the piece of paper the woman threw on the ground.

"Wait!" Jack yelled, finally recognizing the assailant from the report Simon had given him earlier. "That's Danny Cavanaugh!"

Peter Drake had his orders and continued to carry them out. Jack was halfway out the doorway when he saw Cavanaugh throw his gun across the street. Instantly, he heard his son's voice in his head.

"Simon says fight them!"

Jack tightened his body and grabbed hold of the doorway. "He dropped his weapon! Goddamn it, he's unarmed now! There's no immediate threat! Stand down! Stand down!"

Peter Drake looked at the TV screen. A Secret Service agent yanked the woman away from Cavanaugh. Several other agents surrounded him. He flipped over on his stomach and held his empty hands up in the air.

Drake let go of Jack and ordered his agents to do the same. "Our apologies, sir. We're simply—"

"I know, following orders." Jack smoothed himself and stepped across the room. He studied the CNN feed.

"Pete," the president started as he pointed at the screen, "the agent who grabbed the paper from her, get him. I want to see that piece of paper immediately."

"Yes, Mr. President."

"I also want to speak to her ASAP. Cavanaugh, too."

"Sir, we have procedures. They need to be searched and questioned."

Jack turned to Peter Drake. "He's not armed any longer, Pete. Unless he's got a bomb buried in his underwear, he's no immediate threat to me or to the White House, correct?"

"Yes, sir," Agent Drake replied.

Simon Shilling placed himself at Jack's side. "Mr. President, why do you want to talk to them?"

"Don't you think it's odd that all these events are happening together?" Jack replied loud enough for the rest of the room to hear him. "The dirty bombs, Fantroy's plane, and now this? They all have to be related."

Simon sucked air in through his nose and then nodded.

Jack lowered his voice so only Simon could hear him. "Besides, why would Cavanaugh hold her hostage and then throw away the gun as soon as she gives up a piece of paper?"

Simon expressed his theory. "He wants to show us that he's not a threat."

Jack agreed and then added his two cents. "It's not about what he wants. It's just like the break-in at Monticello and the attempted robbery at the Library of Congress. It's about whatever is on that piece of paper. It's about the written word."

Chapter 75

Danny sat next to Sydney on one of the two couches inside the Oval Office. He crossed his legs uncomfortably in a borrowed suit from one of the Secret Service agents. He checked his watch, which was given back to him after being examined by the Secret Service agent hovering over them. Danny was still surprised that his plan had actually worked, but here they were.

He trailed his eyes over to Sydney, wondering just how much she was made to take off during the standard Secret Service search procedures. Danny held a chuckle inside. *That woman just can't keep her clothes on.*

A section of wall on the far side of the office swung open. The president of the United States and his chief of staff strode across the room. As they did, the agent came to attention and whispered into his wrist radio. "Devon has POTUS in Oval."

Danny stood up, and Sydney followed his lead. "Mr. President," he said, extending his hand.

President Jack Butcher switched the folder in his right hand over to his left. He shook his guests' hands. "Sergeant Cavanaugh, Ms. Dumas. This is my chief of staff, Simon Shilling." After everyone pressed the flesh, the president motioned for everyone to sit. He looked at his Secret Service agent.

"That will be all, Peter. Thank you."

"Yes, sir." The agent walked out of the room and closed the door behind him without a sound.

A nervous warmth filled Danny's gut. He couldn't believe it. Regardless of his situation, he was in the White House, in the Oval Office for that matter. If only his dad could see him now.

President Butcher eased back into the rocker at the head of the coffee table. He glanced at the door the agent just used. "That was Peter Devon, the head of my Secret Service detail. He informed me of the extreme measures you've taken to get here."

"Yes, sir," Danny said.

"I feel obligated to listen to you, since you've risked life and limb to gain my attention."

"Yes, sir."

"I especially liked that neat trick you pulled outside, Sergeant. Stripping down to your skivvies."

Danny couldn't help smiling as he acknowledged the president's praise. "I wanted your people to know that other than the gun in my hand, I wasn't otherwise armed or wired with anything."

The president chuckled. "I'm sure you also got every woman watching the news clip of your stunt all hot and bothered in the process." He unfolded a piece of paper from his jacket pocket and laid it down on the coffee table. The president allowed Danny to scrutinize it for a moment before continuing. "You know how the ladies love bad boys."

The warmth in Danny's stomach gave way to a clutched panic. At the top of the paper was the title:

FBI TEN MOST WANTED FUGITIVE

Below it, there were three pictures of Danny: one from the academy with a crew cut, one of him in his dress blues taken when he was still with the Houston Police Department, and one he didn't recognize. It was the most recent of the three, and he was crossing a city street dressed in a long sleeve shirt and jeans. It looked to him like a surveillance photo.

Danny's description was listed beneath the photos: his height, weight, eye color, date of birth—everything down to the scar on his knee from arthroscopic surgery. He was surprised that his aerophobia wasn't listed. Below his description, his three stints in law enforcement were listed: Houston Police officer, Dallas Police detective, and sergeant with the Texas Rangers. Below all of that, the word "CAUTION" had been centered in bold blue typeface. The next part listed Danny's crime:

Daniel James Cavanaugh is wanted for murder.
Cavanaugh allegedly killed an FBI agent in Laredo, Texas.

Danny read on. The FBI was offering a hundred thousand dollar
reward for information leading to his capture. Of all the accusations
on the page, the next words—also in bold blue typeface—were the
hardest to swallow.

CONSIDERED ARMED AND EXTREMELY DANGEROUS

Danny looked up at the president. "I guess you just made a
hundred grand, Mr. President."

The president smirked. "Except that's not why you're here." He
grabbed the FBI flyer, folded it up, and stuck it back in his jacket
pocket.

"Then why did you show it to us?" Sydney quipped.

Simon Shilling finally spoke. "We wanted to remind you that
you have no other choice than to help us."

Sydney replied to the president. "That's why we *are* here, Mr.
President. There are people who want to cause the United States
irreparable harm."

Danny gave Sydney a look. *Don't ever show your cards until
it's absolutely necessary. Shilling just asked for our help, but help with
what?*

"Yes, about that." The president reached into the folder that he
had set beside his chair. He pulled out a familiar stack of documents
and laid them on the coffee table. "I read your note and had White
House counsel review the lawsuit. She determined it's valid. We
compared Booker's signature with the one we have on file. It's
authentic."

Sydney reached for the lawsuit's summary page that was on top
of the stack. She flipped it over and began reading Danny's note.
Danny saw every word of the note in his mind as he waited for her
reaction.

Mr. President,
My name is Danny Cavanaugh. I am a sergeant with the
Texas Rangers. The woman that I am holding hostage is

Sydney Dumas. She has told me that she is a representative of the International Court of Justice and that members of her organization are trying to kill her because of her involvement with a case summarized on the back of this message. I have had no way of knowing if this is true, I've only gone on blind faith. I hope that you do the same and agree to meet with us ASAP to discuss what we know. I am not exaggerating when I say that the fate of the United States may well rest upon what we have to tell you.

Sydney glared at Danny after she was finished reading. "That's why you didn't let me see your message! You still don't believe me!"

"I don't think that you were lying to me, Sydney. I needed to show President Butcher that, just like me, he needs to have faith."

The president regained their attention by clearing his throat. "Ms. Dumas, can you tell me what led you to believe that members of the ICJ are trying to kill you?"

Sydney sat up straight and remained rigid as she recapped the story about the Bilderbergers and how the lawsuit was the sign that Fed chairman Dexter Walsh was engineering America's demise.

When she was finished, the president turned to his chief of staff. Sydney kept her eyes off Danny.

"Any thoughts, Simon?" he calmly asked.

Simon Shilling's poker face was not nearly as good as the president's. He sat motionless on the couch while an amazed look solidified in his eyes.

"Simon?" the president urged again.

"Yes sir. I ..." Nervous laughter escaped his mouth. "I mean, I've never heard of such a thing."

Sydney erupted again. "You do not believe me?"

"Easy, Ms. Dumas. I didn't say I didn't believe you. It's just a lot to take in all at once. I mean Bilderbergers wanting to take over the world, a secret lawsuit, Dr. Walsh being in on the whole thing with his—what did you call it again?"

"The Markov Monte Carlo model," Sydney declared. "It is a real economic theorem, one he has used before."

The president stayed quiet for a long time and then said something that made the collective attention of the room fall squarely on his shoulders. "Simon, what Ms. Dumas is telling us, it fits in with our problem."

"Sir?" Simon blurted. By the way he said it, Danny could tell that half of Simon's response was a question and the other half was a plea for the president not to go any further.

Danny's instincts vaulted to red alert. He fell right into interrogation mode. "Mr. Shilling said something about helping you, Mr. President. What's he talking about, sir?"

President Butcher didn't flinch. He continued staring at his chief of staff. Simon finally nodded at him, and the president swung his eyes over to Danny and Sydney.

"What I am about to tell you does not leave this office. If it does, I guarantee that you will be tried and convicted of treason against the United States of America. I promise that you will be given the maximum allowable sentence for that crime, which is a life sentence in a maximum security federal prison." The president stared into Danny's eyes. "Considering the trouble you already face, Sergeant, a charge of treason would guarantee your spot on death row." Then he switched his gaze onto Sydney. "Don't think you get out easy because you are not a United States citizen, Ms. Dumas. Justice in this country is blind to many prerequisites, including citizenship."

"Okay," Sydney said, "now that you've got us both shaking in our boots, Mr. President, why don't you explain you problem."

Simon Shilling blurted, "Watch your tongue, Miss Dumas. Don't forget you're talking to the president of the—"

Sydney's eyes flashed at Simon. "He's not my president. And even if he was, he's just a man, not a god."

"Let's all just calm down," the president said. He let the room cool before continuing. "Several events have transpired over the past few days that you may or may not be aware of. We started off on Wednesday with a sarin gas attack in L'Enfant Plaza. While the terrorists had the wrong mixture of gas to produce any harm, the fact remains that it was a terrorist attack on American soil. Then there was the discovery of the two dirty nuclear bombs, one at the Washington Monument and the other under the Lincoln Monument. Then, the explosion of Prime Minister Fantroy's plane over the Potomac. Stop me if you haven't heard about any of this." The president breathed in to begin another sentence. Before he did, he glanced over at his chief of staff, who offered another reassuring nod. "Most disturbing of all is that the nuclear material contained within the dirty bombs has been traced back to Great Britain. I was going to announce that nugget to the American public as soon as Tony got here."

"But someone didn't want him talking to you about it," Danny guessed.

"There's more, Sergeant," the president replied. "Perhaps the biggest piece to this puzzle is the fact that three weeks ago, two men broke into Thomas Jefferson's home in Monticello, Virginia, killing both security guards on duty. They had only one objective—a drawing table. It was ripped to pieces, and from what our experts told us, they found a small, secret compartment inside."

"What was inside the compartment?" Sydney asked.

"While we can't know for sure, our experts believe it was copies of the same documents that a man tried to steal from the Library of Congress on the same night."

"Oh yes, I heard about that," Sydney said. "Half-baked theories flooded the Internet as to why the two events happened simultaneously. It was supposedly about some rare book, right? But the book had no connection to anything at Monticello; at least that's what the conspiracy theorists believe."

"That story was a cover for what the suspect failed to steal." President Butcher got up, stepped behind his desk, and faced his credenza. He unlocked the lower cabinet and retrieved a black portfolio. He carried it back to the conference area and set it down on the coffee table. A thick rubber band was stretched around it. The words "TOP SECRET" were stamped across the front in blood red ink.

"The documents in question were hidden in one of William H. Seward's journals, which was, unbeknownst to any of the librarians, housed in the Rare Book section. Seward was President Lincoln's secretary of state. During that escape attempt, the assailant dropped the journal and the documents therein, which were recovered and turned over to this office." The president pulled off the rubber band, opened the portfolio, and slid it in front of Danny.

Danny stared at a folder inside the portfolio. It, too, was stamped "TOP SECRET." It reminded him of the type of people he was dealing with. Powerful people. Powerful and very dangerous.

Danny wiped his sweaty palms on his knees and scooted to the edge of the couch. He looked at Sydney. It felt like he was looking at her for the last time before his world would once again change forever. He opened the folder and that's exactly what happened.

Chapter 76

Article VIII.

Should an overwhelming vacancy of government, including the absence of legislative, executive, or judicial powers therein, deride the ability for those branches of government to carry out their responsibilities stated within this Constitution, the United States of America, at that time, and the citizens thereof shall be returned to the rule of Great Britain and governed under her command.

The bottom of the page was dated September 17, 1787, and was signed by some very famous men, guys like Hamilton, Madison, Franklin, and Washington.

Danny lowered the document back down to the open folder and carefully took his fingers off the edge of the plastic sheet protecting it.

"This is fake, right?" he asked.

"I'm afraid not," Simon Shilling responded. "It's the eighth article of the United States Constitution."

The hairs on the back of Danny's neck stiffened. He leaned over and examined the document again. The aged paper, lambskin or whatever the words had been written on, looked to be over two hundred years old. "But it's by itself. It's not with the rest of the Constitution. In any copy of the Constitution I've ever seen, I've never seen this article."

The president responded. "Read the letter, Sergeant. You'll see why it was kept by itself."

Danny turned over the eighth article. His eyes fell to the bottom of a second plastic sheet that contained a letter signed by those same famous signatures.

He scrolled back up to the top of the letter and began reading it.

Friends and Countrymen,

Several years have passed since our victory over those Englishmen who tried in vain to suffocate our liberty. We stand together as a nation that has suffered greatly but has won a war without equal. However great the injustices that our English foes hath brought to our shores, the cruelties by which other nations may bring to the United States should we be again defenceless merits an unusual clause to our Constitution. Article VIII carries the provision within it to deliver our nation to the bosom of Britain if, in fact, the United States cannot sustain itself as a nation until such a time that it can. King George may have all but forced us to drink from the bitter cup of slavery, but we are assured that Parliament values the pursuit against savagery – a savagery that may overwhelm America during her gravest hour. The Kingdom of Great Britain has flown its colors over every continent. It can protect America from our most tenacious of foes. But rest assured dear countrymen that if this darkest of days ever comes, a time will follow that will allow us to again sever ties from mother England – by simple decree or by bloody revolution.

The powers contained within the executive branch allows the president to restrain this article of the Constitution until the time it is warranted to be made public.

We the members of the Philadelphia Convention agree by a majority vote to ratify Article VIII of the United States

Constitution on this day seventeen of September, seventeen hundred and eighty seven.

Danny opened his mouth to speak but had no words.

"I had the same reaction when I first saw it, Sergeant," the president said.

"Our expert thinks that Article Eight was created in secret by the Founding Fathers because, above all else, they had a sense of enlightenment about them," Simon Shilling explained. "The last thing they wanted to see was their new nation fall into the hands of unrefined savages."

President Butcher interjected. "The English were bastards in the eyes of the Founding Fathers. But at least they were genteel bastards who would ensure the continued enlightenment of America until the colonists could again rise up against them."

"But how could they keep something like this secret?" The question blurted from Sydney's mouth. She had been deadly silent, studying the documents ever since Danny had opened the folder.

The president eyed his chief of staff to field her question. "Our expert believes that Article Eight passed from president to president until it reached Abraham Lincoln. Contrary to popular belief that Lincoln was a melancholy fellow, he was actually a spirited leader who despised Great Britain. Once Article Eight was presented to him, he saw it as a treasonous paper. As his secretary of state, William Seward was privy to all discussion and actions that pertained to international relations, treaties, and alignments. Our expert's theory is that Lincoln ordered Seward to destroy all evidence of Article Eight, which he did because there is no mention of it anywhere in history. Except he must have kept at least two copies, because he thought that Lincoln's resentment for England clouded his judgment.

"Seward had traveled all over the globe, witnessing firsthand the desperation of collapsed governments. Seward thought that America might need to call on England for assistance one day and that this document would help entice the Brits to help if they knew they would receive America itself as payment. So, he decided to keep at least one copy of the article and this Philadelphia Convention letter under lock and key inside one of his own journals."

"When you say the documents were inside the journal, where exactly were they?" Danny asked.

Shilling looked at the president. They briefly carried on a silent conversation with their eyes. The president then turned to Danny. "You know all the right questions to ask, Sergeant."

"Comes with my job, sir," Danny replied.

"They were in a leather pouch sealed inside the back cover. The suspect had to cut it open to retrieve them."

"This may seem like a stupid question, but why wouldn't one of the librarians have discovered them before now? I mean it wasn't like they were tucked inside a copy of *Horton Hears a Who!* in some city library. Aren't items in the Library of Congress examined or x-rayed or something?"

Simon Shilling answered him. "As for who would know they were sealed inside the cover of one of William Seward's journals, we have no idea. This particular journal wasn't logged in the system. But that doesn't say much. The Library of Congress is the largest library in the world, Sergeant. It contains over a hundred million items, nearly five million of which are considered rare and housed in the Rare Book and Special Collections division in the Jefferson building. Several thousand of those books, pamphlets, and other documents are considered lost, missing, or misplaced. So no. To answer your question, the librarians can't even keep up with cataloguing them, let alone find the time to examine each item."

"There must be video of the man trying to steal the documents," Danny assumed. "Or he must have shown ID to get into the rare book area."

The president took this one. "He passed himself off as a GWU student. College students are granted access all the time. He presented his GWU ID both at the library's entrance and again at the Rare Book Reading Room circulation desk. It was scanned and recorded at both spots." The president motioned at Simon, who opened his portfolio that was lying on the couch next to him. He extracted a photocopy of the ID and set it on the coffee table. "While the ID is a fake," the president continued, "the photo has already been put through every facial recognition program used by every federal agency that has such technology. A match has yet to turn up."

"It's like he appeared out of thin air," added Simon Shilling.

"Was this his first visit to the library?" Danny asked.

The president nodded. "Using that ID at least."

"And the tapes?" Danny asked.

"We've had our forensics people examine the security tapes," Simon replied. "The suspect knew where the cameras were. He knew to keep his head down inside the building. He never once looked up at a camera. Once he was outside, he pulled a hood over his head. The officer who chased him and retrieved the documents worked with a sketch artist to make a composite, but so far no hits."

"What about fingerprints?" Danny asked.

The president nodded. "They dusted for prints, but he never took his gloves off. It was a cold night, so no one thought it was suspicious. Still, we're reviewing every fingerprint found at the locations where he went inside the library."

"Just in case he had a partner who cased the place for him," Danny said.

"Or if he himself had been there before, in disguise," The president replied. "So far, no nefarious characters have turned up."

Danny's turned his eyes up, focusing on his thoughts. "Okay, so the perp goes to all this trouble; he somehow finds out about hidden documents inside a lost journal that even the librarians don't know is in the Rare Book Reading Room inside the Library of Congress. He probably uses disguises and fake IDs to case the place for weeks or even months, considering every detail of the robbery. Then at last, when he has his prize, he simply drops the documents before he escapes?"

"It was the only way he *could* escape, Sergeant," Shilling answered. "He dropped them in the Neptune water fountain just outside the library. The officer chasing him had to rescue them instead of pursuing him."

The president gave Danny a knowing look. "You're thinking that he wanted to drop them all along, that he wanted to show us what his cronies at Monticello had taken."

"The thought had crossed my mind, yes sir," Danny replied. "How did he get caught with the documents in the first place?"

"A library police officer saw him holding something inside his coat. When he tried stopping him, the thief ran."

"Like I said, the thief goes to all that trouble and then makes a rookie mistake like that? No way. It was on purpose."

"But why?" Simon asked both of them.

Danny eyed both men. "At his news conference, King Edward's threat about Prime Minister Fantroy's death was squarely aimed in our direction. Anyone have a vested interest in Great Britain and the United States going to war?"

"Almost every terrorist on the planet would love to see that happen, Sergeant," the president replied. "I spoke to the king and he admitted his comments were fueled by heavy emotions."

Danny nodded. "Let's just focus on finding the thieves then. Any evidence from the Monticello break-in?"

"Nothing," Simon responded. "No fingerprints or any other hard evidence. They don't even have cameras there."

"We've been over every piece of evidence we have ad nauseum, Sergeant," the president added. "You're welcome to look at the library tapes and the forensic reports all you like. Another pair of eyes may help."

"Who all knows that these documents exist, sir?" Danny asked the president.

President Butcher motioned to Simon and then himself. "The two of us, a handful of my closest advisers, a National Archives expert, a couple constitution experts, and now the two of you. Everyone's under a gag order."

"Except whatever group is responsible for bringing them back to life," Simon added.

The president gave him a look. "Yeah, those bastards, too."

Danny sighed. It just didn't make any sense. But did anything in the world make much sense anymore? Danny needed to only look at his own situation to answer that question.

Sydney piped up again. She clutched Article Eight and waved it around like it was nothing more than a flyer shoved underneath her windshield wiper. "But you don't have to abide by this article. Can't you just convene an emergency session of Congress to get it deleted or amended?"

Simon Shilling vaulted to her, snatching the article from her with a venomous look. "Careful, Ms. Dumas. It might not mean much to you, but this is a priceless document."

Sydney paid almost no attention to Shilling. She waited for the president to answer her.

"I could go to Congress with this and make it public, but there are several reasons why I'm not. While we've had it examined by experts and those experts believe that it is real, we have yet to put it through a complete battery of tests."

"So why don't you?"

The president motioned to the documents as Shilling carefully laid them out on the table. "Because, Ms. Dumas, there are already enough people that know they exist. More testing means more people in the mix and we don't want this information getting out just yet. But it really doesn't matter whether these are legal documents created by the Founding Fathers or counterfeit scraps of parchment. Whoever stole a copy from Monticello and tried to steal another copy from the library thinks that Article Eight is a way to dissolve the United States of America. We don't want to let them know that we are reacting to it. That could make them advance their timetable for whatever they're planning. Besides, even if I convened, to use your words, an emergency session of Congress, we would still need at the very least a two-thirds vote from Congress to nullify or even amend a Constitution article. I could name members of Congress on both hands who would want to conduct independent investigations that would take months to complete. Others would no doubt scream to convene a constitutional convention, which would take months to even arrange. Whatever is about to happen would be long over by then. Believe me, secrecy about Article Eight is the best policy for now."

Danny turned to Sydney. "You know what I'm going to say."

"That the Bilderbergers are responsible?" she replied. "Danny, I told you—"

"I know. They move in covert ways. They don't do the murder and mayhem thing. But what if you're wrong this time, Sydney? Think about it. They're trying to destroy the world's only superpower. What if this is Plan B?"

"What if what is Plan B?" Sydney replied.

"Plan A was to try it through economics. You've thrown a considerable wrench in that plan. What if Plan B is to have someone steal nuclear material from Great Britain and use it to try and blow up Washington, D.C.? What if Plan B is to make the United States and Britain go to war?"

Simon presented a question that Danny hadn't pondered. "Who said it was stolen from Britain?"

"You're saying that the British government is responsible for these bombs?" Danny asked.

"We can't rule it out until we find out who shot down the prime minister's plane and get to the bottom of things," Simon answered.

"Like you said, Sergeant," the president added, "we think someone didn't want Tony talking to us about the bombs. Who knows, King Edward could be one of these Bilder—"

The president didn't get a chance to finish. A gray-haired man with glasses stormed into the Oval Office and then hesitated a few steps inside the doorway. Two other men stood in the doorway behind him. Danny could see Agent Peter Devon out in the hallway, his cold stare attempting to penetrate inside Danny's head.

The president addressed the first man. "What can I do for you, Admiral?" The man crossed to President Butcher and whispered something in his ear. The president looked off in the distance for a split second before he stood. "Is everyone in the Sit Room?" he asked.

"Yes, sir," the man responded.

"Good," the president replied. He turned to Danny and Sydney. "Something's come up. We'll continue this later."

The president left the Oval Office with everyone trailing him. The train of bodies stopped as Danny watched President Butcher address Peter Devon. Devon waited for the president and his entourage to file past him before he entered the Oval Office. He stood tall in front of Danny and Sydney and spoke at a near whisper.

"The president has asked that you come with me."

Chapter 77

Danny was caught red-handed. The Oval Office cracked open and he froze. The president crossed the room with Vanessa Dempsey stuck to his side. She bulldozed her way through the notes in her hand, handing him each one as she summarized it. Neither one even glanced in Danny's direction.

Danny turned from his crouched position over President Jack Butcher's credenza. It was overflowing with framed pictures of the president's life, both personal and political. There were several photos of him shaking hands with various celebrities: Sylvester Stallone on the steps of the Philadelphia Museum of Art, Mel Gibson at some formal event, even Steven Spielberg, the two of them dressed in tennis togs, no doubt at some celebrity fund-raiser. Another photo was of the 1975 Trinity College graduating class at Oxford. Danny spotted Butcher's young, handsome face in the large crowd moments after looking at it. But he was especially taken with the photo of Jack Butcher with his son. Danny was vaguely familiar with how Simon Butcher had died from some horrific disease. In the picture, Simon was lying among a cluttered sea of tubes and machines in a hospital room. His frail body was nearly as white as the dingy sheets draped over him. Nevertheless, their hands were clenched together in a victorious apex. Danny could only imagine what a father would think at seeing his son in such a predicament. It could only be optimism coated with denial.

We will beat this disease. We will be throwing the football around again. We will go on fishing trips. There is no chance my son will die.

As the president approached him, Danny scrambled for the right thing to say.

Your friends certainly cross the entire spectrum, Mr. President.

I was just trying to pass the time by looking at your fantastic photos, Mr. President.

You certainly have a beautiful family, Mr. President.

Danny scratched the last one from his options. The president stopped short of him and sat in the rocker at the head of the conference area. Vanessa handed him a file folder and excused herself.

"You know it's a federal offense for you to be back there," the president said, still examining the papers in his hands.

Danny took a few steps away from the president's desk. Not knowing where to go, he just stood as still as he could and tried to find something to say.

The president finally looked up and laughed. "I've used that one a half dozen times now, and no one's ever challenged me on it."

"It's hard to challenge the president of the United States, sir."

The president nodded with a distant look in his eye. "I'm sure Ms. Dumas would if she was here."

"About that sir, where is Sydney? They separated us as soon as you left."

"I assume that's the Secret Service's standard operating procedure. You can rest assured that she's fine. My administration doesn't condone waterboarding, especially not here." The president stood and switched to the guest chair on the far side of his desk. He motioned for Danny to sit in his own chair. "Why don't you take a load off?"

Danny looked down at the actual, physical most powerful seat in the world—*the* catbird seat. "Oh no, sir, I couldn't."

"Come on, Sergeant. It'll be your only chance, for I'm sure that you're no politician. You're too honest a man for that line of work."

It's hard to challenge the president of the United States. Danny accepted his host's offer and took a seat. He eased into the chair timidly, as if it was wired to explode at any moment. Once he let his full weight down, he took a deep breath and relaxed. His position behind the desk in the Oval Office gave him a shot of confidence.

"Sir, about the Bilderbergers, we never really got your thoughts on them."

The president sighed and stared at Danny for a long moment. "If you're asking do I know of their existence, then the answer is yes. They are real, and they are dangerous."

Danny didn't know how to ask the next question. Fortunately, President Butcher seemed to read his thoughts. "You're wondering if I'm a member?"

"The question did come up, sir."

"They courted me when I became senator of Pennsylvania. I guess they thought I was someone special, because I was the ranking member on the Senate Intelligence Committee. I went to a meeting of theirs in Istanbul. Guests are given a dog and pony show, but any halfway intelligent person could read between the lines. They want to exterminate whole populations of people. They're even involved with eugenics. That's the—"

"Engineering of superior human beings," Danny interrupted. "Sydney told me, sir."

"It's like Hitler and the Nazis all over again, but instead of tanks and propaganda, they are using complex economic theorems and clandestine foreign policies. I politely turned them down."

"So you believe Sydney's story? About their agenda to take over the world?"

The president nodded. "Although the PC term is creating a one-world government."

"Is that what you got pulled away for, sir?"

"Could be our Bilderberger friends." A wave of dread rolled across the president's face. "We found a third dirty bomb."

The words plummeted into Danny's core. "Where?"

The president shuffled through his papers. He plucked out a photo and placed it on the desk. Danny recognized the building, which had an uncanny resemblance to the White House.

"That's the Greenbrier Hotel."

"You've stayed there?"

"My parents did, a long time ago."

"CEOS, the Congressional Emergency Operations Shelter, is there."

The memory of his parents telling him about a strange tour they took during their stay at the hotel poured into the forefront of Danny's mind. "It's a bunker, underneath the hotel, right?"

"Most of it's underneath the eighteenth hole, yes."

"Mr. President, how can it be an emergency shelter? It's open to the public. My parents took a tour of it."

"After 9/11, the previous administration realized that most of our emergency operations facilities had blown covers, including Mt. Weather in northern Virginia, Area R just outside of Camp David, and the Greenbrier. So, the powers that be at the time decided why not use one that the public already knows about. CEOS is located in a section of the bunker that's still off-limits."

Danny huffed. "Hidden in plain sight. Smart."

"The Greenbrier is the safest and strongest of them all. Not to mention it has a hell of a golf course."

"That's where the bomb was found?"

"Not inside CEOS." The president pulled another photo from the papers and laid it on the table. A door at the end of a concrete walkway was in the center of the shot. A sign to the left of the walkway read, "Danger—high voltage." A second sign to the right of the walkway read, "The bunker is a sealed facility. There is absolutely no smoking. Violators will be asked to leave." Behind it, a cast of federal agents, some in plain clothes and others in hazmat suits, were standing around a jagged hole dug into the earth.

Danny looked up from the photo. "It was buried?"

The president nodded. "Just outside the bunker."

"But CEOS is fortified. It could take a hit from something as small as a dirty bomb."

"Yes, but the entire area, including the only entrance to CEOS, would remain contaminated for at least thirty years."

"I'm guessing CEOS is vital?" Danny asked.

"It's on a short list of facilities we have to ensure the continuation of government if something happens in D.C. But it's at the top of that list. We've sent NEST teams to the other sites to make sure they're still secure."

"How many people know about the list of sites, Mr. President?"

"Again, it's a short list. It's classified information."

Instantly, the realization slammed into Danny. "It's an inside job, Mr. President."

The president nodded. "That's why you and I are the only ones sitting here in the Oval, Sergeant. If all these events are connected, then the information Ms. Dumas has concerning the lawsuit and Federal Reserve chairman Walsh only bolsters that conclusion. I can only trust someone outside my administration and outside the federal government to move forward with this investigation." The president raised an eyebrow and cocked his head at Danny.

"Me?" Danny asked.

"Bingo. You're going to help me find my traitor, Danny. You will tell no one else of your investigation, and you will report only to me."

"Sir, although I appreciate your confidence I'm not the best choice right now. I'm wanted for killing an FBI agent and a senator."

"Did you kill Booker?" the president asked flatly.

"No. In fact, I'm sure that whoever shot him was aiming for me."

"I believe you."

"Just like that?"

"Just like that, Sergeant."

"What about Agent Ripley?"

The president said nothing. Instead, he shuffled through the rest of his papers. He plucked one out and laid it on the desk in front of Danny. It was a copy of an e-mail sent from a deputy FBI director to director of National Intelligence Howard Fielding. The subject line read, "Ripley Investigation." Danny couldn't read the e-mail fast enough.

"Crayton Ripley was under investigation when I killed him?"

"For months," the president replied. "The FBI knew he and other agents were in bed with Rafael Espinoza."

Danny's anger flared, damn the fact that he was in the Oval Office talking to the president of the United States. "The FBI knew Ripley was dirty and yet did nothing for months?"

"You know how these things work, Sergeant. The FBI wanted Espinoza. Take out Agent Ripley, and you only take out a cog in the wheel while, in the process, making your own organization look bad.

But take out Espinoza, and you practically wipe out the Juarez cartel, get tons of drugs off the street, and hopefully prevent hundreds, if not thousands, more murders. Most important, you make the headlines for all the right reasons."

"But the op blew up in everyone's face."

The president nodded. "I know. What I don't know is why you ran. You must have known that running only makes you look guilty, Sergeant."

"I didn't know who to trust, Mr. President. I would rather have been considered guilty and alive than be innocent and dead."

A knowing look came over the president. He leaned forward. "Danny, I want you to know that I believe you. You now have the full weight of the president of the United States behind you. You will be exonerated of all the accusations against you. I only ask that you do me a favor in return. Help me figure out who's behind planting these bombs. Help me figure out who wants to destroy the United States of America."

Goosebumps wicked throughout Danny's skin. He would be exonerated of the crimes charged against him. He had the most powerful friend a person could have in his corner. His mind immediately went to work.

"Sir, the first thing I have to do is take a look at L'Enfant Plaza."

"Why?"

Danny recalled the story of a particularly daring smuggling operation, one for the record books, which happened before his time at the border. A small team of coyotes, men that helped smuggle people into the United States, had blown up several warehouses on the far northern side of downtown El Paso. Thinking it was a terrorist attack, all area law enforcement agencies were called to respond to the explosion. At the same time, as the story goes, somewhere between two thousand and ten thousand illegals simply walked out of a mile long tunnel that began in Ciudad Juarez onto the streets of El Paso's east side.

"Because I think your terrorists could have used the gas attack as a cover," Danny said.

The president's eyes widened. "A cover for what?"

"You said it yourself. CEOS ensures the continuation of government should a disaster happen in D.C. I believe the terrorists delivered more nukes underneath the city, and not just dirty bombs either."

The president turned white. "Jesus," he murmured. "Hidden in plain sight."

Chapter 78

It was a first in the history of The Group: they were meeting in the same place twice. There was no time to make other arrangements. Lars Karlsson stood at the front of their private meeting room at the Westbury Hotel, held up his hand, and cleared his throat. "Ladies and gentlemen," he announced. The hushed whispers that snuck around the room ceased. Lars tightened his back and slowly rolled his shoulders. He knew the room was clean. The Group could talk openly.

"As I am sure everyone is aware, our great friend and colleague Anthony Fantroy was murdered. Our source inside the White House has assured me that no one in President Butcher's administration is aware of our plans. Furthermore, there was no White House directive to kill the prime minister."

Our source inside the White House. Lars was well aware that most of the people present in the room had no idea who that was, and for good reason. The Group's board of directors rarely wanted to expose names of their contacts for fear of someone leaking that name, either on accident or on purpose.

"What about King Edward's statement this morning?" the French foreign minister called from the back of the room. "It was a hostile, direct message to the Americans. Do we know if King Edward thinks that the president is hiding something?"

Lars didn't get a chance to answer the question before another concern was raised.

"And what is the status of the hunt for Sydney Dumas and Danny Cavanaugh?" the finance minister of Luxembourg wanted to know.

The whispers returned, weaving throughout the attendees. Lars again held up his hand and the room fell silent. "Prime Minister

Fantroy was our link to the Crown. With him gone, I do not have an answer as to the King's thought process. As far as Ms. Dumas is concerned, our White House contact has let me know that both she and Danny Cavanaugh are now at the White House."

Lars paused. The gap in his speech was filled with what he expected, a few concerned gasps and gruff whispers. "Ladies and gentlemen, if I may continue. Ms. Dumas has been placed under house arrest."

"And what of Cavanaugh?"

Lars chose his words carefully. "All that our man knows is that he had a private meeting with the president and then was issued a White House vehicle. Our man is tracking that vehicle as we speak." His explanation quieted the room. "I know that we all are concerned about the events that are unfolding, but we need explanations just as much as the president does. Why was Anthony's plane shot down? Who did it? If White House officials have arrested Ms. Dumas, she either hasn't told them anything about what she saw in Mexico or, if she has, White House officials do not believe her. We need to wait and see what happens with Cavanaugh. He may find out something that is vital to our needs as well. We need to be patient. Our operative Stefan Taber is also in Washington, D.C. Our White House man is keeping in contact with him concerning all relevant events. Taber has assured me that he will monitor Sergeant Cavanaugh and will get back to me with any pertinent information."

"What if Taber fails?" the French foreign minister asked.

Lars smiled. "You all know as well as I do that our operations always have fail-safes. If Taber fails then we will follow our backup plan." Lars cut off a Russian oil baron who was about to speak. He could read the man's mind.

What is this backup plan?

"You all know as well as I do that information is our most valuable asset," Lars continued. He glanced over at the board of directors. They each gave him an approving stare. "Only when the time is right and if it is needed will our fail-safe be discussed."

Chapter 79

Nobody had come out and actually said it; they didn't have to. Sydney was under some sort of house arrest. Because it was the White House, she knew that any number of reasons could be used as an explanation of why she was being held against her will. Her mind was spinning with questions. *Where was Danny? Were they questioning him about killing the FBI agent? Were they trying to blame him for Senator Halsey's death?* Sydney had no answers. Whatever was happening to Danny was out of her control. She had to concentrate on her own situation.

She had been sequestered in a windowless room for what seemed like two hours now. There were no clocks on the walls, and her watch had been taken from her and scanned for explosives when they first entered the White House. She had yet to get it back.

Sydney was tired of sitting at the end of the Lucite table that was bolted to the floor. She pushed back the metal chair and walked toward the only other object in the room. She stared into the wall-length mirror, wondering if people were behind it, staring back at her.

She cupped her hands on the mirror and tried looked through it. It was no use; there was only darkness. She returned to the table and leaned against it. She closed her eyes and prayed to her real father.

I'm here, Father. I'm inside the White House. But I'm still far away from our goal. I need your help. Help me figure out how to succeed.

Sydney opened her eyes and began examining her palms, hoping whoever was watching would think that she was checking the fresh bandages the White House nurse used to dress her wounds. Instead, she used the time to try and figure out how to best confront the villain from Knobby's stories. He was here, inside the White House. It was finally time for Sydney to avenge her parents' death. Only walls, a locked door, and probably fifty armed guards stood in her way.

Chapter 80

Except for a handful of riders striding through the turnstiles, the street level of the L'Enfant Plaza Metro station was empty. Danny approached the station manager's booth still reviewing the Library of Congress security tapes in his mind. Before leaving the White House, he viewed them alone in the Secret Service's conference room. From the high camera angle, Danny saw the backside of a man huddled over a small table in the corner of the Rare Book Reading Room for fifty-six seconds. The scene screamed as to the thief's shrewdness. His body barely moved as he removed the documents from Seward's journal. He was a well-trained thief, an expert lift man. The incident gnawed at Danny.

There's something not right about that scene.

Danny pictured the thief's fake GWU ID. The only feature that anyone would remember was his olive complexion. Every other detail, his common nose, his normal eyebrows, the unimpressive shade of his brown eyes, was achingly forgetful. The thief had used the name Joel Basher. It was easy to remember but hardly worth remembering. Why did he pick it? In Danny's experience, people who used aliases chose the names for a reason, either consciously or subconsciously. What was Joel Basher trying to tell him? And, besides stealing lost documents, was it also Joel Basher who had launched the missile that destroyed Prime Minister Fantroy's plane?

Danny had received the information about the missile attack from the president himself just before he left the Oval Office. The boat from which the missile was launched was a Sea Ray 300 Sundancer. It had been stolen from a marina in Annapolis, Maryland six months ago and moored at the Georgetown Marina only two weeks ago. The slip had been rented three months ago but was left empty, which wasn't unusual. Many of the smaller boats in the marina had been dry-docked over the winter. The yearly cost of renting the slip was paid upfront, in cash, something that wasn't unheard of in a town where privacy concerning such transactions was a necessity. The marina manager remembered that a man, probably in his early forties, had paid the bill, but he couldn't remember any description beyond that. Slip renters were given a keycard to access the portion of the docks that contained the smaller boats, anything less than 40 feet, so no marina worker had interacted with the assailant before he started his mission. The only fingerprints on the boat had matched those of the rightful owner, his family and friends. The shoulder fired missile launcher, which had been found at the bottom of the Potomac River, was garden variety military issue, the kind that was bought and sold on the black market everyday.

Danny pictured the assailant, throttling away from the marina, smiling in the wind on the way to complete his task at hand. *Whoever he was, he was hired to pull this job. But who hired him?*

Danny had to switch gears and concentrate on his new task. He looked inside the station manager's booth. It was empty. He tried the knob. It was locked. He cupped his hands to the glass and peered inside. He was greeted with the strange sight of Post-It notes everywhere. It reminded him of one of those promotional booths that blew money around as the person inside frantically grabbed for every dollar.

"Can I help you?"

Danny spun around to see a black man with mostly gray hair and a wrinkled face standing in front of him. The nametag on his uniform read, "Luther Smalls, Station Manager."

"Luther, I'm Sergeant Danny Cavanaugh with the Texas Rangers." Danny paused. It was good to hear that title flow from his mouth again. "I believe you just got a phone call from the White House ..."

Luther held up his hand. "Say no more. I was told to be an open book for you, Sergeant."

Luther extended the key ring from his belt and inserted a key into the booth's lock. He unlocked it and let the retractable tether yank the ring back to the side of his thick waist.

"After you," Luther told his guest.

Danny immediately crossed the booth to the bank of small monitors that helped Luther keep tabs on various locations around the station. Luther took a load off on a rickety stool in front of the radio equipment. He crossed his arms on his chest. The look in his eyes told Danny that he remained tight-lipped to strangers, especially ones who would question the manner in which he performed his job.

"Were you working when the station was gassed?" Danny asked.

"Yup," Luther replied.

"Did you see anything unusual at that time?"

"You mean other than a yellow fog?"

"Did you get a look at anyone who was acting suspicious? Did you see anything that was not part of the normal day-to-day scene?"

"They already asked me these questions, Sergeant."

"Who did?"

"FBI and TSA." The noise of an approaching train on the lower level caused Luther's eyes to wander over to the bank of monitors. "I didn't see anything unusual."

"What's with the Post-It notes everywhere, Luther?"

Luther's eyes darted back to Danny. "They're for training purposes. But I have to admit, they're cluttering up my sea of tranquility here."

"Training for whom?"

"Training for my replacement. I'm retiring after thirty-four years of faithful service."

"Congratulations."

Luther huffed. It was obviously forced retirement. That was Danny's hook. He would make the old man feel useful, something he probably hadn't felt in a long time.

"Listen Luther, I'm going to be honest with you here. I was told by the president himself not to tell you this, but my instincts tell me otherwise." Luther's eyes came alive. He straightened up on the stool. Just like that, Danny had him. "We think that the gas attack was really a diversion to deliver a nuclear device, or perhaps several nukes, underneath the city. I need you to think like a terrorist. If you were trying to do that, where in this station would be the best place to hide the device without it being detected?"

Luther searched his thoughts. He looked over at the monitors. Then he stood up and peered out the dull window that gave him a full view of the station's upper mezzanine. His stare lasted for nearly a half minute before he moved a muscle. He reached behind Danny, grabbed a rolled-up blueprint, and unrolled it across the radio equipment.

Luther craned his neck around and smiled. "I hope you don't mind getting dirty, Sergeant."

-

While Danny and Luther studied the blueprints in the station manager's booth, a handful of well-trained men tensed in their tight quarters underneath L'Enfant Plaza as the echo of radio squelch bounced around them. Instantly, they all knew the same thing. Something was wrong.

Three long beeps followed by two short ones and then one more long one came over the radio. It was the correct code.

"Copy code. You are go for instructions," their leader whispered into the radio.

A calm, almost chilling voice replied. "You might have a visitor soon."

Chapter 81

Luther sat down on the edge of the platform, dangled his legs over the side, and shoved off. He dropped two feet before hitting the track bed below. He motioned to Danny to throw him the blueprint roll.

"Is it safe for us to be doing this?" Danny asked as he threw him the plans and then jumped down.

"Oh yeah." Luther pointed at the conduit that ran along the far rail. "Just don't touch that, or you'll go up like a pack of firecrackers." He turned and began walking down the tracks toward the far end of the platform. "The next train doesn't come down this line for another three and a half minutes. But that's not a guarantee it won't show up a little early."

Less than a minute later, they had turned the corner of the platform and were squeezing through a narrow passageway that continued underneath the platform. Light faded with every step, while the stench of sewage grew more pungent.

Danny bumped into Luther as he came to an abrupt stop. Luther pulled a mini Maglite flashlight from his belt, clicked it on, and pointed it down at a square sewer grate. The far side of the grate caught Danny's attention. Luther noticed it, too. He was about to say something, when Danny put his finger to his lips and shook his head. He motioned for Luther to follow him back out to the edge of the platform.

The train Luther had warned Danny about was approaching the station. Its abrasive racket camouflaged their conversation.

"Those are fresh scratches," Luther declared over the noise.

Suddenly, the train exploded into the station. It blasted musty wind around them, as its screaming brakes split through Danny's head. He covered his ears and yelled, "When was the last time—"

Luther leaned into Danny's ear as he cut him off. "The sewers under here are inspected every summer and only every summer."

"So, you're saying no one should have been down here this time of year?"

"Except for when the FBI and TSA people were down here after the gas attack."

"Did you see them come down here?" Danny asked.

"No, but I overheard one of the guys talking to his boss. He said they searched every inch of the station. If they did, they should have caught it."

Absolutely, Danny thought. If nothing else, FBI people were thorough. *Maybe they did, and didn't report it. Or maybe, like Crayton Ripley, there were a few more bad FBI apples up here in D.C.*

"You remember any names of the FBI or TSA investigators?" Danny asked.

"I'm just a lowly subway grunt, Sergeant. They didn't so much as say boo to me."

Danny wanted to inform someone of this new twist, but there was no one. He was by himself investigating what more and more looked like an inside job. He peered toward the platform as the train noise began dying down while he imagined the solitary scene of the Mexican wilderness from the cabin's porch, the scene that was almost the last one of his life. He had an uneasy feeling he was in those same dire straits here. Only this time, he had to worry about someone else taking his life.

He turned back to Luther. "Let's have a look at those plans."

The train finally came to a stop, and so did all the noise. Luther squatted and unrolled the blueprints on the ground. "These map the sewer system from 395 to Constitution Avenue and from 2nd to 9th Street," he muttered as he shuffled through the prints before he came to the one he needed, "including the part that runs directly underneath us."

Danny studied the page as the train began rolling, causing noise to fill the station again. The sewer grate was the starting line of a maze of tunnels that fanned out in every direction. But Danny needed only seconds to see the layout before it was tattooed on his brain.

"Which way's north?" he asked Luther as he stood up, ready to move.

Luther pointed. "That way."

"Great." Danny took a few steps back toward the sewer grate.

"Wait a second," Luther yelled. The train snaked its way out of the station, and Luther continued in a whisper. "There are at least two dozen different tunnels down there. Not to mention all the service passageways and utility corridors. You need to take the prints with you."

"They'll just slow me down."

"But you only looked at them for a second. You won't know where you're going."

Danny motioned for Luther's flashlight, and Luther gave it to him. "Let's just say I have a pretty good memory."

Chapter 82

Sydney knocked on the door, but there was no reply. She knocked again. Still nothing. *The door must be guarded*, she thought. Someone had to be out there.

"How much longer will I be in here?" she asked to whoever was beyond the door.

Silence.

She turned to the mirror on the far wall. "I have to use the bathroom," Sydney said as she clutched her stomach. "Please. I'm not feeling well." Finally, there was a buzzing sound and then the door opened. A Secret Service agent stood in the doorway. A woman. Blond, steely-eyed, and not likely to be charmed by Sydney's feminine wiles. Sydney may have been disappointed, but she played it off well. She clutched her stomach again and winced.

"This way, ma'am," the agent ordered, a submachine gun tucked in her armpit. The agent motioned down the hall with her gun barrel. "Let's go."

As they walked down a barren hallway, Sydney eyed as much of her surroundings as she could. The holding room was located in the basement. Naked lightbulbs were covered by wire cages and stuck high on the concrete walls every ten feet. Several pipes that ran along the walls provided the only color to the area. Each one was painted with different colors and labeled Air, Water, Sewer.

They turned down a narrow hallway lined with office doors and tiny nameplates too far away to read.

"Hold it, ma'am," the agent barked. "Make a right."

Sydney did as she was told. They moved into a shorter hallway. A men's room door was to her left, and a ladies' room was to her right. Straight ahead was another office. A black and white nameplate hanging on the door read, "White House Military Office." Below it, in print that Sydney could read, was a name that had been burned into her mind long ago.

Sydney's father was listening after all. He had answered her prayers. The target of her lifelong search was right in front of her, only steps away.

Sydney was an instant from breaking into a run when the agent grabbed her by the arm and turned her toward the ladies' room.

"Make it fast," the agent said. Sydney entered the bathroom with the agent on her heels. There were three stalls, and Sydney took the one at the far end. She shut the door behind her and sat down on the toilet. Her whole body began shaking. She opened her mouth to let soundless cries escape. Hot tears plummeted from her eyes, staining her cheeks. Her anger clouded her thinking.

How? How? How?

The question that pounded in her head was as much for her parents' senseless death as it was for how she was going to proceed.

Don't blow it now, Sydney. You're too close. Stay calm and think.

She turned around, sank to her knees, and stared into the small pool of water in the toilet bowl. She imagined it was a hundred times its size. She closed her eyes and pictured herself immersed in refreshing water. She could feel the water supporting her, challenging her. It was the only place where her thoughts ran clear. It was the only place where Sydney Dumas could really breathe.

Sydney's eyes shot open. *Of course*, she thought. She tightened her stomach and swallowed enough air to fill her lungs. Then she opened her mouth and heaved.

The agent remained silent, but Sydney heard her approach.

Sydney heaved again and followed it with several hacking coughs.

"Ma'am, are you okay?"

Sydney kept her eyes in the toilet, but she heard the door open. Then she felt the agent hovering over her. "Could you please hold my hair back?" Sydney paused to breathe hard. "I don't want to get vomit in it."

Sydney heaved again for the exclamation point on the end of her request. Then she felt the agent pulling her hair back with both hands.

Sydney took in a deep breath and heaved again. But this time, she exploded off the toilet like it was a starting block. The back of her head caught the agent on the chin. Sydney shot up next to the stunned agent and grabbed the back of her shirt. Then, with every ounce of strength, she rammed the agent headfirst into the tiled wall. The agent hit the wall just as she tripped over the toilet. Her limp body slid down between the toilet and the side wall. She was motionless.

Sydney bent down to check the agent's vitals. She thought about her friend Gabrielle back home. When they were still teenagers, Gabrielle was on the diving team while Sydney was on the swim team. Sydney was watching as Gabrielle was practicing her diving one day. As she began a reverse one and a half somersault, Sydney noticed that she was too close to the board. She started to scream to Gabrielle, but it was too late. Her head cracked against the board, and she plunged lifeless into the water. Sydney was first in the pool after her. When they got her out, she was concerned that Gabrielle was dead, but the diving coach reassured her that she had only been knocked unconscious. "The head can take a pounding," he had told her. The agent's beating pulse confirmed the diving coach's words once again.

Blood began trickling down from the agent's forehead, but Sydney couldn't worry about that now. The agent was alive, and that's all that mattered. Sydney took the agent's submachine gun and ran out of the stall. She eased open the bathroom door and took one step into the hallway. She gazed at the submachine gun in her hands. *I will kill him if I have this*, she thought. Sydney Dumas was not a killer. She would not murder another human being and then spend the rest of her life behind bars. She stepped back inside the bathroom and shoved the gun into the trash can.

Unarmed now, Sydney stepped back into the hallway, took a deep breath, and walked purposefully toward the door that held the name of the man who killed her parents, gathering courage with every step. As she stood outside the office door, Sydney could feel the weight of revenge in every cell of her body. Her legs were brimming with nervous energy, but nevertheless felt incredibly heavy. As she put her hand on the doorknob, Sydney fueled herself by the memory of Knobby's final story on his deathbed. It was about the man who killed her parents. Knobby started off with his name.

"I know the man that killed your parents, Sydney. I didn't want to tell you his name, but I can see that you will never rest until you know."

The name that crossed Knobby's lips all those years ago now echoed in Sydney's head, rekindling the promise that she made to herself in that hospital room as the warmth from Knobby's hand slipped away.

I will seek vengeance for what that man did to my family.

Sydney felt a surge of adrenaline wash over her. By the time she swung open the door, Sydney Dumas was ready for her ultimate confrontation.

Chapter 83

Danny dropped down into complete blackness. He heard his feet splash and then seconds later felt cold liquid ooze around his borrowed dress socks. *I can't believe I'm in a sewer in a suit,* he thought. *I can't believe I'm in a sewer at all.*

He propped his feet up on the sides of the pipe, straddling the sewer water. He looked up and saw Luther's head eclipsing most of the deadened light that fell through the hole from the Metro station. The voice inside Danny's brain was begging him to climb back up the pipe and go for reinforcements. But he couldn't. The president didn't know whom to trust besides a stranger; that meant Danny had to fly solo. He tried looking on the bright side. He had the element of surprise on his side. The presence of more bodies would only chase away that advantage.

From his armpit holster, Danny yanked out the SIG Sauer Tactical 9 millimeter that Peter Devon had given him. As he gripped it, he remembered the similar gun the Texas Rangers had issued him what seemed like an eternity ago. *Feels like old times,* he thought as he began an awkward hike down the pipe.

He was counting each step and figured he had made it a full city block. He had to be nearing the Air and Space Museum. After hearing Danny's theory back in the Oval Office about delivering a bomb underneath the city, the president showed him the map of the Capitol escape tunnels. One of the exit points was in the Air and Space Museum's basement. The sewer system ran right by it.

Danny continued shuffling north until he felt air blast him from his left and right. He inched forward in the pitch dark until his shoes reached a small ledge. He had reached a major pipe intersection. *Must be the one under Independence Avenue.* He continued his hike north for what he thought was another two hundred feet, when a stream of cool air hit his right side. He stuck out his arm and felt a grate protrude from the wall. He visualized the sewer system map. Behind the grate had to be the access pipe that led to the utility corridor. On Luther's blueprint, the utility corridor ran north and south for several thousand feet, sandwiched between the sewer tunnel and the Air and Space Museum basement. If someone wanted to gain access to the Capitol tunnels, this would be the starting line.

Danny felt around the grate's edges and found hinges on the right side. Then he felt the left side and found the handle. He used Luther's flashlight to illuminate the handle. It looked like it had recently taken a beating. The thin metal was battered and cut, the fresh scratches gleaming in the flashlight's beam. Then Danny noticed the handle hung on a round clasp. It didn't take a detective to realize that someone had recently beaten off a padlock.

Danny turned off the flashlight and rolled away from the grate. He had two choices. One, he could explore the pipe without any light, or two, stay behind the grate and use the flashlight to get a good look before leaping into total confusion.

There was really no choice. He peered past the grate and switched the flashlight back on. He followed the pipe past the end of the flashlight's beam into the darkness. He squinted and thought he saw something. He fooled with the flashlight, tightening and then widening its beam. He edged closer to the grate. He was more interested in trying to see what was at the other end of the tunnel than in his own safety. That's when a gun was aimed at him, and the shooter pulled the trigger.

Chapter 84

The gleaming pistol aimed at Sydney had no effect on her will. She stared into the eyes of C. Benjamin Speakes.

Speakes didn't say a word. He had already slithered around her to shut his office door. A razor-sharp blankness was etched on his face. Sydney could tell that things like killing were all in a day's work for the director of the White House Military Office. But could he do it here in the White House? Supposedly the safest place on the planet?

Speakes eased over to his desk and leaned against it. "You have your father's eyes." His southern accent rolled like a paddlewheel boat lulling along the Mississippi. He maintained the relaxed confidence of a man interviewing her for a job, not as someone who had just been exposed by an outsider. He coolly waved his weapon at her. "I thought you might pay me a visit down here, so I took the necessary precautions."

"You killed my parents, you bastard," Sydney spat.

Speakes shook his head. "Your father killed himself and your mother with his betrayal."

"That's bullshit." Sydney's rage amplified. She now longed for the agent's submachine gun, damn the consequences.

Speakes cocked his head and sighed. "Life is about choices, Ms. Dumas. Your father chose to become one of us. Then he chose to walk away. He knew the consequences of his actions."

Sydney's anger engulfed her now. She balled her hands into fists. She didn't care if she lived or died now. All she wanted to do was to hurt this man who took the parents she never knew from her.

She charged Speakes. Even though the barrel of the gun was right in front of her, she kept her eyes locked on his. He never flinched, never twitched, never even blinked. Sydney was only steps away from him when someone grabbed her from behind and slammed her against the floor.

Chapter 85

The bullet ricocheted off the grate before the gunshot registered inside Danny's head. He lunged sideways and tried to steady himself as two more bullets ripped through the rancid sewer air.

Danny stuck the SIG Sauer's barrel through the grate and blindly fired twice. Through the echo from his two rounds, he heard a voice travel down the length of the pipe.

"Should we take him or retreat?"

Danny helped them out with their decision. He fired two more shots into the tunnel and listened intently. He didn't hear any more voices. But he did hear movement, and it was fading fast.

He yanked on the grate, and it swung open. He leaped up into the access tunnel and banged his head on the roof. He bent down and began racing down the pipe, with only the tiny flashlight lighting his way.

The access tunnel emptied into the utility corridor. Danny aimed the flashlight and his gun in both directions. What he saw a few feet away to his right confirmed his suspicions. Someone had pierced a hole in the corridor's east wall.

It would be suicide to chase after them, Danny thought. Not only was he outnumbered, but whoever was down here, they knew their route where he would be flying blind.

Danny hiked back to the main sewer tunnel and then sprinted through the soggy mess until he came to the L'Enfant station access ladder. He climbed up it and pulled himself out into the station, where Luther was waiting for him.

"I heard gunshots. Are you okay?"

Danny nodded while he caught his breath. "Yeah, I'm fine. Listen, can you contact the agents who investigated the gas attack?"

"Yeah."

"Call them and tell them you have a security situation."

"What do I do once they're here?"

Danny pointed to the sewer grate. "Tell them to investigate the sewers. The first utility corridor access pipe north of Independence Avenue; someone punched a hole in the corridor's wall and gained access to the Capitol escape tunnels."

"How'd you know about the escape tunnels?"

"Who do you think sent me down here, Luther?" Danny paused as the revelation nearly knocked the wind out of him. The president was the only one who knew he was coming here.

"Sergeant, you okay?" Luther asked.

"Yeah. You got a cell phone?"

"Do dogs have fleas? 'Course I do."

"Let's exchange numbers." They did, Luther writing Danny's down, and Danny only needing to hear Luther's once.

"Who shot at you?" Luther asked.

"Don't know. Hopefully, we'll find out once the agents do their thing." Danny stared into Luther's eyes. "Luther, whatever you do, don't give the agents details over the phone. Keep them in the dark until they get down here. Just tell them it's a security situation, that's all."

"Why?"

"Because I need some time."

"Time for what?"

Danny thought about the timing of the next events. He should be arriving at the White House just as FBI and TSA agents swarmed L'Enfant Plaza. "Time to question my only suspect."

Chapter 86

Someone must have seen us. Someone must be coming.

The calm look on Speakes's face gave Sydney her answer. He had been waiting for her with a gun. A Secret Service agent was also hiding inside his office, ready to subdue her. Speakes had tied up all the loose ends.

They had proceeded past a thick steel door and had been walking down a darkened concrete hallway for a full minute now. A little more than a hundred feet in front of her, the hallway split into five different directions.

Wherever they were going, Sydney knew it might be the last place she would ever see. She had to think fast. If it was just she and Speakes, she might have been able to overpower him. But it wasn't. Her hands had been bound together with a plastic zip-tie, and she was sandwiched between Speakes and the muscled Secret Service agent.

They were now fifty feet from the intersection. Sydney figured they were moving away from the White House. She pictured the park across Pennsylvania Avenue, where the green pup tents were. Could they be underneath it? The memory of Danny exploding from the tent in his underwear and grabbing onto her stung Sydney. *Danny has to find me.* She concentrated on the five smaller hallways in front of her. The most important question dawned on her.

How can I let Danny know where they've taken me?

Sydney looked down at her hands. She felt useless with them bound together. She balled them up in tight fists and applied as much pressure to the bands around her wrists as she could. It was no use. Then, looking at her bandaged palms, Sydney had an idea. *Leave Danny a trail of breadcrumbs.*

She could stain the pathway through the hallways with her blood. But how would she get the blood flowing? She thought about the acting that she had performed so far. She could act once more, couldn't she? Speakes and the agent wouldn't blame her if she started crying. They probably expected her to. She's just a poor, scared girl after all, they would think. So, Sydney gave it to them. She began to sniffle and then she put her palms to her face. To make herself cry, Sydney recalled Knobby's details about her parents' death.

"Speakes rammed their car and pushed it off the bridge into the river. The impact crushed the car around your parents. There was no way they could escape."

In trying to make herself a better swimmer, Sydney would hold her breath under the water, breaking her previous records again and again. She would stay down, her lungs nibbling on the last bits of air inside them. But soon she would be spent. Her lungs would be aching for air, her body doing anything it could to feed itself. Her cheeks would hollow, and her throat would close in on itself. Her arms and legs were free to jettison her back to the surface and grasp the oxygen her lungs so desperately needed. It was at that point that she always thought about her parents. They were trapped underneath the water. They weren't able to grasp air from the surface. They went past the point of no return.

The tears began to flow. Sydney let herself feel the pain as she kept her face in her palms. She stopped walking and bent over. When she did, her tears turned into sobs, and she went to work on her hands. She used her teeth to tear through the bandages and then bite at the scabs on her palms.

The agent ordered her to move. She felt pain throbbing in her hands, but she didn't want to look at them for fear of getting caught. They were at the intersection now, and the agent pulled her to the second hallway on the right. This was Sydney's only chance.

"No," she screamed. "I'm not going anywhere! Help! Someone! Help!" Sydney clawed at the side of the tunnel, making sure her palms came in contact with it each time.

"Shut her up," Speakes ordered.

The agent was trying to control Sydney's arms from the side, but it was no use. He finally got her in a bear hug from behind,

clasping her arms against her body. They continued down the next
hallway, the agent having to heave her along. Speakes turned around,
his molasses words dripping from his mouth.

"Don't worry, Ms. Dumas. It will all be over soon."

Chapter 87

"May God bless you all, and may God continue to bless the United States of America."

President Butcher looked up from the podium after finishing the conclusion to his State of the Union speech. He was alone in the Family Theater. The speech was written out on paper in front of him and had been scrolling across the teleprompter, but Jack didn't need either crutches. Jack Butcher forced himself to memorize every political speech he had ever made. It started out as the method he used to get Simon to go to sleep as a toddler. All Jack needed to do was start in with his ideas about bureaucratic reform or fixing budget deficits in Simon's darkened bedroom, and soon his son would be sawing wood. Reading his speeches to Simon proved to be good luck, and before every speech Jack made, the final version would be run by Simon first. As the years passed, Simon would no longer fall asleep. Instead, he would applaud after his dad finished speaking, while at the same time offering constructive criticism. Even when his disease burrowed pain deep into his bones, Simon still managed to clap for his dad as tears filled his wincing eyes.

As he stood at the podium, Jack pictured his son in the front row, clapping for his dad once again. Jack swore that he could even hear Simon's applause. His eyes caught movement at the back of the theater. Jack squinted beyond the stage lights and saw two bodies emerge from the shadows. The first was Vanessa Dempsey. She was escorting Sergeant Cavanaugh down the side aisle. He was the one who was clapping.

Jack stepped down from the stage. Vanessa could tell that he wanted privacy. She turned and left the theater.

"I'm glad you like my speech," Jack said.

"I wasn't applauding for that, Mr. President. I am clapping for the way you played me. Bravo, sir."

"What are you talking about?"

Danny stepped toward the president from the end of the aisle. "There were men in the sewers underneath L'Enfant Plaza. They knew I was coming. You set me up."

"Freeze!"

The order came from the back of the theater. Jack recognized Peter Devon's voice before he made it out from the shadows. He bounded halfway down the aisle and aimed his pistol at Danny. Danny stopped moving, but his eyes never wavered. They continued piercing through Jack.

"On the floor, Cavanaugh! Now!"

Danny didn't move. He didn't even blink.

Peter Devon cocked his gun. "I'll give you two seconds, Cavanaugh. You won't hear number three. One ..."

Even though Danny was required to relinquish his weapon as soon as he entered the White House grounds, he acted like a man who still had the upper hand.

"Two ..."

Jack held up his hand. Peter Devon nodded but kept his gun firmly affixed on his target.

"Can you tell me why they knew you were coming?" Jack asked.

Danny maintained his grip on Jack's eyes as he explained himself. "I heard them talking. One of them asked, 'Should we take *him* or retreat?' They knew only one man that was there. You and I were the only two who knew I was going there alone, Mr. President. And I didn't rat on myself."

"I'm sorry, Danny," Jack said, his words nearly whispers. Danny finally blinked as he unfurled himself from a tensed ready position. It was obvious he thought the president of the United States was about to confess. Jack continued. "But I did tell one other person about your mission."

Chapter 88

Simon Shilling was in the middle of a phone call when the door to his office cracked open. Jack only saw the look on his face for a moment before Peter Devon's shoulders eclipsed the doorway.

Seconds later, Devon was standing over Simon. Jack had specifically requested that he not draw his weapon, for there was no need. Devon could probably kill any one of them in a matter of moments with his bare hands. Jack didn't want to make this moment more of a spectacle than it was already.

"I'll have to get back to you," Simon uttered into the phone. He slowly hung it up, his eyes never wavering from Jack's. "Is there something you need, Mr. President?"

Jack felt his pulse throb in the back of his head. He could barely get the words out. "Simon, I think you know why we're here."

Simon gazed at the other two men in the room. Peter Devon remained motionless next to him. Danny stood in the back corner, his eyes at his feet. "No, Mr. President. I don't have a clue."

"Simon, you were the only one I told about Sergeant Cavanaugh going to investigate L'Enfant Plaza." He paused and shook his head. "You were the only one."

Simon mashed his teeth together. "I don't like the sound of what you're getting at, Mr. President."

"Sergeant Cavanaugh was ambushed at the station, Simon. How could that happen?"

Simon squinted at the man who was both his boss and his friend. "I don't know, sir."

"A hole was punched through a utility corridor down there that breeched the Capitol tunnels. Whether or not someone delivered a bomb down there doesn't matter now, Simon. The entire NEST team is headed there as we speak to check it out."

"Better safe then sorry, Mr. President."

Jack lunged at his chief of staff. "Goddamn it, Simon! What did you do? Tell me what you've done!"

The president had a death grip on Simon's suit jacket and was only inches from his face. Out of the corner of his eye, he saw Peter Devon move his wrist to his mouth and whisper. Devon was concentrating on whatever information he was receiving through the transmitter that snaked up from his collar into his ear.

Peter Devon eyed the president. "Sir, we have a security breech inside the White House. I need you to come with me."

Devon was already steaming at Jack like a linebacker before he started his objection. "I'm not leaving this room until I get some answers, Pete."

Jack's words had no effect on the Secret Service agent. "Sir, I can't do that. We need to follow procedure. I will see to it that Mr. Shilling is placed under house arrest, but I must get you to a secure location now."

Jack turned to the other law enforcement officer in the room. He hoped Danny could read his burning glare.

Do something!

Peter Devon clamped his hands on the president. He was practically carrying Jack across Simon's office when he suddenly stopped. Jack felt Peter's solid grip release from his right tricep. The locomotion that burned into the small of his back vanished. Jack turned around and saw Sergeant Cavanaugh standing there with Peter Devon's gun in his hands.

"You heard the president, Agent Devon. We're not leaving this room until we get some answers. Now tell us what you heard in your earpiece."

Devon remained silent.

"Goddamn it, Pete," Jack snapped. "Answer him! This is no time for SOP bullshit!"

Devon was staring at Danny with hollow eyes. Jack could tell that he was burning with rage that Cavanaugh got the better of him. He gritted his teeth as he leveled his voice. "Sydney Dumas is missing."

Chapter 89

It was obvious Benjamin Speakes had performed this procedure many times. He stepped ahead of the Secret Service agent and set his eye at the end of a scope that jutted out from the wall. Like he did on the steel door they passed through just before the hallway intersection, Speakes hit a sequence of numbers on the keypad beneath the scope. He then pushed on the wall that Sydney thought was their dead end. The wall heaved open, and she was ushered out into a storage room.

She continued to let herself be manhandled as the three of them ducked out of the storage room door and shuffled down a short hallway to a stairway. Speakes showed little sign of his age as he vaulted up the stairs two at a time. At each landing, he checked the stairs in front of him and then motioned for the agent to bring their prize.

Where were they?

Sydney tried to piece together their location from her surroundings. The stairway wasn't distinct. It was bare concrete; the only markings were "Floor 1, Floor 2, Floor 3" at each landing. They stopped on the fifth-floor landing.

"Wait here," Speakes instructed. He opened the door and coasted through it before it closed on its pneumatic hinge. Sydney caught a glimpse of a red patterned carpet before the door shut. Were they in a government building? Perhaps one of the memorials? She ached for a sense of direction. She tried remembering the scenes around the White House perimeter as she scrambled around it earlier that day. Had they gone north, south, east, or west?

As they stood there waiting inside the stairwell, Sydney stared at the agent. He stared back without emotion. She stretched her fingers and felt pain in the wounds. Pain meant they were still open. Pain meant there was still blood ready to flow. She started sobbing again and turned away from him, putting her hands on the door to steady herself.

"Step back from the door," the agent ordered, grabbing her shoulder. Sydney spun back around and collapsed in the agent's arms. She kept crying as she maneuvered in the agent's grip, turning him around so that his back was to the door.

Just then, the door flew back open. "What the hell is going on?" Speakes asked. He stood there with a towel in his hand. Sydney stared at it, and her questions were answered. Embroidered at the bottom of the towel was the crest of the Willard Hotel.

We are at a hotel. But why such a public place?

"She collapsed sir," the agent replied.

Speakes smiled. "Right." Then he gazed into Sydney's eyes. "Trying to seduce your way to freedom, Ms. Dumas?" Speakes threw the towel to the agent. "Stuff it in her mouth," he ordered. The agent did as he was told. Speakes glared at Sydney. "Not a peep, young lady. Like I said, it will all be over soon."

Sydney normally wouldn't have complied, but she wanted to get out of the stairwell before they noticed she had marked the back of the door with her blood. Speakes motioned to the agent, and he began shuttling Sydney through the doorway. Speakes was out on point, five paces in front of them. As they ventured further down the open hallway, the agent's grip tightened around Sydney's tricep and shoulder, steering her in Speakes's wake.

Speakes made a sharp right down the only other hallway on the floor. The agent and Sydney followed. As they made the turn, she heard the stairwell door finally shut. She prayed that Danny would find the marks she had hopefully left on it.

There were only four doors on the entire hallway. They stood much farther apart than normal hotel room doors. Speakes rapped his knuckle only once on the closest door to his left. It opened and Sydney's heart dropped into her stomach. Standing before her was Stefan Taber.

"Ms. Dumas," Taber purred. "I finally caught up to you."

Chapter 90

Danny pictured the five Secret Service agents that just burst in the room like they were five gang members ready to take him out. They all had the latest in weaponry; each Beretta Px4 Storm was equipped with laser sights and all five laser sighting dots were aimed at Danny's head. Danny had backed himself into the corner of Simon Shilling's office. The only thing between him and a hundred rounds screaming from the agents' pistols was the president of the United States.

While Danny's body pumped adrenaline, the president seemed relaxed. Of course, it was his idea for Danny to take him hostage.

"Stand down!" President Butcher yelled to the agents. They didn't budge. "Peter! Tell them to drop their weapons and stand down!"

Using Devon's handcuffs, Danny had shackled Peter Devon and Simon Shilling, kneeling together, through the arms of Simon's desk chair. Every vein in Devon's reddened face bulged. It seemed like he could burst out of Danny's impromptu cage any second.

Danny put his thumb on the gun's hammer. He imagined cocking it before he did it. It would then only take the slightest bit of pressure, and Jack Butcher would be dead. Danny couldn't have the death of a president on his hands, accident or not. But he didn't dare take his thumb off the hammer either. He knew the mind games that spun during moments like these probably better than the Secret Service agents did. He had no doubt seen more action in the line of duty than they had. He couldn't do anything that looked weak. He decided the only thing to do was to stare down every agent, starting with the short, balding one to his far left.

From left to right. Read them like the open books that they are.

"You heard the president. Stand down." It was Peter Devon. The words shot purposefully from his mouth.

Like showgirls in a line, the agents moved one by one, laying their guns on the ground.

"Now your radios, earpieces, and mikes," the president ordered. "Take them off and throw them in the middle of the room."

President Butcher tugged away from Danny. He collected the communication equipment and, except for one set that he gave Danny, threw them into the empty fireplace at the far end of the room. He did the same with the agents' guns except for one, which he held firmly in both hands.

"What's the best way to make sure they stay here, Sergeant?" the president asked Danny.

Danny thought for only a moment before ordering the agents. "Take out your handcuffs, both sets, and your keys to them. Throw the keys in the middle of the floor and then handcuff yourself to the person next to you with both sets of cuffs." Danny waited for them to perform the procedure. "You two on the end, take your empty handcuffs, strap one shackle to your wrist and the other one to the radiator."

Simon Shilling spoke as the agents trudged over to the radiator and shackled themselves to it. "Honestly, Mr. President, is this really necessary? Now you're tying up your own detail when there's a security alert in the building? You're not thinking—"

"Shut up, Simon! You were the only one I told about Cavanaugh going to the Metro station!"

Simon's eyes became slits. "I didn't tell anyone about him going to the station, Mr. President."

"We'll see if that's true then, won't we?"

"Mr. President, I agree with Mr. Shilling," Peter Devon said. "There is a security breech in the building, sir. You need at least one of us—"

The president cut him off. "Pete, I don't know what's going on here in my house, on my watch! Sergeant Cavanaugh is the only one who isn't a part of us! He's the only one I can trust!" The president smirked. "Besides, I'm a big boy and we've got guns. I'm sure we can take care of ourselves."

Danny collected the keys from the floor and tucked them into his pocket. "Agent Devon, give me the details of the security alert."

Peter Devon was no longer trying to show off for his crew. He had witnessed a president throw himself into harm's way for something other than himself, much like Devon had been doing for most of his career. He looked over at the president, and Jack Butcher nodded.

"Ms. Dumas needed to use the restroom. The agent assigned to guard her, Laura Downing, was found unconscious in the ladies' room on the East Wing basement level. Her weapon is missing."

"You know how to get there, sir?" Danny asked the president.

The president nodded. "Let's get going." He started for the door that led into the Oval Office and then stopped. "Pete, how's Agent Downing doing?"

"She's stable, sir. They're taking her to the infirmary now."

The president jogged out of Simon's office with Danny on his heels. They were halfway across the Oval Office when the president tucked the agent's pistol in his waistband underneath the back of his suit jacket.

"You better hide your weapon unless you want to have every member of my staff on you like stink on shit."

Danny tucked Devon's pistol underneath his shirt. "Mr. President, I don't want to kill our momentum here, but Simon and the agents could just start yelling for help."

"Pete won't let them." The president reached the door that led into the Oval's waiting area.

"Why not?"

The president turned to Danny. "Because Agent Devon realizes I need to do this."

"What about Simon, sir?"

"I can't … I just don't know. I have a hard time believing that Simon's got something to do with this mess. Someone may be using Simon, setting him up. They may have his office bugged, who knows. But I have to play this thing out for whoever's pulling the strings."

The president cracked the door and looked out into the waiting area next to Vanessa Dempsey's desk. It, along with her chair, was empty.

The president faced Danny again. "We need to hurry."

Danny gave him a fairly obvious look. "Don't wait on me, sir."

"You don't understand. We've got another problem."

"What's that?"

"The Capitol's not the only building that has escape tunnels."

Chapter 91

A smile crept onto Benjamin Speakes's gray lips. He was sitting in an elegant winged-back chair that matched the hunter green stripes in the hotel suite's wallpaper.

Sydney was sitting down on the unmade bed. She watched Stefan Taber wander in through the French doors that separated the bedroom from the rest of the suite. He sipped on a crystal glass of ice water as he sat down on the crumpled white sheets next to her. They were trying to intimidate her, using the bed as leverage. They wanted her to think that they might molest her, even rape her, if she didn't give them what they wanted. Sydney willed herself to think positive thoughts.

Danny will come for me.

She had to keep these two men guessing. She had to keep them going in circles for as long as possible. She looked Speakes straight in the eye with no fear and zero respect. Then she used the same look on Taber. "Let me guess. There's a piece missing from your puzzle, and you think I have it." She settled her eyes on Speakes again. "But if you ask me, you're missing more than just one piece."

Speakes ignored her taunt. "You've surmounted incredible obstacles to reach the president, Sydney. Why did you feel the need to see him?"

"So there it is," Sydney managed an irreverent smile. "Take a guess, Speakes. Take a wild guess." Speakes remained silent. "No? Here's a hint, I told him all about the Bilderbergers. I told him what I witnessed in Mexico."

"So what did you tell him?"

"I told him about the lawsuit that Japan issued against the United States."

"Countries sue each other all the time."

"But not for payment in gold. Not when they already struck a blow against the U.S. by stopping their debt purchases." Sydney narrowed her eyes at Speakes. "I worked for Dexter Walsh. I know what he's capable of."

"And what's that?"

"He's engineering the financial collapse of America."

"Did the president believe you?"

"Yes. Especially since I also showed him Senator Booker Halsey's signature on the lawsuit. Like you, Halsey was a bottom feeder, a pawn the Bilderbergers play with."

Speakes eyes flashed. "You have no idea what you're talking about, young lady."

"Really? I know you work for the Bilderbergers."

Speakes laughed, but his nervous eyes gave him away. "I'm not interested in your fantasies, Ms. Dumas."

"What I have to say is the furthest thing from fantasy, Speakes. Before his death, Colin Tanner filled me in with explicit details about who you are and what the Bilderbergers do. As soon as I saw the lawsuit in Mexico, I knew what it meant. I beat you, *fichu bâtard!*"

Speakes laughed again. But this time, his eyes were steady as he leaned forward. "You're not as smart as you think, Sydney," he whispered. "We know everything about you. Let me ask you a question. How do you think a lowly economics professor at a second-rate institution becomes an ICJ judge?"

Sydney jumped ahead. She couldn't believe she didn't see it. Her ex-boyfriend, Alexandre Lacoste, the prince of Monaco, the one who nominated her supposedly because of her talent and her intelligence, was he one of them?

"Alexandre Lacoste is a Bilderberger," she stated flatly.

Speakes saw the realization crash into Sydney. "You thought you knew everything, but you didn't know Lacoste is one of us? Tsk-tsk-tsk. Oh well, what's that old saying, love is blind?"

"So what? This was all some kind of test?"

"If you want to think of it that way. There's more than one way to skin a cat."

Sydney's mind scrambled. *Is he telling the truth? Or is he just trying to confuse me?* Sydney recognized her situation. Speakes thought he had won. There was no reason for him to play games with her any longer. All she could do was keep him talking.

"How's that?"

Speakes shook his head. "Uh-uh, Sydney. You'll just have to die guessing." Speakes only needed to look at Taber. In an instant, his powerful hands were on her.

Chapter 92

As soon as they entered the West Wing basement, the president broke into a run. When they reached the East Wing basement, the president explained to Danny that there was only one possible way that Sydney could get out of the building without anyone seeing her. The tunnels.

Danny took the lead as they came upon the women's restroom in the East Wing basement. Blood covered the tiles in the corner of the stall where Agent Downing had been lying. He eyed everything in the room, trying to get a sense of what happened.

"Sergeant." The whisper trickled in from just outside the restroom.

Danny retreated to the hallway. The president was staring at the door in front of him. "Yes, Mr. President?"

"Jesus. Why didn't I think of him sooner?"

"Who?"

The president pointed to the name on the door. "Ben Speakes. The Wizard of Oz."

"Wizard of Oz?"

"As director of the White House Military Office, Speakes's hand reaches almost everywhere. He controls Air Force One, the marine helicopters, Camp David, all communications and computer systems, the White House mess." The president's gaze hardened. "He even controls the nuclear football."

But while the last part of the president's statement made dread clutch Danny's core, his next words wiped away the confusion that had blurred his thoughts ever since L'Enfant Plaza.

"Speakes also controls the White House garage."

"How much do you want to bet that all White House vehicles are LoJacked?" Danny asked, already knowing the answer.

"You took a White House car to the L'Enfant station, right?"

"Yes, sir."

"He used the GPS to find out where you were going." Realization waved across the president's face. "It wasn't Simon. Speakes told the people in the sewer you were coming."

Danny reached for his pistol and motioned for the president to take cover. He approached Speakes's office door and stood to the side with his back to the wall. He tried the doorknob. It was locked. He spun off the wall and kicked in the door. He wasn't surprised to find an empty office.

Danny whipped around. "Sir, does Speakes know about the tunnels?"

"Ben Speakes has worked here under seven presidents, close to forty years. He probably had a hand in building the goddamn things."

Great, Danny thought. "Can you lead the way, sir?"

"Absolutely."

The two of them made a left and scampered down the hallway. They came to an unmarked, gunmetal gray door with a keypad on the wall. The president entered his code and opened it. They shot inside, only to reach another gray door. This time, an eye scanner jutted out from the wall with a keypad underneath it. The president jammed his eye into the scanner and waited. A bell chimed and then he punched a code into the keypad. An electronic lock buzzed, and the president yanked open the door.

Danny followed him past the open door and couldn't believe what he was seeing. A long concrete hallway stood in front them. At the other end, the hallway split into five smaller passageways. The president was already moving, running at a solid clip with his gun in his hand, down the hallway. Danny caught up to him at the hallway intersection.

"Now what?" President Butcher asked.

Danny produced the Secret Service agent's radio from his pocket. "We call for backup." He put the radio to his lips and was about to talk when he stopped. He walked toward the edge of the fourth passageway.

"What is it, Sergeant?" the president asked.

Danny moved over so the president could see the thin slivers of blood that stained the concrete wall.

"Is it blood?" President Butcher asked.

"Yes, sir. More important, it's Sydney's blood."

"How can you be sure?"

"She had cuts on her palms." Danny put his own palms on top of the bloodstains and then held them up. Thin streaks of blood stained his skin. "She was trying to tell us which tunnel they used."

The president lunged into the tunnel. "So let's go."

"Mr. President."

The president stopped. "What?"

"Sir, I've been in situations like this one before. It's still time to call in the reinforcements."

Chapter 93

Taber had Sydney locked in a full nelson submission hold. Panic all but paralyzed her entire body. She tried to gather enough air to scream, but it simply wasn't there.

Taber dragged her toward the bathroom. As they crossed the threshold, Sydney's eyes bulged. The claw-foot tub was filled with water. Her heart doubled its pace. In her panic-stricken state, she wouldn't be able to catch much of a breath. She tried everything in her power to calm herself, but she couldn't. She tried locking her knees and planting her feet, even sliding her legs out from under her to stop him, but Taber was too strong for her.

He muscled her over the side of the tub, forcing her down on her knees. He slid out from behind her. With his arms gone, Sydney's torso was free to expand. She looked up and saw Taber standing over her. He cocked his head and winked. *What the hell did that mean?* she wondered. But the moment of speculation passed as he raised his boot and slammed it down on Sydney's bound wrists.

Sydney's stomach dug into the side of the tub as her head plunged under the water. She tried yanking it up above the surface, but she felt both of Taber's hands on the back of her skull. He forced her chin into her chest. He was standing firm on her wrists, which stretched her useless arms out in front of her. She tried lifting up with her legs, but she was still on her knees. Her powerful legs were worthless.

Sydney thrashed about at first, but then her instincts kicked in. *You must stay calm in order to survive!*

As she desperately tried to calm herself, she closed her eyes and tried to picture herself in the water off Monaco's coast, swimming down underneath the water, diving deeper and deeper and deeper still. Suddenly, an idea popped into her head. Could she fool Taber into thinking she had drowned before she was actually dead? It would take a few minutes to carry out that plan, and she didn't have enough air. She'd be surprised if she could last two full minutes. But she had to try.

Sydney made her body go completely limp. By the time she started counting the seconds, she figured she had been down for nearly a minute already.

Ten, eleven, twelve …

Sydney willed herself to clear her mind. She couldn't think of possible rescue attempts or what the Bilderbergers were still planning.

Eighteen, nineteen, twenty …

Suddenly, a hand slipped around her neck. She heard a voice vibrate through the water. It was Taber. What was he saying? His touch was gentle. Was he feeling for her pulse? Sydney could feel it throbbing in her neck. Certainly Taber didn't think that she was already dead. But then he lifted his boot off her wrists. She opened her eyes and saw Taber's boot rise from the water. Seconds later, she felt his hands on either side of her head, raising it.

Sydney couldn't believe it. Taber did think she was dead. She decided to play along. She shut her eyes and played possum. As Taber pulled her up out of the tub, Sydney stayed limp. He placed her down and Sydney let her body spill out across the floor.

A few moments passed. Sydney could hear Speakes talking on a phone in the bedroom. Sydney almost opened her eyes when she sensed Taber's lips next to her ear.

"You're doing great, Sydney," he whispered. "Just keep up the act for a little longer."

Confusion flooded Sydney's head. Taber breathed in to speak again.

"Knobby would be very proud of you right now."

Sydney's eyes jumped open. Taber's face was only inches from hers. He was smiling at her.

Knobby.

Stefan Taber knew the nickname she had given Colin Tanner. Besides Danny Cavanaugh, she had never told anyone else about that nickname. Knobby must have told Taber to disclose that information to show Sydney that he was a friend.

Taber whispered again. "Whatever you hear in the other room, just stay here. I'll come and get you when it's safe."

Knobby.

Sydney didn't move. She closed her eyes and remained in a fetal position. She heard Taber's footsteps cross the tiled bathroom. He left and closed the door behind him. She could still hear Speakes talking on the phone. Finally, there was silence. Sydney then heard Taber's voice, but she couldn't make out his words.

There was a heated exchange and then the unmistakable sounds of a struggle. Finally, three quick, mechanical pulses jabbed across her eardrums. The struggle ended, and Sydney figured so had the life of C. Benjamin Speakes.

Sydney opened her eyes. The bathroom door opened and Stefan Taber appear in the doorway. A pistol was dangling in his right hand. Smoke rose from the end of its silencer.

"Are you okay?" he asked her.

Sydney was the furthest thing from okay. She was soaking wet on the floor of a strange bathroom while a man she didn't trust was standing over her holding a gun. So many questions filled her head that she feared if she opened her mouth, they would all come rushing out at once. Instead of talking, she simply nodded.

Taber cut off the zip tie that bound her wrists. Then he pulled an impeccably white towel off the rung above the bathtub and offered it to her. Sydney took it and began dabbing it against her face. Taber sat down on the side of the tub and rested the elongated weapon across his lap.

"Sorry about the rough stuff, but I needed Speakes to think you were dead. He just told the others that I killed you. Hopefully, they'll stop gunning for you now."

Sydney remained silent, but Taber no doubt saw the utter confusion in her eyes. He smiled.

"You're wondering what the hell is going on," he started. "Let me begin by telling you who I really work for."

"Who?" Sydney heard herself say.

"The president of the United States."

Chapter 94

Sydney's sign.

Danny was the first one through the bloodstained door on the hotel's fifth floor. All six of the agents on the president's Secret Service detail were tiptoeing behind him with their weapons drawn. The president himself brought up the rear.

By the time they made it to the intersection of the hallways, Peter Devon was shoulder to shoulder with him. Danny had no idea what kind of training Devon had for situations like this one, but he wasn't going to ask him to run through his résumé right quick. He could only hope that Devon knew what he was doing.

Peter Devon flattened his back against the wall and slid over to the corner. He peeked around it and whipped back with a disgusted look on his face. Before he even uttered the words, Danny knew who was standing guard in the hall.

"One of mine," Devon mouthed.

He pulled his Beretta into his chest. Danny read the intensity in Devon's eyes. *This is my guy; it's my show.* Danny took a step back and nodded. He didn't have a dog in this particular fight. Besides, a compromise here would gain him leverage in the future.

Devon wheeled around the corner and leveled his weapon at the man standing at the far end of the hallway.

"Stefansky!" Devon growled. "Drop your weapon and get on the floor, now!"

Danny peeled around Devon and looked past him, checking the hallway for exits. The only exits on the entire floor were the stairway and the elevators. Six Secret Service agents, a Texas Ranger, and the president of the United States stood between whomever Stefansky was guarding and freedom.

The sight of seven armed bodies pouring into the hallway made fear shiver across Stefansky's face. He immediately followed Peter Devon's command. Devon ordered one of his agents to cuff Stefansky and then Devon pushed him up against the wall.

"How many are in there?" Devon barked.

When Stefansky didn't answer, Devon dug his fingers into Stefansky's eye sockets. The agent let out a hideous yowl.

"Three! Three including the girl!"

Devon released him. He faced the door and was through it with one well-placed kick under the doorknob.

Years of protecting partners and covering fellow officers in dangerous situations had been hardwired into Danny's body. He flew through the doorway. Peter Devon was standing in a firing stance in the suite's foyer, an elaborate oval-shaped parlor. Sitting atop an oval carpet was an enormous oval table made of Brazilian cherry wood. The smell of fresh wood polish tangoed with the perfume of the color-coordinated flowers perfectly arranged in a giant crystal vase at the center of the table.

There were two open doorways at either end of the parlor. Suddenly, they heard Sydney's voice. "Danny! I'm in here!" It was coming from the hallway to their left.

Devon churned down the narrow hallway first, with Danny close behind him. They spilled out into the master bedroom. Sydney was guarded by a taut man dressed all in black. Danny recognized him immediately. Stefan Taber, the ICJ guard. *He finally caught us.*

Taber and Sydney stood together just inside a doorway on the far side of the bedroom. He held a gun to her head. Benjamin Speakes was lying face down on the floor next to them, his eyes glazed over with death. Blood trickled out from his body, widening the pool already on the floor.

"Drop your weapon and let the woman go." Peter Devon's command was calm, almost monotone.

Taber stared at Peter Devon. "All I want to do is leave. My work here is done." His words were just as calm as Peter Devon's. But with his British accent, the man sounded even more composed.

Danny studied Sydney. She looked oddly peaceful for a woman with a gun to her head.

Something isn't right here.

"You heard Agent Devon. Drop your weapon. There's nowhere to go." The words came from behind Danny. He turned and saw that the president had made his way into the bedroom.

With the four agents corralled around him, Danny could only see the president's face.

Taber lowered his weapon. "You are the president of the United States," he said. The president stood still, neither affirming nor denying the man's statement. Taber dropped his gun to the floor. Peter Devon took a step forward to collect it when Taber shoved Sydney at him. From his viewpoint, Danny saw the gleam of black metal behind Sydney's back.

"Gun! Gun!" Danny yelled.

Taber ducked behind Sydney, using her as a shield, as he fired at the most important target in the room. The agents piled on top of the president. Peter Devon pivoted to his right, putting his body in the direct line of fire. Danny aimed his gun, but he couldn't pull the trigger. Sydney was still standing in the way.

Taber ducked behind the doorway and into the sitting room. Danny fired three rounds into the wall, hoping at least one of them would find its way through the drywall and into Taber's body.

"Sydney!" Danny yelled. "Over here!"

Sydney looked at him but didn't move from the doorway. Danny scurried over and shoved her behind an antique club chair in the corner of the room. He turned back and crept to the edge of the doorway. He sucked in and ushered the standard police ultimatum.

"There's nowhere to go, Taber! You're surrounded! Drop your weapon and come out with your hands on top of your head!"

Danny heard nothing. He sensed no movement. From the corner of his eye, he saw Peter Devon squirming on the floor, still trying to get to his president to make sure he was okay. He remained a target out in the open. Danny ran over to him, firing three cover shots into the sitting room along the way. He grabbed Devon and pulled him to safety behind the bed.

"The president?" Devon uttered out of breath. He ripped open his shirt and clawed at his bulletproof vest. Danny saw two bullet holes in it, just below Devon's sternum.

The amoeba of bodies around the president had carried him to the far side of the bedroom. They disappeared back down the hallway toward the parlor.

"He's okay. He's out of harm's way," Danny said as he helped Devon loosen his vest, allowing his lungs to expand.

"Get … that … son of a bitch."

Danny nodded and got ready to move. Devon wobbled to his knees. Danny crept toward the sitting room, making sure to hug the wall. Devon nodded and readied himself to cover Danny. Danny lunged out into the doorway, his weapon covering the entire sitting room in a split second. He ducked back against the wall. He thought about his ultimatum as he visualized what he just saw.

There's nowhere to go!

But there was. Beyond the sitting area next to the bathroom was a short hallway with a closed door at the end. Hanging on it at eye level was the familiar hotel rate sheet underneath a sheet of plastic, similar to those sheets he had noticed on every exit door of every hotel room in which he had ever stayed.

Danny rushed through the doorway and through the sitting room. He flew through the exit door and was back in the main hallway of the fifth floor. He pointed his gun in every direction. No one.

To his left was the end of the hallway and the main entrance to the Oval Suite, the one Peter Devon had shattered only moments ago. Danny took off to his right, sprinting down the hallway. He burst through the stairwell door and shuffled down the stairs until he reached the ground floor. He threw open the door and sped out into the empty hallway. He ran past the storage closet, came to another door, and opened it. He was now in a darkened corner of the front lobby. He moved through an alcove and past the restrooms. Restrooms really were dead ends. Taber wasn't that dumb.

Danny entered the lobby. It looked oddly deserted. He pictured Taber ripping through it, waving a gun. *You see a gun, you take cover.* "This is the police," Danny announced to no one. "Did anyone see a man with a gun run through here?"

"Yes."

Danny wheeled around and saw a young black girl in a hotel uniform peer out from behind the front desk. She pointed at the hotel's revolving front door.

Danny bolted through the lobby and churned through the revolving door. He leaped down the front stairs until he came to a stop underneath the stained-glass canopy. The regular cast of hotel characters that adorned the receiving area of a four-star hotel was nowhere to be found. Neither was Danny's target.

The stench of failure began choking him. Danny darted out into the middle of Pennsylvania Avenue. He could see for blocks in both directions. People and cars were moving at their normal paces. No one was running. No one fit Stefan Taber's description.

Chapter 95

Danny was nearly delirious from the marathon debriefing period. Six different agents, two from the Department of Homeland Security, two from the CIA, and two from the NSA, had grilled him all afternoon and late into the night. As soon as he woke up this morning, he endured more grilling from two State Department agents. His last meeting was with a couple FBI agents. They all wanted basically the same thing, for Danny to plot a near minute-by-minute timeline from the time he met Sydney in Mexico. They wanted to know why he was in Mexico in the first place. They wanted to know every detail about the smuggling sting and how much he knew about Rafael Espinoza's operation. The FBI agents had been especially interested about how he ended up in a kill or be killed situation with a colleague of theirs, no matter how dirty Ripley was.

"Did your people find more bombs in the capitol tunnels?" Danny asked the FBI agents as they had closed their notebooks and capped their pens.

"We cannot answer that question," the one agent answered.

"Did they find anything in the tunnels?" Danny pressed.

After a momentary silence, Danny answered his own question. "Let me guess, you can't answer that question either." The two agents exchanged looks. Not a word crossed their lips.

"Can you at least tell me if they found the men that I encountered?"

The one agent began giving the standard answer. "We cannot—"

Danny slammed his fist on the table. "I almost get killed down there, and you can't give me a fucking thing!"

The second agent sighed. "The tunnels are connected to secret access points in every building along the mall. They could have escaped out through any one of them."

Great, Danny thought. Information he already knew. By the time the meeting was over, Danny was exhausted. He tried to clear his head touring the White House grounds.

A crushed gravel path eventually led him to an elongated trellis wall covered in gnarled trumpet vines. It was impossible to see through it, but Danny heard the faint sound of human limbs cutting through water. He followed the wall until he came to a wrought iron gate. He unlatched the gate and walked through it, ready to confront the only person who could answer the questions that still loomed in his mind.

Danny walked to the edge of the pool just as Sydney finished another lap. She flipped to start another one and then stopped, seeing him standing there. A dark blue swimmer's cap with the official White House seal broke the water's surface.

Sydney smiled. "Good morning, Sergeant Cavanaugh."

Danny squatted next to her. "Ms. Dumas."

"Are they finally done interrogating you?"

"For now. You?"

She nodded. "For now."

"Anyone from the ICJ call to say they recognized you yet?" Danny was aware that while Sydney had been filmed on TV during their hostage stunt outside the White House, a good shot of her face was never captured. She was still referred to as an unidentified woman in the news about the incident.

"No. Mr. Shilling already dispatched a team down to the monastery. They said they found two bodies. I'm sure it's Joseph and that bastard Broederlam."

"I'm sure they'll come up with something about why you aren't with them."

Sydney nodded. "I am to consider myself a guest of the president until further notice."

"So you're a prisoner of the White House?"

Sydney looked around. "Is there a better place to be one?"

"And after Butcher's done with you?"

Sydney's coy smile vanished. "They want to put me in protective custody until they can figure out just how far the Bilderbergers' reach extends."

Danny reacted. "That will take months, maybe years, Sydney. Are you prepared to put your life on hold for that long?"

"I don't see it as putting it on hold, Danny. I've finally brought justice to my family."

Danny could only imagine what the various agents interrogating her had used as part of their sales pitch for Sydney to agree to be their snitch. She said her life wasn't about revenge, but Danny could see it in her face. She would do anything to avenge her parents' death, including existing in the purgatory that is protective custody. Well, so be it.

"How's your swim treating you?" he asked.

Sydney looked behind her at the perfect, Olympic-sized White House swimming pool. The space held a sense of privacy within the eighteen acres where there was none.

"I was just finishing up." She pulled off her cap, along with her goggles. The clear water danced around her amazing eyes, making them sparkle even more brilliantly in the late morning sunlight. "I can't believe I'm swimming at the White House. This will definitely be a story for my *petits-enfants*, my grandchildren."

"Where'd you get the suit?"

Sydney eyed the sleek one-piece that covered her body. "President Butcher. He said they keep a complete wardrobe of all clothing options in a range of sizes for visitors."

"That's gotta be one hell of a closet."

Sydney giggled. "Care to join me?"

"I do have some time to kill until the State of the Union."

"You're going to the State of the Union speech?"

"As a special guest of the president."

Sydney clapped. "Congratulations. Even more of a reason to take a few victory laps."

"I don't have a suit."

Sydney looked behind her again. Then out to each side. "You don't need one." Her lips curled, creating a wicked smile. "In fact, neither do I."

She pulled down one shoulder strap, then the other. She began cinching her swimsuit down slowly, teasing Danny. Her eyes never left his. "I'll make sure to keep this next part out of the story to my petits-enfants."

Danny was glad he wasn't armed. For if he was, he could shoot himself for what he was about to say.

"It's easier for you to bare your skin than your soul, isn't it Sydney?"

Danny's words wiped the mischievous look off Sydney's face. She quickly yanked her swimsuit back up, securing her tanned cleavage behind the wall of spandex.

"What are you talking about, Danny?"

"The lying never stops, does it?"

She didn't answer him. She lunged for the pool steps. Danny met her as she leaped out.

"I never lied to you, Danny," she declared and then began drying herself with a towel.

"You knew Benjamin Speakes worked in the White House, and you never told me."

Sydney glared at him. "Do you know how long I've waited to confront Speakes? My whole life, Danny. I didn't play by your rules, but I'm not sorry. I had to do it my way."

Sydney pulled on a white robe emblazoned with the White House seal and tied it around her waist. She slipped her feet into slippers also bearing the seal and began walking away.

Danny followed her. "Is that why you helped Stefan Taber get away?" Sydney stopped in her tracks, but she didn't turn around. Danny continued. "Back in the hotel suite, when Taber escaped, you stood between him and anyone getting a clean shot. At first, I thought you were frozen in fear. But then I saw it in your face. You weren't scared; you did it on purpose."

Sydney turned and faced Danny. Her eyes were wet with tears. She moved toward him. Danny grabbed her forearms to stop her.

"Tell me, Sydney. No bullshit."

"He saved my life."

Danny shook her. "I said no bullshit."

Sydney gazed deep into Danny's eyes. "He knew Knobby."

"He knew Colin Tanner?"

Sydney nodded. "He was working undercover and infiltrated the Bilderbergers. He knew Knobby was trying to leave them."

"Who was he working for?"

Sydney's eyes instantly cleared. "For the president."

"Hold on. Stefan Taber, the ICJ guard, the one who chased us across the country and who tried killing us at every turn, was working for Jack Butcher?"

"At the Potomac, after we jumped off the plane and Fantroy's plane exploded, I never told you that I encountered a diver under the water. He held a knife to my throat, but he didn't kill me. It was Taber. He was the one who launched the missile from the boat that blew up Fantroy's plane. He knew Fantroy was a Bilderberger—"

Danny held up his hands. "Stop."

"Danny, I know it's hard to believe—"

"There's too much damn mystery surrounding you, Sydney."

"You don't believe me?"

Sydney had asked that question to not only him but to several people during their adventure together. Danny had always sidestepped it. But now he was about to answer it once and for all.

"No, Sydney. I don't."

While she looked as if he had just slapped her, Sydney allowed him to kiss her on the cheek. "Good-bye Sydney," he whispered. "Take care of yourself."

He slipped away from her without looking into her face. He knew that if he did, her eyes held enough power to draw him back.

Danny stepped around the pool, keeping his eyes locked on the gate in front of him. Whether or not he had shut off his hearing, he didn't know. But as he walked through the gate and out of Sydney Dumas's life, he didn't hear a word.

Danny wove along the pathway toward the White House Rose Garden. He finally looked back toward the pool. The trumpet vines blocked any attempt to see Sydney. *What if she's telling the truth?* Danny couldn't go back and ask her. But there was another way to find out.

Seeing that he was steps away from the Oval Office and that his movements were no doubt being monitored, Danny tried as best he could to look nonchalant as he reached for the cell phone that Carver Sutton had given him, which he finally got back after the Secret Service was done examining it. He called Chip's cell number.

"Well finally," Chip answered. "Where are you calling me from? Are you in the Lincoln bedroom with that gorgeous creature? Tell me you are."

Not knowing if he was being recorded as well, Danny whispered his reply. "Not quite. Listen, I need you to get me some more information."

"More information? You're a hero, Danny boy. Just sit back, relax, and enjoy it."

"Chip."

Chip sighed. "A cop never sleeps, right? That goes for the retired ones, too, I guess. What do you need?"

"I need everything you can get me on Sydney's godfather, Colin Tanner."

Chapter 96

Danny answered the knock on his hotel room door. Simon Shilling stood in the hallway, holding an ID badge at the end of a lariat.

"You clean up nice, Sergeant," he said, giving Danny the once over.

"It's not hard to do in a custom-made suit." Danny smoothed the lapels on the charcoal gray jacket and buttoned its top button. "And one made in record time. Please pass along my thanks to the president."

"The White House has a clothier on call. He's actually been through four different administrations."

"So, I guess he's used to last-minute tailoring emergencies."

"Presidents and their administrations come and go. But the staff, the ones who really run the White House, they're permanent." Danny nodded, thinking about Benjamin Speakes and his long service record. Simon handed Danny the lariat. "This is your security pass for the evening. You ready to go?"

"Yes, sir." They walked down to the elevator and got in. "So what's the plan for the speech this evening?" Danny asked after the doors shut.

Simon smiled. "The president wants to keep everyone in the dark about what he's going to cover tonight. He and I are the only two who have been privy to the final draft. It's driving the rest of the staff crazy, especially Blake Conway, the president's press secretary."

"I guess that means I can't get a sneak preview?"

Simon chuckled. "Can't do it. Not even for our hero. What I can tell you is that the president will acknowledge you during his opening comments, about three minutes in. My advice is to just stand, look appreciative, and let the applause soak in." Simon rested a hand on Danny's shoulder. "Let it wash away the sins of the past, Sergeant. From now on, you've got a clean slate."

Goosebumps rolled across Danny's skin. The elevator doors opened at the lobby level of the Willard Hotel. The lobby looked foreign to Danny. It was bustling with bodies in motion. Simon led Danny through the revolving door and into a waiting black Suburban. The driver whisked them through the D.C. streets on the relatively short trip to the Capitol. The driver stopped in front of the Capitol Visitor Center's entrance, where a throng of reporters immediately swarmed the vehicle.

"No comment is your answer to everything until further notice," Simon told Danny.

"Got it," Danny replied.

They got out of the Suburban. Simon kept a smile on his silent lips as he hustled past the reporters and through the revolving door. Although it was only steps to the relative peace inside the center, the reporters managed to fire several questions at Danny about the smuggling case, about Rafael Espinoza, and about killing Crayton Ripley. Danny wanted to scream, "I'm an innocent man! Leave me the fuck alone," but he followed Shilling's advice and spoke two words through a forced smile.

"No comment."

Minutes later, Simon was leading Danny down to his seat for the evening. It was on the front row of the mezzanine overlooking the floor of the House of Representatives.

"You need anything before I leave you, Sergeant?"

Danny looked around. Most of the seats around him were still empty. "Actually, yes." He leaned toward Shilling and lowered his voice. "What'd y'all find in the capitol tunnels?"

Simon squinted at him. "What did the FBI agents tell you when you asked them?"

"How did you know ...?" Danny knowingly stopped before finishing his statement. Simon Shilling probably knew about some things before they even happened. "Don't you think your hero has the right to know?"

Simon looked around before leaning into Danny. "You don't like surprises, do you, Sergeant?"

"I've had enough to last a lifetime."

Simon laughed. "The president is going to divulge that information to the American people tonight as a reminder that we live in a new age where caution and vigilance are the watchwords."

"Where is the president?"

"He's giving the speech to Simon in the Senate chambers one last time."

"I'm sorry?"

"Every speech the president has ever made, he's given it to his son before the public hears it, for luck."

Goosebumps wicked across Danny's skin. *Jack Butcher still talks to his dead son.* He immediately wished his dad had loved him that much instead of leaving him to flounder through life wondering why he chose to kill himself.

Suddenly, a face caught Danny's attention from the House floor. "There's Dexter Walsh," he exclaimed before realizing the volume of his voice.

Simon turned and looked at the Fed chairman as he shook a few hands on his way toward the front row. "In the flesh."

Danny ratcheted his voice down to a whisper. "But what Sydney told you about him … why the hell isn't he in a jail cell?"

Simon gripped Danny's shoulder as he gazed into his eyes. "Sergeant, with your years of service in law enforcement, you should know by now that timing is everything. Especially when it comes to office politics." Simon stayed silent for a long while, his eyes never wavering from Danny's. It was like he was trying to put him in a trance.

"So, you're saying that this isn't the right time to start an investigation on him?"

Simon nodded. "It would take steam away from the president's message tonight. But make no mistake that Dexter Walsh will get his. Trust me." Simon patted Danny's shoulder again. "Just try to sit back and enjoy the night. Like I said, from now on you've got a clean slate." He turned and vaulted up the stairs before Danny could ask him any more questions.

Danny watched as the House floor began filling up with representatives, senators, their minions, and media people. He should have been relaxing, waiting to be exonerated by the president of the United States. But all he could think about was what happened underneath L'Enfant Plaza.

"The president is going to divulge that information to the American people tonight as a reminder that we live in a new age where caution and vigilance are the watchwords."

Danny couldn't wait to hear what Jack Butcher had in store for everyone.

Chapter 97

An unusually chilly breeze for this time of year wandered across the steps of the Lincoln Memorial. Stefan Taber, prepared as usual, tucked the lapel of his suede barn jacket up against his chin as he checked his watch. He considered the sky behind him. The setting sun melted the blue sky into intermittent bands of purple and pink.

Tourists clad in thin jackets and comfortable walking shoes trudged all around the monument. Children scampered over the granite stairs as if these hallowed grounds were a simple playground. Several teenagers chattered away on their cell phones, oblivious to the history and meaning of this place. Only when an elderly man shuffled along the edge of the setting in front of him did Stefan Taber finally feel reinvigorated.

From this distance, Taber recognized the man's military beret. The middle-aged woman who had been helping him climb each step knew enough to leave him alone when they reached the top. The man was able to overcome his perpetual stoop an inch at a time. Taber witnessed the pain etched in his face as he stuck out his chest and stared straight ahead out over the Reflecting Pool, toward the National World War II Memorial, the Washington Monument, and finally the Capitol. After a few moments of silent reflection, the man brought his shaky right hand up to his eyebrow and saluted. He tottered around and contemplated the Lincoln Memorial. He saluted it as well. Moments later, he nodded to the woman to begin their long journey down the stairs.

Taber wanted to stop the man in the worst way. He wanted to ask him why he was saluting. He wanted to talk with this man awhile, soldier to soldier. Only a soldier could appreciate what Taber's comrades had done underneath this very place. Only another soldier could truly realize the words that Taber lived by.

Sometimes one must engage in evil to do the most good.

What kind of evil had this man done? Taber knew that whatever sins a man waged in the throes of battle could never be forgiven in a house of God. They could only be cleansed at places like these, where the ideas and ideals for which they fought were tangibly cast in marble and stone.

Taber watched the old soldier hobble away. He checked his watch. He thought about the other old man that helped put him on this mission in the first place. Colin Tanner. Taber had met the man and heard his story only weeks before he died. Colin "Knobby" Tanner. The nickname was the old man's password for nearly everything in cyberspace. After Taber's computer people hacked it, Taber had wondered what the silly word had meant. He only needed to Google "Colin Tanner" and "Knobby" for his the answer. Sydney Dumas had mentioned it years ago in an article for some French magazine about women in education. She had probably forgotten all about letting his nickname slip when she answered the question about people who had influenced her life. But Taber used that tidbit to his advantage. Simply knowing it had turned Sydney into a temporary ally, allowing Taber to escape certain capture at the Willard Hotel. Ah, the power of information.

Taber checked his watch again. It was time. He reached into his jacket pocket, pulled out a disposable cell phone, and dialed an international number.

"Lars Karlsson," the unsure voice blurted into Taber's ear.

"Lars, it's Stefan."

There was a long silence. "Stefan, where the hell are you?"

"Don't worry about that."

"Everything has gone to shit. Do you know that Ben Speakes has been killed?"

"Yes. I was the one who killed him."

"What?"

"Lars, listen to me. I only called to tell you one thing. You treated me like a son, and I thank you for that. You made the mistake of letting your emotions blur your judgment. You should not have trusted me. But I thank you that you did."

"What are you talking about? What in the world is going on?" Lars snapped.

Taber wasn't listening. He stared at his watch as the seconds ticked away. Then he said, "I was never married, Lars. There was never any baby."

There was another long pause, as Lars undoubtedly computed this revelation. "You son of a—" Suddenly, Lars stopped in mid-sentence. Taber could hear him questioning someone in the room. "Who are you? How did you get in here?" Then Taber heard the unmistakable *thwoop, thwoop* of two bullets being fired through a silencer. Two more, *thwoop, thwoops* finished the job. Taber ended the call still staring at his watch.

Like clockwork.

Taber tucked the phone back into his pocket and bundled the jacket tighter around his torso, trying to fight off the momentary chill that ebbed into his soul. He stared out past the memorials to the building where he hoped his comrades' operation would be pulled off with similar precision in a matter of minutes.

Chapter 98

The clanking behind him nudged Danny out of his dazed state. A little boy strapped in a wheelchair was being lowered step by step by two Capitol policemen. They shuttled him down to the end of the aisle in front of the balcony. A female page ushered a woman over to the empty chair at his side. The woman was in her mid-thirties. She had bottle blond hair cropped short and an easy smile, which she sported as she made eye contact with Danny.

"Will this spot do, son?" the one policeman asked.

The boy strained to lift his head off the headrest. He peered down over the balcony through a pair of chunky eyeglasses. His reddened face lit up. Noise from a ventilator machine squeezed air into a tube fixed in the side of his neck.

"Yes, sir," the boy croaked. He pulled his left hand over to his right and began lifting it up in the air to shake hands. The policeman knew what he was trying to do. He grabbed the boy's trembling hand and shook it.

"Thank you," the boy uttered. The other policeman leaned around the wheelchair and shook the boy's hand as well.

"You're welcome," they said simultaneously. Danny saw the one cop's lower lip trembling as he walked back up the steps. Danny noticed he was wearing a wedding ring. He was probably a father as well. He could only imagine what the cop was thinking.

Thank God that's not my son.

The mother noticed Danny's eyes on her son. "Good evening," she said to him.

"Evening, ma'am," Danny replied.

She extended her right hand over her son's lap. "I'm Elisha Goodnight, and this is my son, Ethan."

343

Danny shook her hand. He noticed that the ring finger on her left hand was naked. "Sergeant Danny Cavanaugh." Ethan moved to pull up his right arm again. Danny went to scoop Ethan's hand out of his lap but stopped himself. Ethan had the look of a determined young man. Danny waited until he raised his right hand up in the air to embrace it. "Nice to meet you, Ethan."

The machine pushed air into Ethan's body. His fixed smile grew. "Like ... wise."

"Sergeant? Does that mean you're a police officer?" Elisha asked.

Danny nodded. "Yes, ma'am. I'm with the Texas Rangers."

"Oh, how exciting. Ethan always wanted to be a police officer. I bet you have some incredible stories."

"I've got a few, yes ma'am."

"So what brings a Texas Ranger to the State of the Union?"

"I'm being recognized for my service."

"Wow. You must have done something special. Of course, in my eyes, people in law enforcement do something special every day."

Danny grinned. He figured that this single mother's life was so full of caring for a child like Ethan, on top of supporting herself, that she had no time to follow current events.

"I just helped the president out of a jam," Danny replied. Even though Ethan was hanging on his every word, he wanted to change the subject. "What brings y'all here tonight?"

"Ethan's the newly appointed spokesperson for President Butcher's healthcare initiative." Elisha's easy smile ramped up into a dazzler, as she gazed proudly upon her son.

Danny smiled at Ethan. "Well congratulations, Ethan. It's about time that someone did something about our healthcare crisis."

Ethan raised his finger to his lips. "Shhh," he sounded. He opened his mouth to speak further, but nothing came out.

"Don't try to talk too much, honey. You need to rest up for your big moment in the spotlight." Elisha turned to Danny. "He's trying to tell you not to tell anyone about his new job. It hasn't been announced yet. Ethan doesn't want anyone to steal the president's thunder."

Danny felt a vibration in his side. He pulled out his buzzing cell phone and checked the caller ID. "Oh, okay, I understand." He put the phone to his ear. "Mum's the word." Ethan nodded. "Excuse me a second." Danny turned away from them. Carver Sutton's unmistakable voice echoed in his ear.

"Mum's the word for what?"

"For mum. It's nothing. What's up?"

"I've got a juicy morsel for you, Sergeant."

"What is it?"

"First of all, I checked to see if Stefan Taber had been a student of Colin Tanner's at Oxford and found nothing. I figured it was an alias anyway. But then I did a little more digging into Tanner's professorial career. Like my pappy always said, it's all about the follow-through."

"Chip, I don't have the time for theatrics."

"Okay, okay. Tanner was an adviser to two young men in the same class. One was at Oxford because of his birthright; the other was there because he was the American Rhodes Scholar that year."

Danny flashed back to the photo he had seen on the president's credenza in the Oval Office. He found Jack Butcher again and then scanned through the rest of the faces in the small crowd. He whispered the names before Chip could spit them out. "King Edward and President Jack Butcher."

"You get the gold star, Sergeant. But how the hell did you know that?"

"I saw a photo of the 1975 Oxford graduating class in the Oval Office."

"Aha. That noggin of yours to the rescue once again."

Danny remembered all that Sydney told him about Colin Tanner. Tanner had realized that however altruistic the intentions of the Marxist student group he started, they became infected by human nature. Tanner couldn't help what they turned into, but he could still influence other Oxford students.

Danny visualized Jack Butcher on the phone with the British monarch after he left his supposedly private meeting in the Oval Office.

I did tell one other person about your mission.

It was as if someone had slapped his face. Danny listened past the words uttered underneath L'Enfant Plaza as he replayed the moment over and over in his mind.

Should we take him or retreat?

Danny nearly jumped out of his chair when he finally recognized the accent. *The man was British!* If they were King Edward's men underneath the plaza, that meant they were also President Butcher's men. He then pictured himself at the White House pool, cutting Sydney off before she could fully explain why she thought Stefan Taber was working for the president.

I never told you that I encountered a diver under the water. He held a knife to my throat, but he didn't kill me. It was Taber.

Taber also had an open shot at Danny back at the racquet club. He could have easily killed them both, which if he was really working for the Bilderbergers, would have been his main directive. And while Taber shot at the president at the Willard Hotel, he must have known that the Secret Service agents would have jumped in the line of fire. All Taber needed was an out.

How could I have been so stupid, Danny thought. He turned and stared at Ethan Goodnight. The boy's bleary eyes were stuck on his mother's kind face as she spoke to him, pointing out the famous policymakers beneath them. Danny focused on the reddened patch of skin around the trachea tube in his neck. Suddenly, all he could hear was the pulse of the machine. He watched Ethan wince every time the machine breathed for him.

Danny caught Elisha Goodnight's eyes and then motioned for her to swing her head behind her son's wheelchair. "If I may ask, what condition does Ethan have?" Danny whispered.

Elisha cocked her head at Danny, like it was a very odd question to be asked in their surroundings. "Dysautonomic mitochondrial myopathy," Elisha whispered back. "It's a form of muscular dystrophy."

Danny mouthed, "Is there a cure?"

Elisha shook her head.

Danny nodded at her politely and then gazed down at the House floor. He visualized another photo on the president's Oval Office credenza, the one of Jack Butcher holding onto his son amid the tubes and machines that kept him alive. There was nothing Butcher could do but watch a painful disease slowly tear apart his little boy cell by cell. But what about this time? What about Ethan Goodnight? Butcher couldn't cure the incurable, but he could provide another little boy with a quick, painless death. The question was how?

"Danny? Danny? You still there, man?"

Danny blinked as he heard Chip's voice in his ear. "Yeah, I'm here," Danny replied as he studied the House floor. Although the power that rested in the hands of the gathering people was awe-inspiring, the most powerful man on the planet was still nowhere to be found. "Listen Chip, I've got to get going. But tell me something, will you? Who would you trust around here in an emergency?"

Chip laughed cynically. "Find Admiral Howard Fielding."

Danny spied him pressing the flesh near the dais on the House floor. "The director of National Intelligence?"

"He was my mentor back when I was at Naval Intel."

"He's a little busy right now."

"Then find a beat cop. The lower on the totem pole, the better. Got it?"

Danny was already out of his seat and vaulting up the stairs. "Yeah. This number good?"

"It goes where I go, Danny boy," Chip replied. "You want to tell me what you're thinking?"

Danny darted out into the hallway and hooked a left. He studied the sea of faces surrounding him. Suddenly nothing was as it seemed anymore. He didn't know who might be listening in on his conversation. Instead of thinking of something clever, Danny opted for a straight "no" answer and then ended the call.

Chapter 99

"Find the lowest man on the totem pole."

Danny took Chip's advice to heart. By definition, the grunts were the least likely to be corrupt. If they were, then they wouldn't be the grunts. Danny just hoped the cops who had carted Ethan Goodnight down to his seat were men he could trust.

"Officers, I need your help."

Neither one spoke. But the younger one looked at the older, alpha dog. Danny looked at the names on their badges. Cannon and Koontz. Danny concentrated on the alpha, Cannon.

"I think we may have a security situation," Danny said in a hushed tone. "Where's the entrance to the escape tunnels?" The two officers looked at each other. "Come on guys," Danny continued, "they're no big secret. Hell, they're even on the Internet."

"You'll have to talk to someone in the Architect of the Capitol's office," Cannon finally replied.

"I don't have time for bureaucratic bullshit," Danny said. He eyed Cannon's sergeant stripes. "Sergeant Cannon, you must know where the entrance is. Can we just check it to make sure nothing's wrong? If everything's okay, then I'll buy you both a steak dinner at Smith & Wollensky's."

"Weren't you the guy sitting next to the kid we took down to the balcony?" Koontz asked. He was pasty, almost sickly white, with pockmarks on his cheeks and the unsure stare of a rookie. He stood slumped over forward, like the accessories on his chest were weighing down his lanky frame.

"That's right," Danny replied.

"You're the Texas Ranger who helped the president, right?" Koontz continued.

"Right again, but I don't have time for this. Y'all going to help me or not?"

Koontz shrugged. He was about to say something when Cannon interjected.

"I'll take you down there." Cannon was staring into Danny. His calm, black eyes matched the color of his hair, his skin, and his uniform. "Randy, you stay here. If anyone asks, I'm in the head. Not a word of this to anyone until I tell you. Got it?"

"You got it, Sarge," Koontz replied.

"Follow me," Cannon said to Danny.

As they waded through wave after wave of lobbyists and Capitol Hill staffers exchanging hollow pleasantries along the massive stone hallway, Danny grew more and more confident with his theory.

Sydney said Colin Tanner grew to be disgusted with what the Bilderbergers stood for. Look at this concentration of power. Tanner taught Jack Butcher and King Edward that this is not the right way to run a society. The only way they could possibly change it is to start from the ground up.

They came to an intersection. Cannon led Danny to the right and then down a flight of steps to a landing. He took another right, and they swerved into a calm alcove. Cannon produced a barrel key and twisted it in a panel next to a set of elevator doors. Then he punched the button and it lit up.

"Thanks for trusting me," Danny said as they waited.

Cannon's face narrowed. "Let's get one thing straight, Sergeant. I don't trust you. I've followed your story. I know about how you killed that FBI agent. Hell, as far as I'm concerned, you're still on the hook for Senator Halsey's death. What I don't know is how you're mixed up with the president."

"You shouldn't believe everything you read, Cannon. I've been cleared of those charges."

"That's what I'm talking about. I've worked on the Hill long enough to know that the shit that fills the papers is just a dog and pony show."

Anger seared Danny's gut. "So why the fuck are you helping me, Cannon?"

The elevator chimed and the doors opened. Cannon thrust out his arm to hold the doors. "Because I've seen that look in your eyes before, in other cops. You've got a credible hunch. I wouldn't be doing my job if I didn't investigate it." Cannon finished with a sarcastic grin. "After you, Sergeant."

Both men boarded the elevator. Danny noticed four floor buttons. The top one, marked 'G' for the ground floor, was lit up. The three others beneath it were labeled 'B', 'SB1', and 'SB2'. There was a biometric scanner protruding from the panel next to them. Cannon didn't bother with scanning his fingerprint and punched the 'B' button.

"We going to the basement?" Danny asked.

"Yeah," Cannon replied.

Danny motioned to the other two buttons. "What's on those other floors?"

"Storage." The answer came too quick, like it was a practiced one used to hide the truth.

The ride to the basement level was a short one. The elevator chimed and Cannon pounced on the "Close Door" button with his thumb.

"You mind telling me what might be out there?" Cannon asked.

Danny had been considering his answer ever since he ended his last phone call with Chip. "I think there's a bomb set to go off under the House of Representatives tonight, in a matter of minutes."

Danny half expected Cannon to bust out laughing, but he didn't even flinch.

"Explain," Cannon replied.

"The sarin gas attack last week, at L'Enfant Plaza." Danny paused to make sure Cannon was on the same page.

"Yeah?" Cannon said.

"I think it was a cover to plant a bomb."

Cannon looked confused. "But bombs were already found under the Lincoln Memorial and near the Washington Monument. There were no bombs found at L'Enfant Plaza. Every agency, from the FBI down to the meter maids, has been sweeping everything around here since the gas attack. There's nothing."

Danny thought of another border story. Several members of the fledging Meridian Cartel had slaughtered a lieutenant of the rival Juarez Cartel, most of his family and several other cartel members at the lieutenant's daughter's wedding. A full revenge assault was inevitable. Every member of the Meridian Cartel was murdered, which is exactly what the Mexican government had counted on. For the killers weren't actual members of the Meridian Cartel. They were Mexican Army officers in disguise.

Deception has always been the true art of war.

"Who said they didn't deliver the bombs here *before* the gas attack?" Danny offered. He pictured the group of men who had fired on him underneath L'Enfant Plaza returning to their cramped quarters in the utility corridor after planting the bombs, before the gas attack. Then he pictured them waiting until after the gas attack and the subsequent investigation to commence the other part of their plan: linking the gas attack to their delivery. He pictured one of them unlocking the sewer grate's lock to gain access to the sewers, relocking it and them smashing it off. He pictured another one scratching the grate underneath the platform in the station. That's why the FBI didn't notice the scratches. They weren't there until after the Metro station investigation was complete. *The assailants wanted to make it look like an outside job, the blame no doubt falling on some terrorist cell.*

Rather than argue with him, or even question his line of thinking, Cannon jumped ahead. "The only security we have down here are the cameras." It seemed Cannon shared Danny's take on cameras: they were too heavily relied upon and were susceptible to tampering, a recipe for a security disaster.

"No guards?" Danny asked.

"Not before the gas attack. But since then, the entrances to the escape tunnels have been guarded 24/7."

"Who works on the cameras?" Danny asked.

"We control them." Cannon's response oozed of contempt, like Danny shouldn't have even thought that a member of the Capitol Police could be mixed up in anything sinister.

"I didn't ask who controls them. Who works on them? Who fixes them when they go down? Who maintains the software, the network?"

"Private contractor," Cannon replied.

"Your chief hire them?"

"No, procurement department does. But I know they're new."

Danny stiffened. "New? How new?"

"They came in with the Butcher administration. But that's nothing different. New contractors always come around with the changing of the guard at 1600 Pennsylvania Avenue."

"How much time until the State of the Union?" Danny asked.

Cannon flicked his left wrist, checking his watch. "Less than 45 minutes."

"Which means we probably only have a half hour to find the damn thing," Danny said. He eyed the control panel. "What's really on SB1 and SB2?"

"Like I said Cavanaugh, it's for storage. Sub-basement one and two are filled with private storage rooms and old offices that aren't used any longer."

"How many rooms are down there?"

Cannon huffed. "Around a hundred on each floor. Some are locked, some aren't. Many of the keys to the locked ones have been missing for years." Cannon eyed his watch again. "No time to search every one, not even with dogs."

Danny didn't fully trust Cannon, let alone a full search team. And Cannon was right. Even with all those resources, there was no way to search that much area in under an hour, and counting.

Danny focused on the control panel again as he asked the next question.

"Who has access to those floors?"

"Some people from the Architect of the Capitol's office. Some Capitol Police staff."

"Do you?"

Cannon shook his head. "Not high enough on the food chain. But trust me, Cavanaugh, security for the sub-basement is top notch. Besides fingerprint recognition here, there are numerous keycard access points that use password and voice verification. If someone smuggled a bomb in through the escape tunnels, it's not in the sub-basement."

Danny wanted to ask the obvious question: if the sub-basement was merely old storage rooms, then why all the "top notch" security? But he didn't have the time for a pissing match. He had to trust Cannon. "How do you want to play it?" he asked Cannon instead.

"Just follow my lead." Cannon yanked his police-issue Beretta from his belt holster. Then he bent over and pulled up his pant leg, revealing an ankle holster. In it was a Kahr PM9 millimeter. He retrieved it and handed it to Danny. "You ever fired a pocket rocket before?"

"A few times." Danny chambered a bullet and sighted the gun before pulling it in tight to his chest.

Cannon finally took his thumb off the "Close Door" button. The doors rolled back and he eased out of the elevator. Danny was on his heels. A set of pea-green double doors stood in front of them. Cannon turned the doorknob, and they spilled out into a long, deserted passageway that contained two rail beds cut into the glazed concrete floor. Both the passageway and the rail beds snaked down a hill and then out of sight. Danny and Cannon shuffled over the width of the passageway, their guns and eyes pointed in all directions.

"We're directly underneath the House chambers," Cannon declared as he stood tall and relaxed, not seeing anything out of the ordinary. "The Capitol is actually three buildings in one. The House, the Rotunda, and the Senate are all separate." Danny eyed four massive support columns, two on each side of the rail beds as Cannon continued. "These columns hold up the entire House building. I'm guessing you were thinking the terrorists would pull another 9/11 and make the building implode on itself? If so, then they'd have to take out these columns. And I don't see any bombs strapped to them, do you?"

Danny didn't answer. He galloped past the columns, looking for the slightest shred of evidence to confirm his theory. The tension coiled in his body evaporated as he came up empty handed.

Directly under the House chambers.

Cannon was right. Danny did think a bomb or bombs would make the building implode, killing all the occupants within it. He pictured the horrifying sight of 9/11, the Twin Towers each collapsing into rubble.

Unless.

The thought slammed into him. *Unless an implosion wasn't what they were after.*

"Did bomb-sniffing dogs go over this area?" he asked Cannon as he walked back toward him.

Cannon nodded. "Every inch of the entire building."

"Can they sniff out nukes?"

Cannon gave him a funny look. "For obvious reasons, they don't train with radioactive material. So no."

"What about testing for a nuclear device?"

"We have radiation monitors everywhere," Cannon replied. Then he unfurled his long, right arm to uncover the strange-looking watch on his right wrist. "Plus, we're required to wear radiation monitors during our shifts." He looked at it and then turned his wrist so Danny could see the '0.0' on its face. "Nothing's been reported by anyone else, either."

Danny noticed a wide stairway to their right. "Where does that lead?" he asked.

"That takes you back up to the ground floor and the first-floor offices. Come on," Cannon said as he started walking down the hallway. "I'll take you to the entrance to the tunnels."

They reached an alcove to their left, and Cannon swung into it. There were three separate sets of double doors, one on each wall. Cannon nodded to the set right in front of them.

"The entrance to the tunnels is beyond those doors," he whispered as he held up his weapon. "There should be a guard just inside."

Cannon moved to a keycard panel hanging next to the doors. He inserted his card, typed in his access code, and the door buzzed. He swung open the door and, as promised, a surprised guard jumped up from his chair.

"Christ, Sarge. You scared the shit out of me."

"Sorry, Pulido. All quiet down here?"

Pulido nodded. "Just fighting my eyelids, Sarge."

Cannon holstered his gun. He turned to Danny. "I don't know about Koontz, but I like my steak medium."

Danny heard Cannon, but he wasn't listening to him. He still trusted his gut feeling telling him something wasn't right here.

What am I not seeing?

He jogged back out into the open area behind them. He ran around the support columns again, looking for anything that he missed.

"What are these railways for?" Danny asked Cannon as he loped back from the escape tunnel entrance.

Cannon's eyes trailed down the railway. "Capitol subway system. These lines run to and from the Rayburn building."

"Is it just for members of Congress or is it open to the public?"

"Just for Congress and their staffers, unless one of them is escorting a visitor."

A subway system. Danny's heartbeat picked up its pace. A major part of the infiltration plan so far used tunnels and a subway, the Metro. *Tunnels and subways.* Could the bad guys have gone to the well twice? He stared down the passageway and pictured it weaving its way underneath the earth to the Rayburn building. Butcher could have recruited a member of Congress or a congressional staff member to share his vision. That person could have escorted a bomber down here. But where could they have planted the bomb? Danny pictured a faceless bomber riding the subway. *Riding the subway. A moving bomb would be harder to locate, he thought.* The only problem with that theory is there wasn't a train car in sight.

Danny started running down the passageway. Suddenly, he froze. Another channel sliced off to his right. He saw a stubby, cream-colored subway train resting in the shadows at the end of a short hallway.

Subways and tunnels.

Danny ran to the train. It was elevated off its track by hydraulic jacks underneath each car. Each of the five cars contained two bench seats facing each other, room enough for twenty people. The top half of each open-air car was encapsulated by sheets of clear Plexiglas.

"What are you doing, Cavanaugh?" Cannon asked, hoofing up behind him.

"Do you know much about these trains?" Danny asked as he stepped into the first car and began examining it. He got down on his hands and knees and looked under each bench.

"Not a clue. All I know is that this car has been out of service for a couple weeks now," Cannon explained.

Danny popped his head up. *Out of service. Of course.* He pictured men dressed in workmen's outfits, men who had manipulated the camera network, gaining access through the tunnel during off hours and then carrying toolboxes over to this train to work on it. But they weren't real workmen, and they didn't have the kind of tools and supplies needed to repair a subway train.

Danny slid down on his stomach and began examining the underbelly of the train.

Exasperation laced Cannon's voice. "What the hell are you doing? I saw the dogs go over this very train myself. And my monitor is still showing 0.0. It's clean."

Danny flipped over on his back and pushed himself into a crawl space between the train and its track.

"Cavanaugh, get out from under there. I don't know if that track's hot. If it is, you're history, bomb or no bomb."

Danny wasn't listening. He stared at every inch of the train's mechanics around him: wheels, rotors, gearboxes, suspension dampers, and thick bunches of electrical wiring. Could someone hide a bomb in all this? Maybe a nuke deep inside, where it couldn't be detected? He had no idea, but he did have a good idea who might know.

Find the lowest man on the totem pole.

Danny squeezed out from under the train, pulled out his cell phone, and quickly dialed.

"Hello?"

"Hello, Luther?"

Luther Smalls grumbled a yes into the phone.

"Luther, it's Sergeant Cavanaugh from the Metro station."

"Yes, Sergeant. I remember you. How could I forget?"

"Listen Luther, I need a favor, and I don't have much time. I'm here at the House of Representatives. Actually, I'm under it. Do you know anything about their subway system?"

Luther laughed. "Know anything? My brother's people did the retrofitting work back in '93 for all the house trains. I heard enough bullshit stories about that job to last me a lifetime."

"That's great, Luther. Listen, I'm going to need you to stay calm and concentrate on what I'm about to ask you. Don't worry about anything else, just focus on answering the question."

"Okay."

"Can you tell me if there is anywhere on one of these trains where someone could hide a bomb without it being discovered?"

"Someone wants to bomb one of the trains?"

"No, Luther. Someone wants to blow up the Capitol."

There was a long silence. Danny thought that the old man may have had a heart attack.

"Luther, you still there?"

Luther came back with a question that stunned Danny. "Is the car in the repair dock?"

"Yes! Yes, Luther, it is!"

"Listen to me carefully, Sergeant. Your problem isn't the train. Your problem is what lies beneath it."

Chapter 100

"It was Steven Fraser Tytler, an eighteenth-century Scottish historian, who said that a democracy cannot exist as a permanent form of government. It can only exist until the voters discover that they can vote themselves largesse from the public treasury. From that moment on, the majority always votes for the candidates promising the most benefits from the treasury. Then it's all over but pinpointing the moment of total ruination.

"Our leaders in Congress have been loose with the purse strings long enough. They have fed for far too long and taken far too much from the public trough. I am not exaggerating when I say that our leaders have guided us down the path toward complete financial collapse. It is time for us, the American people, to take back the reins of fiscal responsibility.

"Each and every American has a responsibility to not only vote but to ascertain an intimate knowledge of the processes and players of their government as if their lives depended on it. Because it does. Thomas Jefferson once said that the tree of liberty must be refreshed from time to time with the blood of patriots and tyrants. While he was referring to battle, I believe that if each American takes the initiative to make our democracy a part of us, to let it flow through our veins like lifegiving blood, then we will keep the tree of liberty healthy forever.

"I have spent my first weeks in office, as my predecessors have, being handled with kid gloves by my critics and by the media. With this speech, I am certain my list of critics will grow exponentially. Tonight, I issue those folks an invitation to bring their concerns to my door. Should they have a better solution to bring America back from the brink of disaster, I will utilize it and offer my deepest appreciation as well as the thanks of a grateful nation. However, before you even draft your critique, I challenge you to stand tall, look me in the eye, and tell me with an honest heart that you too are not concerned about the kind of nation we are leaving our children. But most of all, I ask you to take the energy you will expend to try and browbeat me and use it for America, not against it.

"I will not lie to you. I stand here before you and the world to say that we all will need to make sacrifices over the next four years and beyond in order to fix our nation. Each and every American will need to make great sacrifices. We will endure much pain. But we will not make those sacrifices and endure that pain alone. We will bear those burdens with our American brothers and sisters. We will hurt together, but we will also persevere together to one day make our democracy great again.

"My fellow Americans, we can no longer afford to be led with blinders on. We can no longer afford to put our democracy on autopilot. It is up to each and every one of us to decide whether we stand teetering on the brink of failure or poised ready to rebuild a new and improved nation. Thank you, and may God continue to bless America."

The echo of a single pair of clapping hands rose up from the back of the Senate chamber. The first floor lights had been dimmed beyond the central dais from where Jack Butcher stood. He squinted beyond the spotlights aimed on him toward the man who was strolling down the aisle.

"Excellent speech. The best I've ever heard," Simon Shilling said, stopping at the foot of the dais.

Jack folded the speech into his pocket as he stepped down. He shook the hand of his closest friend as they met on the Senate floor.

"Thanks," Jack replied and then brought his voice down to a whisper. "Too bad no one will hear it."

"Maybe not tonight," Simon replied in his own soft voice. "You're doing the right thing, Mr. President. We're doing the right thing."

Jack nodded. Simon glanced at his watch. "We've got time to hear it once more, from the top."

Jack returned to his perch on the dais. Simon slid over to the second desk on Jack's right. He knew that the first one was already occupied.

Jack's heart fell as he stared at the empty desk next to his chief of staff. He pictured his young son like he always had after his death, without the tubes and machines tied to him. Jack put his hand in his jacket pocket to retrieve his speech but then stopped. He gripped the podium atop the dais with both hands and began his speech from memory for his audience of two.

"Mr. Speaker, Vice President Mulroney, members of Congress, fellow citizens ..."

Chapter 101

A forgotten room.

Danny's cell phone had already lost service twice since he crawled into the space beneath the congressional subway train. Except for the tiny beam of Sergeant Cannon's mini-flashlight and the weak glow that fell from the open hatch at the end of the service bay, Danny was submerged in complete darkness. He stepped back over to the hatch, stood tall, and poked his head up into the service bay. He called Luther again and waited. Luther picked up after two rings.

"I keep losing you down there," Danny said.

"Where are you now?" Luther replied.

"I'm at the opening in the service bay floor."

"Then I'm going to have to walk you through it from there."

Danny listened to Luther's explanation. As he heard the words, he tried to visualize the spatial arrangement of the room.

"That's it," Luther surmised.

"Wish me luck."

"Good luck, Sergeant. We'll grab a beer later, and you can tell me all about it."

"Thanks, Luther."

"I'll be glued to the TV to see how you do."

Danny ended the call and looked at the empty service bay. He had instructed Sergeant Cannon to get a bomb expert down here as fast as he could. Normally Cannon would have used the radio, but he had agreed with Danny's sentiment. Nothing was as it seemed anymore. They didn't know who could be trusted, so broadcasting a plea for help over an open line was out of the question.

As if he was about to go underwater, Danny swallowed a deep breath and plunged back down through the hatch. He used

the flashlight to light up his feet. He shuffled to the edge of the
platform he was standing on and used the ladder bolted to its side
to climb down. When he reached the floor, he felt openness around
him. Instead of wasting time swinging the flashlight around in all
directions, he followed Luther's instructions.

"Look for a light switch on the wall close to your point of entry."

Danny widened the beam as much as possible and plastered a
ring of weak light on the wall. He found a panel of switches and
flipped each switch up as fast as he could. Row after row of florescent
tubes sputtered to life, their electrical whine aching above his head.

Danny nearly dropped the flashlight as soon as he saw what
was around him. The room was the size of a hockey rink. His eyes
immediately focused on the strange looking machinery at the far
end of the room. Luther had explained that the hulking linear
induction motor, complete with its massive transmission gears and
a steel support structure that was attached to both floor and ceiling,
had been installed back in the 1950s to power a monorail system
that highlighted U.S. technological advances at that time. The single,
knee-high track that extended from the motor and suddenly stopped
in the center of the room supported Luther's claim. But the monorail
was stopped in mid-construction due to cost overruns. It would have
been more expensive to remove the track and machinery and repair
the damage they had caused to the floor then to just build a new
basement level on top of everything and start over.

Danny pulled back and saw the four massive support columns
that continued through the basement floor into this level. He saw
nothing but smooth concrete on the two sides he could see from his
position. He ran over to the first one, slid along its side, and turned
the corner. A mixture of dread and adrenaline rocked his body as he
nearly ran into a bomb attached to the back of the column.

He raced around the other columns. Eight bombs had been
attached to the backs and sides of the four columns. Danny returned
to the first one he saw and studied its guts. Four sets of red, green,
yellow, and blue wires ran from a small silver box to what looked to
be a 25-pound brick of C-4 explosives. Another thick, black wire ran
from the silver box to a smaller black box. The absence of anything

that looked like a timer made Danny's heart drop even further. These devices were controlled by a remote. They could go off at any time.

Although he had seen C-4 bombs before, Danny didn't have the first clue about how to deactivate them. Besides an antenna, the silver box undoubtedly also contained an amplifier to reach through the thick concrete walls of the Capitol, ready to receive its detonation signal. The smaller black box tied to it housed a fail-safe switch that tripped the device in case it was tampered with.

How in the hell am I going to deactivate all these bombs in the next few minutes?

Danny checked his watch. *The House chamber had to be near its scheduled capacity by now. I've got to find Cannon,* Danny thought.

He ran for the ladder and raced up it. He tore across the platform to the hatch and stuck his head up. The service bay was still empty. Danny swiped his cell phone from his pocket and dialed in Cannon's number.

"Cannon," he answered breathlessly.

Danny yelled into the phone. "Where the fuck are you?!"

"Right around the corner." Danny heard it both in the phone and in his other ear. Cannon raced toward him with another officer hot on his heels.

"Come on!" Danny shouted, waving his arms. "I found the bombs!"

The officer behind Cannon began sprinting toward the hatch. He was dressed in a bomb squad outfit, complete with full body armor and a helmet. "Name's O'Brien," he called. "I'm with the Capitol Police Bomb Squad."

"Get down here now!" Danny ordered as he collapsed back down inside the hatch. "These things could go off any second!"

O'Brien wriggled out of his backpack and handed it to Danny through the hatch. "Take this," he said.

Danny took it from him and then scurried over to the ladder. O'Brien was right behind him but instead of taking the ladder, the baby-faced bomb expert jumped down to the concrete floor. He walked to the nearest bomb and examined it for only a moment before walking back to Danny.

"I need the backpack, please," O'Brien said. His words were calm, as if he was asking Danny to pass him a wrench to do an oil change.

He unzipped the backpack and pulled out a laptop. He turned it on and then reached back into the pack. He unfurled a long cord and stuck it into the back of the computer. He typed in his password, and the laptop automatically launched some kind of scanning program.

O'Brien dug into the backpack one more time and produced a small tripod with a silver ball at the end. He plugged the other end of the cord into it, hit the "Enter" button, and then gazed into the laptop's screen.

Eight green dots popped up on the screen in the same formation of the explosives in the room. O'Brien fingers flew across the keyboard. Numbered and lettered codes appeared on the screen. O'Brien turned to Danny and grinned wide as he hit "Enter" again. All eight green dots turned red.

"We're good to go. All the bombs have been suspended."

A sense of relief washed over Danny. "What the hell is that thing?"

"We call it the Terrorist Trap. It's a bomb jammer. It uses open-ended RF architecture to interrupt signals as low as 20 megahertz and as high as 2,000 megahertz. We've got a bigger unit on the top of the Capitol dome, but it seems that its signal can't quite reach down here."

"So what now?"

"Well, let's see." O'Brien left the laptop and walked back over to the closest explosive. "I'm glad as hell you didn't try to deactivate these bad boys." He pointed to the black box. "See this little jewel? It's a tamper relay, what we call a tinker blinker. If you had cut any of the wires on this one device, it would have sent a signal to the rest of its buddies here and boom." O'Brien gave the tinker blinker a second look. "Looks like they splurged for the upgrade and got the gyroscope package, too."

"Gyroscopes? For what?"

"If you would have tried to remove this bomb from its position, the gyroscope would have moved."

"And there goes the neighborhood."

"Bingo."

"So how can you deactivate them?"

"We can't. We'll have to blow them. But don't worry. As long as the trigger signal's jammed, we can transport them over to our detonation room and set them off there."

"What about the gyros?"

"I can bypass them right here." O'Brien used his fingernails to pry off the relay's cover. He already had a pair of wire cutters out and snipped a black wire that looked like several others, which ran into a tiny rectangular component. "This one's all set." O'Brien didn't waste any time. He moved around to the next bomb and pried off the relay cover. Danny was impressed. This kid had obviously been around the block a few times, and had the confidence to prove it.

Danny followed him and winced as O'Brien nonchalantly cut another wire. "Hey, O'Brien, let me ask you something."

"First name's Jimmy," he replied, moving to the next bomb.

"Okay, Jimmy. Can you tell if there are any other explosives down here, say a dirty bomb or other nuclear device?"

O'Brien motioned to the tripod. "The double T scans for everything. Besides these babies, the room's clean."

"Any idea who could rig up something like this?"

Jimmy had already pried off the next relay cover. He talked while he hunted for the right wire to cut. "Hell, I've been racking my brain ever since I first saw these beauties. But I can tell you this; the bad guys knew what they were doing. These bombs were set up to act like one giant knife." He swiped through the air with the side of his hand. "Once these babies went off," he pointed toward the ceiling, "it would have caved in the entire House chamber and killed everyone inside. The guys who did this knew how to set up a picture perfect implosion."

Danny remembered what Cannon said about the architecture of the Capitol.

"The Capitol is actually three buildings in one. The House, the Rotunda, and the Senate are all separate."

He also remembered what Simon Shilling had told him about the president's whereabouts.

"He's giving the speech to Simon in the Senate chambers."

All the evidence Danny had racked up confirmed his theory. President Jack Butcher and his chief of staff wanted to carry out the most egregious act of terrorism in the history of the country.

"How many of these setups have you seen, Jimmy?"

Jimmy finally cut the wire and moved on. "I grew up in the demolitions business back in Philly. Then I graduated from the school of 'Blowing up Iraqi Shit.' I've seen one or two in my time."

"So who could pull off this job?"

"Job this big? This much planning? Maybe a dozen guys could do this work."

"Any idea where I could find them?"

Jimmy popped off the next cover. "You got access to a private jet?"

"No."

"Well, I suggest you start cashing in your frequent flier miles, 'cause they're military. Specialists in different countries that I met during my tours in Iraq."

Danny rolled his hand. "Countries like?"

Jimmy was much quicker finding what was hopefully the right wire on this one. "Like Germany and France, if you can believe it. Russia's got a hell of a guy. England, hell there was a guy there from one of the 'Stan' countries." Jimmy cut the wire as he tried recalling. "Uzbekistan, Kreplakistan, something like that. Anyway, he could blow the stink off of shit. He was a fucking wizard with directionals."

"Anyone work with nukes?"

Jimmy moved to the next bomb and went to work on it. "Straight nukes, no."

"What about dirty bombs?"

"Dirty Debbies? They all talked the talk about Dirty Debbies. Every one of those bastards said that they'd killed at least one or two double Ds."

"But you never saw them actually work on one? Either to activate one or defuse one?"

Jimmy shook his head. "We never encountered Dirty Debbies in Iraq. Shit, in the sandbox, it was all about sniffing out IEDs."

Just like that, Danny had answers to all of his questions about the bombs. An English military explosives expert could have rigged them. Both the Dirty Debbies and these explosives in here as well.

"Should we take him or retreat?"

The bomber could very well have been supported by a small but well-trained force acting on secret orders directly from King Edward, England's commander in chief.

"Thanks, Jimmy. And thanks for saving our asses."

"Sure enough, Sergeant." He grinned as he snipped the right wire once more. "All in a day's work, right?"

Danny started for the ladder. Halfway up it, he called over to Jimmy. "Name's Danny Cavanaugh by the way."

O'Brien saluted him with his wire cutters. "Nice to meet you, Danny. Maybe us two Irish boys can go tear up Adams Morgan some night, if you're still around."

"Sounds like a hell of a plan," Danny replied. He stepped over to the hatch and stuck his head up to see Sergeant Cannon standing over him. He was holding a walkie-talkie out in front of Danny's face. "I thought you might like to hear this."

Danny heard the Speaker of the House's voice in the distance. "Are you ready, sir?" There was no answer. A few moments passed and then the Speaker's voice rung out through the walkie-talkie.

"Ladies and gentlemen, the president of the United States."

The tiny speaker inside the walkie-talkie crackled with static as the applause overwhelmed it. Danny almost forgot about the speech. Cannon kept his thumb on the button until Danny motioned for him to turn it off. He climbed up out of the hatch and dusted himself off.

"Looks like you get to be the hero all over again, Cavanaugh."

There was no hint of gratitude in Cannon's voice, no recognition of Danny's hunch that had just saved hundreds of lives, including Cannon's. But Danny didn't expect as much.

"You still don't trust me do you, Cannon?"

"I'd like to know exactly how the hell you knew to check the basement. You get a call or something?"

Danny shook his head. "No."

Then how'd you know?"

"Instincts."

Cannon huffed. "Instincts, huh? Bullshit."

Danny stared at Cannon for a while. Then, he simply turned and started walking away.

"Hey. Where you going Cavanaugh?" Cannon asked.

"Where my instincts are leading me."

"We've got to tell people what's happened. You've got to explain how you knew what was going on."

Danny kept walking. "You do it, Cannon. You've got a way with words."

Cannon called out after Danny. "Wait a minute. What are you going to do?"

Danny kept walking and called out over his shoulder. "Be the hero again. Third time's the charm, right?"

Chapter 102

Danny lifted his head up off the cot and was momentarily confused by his surroundings. Then he saw the lockers in small employees' locker room, and it all came rushing back to him. Chip had put him up for the night.

Danny checked his watch. It was seven thirty in the morning. He looked over at a chair in front of one of the lockers. On it, Chip had left him a towel, a can of shaving cream, and a disposable razor. A note was on top of the towel. Danny rolled off of the inflatable mattress, trudged over to the chair, and read it.

"No man ever looked good in his casket with a five o'clock shadow. Love and wet kisses, Carver."

Danny chuckled and then headed to the shower. As he took the next twenty minutes soaking his head, he reviewed the plan that he and Chip had devised in the late night that turned into early morning just hours ago.

A couple pints of Shiner Bock had moistened Danny's brain just enough to make their idea seem plausible, damn near successful. If everything went according to plan. But, as Danny knew all too well, things hardly ever went according to plan.

Danny emerged in the kitchen with a towel around his waist and beads of water still clinging to his chest. Chip was cooking ham and cheese omelets. As soon as he saw Danny, he put both hands on his hips and thrust out his ass.

"Morning, sugar. Thank you so much, but I don't need any more heat for my fire," he said, lisping his words.

"It's too early for that shit, Carver."

Chip produced two pints of beer from behind an industrial-sized bottle of Heinz ketchup. He handed one to Danny. "Here you go, breakfast of champions."

"Thanks." Danny took it from him and glanced at the TV hanging in the corner. It was tuned to CNN Headline News. "Anything new on the news?"

Chip looked up at the TV. "Just more pundits adding to the nauseating river of analysis about Butcher's speech. They all loved the hell out of it, said it was just what this country needed to hear." Chip laughed. "Chris Matthews actually said it was as refreshing as making love to his wife after sipping on a mint julep. But they all agreed Butcher killed any hope for reelection."

Danny had listened to a rebroadcast of Butcher's State of the Union address in the wee hours after the bar had closed. "Americans don't like hearing the truth."

"Americans don't like making sacrifices," Chip rebutted. "At least not in the twenty-first century."

Danny held up his glass. "Truer words have never been uttered." Chip clinked Danny's glass with his own and the two swigged their beers. "Anything about the bombs under the Capitol?"

"Not a word. Nothing in cyberspace either."

"The Capitol police are a tight-lipped bunch."

"No doubt."

"You think they'll be able to bury the story forever?"

Chip grinned. "That depends on you, doesn't it?"

Danny huffed as the impossibility of his next task flooded his brain again. "Yeah."

"Just think of the ass you'll get if you pull it off," Chip said. "Chicks dig heroes." He put his pint glass back in the air. "Here's to the women, the wonderful wine. They bloom once a month and beer twice a nine. They're the only creatures this side of hell, to get juice from your nuts without cracking the shell."

They clinked glasses again and gulped their beers. "That's beautiful, Chip. You just make that shit up?"

"I'm not that clever." Chip put his finger and thumb to his mouth like he was smoking a joint and assumed his best Jamaican accent. "I learned it from a Rasta man during my visit to the mother country, mon."

"And here I thought you were going to toast our mission."

Chip grabbed the salt shaker and pepper grinder off the rack above the grill. After dusting both omelets with the salt and then cranking the pepper grinder several times over each one, he threw some salt over his shoulder. "Absolutely not. That's bad luck."

"It is?" Danny asked, swigging another sip of beer.

Chip folded both omelets and then sprinkled shredded cheese on them as he assumed a thick Texas accent. "Shoot, I don't know about in the land of steers and queers, but us Yankees think it is." He slid the omelets out of the skillet onto two plates. Then he grabbed a handful of chopped scallions off the butcher block and sprinkled them across each plate. A look of utter satisfaction crested Chip's face as he handed his friend his finished product.

"Thanks, Chip," Danny said. He grabbed a fork off the chopping block and dove into the omelet. "Delicious as usual."

The two of them talked about everything except their mission for the next several minutes. They updated each other about their personal lives, their triumphs, and tragedies. They recalled their adventures in this very bar this last time they were together, reminiscing about the women who hit on Danny and the ones Chip tried to talk into his bed. It was a moment that Danny would remember for the rest of his life, no matter how long that was.

An hour later, Danny was shaking his friend's hand inside the door that led out into the back alley. They both knew that this could be the last time they saw each other. They didn't speak. The look in Chip's eye said everything as he handed Danny a new disposable cell phone to replace the one that Danny had trashed before getting anywhere near the bar last night, along with a thick wad of cash. *Good luck, my friend.* Danny hoped his eyes were conveying the same message.

Danny eased out the door. He imagined FBI agents appearing out of nowhere and swarming him. But that didn't happen. He hurried down the alley and stopped at the edge of 19th Street. He looked in both directions. A jogger ran up the sidewalk across the street. A cab was about to pass him when he flagged it down.

Eight minutes later, the cab stopped in front of the Connecticut Avenue entrance to the National Zoo. Danny told the cabbie to wait for him and he got out. He took a few steps toward the entrance, making sure to stop short of the reach of the cameras attached to the entrance gates. He dialed a number on the disposable cell; the same very private number he memorized just before he had left the White House to investigate L'Enfant Plaza. It rang five times. Danny was about to hang up when he heard someone on the other end.

"Hello?"

Danny recognized the voice. "Hello, Jack."

There was a long pause. Finally, the president replied. "Good morning, Sergeant."

"I believe that you and I need to have a conversation."

"I agree."

Danny had the place and time ready to go. "Arlington Cemetery, the JFK Memorial. In two hours."

"I can't possibly—"

Danny cut him off. "Find a way, or I go public with what I know."

Another long pause. "I'll be there," the president finally said.

"One more thing, this is the deal breaker."

"What?"

"Bring Sydney along."

Danny didn't give the president a chance to say no. He ended the call and turned the phone off. Even though it was powered down, as long as the battery was still connected, a cell phone still sent out a signal that could be tracked by GPS. That's why Danny chose to place the call at the zoo. He figured the president would track the call to a nearby tower and assume that Danny was hanging out in the zoo, a very public place, until their meeting.

As he walked back toward the cab, Danny pried the battery out of the phone and threw it in a nearby trashcan. He broke the phone in half, tossed the parts into another trash can, and jumped back in the cab.

"Where to now?" the cabbie asked.

"GWU," Danny told him.

The cab stopped across the street from the George Washington University Visitor Center. Danny got out and crossed the street. He was dressed in a navy blue T-shirt and camouflage cargo shorts he borrowed from Chip. He pulled the navy blue Washington Senators cap low on his head, his eyes everywhere behind Chip's aviator sunglasses. No one even glanced his way.

Danny entered the Visitor Center. The university's spirit shop was just inside to his left. He strolled into it like he didn't have a care in the world. A cute coed in full GWU apparel approached him from behind the counter.

"Is there something I can help you with, sir?"

"Do y'all sell disposable cell phones?"

"We do." She motioned to the side wall of the store where various electronics hung.

"And do y'all have warm-up suits? Both men's and women's?"

"We do. Just follow me." She turned and led him toward the back of the store. "Are you with the tour group?"

"Tour group?"

"The alumni tour group."

"No, why?"

"Oh, it's just some of them have stopped by to make sure we haven't canceled it because of the weather."

"What weather?"

"There's an 80 percent chance of thunderstorms moving in." Seeing a sales opportunity, the girl stopped at a nearby display and grabbed a buff and blue-colored umbrella. "Do you need an umbrella?"

The weather. Danny didn't even think about it. Instantly, he visualized how rain would affect his plan.

Danny grinned at the salesgirl. "I'll take two if you tell me a little more about this alumni tour."

Chapter 103

Jack Butcher popped open the black, double canopy umbrella as he stepped from the passenger seat of the late-model Mini Cooper, a vehicle in which the president of the United States wouldn't normally dare ride. He looked around, as he pulled the lapel of his tan trench coat up around his chin. He tugged on the brim of the matching fedora, lowering it until it touched the pair of sunglasses concealing his eyes.

He pulled the seat back forward and Sydney got out. She was dressed in a Jones of New York belted trench coat. There were several colors and sizes from which to choose in the White House's inventory, but Sydney chose the very form-fitting one with the leopard print so loud it might as well have growled. Jack thought back to the words he used on Cavanaugh to persuade him to investigate L'Enfant Plaza, words that Cavanaugh himself had used in the same conversation.

Hidden in plain sight.

Jack was confident that he had also conned Sydney the same way now.

Danny's lost it, Sydney. I need to help him. I need you to go with me.

Jack leaned down and nodded at Simon, who was behind the wheel. Simon returned the gesture. Jack closed the door and Simon sped off, spinning the tires slightly on the wet pavement.

The rain drizzling from the gray sky couldn't keep visitors away from Arlington Cemetery. Jack and Sydney fell in behind a tour group wrapped in ponchos like action figures sealed in shrink-wrap. They were all intently listening to their guide's respectful whisper as she led them up the granite stairs to the viewing platform next to the JFK Memorial.

374

Jack tightened his grip around Sydney's waist as he steered past the tour group and moved in close to Kennedy's Eternal Flame. A woman clutching her young daughter's hand stood to his left. They were both bowing their heads. To his right, some asshole was chatting away on his cell phone. Jack wanted to rip the phone right from the guy's ear. *How dare he be so disrespectful!* Seeing that guy only reaffirmed Jack's intentions last night.

The only thing that will change this country is revolution.

The asshole moved, and Jack saw Danny. He was dressed in a black trench coat. Sydney's body tensed as she gazed upon him.

It was smart to choose this location, Jack thought. It was a very public yet hauntingly private place. Jack gazed across the endless formation of white headstones and up toward Arlington House. He looked for Stefan Taber, who should have been in place by now.

Danny, who stood off the concrete pathway next to a headstone adorned with fresh roses, motioned Jack toward him. Jack kept Sydney close underneath his umbrella. They stepped over the knee-high black chain that separated the gravesites from the path. Jack could feel Sydney's heartbeat accelerate. He had to admit his own heart was racing as well.

"Hello, Danny," Jack said with a sympathetic tone. Once again, he glanced up at Arlington House. Just beside it, Jack caught Stefan Taber's camouflaged hand wave to him from a thick grove of cypress trees. Jack didn't need to act like Danny's savior in front of Sydney any longer. He gripped her as hard as he could, and she glared at him, wincing in pain.

"Don't say a word," he whispered to the both of them. "There are guns trained on both of you. Try anything and, well, let's just say it would be appropriate we're in a cemetery."

Chapter 104

"You get that costume from the CIA?" Danny asked the president. He intentionally kept his eyes off of Sydney as she took a small step back from both men.

The president smirked. "I'm glad you like it." He stepped to his right. Danny was well aware that the president was probably telling the truth. There had to be at least one person watching them. He was also aware of the cemetery's topography, and the abundance of memorials surrounding them allowed for an endless list of locations that a trained sniper could use as cover. Danny would only know where he was when the president stopped moving and made some kind of signal. Then he would only have milliseconds to react.

"I also liked the speech. No one was supposed to hear it, were they?" The president didn't reply. "You're the one behind all of this; you and your old Oxford buddy King Edward. He supplied the dirty bombs, and you supplied the fake eighth article. Those two things were enough to get Fantroy on a plane so you could kill him." Danny stopped to examine the president's reaction. He remained as motionless as the headstones around him. "Why was Fantroy so important? Was he the roadblock to your creation of some perfect society?" Danny finally stared at Sydney. "One that was inspired by the teachings of Professor Colin Tanner?"

The president still didn't say a word. Instead, he shifted further to the right.

"There are guns trained on both of you."

Danny once again reeled back to Sydney's confession at the White House pool. *"Stefan Taber told me he's working for the president."* The Secret Service would have never gone along with this stunt. If anyone was really out there, Danny had to believe it was Taber and only Taber.

"The eighth article was never in the Library of Congress, was it?" Danny continued. "Your thief had Seward's journal with him the whole time. He only made it look like he took it off the shelf in the Rare Book Room. You knew the documents would stand up to simple examinations performed by a professor, a writer, and even an expert from the National Archives. But you also knew that any in-depth scientific testing would prove them to be fakes. That's the real reason why you controlled access to them." Danny was rolling now. He felt like he was back in an interrogation room trying to break a witless perp. "You also made sure the gas mixture at L'Enfant Plaza wouldn't harm anyone, because those hard working stiffs weren't the people you were trying to kill." The President smirked, but again said nothing. Danny pressed on. "Sucks your men didn't clip me under L'Enfant, though. They were almost home after rigging the columns under the House of Representatives *before* the gas attack. Of course, the Capitol basement is monitored, but being the former head of the Senate Intelligence Committee, you have access to all kinds of hi-tech goodies, including camera bugs that can loop recordings, so your boys could have held a keg party down there and no one would have known the difference. They even set up L'Enfant Plaza to look like the gas attack was used as cover to access the sewers and the Capitol tunnels." Danny took in the president's stoic reaction. He hoped his next words would strike the president's Achilles' heel.

"I had all the pieces, but do you know what was the glue that brought them all together? I was sitting in the balcony of the House chambers when two officers wheeled down Ethan Goodnight. Your son suffered from the same form of muscular dystrophy Ethan has. You couldn't save Simon from endless pain, but you could have saved Ethan by providing him with a quick death."

Anger finally flashed across the president's face. "Do you know what you did last night?"

"I saved people's lives," Danny said sternly. "People you wanted dead."

"All you did was ensure the demise of America, Danny."

Danny heard the words, but they took a backseat to the president's actions. Danny watched his head shift. He was looking up toward Arlington House.

"So, if things had gone according to plan and Congress had perished last night, you would have blamed Great Britain, what with King Edward basically throwing down the gauntlet after Fantroy's death, how could you not?"

Sydney gasped. "King Edward knew all along that Fantroy was a Bilderberger. That's how you knew to time the burglaries at the library and Monticello with the lawsuit filing."

The president remained silent. Danny continued. "The King then does a little snooping and finds that Fantroy and his Bilderbergers were behind all the bombs. You and King Edward kill two birds with one stone. The late Anthony Fantroy is blamed for blowing up the House of Representatives, and an unprecedented investigation into the Bilderbergers operations would have put them out of business."

The president wiped a patch of dirt off the top of the nearest headstone and then looked out over the cemetery toward the White House. "Presidents are temporary. We only have four years, eight if we're lucky, to make things happen."

"But others were there last night besides members of Congress," Danny reminded him. "I know from experience, Jack. Having blood on your hands is a hard thing."

The president focused on Danny. "Exactly who all was in the House of Representatives last night, Danny?"

"Members of Congress, people on their staff. A ton of lobbyists. Little Ethan Goodnight and his mother, who I'm pretty sure didn't want to take over the world."

The president smirked. "You're forgetting a whole group of people seated around you in the mezzanine. Those people were given special invitations by the president to be there."

Danny pictured the faces in the mezzanine from last night. Mostly white, mostly middle-aged and older. They were all dressed in their best suits and chatted with each other in familiar ways.

"I give up," Danny said.

The president turned and stared into Sydney's eyes. "They were people like Ben Speakes and Dexter Walsh. They are the career bureaucrats, the true power brokers, the Washington establishment. Like I said, presidents may have power, but we're very temporary compared to a man like Speakes, who has remained an insider for forty years or a congressman who serves a twenty-year term and then goes on to become a seven figure a year lobbyist."

"You wanted a revolution," Sydney uttered. "You wanted to start America over."

No one spoke for several seconds after her declaration. It was so silent that Danny could actually hear the drizzling rain strike the president's umbrella.

The president finally broke the silence. "History has taught us that failed democracies were not toppled from outside forces. They rotted from the inside."

"So, last night was about removing the rotten apples from the bunch?" Danny asked. "But not all lobbyists are greedy, not every member of Congress is corrupt."

The president chuckled. "Like a surgeon friend of mine once told me, there's only one good way to rid a body of cancer. You've got to cut it out, even if you take some good tissue with it."

Sydney piped up. "History also proves that this is the way democracies work. The two parties would elect new representatives, and the jockeying for position would begin all over again. The fight for control would be worse than ever."

The president considered Sydney's statement. "After 9/11, there was a brief time when America truly acted like one united country. The events from last night would have dwarfed 9/11. The country, led by their president, would call for a total revisal of what a democracy is. No Democrats, no Republicans, no red, no blue. Just one big purple heart beating with civility, courage and compassion." The president paused and looked up at Arlington House again. "Thomas Jefferson said that for America to work, a revolution must occur every twenty years. I'd say we're more than two hundred years overdue."

The president shifted his weight back and forth. He was obviously edgy. He would make his signal any second. Danny had to keep him talking. "The country's already on life support. Without Congress, America would have flatlined altogether."

"It's brilliant." The words came from Sydney's mouth. Her calculating eyes hung on the president for several seconds and then she looked at Danny. "If America fails due to market forces, then so be it. However much governments try to prop up their economies in bad times, the presiding philosophy across the globe is still laissez-faire, let the markets correct themselves. However if a political catastrophe, such as a mass murder of Congress, causes economic calamity then political forces step in." Sydney turned back to the president. "The UN would wipe away your deficits. Much of your debt would be written off as well. Financially speaking, it would be as fresh a start as a government could get."

"But now all that can't happen," Danny said.

The president grinned. "I've got at least four years, Sergeant. Four years is a long time. Who knows what can happen."

The glow that surrounded the president's face suddenly evaporated. Danny noticed his right hand move. A split second later, two gunshots echoed across the cemetery.

Chapter 105

The sound of gunfire caused people at the JFK Memorial to run for their lives. Danny grabbed Sydney and galloped toward the Visitor Center. He didn't look back to see what the president was doing. He kept his eyes on the tree line in front of him, making sure to hug it as they ran. He was sure the president's sniper wouldn't be able to get a clean shot through the tree branches from his position.

By the time they reached the Visitor Center, chaos had fully erupted. The scene of people scrambling in every direction, panic etched in their faces, was exactly what Danny counted on as he and Chip made their plans only hours ago.

Danny led Sydney inside the center and then into the men's room. It was empty. He took her into the last stall and closed the door behind them.

"You okay?" he asked her.

She was obviously still shell-shocked. "What the hell just happened?"

"Back at the pool, I should have listened to you about Taber being with the president."

"Danny, you don't have to—"

Danny interrupted her. "When I left Chip's bar this morning, I knew that I could trust you."

"Why?"

"Because no one came there for me. You could have told the president about Chip, but you didn't."

"There was always something I didn't like about Butcher." Sydney smiled. "Plus, a girl has to have her secrets, no?"

Danny smiled at her. "Chalk up one more to women's intuition."

381

"Thank you for rescuing me, Danny. Again."

"You're not rescued just yet." Danny stood up on the toilet. He pushed up on the ceiling tile above his head and slid it over.

"What are you doing?" Sydney asked him.

Danny felt around for the three items he had placed up there before his meeting with Jack Butcher. He grabbed the GWU bookstore shopping bag and handed it to Sydney. Then he gripped the two GWU umbrellas and dropped down off the toilet.

"Here, put this on over your clothes," he said, reaching into the bag. He handed her a warm-up suit and baseball cap. She stripped off her coat and quickly put them on. Danny did the same.

Minutes later, they exited the bathroom. Several people had taken refuge inside the nearby gift shop. Even if anyone recognized Danny or Sydney, they were too busy crowded around two sets of windows that looked out on the cemetery.

Danny led Sydney toward the north exit. They stopped short of the double doors. As he whispered the next part of his plan into her ear, Danny looked through the windows. The rain had intensified. Some National Park police were trying to keep order near the cemetery's exit. Beyond the two D.C.P.D. cruisers that had pulled up on Memorial Drive, Danny spotted the GWU alumni tour group.

"You ready?" he asked her.

She turned and gazed into his eyes. "Can we make sure this is the last time we're in a life and death situation?"

"What? You don't like being the damsel in distress?"

Sydney huffed. "I'm just tired of playing to the male ego."

They both grinned. Danny blew out a quick breath before he opened the door. As he stepped outside, he opened his blue and buff umbrella. He held the canopy close to his head as he scurried toward the GWU group. From the corner of his eye, he saw Sydney emerge from the Visitor Center exactly thirty seconds later and open her umbrella.

Soon, they were both cloistered among two dozen other people holding blue and buff umbrellas and were heading down the stairs that led to the Arlington Cemetery Metro station. As they boarded the waiting Metro train, Danny couldn't help thinking about Chip. Something was wrong. Chip should have made contact by now.

Chapter 106

Stefan Taber's shot hit the small man exactly where he had aimed. The man's right leg buckled, and he went down into an outcropping of cedar trees just outside the Memorial Amphitheater.

Taber had been less than fifty yards from him when he heard the two gunshots ring out. His instincts compelled him to check the nearby woods from where the sounds originated. Through his scope, he saw a man wearing an eye patch stand from a prone position next to an exposed bolder. He left his rifle on the ground and shucked off the camouflage coveralls he was wearing. He then bent over and picked up a recorder wired to a shotgun microphone. The familiar device was super-directional. It could pick up private conversations that were over two hundred yards away. It was the perfect tool to record the conversation taking place between Cavanaugh and the president.

Taber wheeled around and gazed at the spot next to the JFK Memorial where he had had a perfect shot of Cavanaugh. Neither he nor Sydney were there any longer. Taber moved on the only target he did have and began sprinting through the trees. He heard the president's voice in the walkie-talkie on his hip but ignored it. He had to get to the man with the eye patch. Even though he was injured, the man might be able to make it to the amphitheater. Memorial Drive snaked right next to it. A car could be waiting there to help him escape.

Taber burst through the cedar trees and dove into the small of the man's back. He had been trying to hop on his left foot up the steep hill that led up to the amphitheater. Taber flipped him onto his back and pinned him to the ground. He searched him and found no weapons. He yanked the recorder out of the man's right hand. The man stared at him with his one eye. Taber could tell he was in indescribable pain, but he didn't make a sound. To add insult to injury, Taber ripped off the man's eye patch. The man winced but then stared at Taber with his clouded, dead eyeball.

Taber held up the recorder. "Who is this for?"

The man remained silent. The look in his ghostly eye said it all. *Go to hell.*

The president's whispered shouts again squelched from the walkie-talkie on Taber's hip. "Cavanaugh's escaped! I repeat, Cavanaugh has Sydney Dumas! They headed into the Visitor Center! Do you read me?"

The man heard it and smiled a shit-eating grin. Taber stood, grabbed his rifle off his back, and leveled it at the man's injured eye. Still not a word. Taber pulled the trigger. The bullet ripped into his eye socket and exploded out the back of the man's head with only so much as a soft *whump.*

Taber yanked his walkie-talkie from his belt and faced the Visitor Center. "I read you."

"What the fuck were you thinking?" the president shot back. "I thought you had a silencer?"

"It wasn't me. Cavanaugh had help." Taber looked down at the dead body at his feet. "Don't worry, I took care of him."

"Get your ass down to the Visitor Center and find him," the president ordered.

Taber had already begun playing the recording. As he listened to stupid Jack Butcher explain himself to Cavanaugh and Sydney Dumas, a better use of his talents came to mind.

He searched the man and found a cell phone in his pant's pocket. He dialed the last received call and waited.

"Chip, thank God," Cavanaugh gushed into the phone.

"Not quite."

There was a long silence. "What have you done to Chip?"

"I killed him, and I have his recording. Just thought you might like to know you have nothing now."

Taber hung up. Then he put the walkie-talkie to his lips.

"Cavanaugh is no longer a problem," he told the president. Taber couldn't help but smile, as he thought about the recorded confession he held in his hand. "But we need to have a chat about increasing my fee."

Chapter 107

Danny doubled over in his seat. He put his thumping head in his hands.

No! God, no!

The Metro train gained speed as it left the Arlington Cemetery station and sped toward the District. Danny wanted to scream. He wanted to bust the train apart. He wanted to get off right now and go kill that bastard Stefan Taber.

"Danny," Sydney peeled his hands away from his face. She had listened to the call that Danny thought was from Chip. "Danny, listen to me."

Danny looked at her. As he blinked, tears spilled from his eyes.

"Danny, it's not your fault."

"I got him—" Danny heard the volume of his voice and then whispered, "I got him into our mess, Sydney. I got him killed."

"He knew what he was getting into, Danny." Danny shook his head. He tried looking away, but Sydney wouldn't let him. She followed his eyes with hers. "He knew the risks, Danny."

"It's not that simple."

"It isn't fair, Danny. We both know too much about loss. My parents and your father were taken from us. Chip was your friend, and now he's gone. I know it isn't fair. But all we can do is finish what he helped us start."

"What are you talking about?" Danny asked.

"We don't have the recording anymore, so we need to get another form of proof."

Danny searched Sydney's eyes. He suddenly realized what she meant. "You're talking about the lawsuit."

Sydney nodded. "With all that has happened, the other copies are no doubt destroyed by now. My copy is the only one left."

Danny lowered his voice even further. "But it's in the White House, Sydney. It's in the Oval Office, for Christ's sake. I saw Butcher lock it up in his credenza. For all we know, he's already destroyed it."

Darkness invaded the car as the train rocketed into the tunnel that snaked underneath Rosslyn, Virginia. But it couldn't overtake the look in Sydney's blazing green eyes.

"Butcher wouldn't have destroyed it. He could still use it as evidence for whatever else he may be planning. You said it yourself back outside the monastery, Danny. Spoken accusations are nothing without hard evidence to back it up."

As Danny's eyes adjusted to the muted light inside the train, he saw the look on Sydney's face. "You're suggesting we break into the White House?" he whispered. She nodded. "It's impossible, Sydney."

"What's impossible is that we're still alive, Danny." She looked toward the train's ceiling. "Someone up there is watching out for us. They'll help us again, I know it."

The Metro slowed, its squealing brakes piercing their quiet conversation. The driver's voice boomed throughout the car. "This is Rosslyn Station. Transfer point for the orange line train."

Help. We need help. In his mind, Danny was already analyzing a short list of candidates who could help them infiltrate the White House. He kept coming back to the same person over and over. "I think we need to count on someone else, Sydney."

"Who?"

"Someone Chip told me I can trust."

Chapter 108

Danny entered the code at the keypad hidden in the back of the storage closet in the Willard Hotel. He heard a *clunk* and then pulled on the corner of the shelving unit bolted to the secret door. It swung open, and he saw the same long concrete tunnel that he had run through only days ago. Sydney blasted by him and began running down it. Danny wanted to yell at her to wait, but he also didn't want to alert anyone of their presence. The door began closing on its pressurized hinges behind him as Danny took off after her.

As they blew through the intersection of the five tunnels, Danny couldn't help noticing that someone had already cleaned Sydney's blood off the wall. They were at the next security door in seconds. Danny entered the new ten-digit numeric code that he had memorized less than an hour ago into the keypad. There wasn't a light that turned color and no sound emanated from the door. Danny looked at Sydney. She shrugged and grabbed the knob. It turned in her hand and she pushed open the door. Fifteen feet in front of them was another gray door exactly like this one. They both realized it as they looked at each other.

We're back inside the White House.

Danny walked toward another keypad that hung next to the second door. Sydney followed and the first door shut behind them. Before typing in his code, Danny looked Sydney over. She was wearing a navy blue pantsuit with a cream blouse. Danny had also dressed up for his White House visit, choosing a pinstriped suit with a solid red tie.

"By the way, you clean up nice," he whispered. She offered him a funny look, obviously not understanding the American saying. "I mean you look beautiful." He reached for her and adjusted the ID badge at the end of the lariat hanging around her neck. It had swung onto her back during their short hike.

"Merci," she whispered.

"You ready?" he asked. Sydney nodded. Danny punched in his code. Again, no light or sound. He tried the knob and it turned. He cracked open the door, halfway expecting they had been set up. He pictured the hallway filled with Secret Service agents ready to take them out. But their new partner had promised that he would make sure their entrance wouldn't be detected by any man or machine. *So far, so good*, Danny thought as he gazed down the sterile, empty hallway that would take them past Ben Speakes's office.

Danny nodded at Sydney. "Ladies first."

Sydney stepped out into the hallway. At first, she walked down the hall like the laminate tiles were eggshells. But as soon as she gazed upon Speakes's door, a confidence washed over her. She looked back at Danny. "We're going to do this."

They weaved their way through the basement hallways of the White House's East Wing. Most of the office doors were closed. The occupants inside the open ones were too busy staring at computer screens or involved in phone calls to even pay attention to them as they walked by. The few White House staffers they did brush by in the hallways had their faces buried in paperwork. White House or not, offices are the same everywhere. Most of the time, people are too busy lost in their own little worlds to notice what's right in front of their faces.

They reached the central stairway that would take them up into the heart of the West Wing. They climbed up to the first-floor landing and Danny opened the stairwell door for Sydney. Of the two of them, her face was the less recognizable. Danny filed in behind her and kept his head down, but he could see a Secret Service agent out of the corner of his eye. He was seated at a desk in the far corner of the room, his eyes glued to a bank of security monitors. He didn't even bother looking at Sydney and Danny. Danny just hoped that the badges around their necks, adorned with bright red A's that stood for "All Access", would continue to be their good luck charms.

Sydney didn't hesitate as she scooted down a long, deserted hallway that would ultimately lead them to the Oval Office.

"Thank God for these badges," Danny whispered as he caught up to her.

"I know. But I feel like Hester Prynne," Sydney replied, keeping her eyes low.

"You've read *The Scarlet Letter*? I'm impressed."

Sydney briefly glanced at him. "Actually, I saw the movie. Demi Moore played her. Gary Oldman played the minister who was her lover."

"Arthur Dimmesdale."

"Right. I used to have a thing for Gary Oldman."

"I wouldn't kick Demi Moore out of bed."

"Me neither." Shock filled Danny's face. Sydney chuckled. "Men. Two words and your penis has now taken over your mind."

"Whatever," Danny replied. Showing her that he was still very much concentrating on their mission, he strode out in front of her as they came to the mouth of the West Wing's communications office.

When the president led Danny in the opposite direction through the communications office, the dozen staffers immediately dropped what they were doing and stood tall as their president clipped past them. But now, those same staffers didn't even glance at Danny and Sydney. They were staring at television monitors, or talking on phones, or typing on computers, lost in the world of information, no doubt attempting to spin it to put their boss in the best possible light.

The cubicle nearest to the archway that separated the communications office from the Oval Office's foyer, the one that Danny's plan centered around, was still vacant. They ducked into it, and Sydney sat down behind the desk. From her viewpoint, she had an unencumbered view of the foyer. The chair behind Vanessa Dempsey's desk was empty. So were the two leather chairs against the opposite wall. On the far wall stood the doorway to the Oval Office. Danny checked his watch. It was supposed to be unoccupied at the present moment, and from the outside, that looked to be the case.

"Point of no return, Sydney. You still want to go through with this?" Danny whispered.

Her eyes blazed as she whispered, "Absolument."

"Okay. Wish me luck."

"Good luck, Danny."

Danny walked as confidently as someone could who was about to break and enter the Oval Office. He strode through the archway and into the Oval Office foyer. A short, empty hallway led off to his right and down to Simon Shilling's office.

Before he could stop himself, Danny darted toward the Oval's door. His vision collapsed on the doorknob less than two feet from him now. He put his hand on it and expected it not to turn. But it did. He opened the door and slid inside.

For a second, he thought he was dreaming. He looked around: JFK's rocker, the enormous oval rug embossed with the presidential seal, sunlight pouring through the windows, illuminating the seat that he himself had sat in only days ago when he had held this office and this president in the highest regard. Danny had really done it. He had just performed a B and E on the Oval fucking Office.

Danny started the timer on his watch and sprang across the room. He ducked behind the president's desk. He checked the credenza drawer to his right, the one he saw Butcher open during their private meeting, the one that contained both the lawsuit and the eighth article documents. He pulled on the handle, and this time he wasn't lucky. It was locked, but the flimsy cabinet lock wouldn't take more than a few seconds. As he dug out a set of pick tools from his pocket and went to work, he thought about Sydney asking him who had taught him to steal cars. They were the same police training officers who taught him how to pick locks. *Sometimes you have to act like a criminal to catch one.*

The credenza door was open in less than a minute. Danny rifled through the file folders lying on the shelf. None were the lawsuit documents. But would the president keep incriminating evidence behind only a cheesy cabinet lock? Especially after he put them in there with Danny watching in the first place? Danny whirled around and dove into the president's desk drawers. Every one of them was open. He only glanced at the contents. File folders hung in the bottom two drawers. The two others above them contained more folders lying in piles. Danny looked at his watch. He had already been in here for almost two minutes. He couldn't burn the time to check all these files. Plus, Butcher would have the documents under lock and key. Would they be in the residence? Perhaps in his bedroom? No, if nothing else, a president controls the Oval Office. It is his command post and his sanctuary. It had to be in here.

Danny's new cell phone buzzed. He took it out and read the text message on the screen.

VD bck.

Vanessa Dempsey had returned to her post in the foyer. He and Sydney had planned for that. When he was ready to leave, he would text Sydney, and she would create a diversion to make Vanessa leave her post so Danny could make a clean getaway.

Danny looked at the paintings on the wall. Could there be a safe behind one of them? No. Danny remembered the way Vanessa Dempsey would barge into the room almost unannounced. Standing at a wall safe would leave Butcher too exposed. It had to be back here.

Danny remembered what Butcher had told him when he was sitting back here.

"I'm sure that you're no politician. You're too honest a man for that line of work."

His eyes shifted back to the credenza. He had yet to check the cabinet on its left side.

This time, Danny had the door open in under thirty seconds. He gazed inside at the built-in horizontal safe that featured an electronic lock. Danny's odd calmness at seeing this new challenge quickly evaporated as soon as his cell phone vibrated on the floor in front of him and his gaze fell on its screen.

Prz cming gt out nw!

Chapter 109

"Less than thirty, people!" The man's voice was coming from the cubicle behind Sydney, the same place where he made his first announcement concerning the president's status that had made her text Danny. She checked her watch. The president wasn't supposed to be back this early. They were supposed to have a twenty-minute window to get in and out. Sydney stared at the Oval Office door. Even with Vanessa Dempsey right there, she wanted desperately for it to open and for Danny to escape.

Hurry Danny!

All the noise, which seemed to be unbearable moments ago, had been extinguished. Even the phones weren't ringing, which they had been nonstop since Sydney had sat down.

"Everyone up and ready?" the same voice behind her asked, but this time Sydney could tell that the guy was now standing. She wanted to stay seated, but her cubicle faced the open hallway. People would see that she wasn't following protocol. She thought about ducking behind the desk, but she would still be seen from the hallway. To hide her face, she pulled her hair around the edges of her chin and stood facing the hallway. Her eyes never left the Oval Office door.

Hurry Danny!

"Good afternoon, Mr. President." The phrase was repeated over and over, the sounds starting at the other side of the room and then rolling agonizingly closer to her. By the time she saw Jack Butcher and Simon Shilling out of the corner of her eye, they were already past her. They remained entrenched in their hushed conversation, the greetings from an entire office not even making a dent.

Do something! she thought. *Don't let them catch Danny!*

"Good afternoon, Mr. President," Sydney said loudly.

Suddenly, the president stopped and turned toward her. He had recognized her voice.

They locked eyes and Sydney made the mistake of glancing for a split second past him at the Oval Office door. The president looked at it and then back at her. He eyed Peter Devon, who was standing next to him, and whispered into the agent's ear.

Sydney didn't have to hear him. She knew what the president's orders were as Danny's instructions rocketed through her head.

"If you get caught, don't run. They will use lethal force to protect the president."

But Sydney couldn't help it. She needed to buy Danny more time. She tore out of the cubicle and then ran down the hallway away from the president. She was only steps away from escaping the communications office when she felt her back explode in pain.

Chapter 110

"Freeze, Cavanaugh!" Peter Devon aimed his Beretta at Danny from across the Oval Office. Danny stayed hunched over the credenza.

"How the hell did you get in here?" the president asked as he whisked by Devon and clipped over to his own desk.

Danny remained silent.

"Hands up! Stand up, slowly," Devon ordered. Danny complied, slowly rising. As he did, he exposed the open cabinet door and the open safe. The president looked at them and then focused on the documents in Danny's hand. He lunged at Danny and ripped them from his grip.

The president studied the documents and shook his head back and forth. "Breaking into the White House and attempting to steal classified documents? This time you really have committed a federal offense, Sergeant."

Agent Devon holstered his weapon and steamed toward Danny while another agent covered him. Devon shoved Danny against the wall and searched him.

"He's clean, sir. No weapons," Devon reported to the president. He pulled Danny's arms down behind his back and slapped handcuffs on his wrists while he read Danny his Miranda rights.

The president glared at Danny. He was about to say something when commotion spilled into the room as a third agent entered. He was trying to control a handcuffed Sydney Dumas, who was verbally assaulting him in French. She paused her ranting only long enough to gaze upon Danny with a silent apology in her eyes.

"President Butcher is a madman!" Sydney desperately shouted as she continued. "He's behind all the bombs! He wanted to kill everyone at the State of the Union!"

Butcher laughed. "Including myself, right?" Shilling laughed as well.

Peter Devon addressed the other agents. "Malloy, you're on POTUS. Dixon, White House is code blue. Full body searches on every visitor."

"Honestly Pete, is that really necessary?" the president asked Devon.

"Mr. President, I have my orders for these situations, and I will follow them."

"What you need to do, Pete, is figure out how the fuck these two got into the White House and how he gained access to the Oval Office! Right now!"

"I will, sir. But this is not the place. We have procedures for questioning suspects."

The president glared at the head of his security detail and finally relented. "Okay." He turned to Danny as Peter Devon began to muscle him across the Oval Office. "I hope you like prison, Danny. You're gonna be there awhile."

Danny had the perfect comeback in mind. But, wisely, that's exactly where it remained.

Chapter 111

The only sounds out of Peter Devon's mouth since they left the Oval Office had been single word directions. "Left." "Right." "Down." They reached the bottom of the central staircase that led into the basement. Devon opened the door and uttered another "right."

Sydney and Danny began walking shoulder to shoulder down the hallway. From the corner of his eye, Danny saw Sydney glance at him and read the confused look on her face. *We're not heading for the interrogation room. We're heading under the East Wing.* As they came to the next intersection, Danny correctly predicted the one word that would escape Peter Devon's mouth.

"Right." They turned and headed for the one place that had been marked off limits. Dark blue tape with the words, "Federal Crime Scene—Do Not Cross" in white remained taped to the doorframe.

"Stop," Devon commanded just outside Ben Speakes's office. He knocked once on the door, and it opened. Standing there was Howard Fielding, director of National Intelligence. As the two of them stood there, Danny remembered the tidbit of news that seemed like nothing at the time, but right now meant everything in the world. After 9/11, the Secret Service department got reassigned from the Treasury Department to the newly created Department of Homeland Security. DHS reported to Howard Fielding. Fielding, not the president, was Peter Devon's boss.

Fielding looked down the hall. "Inside, quick." They ducked under the tape, and Fielding closed the door behind them. "Did you get it?" The question was aimed at Danny. Peter Devon shot him a look. Danny lifted his shirt and pulled out a manila envelope, the same one that Devon undoubtedly felt as he patted down Danny back in the Oval Office.

"What's that?" Sydney asked Danny as he handed the envelope to Fielding. Fielding wasted no time tearing into it and examining the contents.

"It's the lawsuit."

Sydney's brow furrowed. "But the president took it from you."

"He took your copy, yes."

"My copy?"

"Director Fielding told us that Butcher was out with Shilling. That meant the chief of staff's office was open. I remembered seeing a copier in there and made a copy of the lawsuit for myself. They caught me putting your copy back in his safe."

A laugh escaped Sydney's lips. "God bless your beautiful memory, Danny."

Danny reached into his pocket and pulled out the device he used to open the credenza safe, along with the pick tool. Fielding had given them to him in the Willard Hotel room where they had planned this mission only hours ago. "Worked like a charm."

Fielding gazed at the electronic lock decoder's tiny screen and read the combination. "*071492*" He looked back up. "I should have known."

"What?" Danny asked.

"His son Simon's birthday."

"So what happens now?" Sydney asked Fielding.

"Like I told you when you called me, you've done your jobs." He held up the lawsuit. "You've produced what you said you would. You're free to go."

Sydney motioned toward Peter Devon. "You mean free to go with your agents to your, what did you call it?"

Danny took the liberty of answering. "Undisclosed location."

Fielding smiled. "I'm a man of my word, Sergeant. You'll be turned loose after a few days."

Chapter 112

Sydney had flirted, whined, and finally threatened her chaperones, as they called themselves, until she got her way. She unlatched the chain-link gate and stepped onto the scummy pool deck. She gazed past the rusty chain-link fence in all directions. The parking lot of the Manassas, Virginia Red Roof Inn was nearly empty in the middle of the afternoon, which was expected at a cheap motel used primarily by weary travelers looking for a place to flop overnight. She looked back at her room, the one she'd been occupying for the past thirty-eight and a half hours. The pulled curtains wiggled. She couldn't see the agents behind them, but she knew they were there watching her every move.

Sydney zipped off her GWU warm-up top and then tugged off the pants. She stood at the far end of the pool. It wasn't exactly inviting. Swirls of yellow algae clung to its sides. The water itself was so cloudy she could barely see the bottom. Plus, it reeked of chlorine. The pool was about as far away from the one at the White House as it could be, but beggars couldn't be choosers.

A man walking out from the lobby to his eighteen-wheeler parked along the side of the motel nearly ran into a light pole as he gawked at her. She didn't think twice of standing there in her underwear; it felt and looked like a bathing suit. Americans. She dove into the pool and coasted under the water toward the other end. The overwhelming amount of chlorine stung her closed eyes. As soon as she hit the far end, she stood and wiped the tainted water away from them. She saw Danny standing at the gate.

"It's time to go."

Chapter 113

Danny didn't think anything of it when Howard Fielding turned the blue Ford Taurus onto the 495 loop from I-66 and headed north. They were bypassing the District, but many government agencies were headquartered on its outskirts. But now that Fielding took the ramp for I-95 north, heading toward Baltimore and then New York, Danny's curiosity spiked.

"Where we going?" he asked Fielding. It was the first words that anyone had spoken since bland pleasantries were exchanged almost an hour ago in the Red Roof Inn parking lot. Sydney had actually fallen asleep in the backseat.

Fielding kept his eyes on the road. "Baltimore."

"What's in Baltimore?"

"You'll see."

Twenty minutes later, Fielding veered off I-95 and drove down 198, heading east. Danny tightened. "This isn't the way to Baltimore, Admiral." Danny glanced in the backseat. Sydney's eyes popped open, and she immediately tensed.

"Relax," Fielding replied. He looked at Sydney in the rearview mirror. "The two of you. I'm hungry and I know a good place to stop."

The name of the place was Champions Sports Bar. Fielding swerved into an open parking space right in front of the bar's double doors. The windowless establishment was divided into two spaces. Six billiard tables and twenty hulking video game consoles on the left side provided the "sports" part. A long slab of cheap Formica with a dozen table and chairs scattered near it on the right side was the "bar" area. Flat screen TVs hung everywhere with what seemed to be every conceivable sporting event being broadcast. Fielding crossed to an empty table near the lone TV broadcasting CNN. Anderson Cooper was talking to Blake Conway, the White House spokesman, about the many rumors that continued to swirl around the events of the past week.

"My treat," Fielding said as they sat. He grabbed three of the four menus crammed between the napkin dispenser and salt and pepper shakers on the corner of the table. "Don't let the ambiance fool you. The crab cake sandwich is excellent, best I've ever had. For appetizers, they have these stuffed jalapenos wrapped in bacon. Really outstanding." He glanced at his watch. "What it makes up for in food, it lacks in service. We better be ready to order when our waitress comes."

Their food arrived a good twenty minutes after they ordered it. No one had appetizers. Fielding's sales pitch had at least convinced Sydney to order the same crab cake sandwich he was having, with a side salad instead of the mixed fruit Fielding ordered. Danny opted for the cheeseburger with onion rings and the biggest Miller Lite they had. Fielding glanced at his watch again before doctoring up his sandwich. After squeezing a wedge of lemon over his crab cake, he coated one bun with tartar sauce and the other one with cocktail sauce. He was finished with both the sandwich and the fruit before Danny had half of his burger down. Sydney had only finished her side salad and hadn't touched her main course yet. That's when a "NEWS ALERT" flashed on the TV screen above their heads.

CNN's White House correspondent, Grace Styles, materialized on the screen. She was covering President Butcher as he was leaving for a few days R and R at Camp David. The shot switched again, and there was Jack Butcher, smiling at the cameras and waving to whomever it was presidents waved to as they performed the familiar photo op of crossing the lush South Lawn toward the waiting Marine One helicopter. As the president walked, Grace Styles provided the mundane details of his trip and even a few background facts about Camp David and Marine One. Danny heard Sydney's fork clang against her salad bowl. She stared at Butcher on the screen. He could read it in her face. The mere sight of him made her lose her appetite.

Danny put his burger back down on his plate, his own stomach twisting as he watched Jack Butcher climb the helicopter's stairs. Butcher paused, turned, and waved from the top. He looked like a man without a care in the world. A split second later, his body slammed backward into the helicopter.

The camera zoomed in on the helicopter's darkened doorway. Grace Styles was yelling to someone off camera, her voice now exploding through the TV speakers. "What happened? What? My God! The president's been shot!"

Danny saw Peter Devon fly into the shot. He bent down over the president and began frantically shouting into his wrist microphone. The TV screen split in half, and another camera angle showed a full shot of Marine One. Several agents scrambled around it, their weapons drawn. The presidential limo raced into the shot, sliding to a stop next to the stairway. Devon and three other agents carried Jack Butcher down the stairs and shoved him into the limo's backseat. Both of Butcher's arms hung lifelessly at his side. Peter Devon had draped his suit jacket over the president's head so that the cameras couldn't get a shot of his face.

Several people from the bar had gathered around their table by now, watching the events unfold as CNN repeated the scene over and over and over. The three of them sat in stunned silence as they watched the TV for several minutes before Fielding wandered over to the bartender to pay the check.

Danny waited until they were back in the privacy of the Taurus before slinging his accusation. "You knew what was going to happen. That's why you ate so fast."

"I always eat fast, Sergeant," Fielding replied. "All soldiers do."

"You killed the president," Sydney blurted.

Fielding's eyes darted to the rearview mirror. "How could I have killed the president, Ms. Dumas? I was in a sports bar in the middle of Maryland when it happened."

"You had him killed," she replied. "Why?"

"Because he didn't want Butcher talking," Danny answered for Fielding.

Fielding stared at Danny. "The country doesn't need another scandal. Not now. Especially not involving its president. Could you imagine what would happen if it came out that Jack Butcher wanted to start a revolution by killing every member of Congress? What if he was arrested in a couple years after trying a stunt similar to this one? This one event might be over, but our country still stands at the precipice of collapse—financially, socially, morally. What do you think would happen to the country if we saw our leader being led from the White House in handcuffs? We needed to see him shot down in a blaze of glory. History shows that when America mourns, we come together. We need that more than anything right now."

"United we stand, divided we fall," Danny added sarcastically.

"Damn right," Fielding reply.

"But he's the president of the United States for Christ's sake," Sydney offered.

"Like Butcher said himself, presidents are temporary. We can always get another one."

Danny's eyes flashed. "The meeting at Arlington Cemetery. That's where Butcher said presidents are temporary." Danny read it in Fielding's face. "You were listening."

Fielding smiled. "You don't miss much do you, Sergeant?"

"How did you—"

Fielding cut Danny off. "All presidents need a break from time to time, even if it's just to walk the streets of D.C. for a while. That was the main reason the White House tunnels were built. JFK had them put in. Of course, his purpose was for something besides strolling the streets. That's why one led to the Willard. He would meet his … friends there. That's how Butcher got out to the cemetery for your little meeting. But what he doesn't know is that we tracked him. When we get the chance, we insert GPS chips into all of their shoes without their knowledge. We've been doing it since Clinton. Where the president goes, at least one Secret Service agent goes with him, whether he knows it or not."

Devon, Danny thought. He pictured Agent Peter Devon hiding at the cemetery, using a similar device Chip used to record their conversation.

"So, if you had his confession recorded, why agree to us going back in after the lawsuit?" Sydney asked, her anger evident in her tone.

"I needed to be sure it was real, that you two weren't just making it up. Plus, having a copy gives me insurance. In case any of the other Bilderbergers get any ideas, we threaten to go public with it."

"But how does that stop them?" Sydney asked.

"We investigate Booker Halsey. We show how he's tied to Phoenix Oil. Then we investigate Phoenix's operations, which will shed some light on people who, above all else, treasure their anonymity. The last thing they want is publicity."

"Sounds like you are intimately familiar with the Bilderbergers, Admiral," Danny said.

"I wouldn't be a good director of National Intelligence if I didn't know who the puppet masters are."

Sydney continued to hound Fielding. "But Danny gave you the copy he made in Simon Shilling's office. My copy is still inside the president's credenza."

Danny took the liberty of answering Sydney's question. "But as director of National Intelligence, Admiral Fielding himself will be in charge of securing all classified documents inside the Oval Office after the president's assassination. I'm sure it's being sealed off as we speak." Danny's eyes met Fielding's. "That only leaves one loose end. Simon Shilling."

"Shilling will resign his post citing emotional distress. You can rest assured that he will live out his life in quiet anonymity."

"All in a day's work, huh Admiral Fielding?" Danny asked.

Fielding couldn't hold back a sly grin. "A little more than the typical day, but keeping the world balanced is a bitch sometimes."

"So what happens to us to keep things balanced?" Sydney asked. "Are we still free to go, like you promised?"

Fielding looked at her through the rearview mirror. "Your employers still believe that you were either killed or kidnapped down in Mexico. Turns out, when the attack on the monastery occurred, you escaped and hitchhiked toward the border. You will be found wandering the streets of Nuevo Laredo in a few days. Then, you will go back to your post at the ICJ and back to your life in Monte Carlo. With Fantroy and other key members now dead, the Bilderbergers have lost their way. I'm sure that if you don't go off making wild accusations about international financial conspiracies or phantom lawsuits, nothing will happen to you."

"Spoken accusation is nothing without evidence to back it up, right?" she asked Fielding. Danny's familiar line made him look at her.

"Something like that."

Sydney pressed him. "What about Danny? What happens to him?"

Fielding kept his eyes on the rearview mirror. "Like I said, he's free to go as well."

Fielding's tone made Danny press him. "But?"

Fielding finally swung his eyes over to Danny. "For things to work out, you gotta remain a fugitive, Sergeant. Sorry."

Chapter 114

Grace Styles shucked off her $400 Jimmy Choo silver platform shoes and sprinted up the sidewalk along Executive Avenue toward the commotion. Two dozen Secret Service agents were swarming a vehicle parked in the lot that faced the southwest corner of the South Lawn. Grace's mind, trained by years of journalism, sought out the easy pieces of information first: the vehicle's make, model, and color. But there were so many agents dressed in tactical gear, all Grace could see was a wall of writhing black.

Her producer's exasperated voice shot through her earpiece, filling her head. "What's going on, Grace? What the hell can you see?"

Where most people's natural reaction was to avoid confrontation, Grace's legs, also trained over the years to chase down stories no matter how dangerous, carried her toward it. A Secret Service agent accidentally shoved her aside as he backed away from the fracas, crushing her toes underneath his heavy boot. Fueled by the same adrenaline she was still hooked on after all these years, Grace barely felt it. She plunged further toward the vehicle. She could finally make out the description. It was a dark green, late model Nissan Pathfinder. But as she looked through the open passenger door and caught a glimpse of what was inside, no amount of training could compensate for the shock that rocked her.

—

As he packed up the computer equipment into a separate black duffel bag from the one that contained his clothes, Stefan Taber watched the jerky shot of Grace Styles on the plasma TV. After being nearly pummeled by federal agents, she steadied herself on

405

those gorgeous legs of hers that were reportedly insured for a couple million bucks each and dove back toward the bedlam that surrounded the machine Taber controlled only minutes ago.

"It appears that the gunman is actually a machine being controlled remotely. The question is from where and by whom?"

Taber grinned as he faced the TV. "I'm right here in Vegas, Gracie. Why don't you bring those lovely legs out here, and we'll spend some quality time together?"

Satisfied, Taber pointed the remote at the screen and hit the button to access the Treasure Island express checkout screen. He completed the procedure, packed up his gear, and headed for the door. He took one last look behind him at the adequate facilities, as he imagined the superior accommodations that would be waiting for him at the Wynn Las Vegas across the street. Even if someone figured out that the sniper machine that killed President Butcher had been controlled from a computer in Las Vegas, which thanks to encrypted connections and false ID information made that all but impossible, the last thing they would think was that the assassin would stick around to enjoy a few days at one of the city's most luxurious hotels.

Although he never got the chance to collect any money from President Butcher concerning the recording of his meeting at Arlington Cemetery, after which he was followed and then kidnapped by four soldiers led by Admiral Howard Fielding, his luck held out. The kidnapping was really a job interview for the task he had just pulled off. The paycheck? A cool $5 million. This time, the two birds in the bush had turned out to be worth way more than the one in the hand.

Stefan Taber pulled open the hotel room door to find two bulging men with crew cuts standing in his doorway. *They found me*, he thought. Taber's gut had told him not to accept this job offer, even if it was the largest paycheck and biggest prize he would ever bag. He thought that even if the old man tried to double cross him, Fielding would never find him. But Taber had made the biggest mistake one in his profession could make: he underestimated his client. Fielding had the world's most advanced technologies and countless military operatives at his disposal.

The soldiers rushed Taber. He briefly tasted the leather from the gloved hand that covered his mouth before everything went black.

Chapter 115

"You've got five minutes to say your good-byes," Fielding said. He turned and walked back into the unmarked hangar at the southern edge of the Baltimore/Washington International Airport to give them some privacy. Even though the four armed government agents were over fifty paces away, Danny felt like they loomed right on top of him.

"So, what's in store for Sydney Dumas?" he asked Sydney.

"I'm going to follow Fielding's plan, all except for returning to the bench."

"You're resigning from the ICJ?"

Sydney nodded. "I'm going back to my professor job at the university. I miss teaching very much."

"Good for you, Sydney. It's the only real way to change the world."

Sydney smiled. "I'll have to remember that one." Her smile disappeared as concern flooded her face. "It doesn't seem fair to you, Danny. All that you've done, and you remain a criminal."

Danny shrugged. "Like Fielding said, it's the only way to make the story stick, for now. They need their scapegoats. Hopefully, he'll be true to his word and not accuse me of being Butcher's assassin."

Sydney stepped closer to him and gripped his forearms. Her eyes got wet. "You won't do anything ... stupid, will you?"

Danny chuckled. "Like killing myself? No. I'm over that, Sydney. Trust me."

"I do, Danny. With my life. I trust you."

"I trust you too, Sydney."

They hugged each other for a long time. Danny wanted the moment to last forever. He could tell Sydney wanted the same thing.

"Will we ever see each other again?" she whispered through her sniffles.

"Count on it," he whispered back.

She took his face in her hands and pulled him to her. They kissed. When they were done, Danny saw Fielding emerge from the hangar.

"That was a quick five minutes," Danny said.

"You all set, Ms. Dumas?" Fielding asked as he approached them.

"Yes." She turned back to Danny, and they kissed one more time. "Good-bye, Danny."

"Good-bye, Sydney. Safe travels."

Fielding stuck out his hand. "Good luck, Sergeant."

Danny shook his hand, but his eyes remained locked with Sydney's, as Fielding escorted her over to the waiting Falcon 50 jet. Sydney finally broke eye contact as she climbed up the folding staircase and ducked into the plane. The door closed behind them, and the engines fired up. As Danny stepped away from the plane, a familiar voice caught his ear from behind him.

"You ready to go, Sergeant?"

Danny whirled to see Agent Peter Devon standing there. He knew that he and Sydney would go their separate ways, but he still didn't know where he was being taken. "Do I finally get to know where you're taking me?"

Devon stood there without emotion and flatly replied, "New York."

Chapter 116

As they crossed through Penn Station's main doors, Danny could tell that Peter Devon had little concern about being recognized by the people hustling around them. They maneuvered through the crowded terminal toward an enormous information board on the far side of a circular waiting area. As soon as they reached it, Devon's eyes scrolled up and down. "Wait here," he instructed Danny without as much as a glance. He walked over to the nearest ticketing agent and waited in a line three people deep.

As Danny waited, he watched all the people scurrying around. Not one seemed to be even fazed that the president of the United States had been shot and killed. The details of the attempt on President Ronald Reagan's life were as fresh in Danny's mind as if he had been the president who was shot only hours ago. He had just arrived home from school. As soon as he walked in the front door after trekking home from the school bus stop, he could tell instantly something was wrong. His mother was glued to the TV. Tears stained her face. She didn't even notice her son was home until he gripped her shaking hand. She grabbed onto him and hugged him tight, her voice almost breathless. "Oh honey, the president's been shot."

Now, all these years later, it didn't seem like anyone cared that their leader had died. Danny thought about what Fielding had said about the country coming together and fixing itself. If Penn Station was any indication, Fielding's theory was dead wrong.

Devon clipped back over to Danny and offered him an envelope. "Here you go, Jeremy Calhoun."

"Jeremy Calhoun? What the hell ..." As soon as Danny pulled out the Virginia driver's license from the envelope, he realized what Devon meant. Fielding had given him a new identity.

"There's also a Social Security card in there along with a thousand dollars in pocket money and instructions to access an account with fifty grand in it. All compliments of the U.S. government."

"For what y'all are doing to me, there should be a hell of a lot more than just fifty grand."

"What can I say; it's an amount that wouldn't be missed. Your ticket's in there, too. It's good for a private sleeper from here to Chicago."

"Why Chicago?"

"It's big enough to get lost in. Plus it's close enough to Canada, just in case you want to head north. Passport's your problem, though."

Danny examined the train ticket. "Private sleeper. Thanks."

"You look like two shades of dog shit. I thought you could use the upgrade, my treat."

"You're a peach, Devon," Danny replied sarcastically.

Devon actually cracked a smile. "Call it an early birthday gift."

With all that had gone on, Danny had totally forgotten about his thirty-eighth birthday. He wasn't surprised that the Secret Service agent remembered it for him. "Can I ask you one thing?"

"What?"

Danny glanced around, then lowered his voice. "Did I kill the president?" Devon raised an eyebrow. "Come on, Devon. This ain't my first rodeo. This whole thing stinks of a set-up."

Devon remained a stone for a moment. Then he motioned beyond the glass wall to the waiting area. "Your train boards in fifty-two minutes on track 4B." He stuck out his hand. "Good luck, Cavanaugh."

Danny realized that Agent Devon wasn't going to give him the answer he wanted. He turned without shaking hands and started walking toward the waiting area.

"Sergeant." Danny turned back to see a business card in Devon's outstretched hand. He walked back and took it. "I'm sorry about your friend Carver. If you need anything, ever, you've got another friend in D.C. to call on."

Chapter 117

Danny found his cabin and locked the door behind him. He moved the pillow on the seat next to the large picture window and sat down. He plopped the envelope that contained his new life into the seat next to him. After passing through the noisy coach and business-class seat sections, he relished the quiet of his own room with its own private bathroom.

The train signaled it was about to leave the station by blowing its horn. Danny could finally rest easy for the time being. He didn't need to think about assassins chasing him or manipulative presidents or Bilderbergers or international financial schemes any longer. He didn't think about killing himself anymore. If nothing else, this case made him realize that there was too much to live for, too many people that he could help. It was his calling. The mess at the border with Crayton Ripley may have made him forget about that for a while, but Sydney Dumas had helped him remember.

The one thing he couldn't shake however was questioning his own actions at the State of the Union. What if he had just let the bombs detonate? What if he had allowed Jack Butcher to carry out his mission? Would that have put America back on the right track? Would the death of roughly a thousand Washington insiders have helped the destiny of three hundred million Americans? Danny knew he wouldn't be able to shake those doubts any time soon. They would only fade over time.

He looked down at the envelope resting next to him. He wasn't going to become this Jeremy Calhoun. He also knew that while Fielding may not want to blame him for any part of Butcher's assassination, Danny was the perfect scapegoat. Again. Whatever Howard Fielding and the rest of the United States government would accuse him of doing or being, it didn't matter. He was going to clear his own name, once and for all. He was going to stay Danny Cavanaugh. In order to do that, he would need to go back down to the border. He would need to investigate Rafael Espinoza's entire operation, nail his American connections, and blow the whole fucking thing wide open.

But more than anything else, Danny was going to find out what really happened to his dad. This case had made new questions surface, new possibilities open up. He had never truly bought the suicide story. Something had made Danny not follow through with blowing his own brains out. The apple couldn't have fallen that far from the tree.

First things were first, however. Danny scrunched the pillow into the corner between his seat and the window, rested his head against it, and closed his eyes. The train didn't even get up a full head of steam before Danny was asleep and dreaming about his next encounter with the lovely and talented Sydney Dumas, who was dressed, of course, only in her underwear.

Epilogue

Three Months Later

Sydney Dumas took a moment to find her bearings before leaving the water. After winding through a hundred laps without a break, she still felt like she was moving. While she wasn't a guest of the Fairmont Monte Carlo Hotel, the manager was an old friend. He had allowed Sydney carte blanche access to its stunning rooftop pool for years. Sydney walked over to one of the teak lounge chairs that lined its perimeter, feeling the rising sun on her skin. She took in the breathtaking view of the Mediterranean Sea as it was waking up for the day. She closed her eyes and yearned for the same power Danny Cavanaugh had to burn that image into her brain forever.

But neither the lengthy swim nor the spectacular view made a difference. She still felt miserable.

Since resigning her post as an ICJ judge, Sydney had nothing but time on her hands until the fall semester started at the University of Monaco. When she wasn't swimming, she spent most of her time glued to the TV in her apartment watching for any news coming from America. Authorities had found the man responsible for President Butcher's death. He had been killed in a firefight with authorities in an abandoned house on the outskirts of Las Vegas. He had used that private location to set up a computer workstation that remotely controlled the sniper rifle found in the vehicle parked near the White House's South Lawn. When the name Carlos Zabien flashed across the screen under a head shot of Stefan Taber, and the story of how he was linked to an Iranian terrorist sleeper cell was broadcast, surprise barely registered in Sydney's mind. "*Just keeping*

413

the world in balance." She could almost hear Howard Fielding saying those exact words.

As far as Danny went, although he hadn't been charged with any crimes, authorities said that he remained a person of interest in the strange turn of events that had gripped Washington, D.C. for several days back in March, a time period reporters had dubbed "March Madness" and "The Ides of March, Part II." Danny's unknown whereabouts only increased the speculation that he was involved in Butcher's assassination somehow.

Sydney missed Danny horribly, which shocked her. She missed his friend Chip, a man without whom this world was truly worse off. But most of all, after everything had finally come full circle, after his predictions and his stories had finally come true, she missed Knobby most of all.

Sydney sat down on the lounge chair and tucked her head in hands. She felt like weeping. Soon, she sensed someone standing over her. She looked up and saw a woman with short gray hair holding a towel. She offered it to Sydney.

"Merci," Sydney said, wiping the tears from her face. As she wrapped the towel around herself, she noticed that the woman wasn't wearing the same outfit of other hotel employees. Sydney looked closer at the woman, studying her face as she spoke in a proper British accent.

"I've watched you come here over the years to work things out. The water is my favorite place, too."

Impossible, Sydney thought. But simply staring into the woman's face, a face her own would resemble one day, there was no denying it. This woman was Sydney's biological mother.

"After all that has happened, I thought it was finally okay to come out of hiding and meet you."

Sydney's words barely came. "But Knobby told me you were killed with my father."

The woman nodded. "I was in the car with your father when it plunged into the Thames. But I was able to get out and swim away under the water. I tried to save him, but he was trapped inside." A tear fell from the woman's glistening eyes. "Colin thought it would

414

be best for all of us if you thought I was dead until a time when we could be safe together."

Sydney's natural inclination was not to trust this woman, not to believe her words. But she made a decision to fight her instincts. She said no words, letting her actions speak for her. They embraced for an eternity, as they both cried all over each other's shoulder. Then, Sydney's mother began her life story. She started by telling Sydney how much she adored Sydney's father and how fond he was of his newborn baby.

Soon, a spotless hotel porter clipped toward them with a cordless phone in his hand. "Ms. Dumas, I have a phone call for you."

Sydney took the phone from him and put it to her ear. "Hello?"

"Enjoying your swim?"

"Danny?" Sydney looked in all directions, hoping against hope. "Are you here?"

"Not quite. Only a few thousand miles away."

"How did you find me?"

"Before being your knight in shining armor, I was—I am—a detective, remember?"

Sydney chuckled. "I seem to recall saving you as much as you saved me."

She could practically feel the warmth of Danny's easy laugh. "Touché, Ms. Dumas."

THE END